Sweetbriar

Sweetbriar

Paula Judith Johnson

If you purchased this book without a cover, you should be aware that this book is stolen property. It was reported as "unsold and destroyed" to the publisher and neither the publisher nor the author has received any payment for this "stripped" book."

Copyright © 2010 – Teresa Brown

All Rights Reserved. This book may not be reproduced or distributed in any printed or electronic form without the prior express written permission of the author. Please do not participate in or encourage piracy of copyrighted material in violation of the author's rights.

ISBN10: 0615393780
ISBN13: 9780615393780

Printed in the United States of America

Dedication

I lovingly dedicate this book to my husband,
Wayne S. Brown.
I cherish you with all my heart.
Thank you for your love, understanding, and support.

Acknowledgments

I would like to acknowledge my friends, Shirley Johnson and Ann Goldeen, and my mother, Joan Johnson, who so graciously agreed to test read this novel and give me their impressions and suggestions for improvement. This story is better for the advice each of you provided.

And I would like to express my special thanks to my brother, Steven W. Johnson, who assisted in formatting this book for publication.

Prologue

Summer 1804, England

So it was war again. War with France was nothing new. Its wrath had been almost continuous for more than a hundred years. But the conflict was as inconvenient as the persistent ache of a rotting tooth, throbbing and pulsating, always there. Attaining power again, the younger William Pitt called for an Anglo-Austro-Russian coalition against France to stop Napoleon's insatiable thirst for conquering the continent. So, war was as inevitable as the sun rising in the east. And that meant, sooner or later, merchant trade with other countries would be affected. And when trade was hampered, everyone suffered—the importers, the exporters, and the multitudes of people who yearned for their merchandise. Yes, war was damned inconvenient.

Fall 1804, England

Thirteen-year-old Beth awakened slowly while a vague feeling of depression weighed heavily upon her mind. Listlessly she crawled out of bed, opened the heavy drapes, and encountered a thick misty fog that shrouded the landscape. The summer birds of the past few weeks had flown, for the only sound she heard was the mournful cawing of ravens in the distance.

Suddenly, the full realization of death flooded back upon her. Tears welled up from the hollow pit of her stomach and burned at the back of her eyes. The long-awaited joy of a baby brother or sister had mutated into a soul-wrenching ache. Her beloved mama was dead. Today they would bury her with the small body of the stillborn baby cradled in her arms.

"I am the resurrection and the life, saith the Lord: he that believeth in Me, though he were dead, yet shall he live: and whosoever liveth and believeth in Me shall never die," the Anglican priest solemnly intoned.

The early morning mist thickened until a cold, drizzling rain engulfed the countryside. Mourners slowly trailed behind the black-clad priest and the coffin to the gravesite. The bare oak trees were skeletal; the ancient tombstones, like ghostly sentinels, waited to welcome another into their midst. Beth shivered. She had always taken pleasure in coming to the family plot in the spring to place flowers on the graves. Reading the names and dates of long-dead ancestors was an amusing pastime for a child. She would never enjoy that task again.

"Lord, Thou hast been our refuge: from one generation to another. Before the mountains were brought forth, or ever the earth and the world were made: Thou art God from everlasting, world without end." Small rivulets of mud from the heaped earth splattered on the coffin, and like the ticking of a clock, slowly tapped the time to eternity.

Chilled to the bone despite the thick black wool of her dress and cloak, Beth tightly clutched her father's hand and felt him quiver. A reserved man, he had no patience with emotional displays, deeming them signs of a weak character. Over the years, when childhood calamities befell, he had always advised Beth to be strong and keep a stiff upper lip. So, she stood stoically beside her father. He quivered again. Beth looked up and was stunned to see him silently weeping.

"Forasmuch as it hath pleased Almighty God in His great mercy to take unto Himself the soul of our dear sister here departed, we therefore commit her body to the ground." Heavy mud thudded hollowly on the coffin. "Earth to earth, ashes to ashes, dust to dust; in sure and certain hope of the resurrection to eternal life through our Lord Jesus Christ..." The deluge roared down in heavy sheets, drowning out the words of the priest.

Beth wanted him done and everyone gone so she could bury the hyacinth bulbs she'd brought in her pocket. She wanted the delicate beauty of the flowers to adorn her mother's grave each spring.

"The grace of our Lord Jesus Christ, and the love of God, and the fellowship of the Holy Ghost, be with us all evermore."

Mourners paused only briefly in the driving torrent to give condolences to the new widower, then hastened away, black capes billowing in the wind.

Beth quickly buried the bulbs and stood. Her father, staring at the grave, appeared rooted to the ground as solidly as the hundred-year-old oaks surrounding them. Gently tugging his hand to gain his attention, she said, "Come, Father, we must go. Now that Mama's gone, I'll have to look after you. If we stay much longer, we'll both catch our death." The bleak words lingered in the cold air momentarily then were snatched away by the ghostly hand of the wind.

Fall 1804, America

The ship's cutter bumped alongside the *Angel Star* and Bradley Anderson clambered aboard, the box that contained his sextant snuggled close to his chest. Exultantly his eyes swept over the decks. The *Angel Star* was a beauty, and she was his. She was of a new design. The high rounded bilge and somewhat flared topsides gave a heart-shaped look to her midsection. The stem and stern were considerably raked and low-sided with a sharp ended hull. This made the deep draft greatest at the heel of the rudder. Forward the draft was half that of the ship's aft end. Being heavily sparred and canvassed put her in a speed class of her own and made her the desire of every merchant captain in America.

Few men received command of a merchant ship at twenty-two years of age, and no one could say Bradley Anderson had not earned his place in his father's fleet. From earliest childhood, the boy had seized every opportunity to accompany his father to the shipyard and the docks, avidly asking questions of the crewmen and officers. Impatient to embark upon a life at sea, Brad was twelve when he stole away from home and signed on board his first ship as a cabin boy. That first voyage lasted eight grueling months, long enough to break a boy or make a man. The youngster who returned home was no longer a child but a young man who clearly knew his course in life. The ensuing years were demanding. Brad was shunned by the common sailors for being the owner's son and considered extra baggage by the officers, even though he labored twice as hard as any man to prove his worth. Captain O'Malley, in trying to break Brad, was ruthless in his demands only to find his young charge possessed the perseverance of few men O'Malley had encountered before. Slowly grudging respect grew between the two and finally, over the years, a genuine friendship.

Now, after three arduous years of serving as Quinn O'Malley's first mate, Brad had earned the right to command a ship. He possessed the leadership needed to obtain instantaneous obedience from every man on board, had learned to make coolheaded decisions, and had acquired the hard bargaining skills needed to make a good profit. These were all important qualities for any merchant captain.

But Charles Anderson did not see eye to eye with his son's desire to work at sea and was appalled by his plea to command the new ship. Brad must learn to oversee the business from shore, the older man contended, and outright refused the request.

Flabbergasted by the idea of sailing a desk instead of a ship, Brad determinedly argued his case for hours. He was steadfastly rebuffed. In the end, exasperation flashed like lightning in Brad's stormy gray eyes, and he thundered, "From the time I was just a boy, I've dedicated my life to learning everything there is to know about commanding a merchant ship. I've worked every job on board and know as much as any gape-tooth old salt alive. Now you want me to throw it all overboard. But the sea is in my blood, and by my word, if I don't receive command of a ship from you, I'll take my services elsewhere."

"I won't be threatened," Charles slammed his palms down on his desk, aggravated by his son's obstinate outburst.

Brad responded hotly, "It is not a threat. I mean what I say."

For ten long minutes, Charles regarded his stubborn son, too livid to speak. Finally, in a tight voice, he growled, "Quinn O'Malley is the best captain I employ, and I see he taught you well. You drive a hard bargain because you know I'll not have you work elsewhere. You may have the new ship. But remember, this business will be yours someday, and you have the responsibility to learn the administration. You can't pursue your present course forever."

"I know, Dad," Brad said quietly with a self-satisfied smile and crossed his arms over his chest. "But I'm still young. Just give me some time."

Fall 1804, American Frontier

Greed for land caused ongoing strife between native Indians and white settlers. Recently a young Sauk brave was imprisoned for murder, and a Sauk council of war sent Quashquame and three other chieftains to St. Louis to meet with the American chief and buy their man's freedom.

Upon hearing of their mission, William Henry Harrison, Governor of the Northwest Territories, ordered kegs of whiskey sent out to the Indian faction.

"But sir, this delegation didn't come to negotiate a land treaty. They came to pay reparation to the murdered man's relatives. This is their custom for redeeming their Indian brethren and restoring him to his family," Colonel Michaels explained.

"Listen, Michaels," Harrison stated sharply, "we've desired western expansion since before our war for independence, and that desire has escalated since the Louisiana Purchase. The President authorized me to negotiate land treaties with the Indians, and that's what I intend to do. Some beads, cloth, blankets, knives, and whiskey are all it takes, especially if they drink plenty of whiskey before we negotiate the treaty."

"But, sir—"

"If they want their murdering red devil back, they must pay in land," barked the governor. "Just keep them whiskeyed up for a few days. That's all we need do to get them to give us the land in exchange for the man's life."

And so, a few days later, the Sauk chieftains agreed to give some land and made their marks on the Treaty of St. Louis. But they didn't realize they were ceding all the country east of the Mississippi River and south of the waters of the Jeffreon to the American government. That realization came later. Much later.

And did they achieve their goal by relinquishing the land? When Quashquame and his party readied for their journey home, their Indian brother was released from prison, only to be shot dead in the street!

Chapter I
Mid-Winter 1805, England

Humming softly so her father could not hear, Louise smoothed and folded the table linens as she tidied the display shelf. Her father's customers had examined every fine Irish table linen in the shop before selecting their purchase. It was her responsibility to restore order. He chatted cordially with his customers while he tallied their purchases but would have harsh words for her if he heard her humming. Louise felt humming was innocent enough, but her father thought it sinful, along with laughing, dancing, and myriad other pleasant pastimes. A staunch, old-fashioned puritan, he believed that hard work and even harder prayer were barely enough to save a soul from perdition.

At a tap on the window, Louise looked up from her work and saw Mr. Emmett. When he smiled and tugged at the brim of his hat, she thought him an attractive man in a peculiar sort of way. He was middling tall with a crooked smile, but the charming twinkle in his eyes signified he didn't take himself, or life, too seriously. He

Sweetbriar

wouldn't think it wrong to hum or laugh or dance. She decided as she smiled in return.

The bell over the shop door tinkled as he crossed the threshold. Rather than approach her directly, he nonchalantly fingered some bed linens.

"Louise," her father called out, "stop fussing with those table linens and see to the young gentleman until I'm done here."

"Yes, Father," she said, hurrying over. "Are you interested in bed linens today, sir?" she asked.

"Not particularly." His eyes danced with amusement. "You had a mischievous smile on your face, Miss Jetter, as if you had a delicious secret all your own." His warm voice softly caressed, "Will you share it with me?"

Flinging a quick peek toward her father, Louise smirked. "Not a secret," she whispered, "only a little humming. Father doesn't permit it, so I hum when he can't catch me. And when I hear music, I tap my foot, but it's not often I have occasion to hear music," she sighed regretfully.

"Ah, then you won't be at the public dance on Friday, more's the pity."

This time a sidelong glance assured Louise her father was still occupied with wrapping his customer's purchase. Lowering her voice, even more, she said, "I have been invited to stay a few days at the home of my good friend, Ellen Struthers. Unbeknownst to my father, her parents sometimes take her to the public dances. If they decide to do so this Friday, I won't have any choice but to attend."

He leaned close, "And do you suppose Mr. and Mrs. Struthers will escort young Miss Struthers to the dance?"

A devious gleam entered her eyes, "I may recall Miss Struthers mentioning something about that, but one can never be sure about such things."

The shop bell tinkled as the previous customers left, and Mr. Jetter approached. "Mr. Emmett, isn't it? What are you doing out and about today? I thought you worked at the tobacco shop. A man would do better than to encourage sinful habits. You should quit that shop and find more honorable employment."

"Yes, I quite agree," the young man acknowledged, "but my father, the tobacconist, wishes for me to learn the trade. Sinners will be sinners whether I work there or elsewhere. And it is honorable to acquiesce to my father's wishes."

"Be that as it may, young man, I shall not permit my daughter to associate with someone who does the devil's work."

"Father!" Hot spots of embarrassment stained the girl's cheeks.

"I'm well aware of Mr. Emmett's interest, Louise. One look was all I needed to convince me he will pursue his pleasures without serious consideration for his immortal soul."

"Oh, Father, please," she pleaded softly, humiliated by his tirade.

"'Tis quite all right, Miss Jetter. I shan't take offense." Laughter flashed in his eyes, "All men have their failings, and pride is as sinful as any other. Wouldn't you agree, Mr. Jetter?"

Anger suffused the older man's face.

Mr. Emmett grinned cheerfully and said, "Good day, sir." Then nodding toward Louise, "Good day, Miss Jetter." He perched his fashionable beaver hat jauntily on his head and departed, giving the door an extra jiggle to rattle the tiny bell merrily.

"You encouraged that young rascal," her father barked. She knew better than to deny his accusation because he would label her a liar and mete out a worse punishment. "Go to your room, get on your knees, and pray to God for deliverance from your wicked ways."

Feigning meekness, she bobbed her head then miserably ascended the stairs to their residence above the shop, yearning for deliverance from her father's strict rules. Unfortunately, escape could only come in the form of marriage, and the only men worthy of her hand, in her father's opinion, were like-minded puritans. Marriage to any of them would be worse than living under her father's control.

On her knees, instead of praying, she pondered what it would be like to have a husband like Mr. Emmett. At length, Louise concluded that a man who was lighthearted and not overly concerned about his immortal soul would make an extremely agreeable mate.

"Half of London must be here tonight," Louise enthused. The animated chatter of scores of acquaintances greeting each other created an underlying rhythm to the music, enhancing her excitement. Colorful gowns, glittering jewelry, and candlelight sparkling from hundreds of crystals on the chandeliers swirled dizzily in her mind like vibrant shards of multicolored glass.

Ellen Struthers had insisted Louise wear a gauze evening gown of midnight blue shot through with silver thread. It was plain enough by most standards but gayer and more elegant than any of her dreary broadcloth dresses. A foot-long peacock feather quivered gracefully above her head, secured by a fancy blue ribbon encircling her brow. She felt like a fairy princess standing there, softly tapping her foot, and gently swaying to the haunting strains of the violins. Louise thought that if a pretty gown, music, and gaiety were the fabric of sin, then the angels of heaven had their work cut out for themselves tonight.

Cautioning her friend, Ellen instructed, "A public assembly is not the same as a gathering hosted in a private home. Here a man mustn't ask permission to dance unless he has been properly introduced through a mutual acquaintance. You, of course, may decline the introduction, if you choose."

"And why would I do that?" Louise posed, scanning the room for familiar faces.

Ellen smiled at such naivety. "For many reasons, dear girl. Perhaps you don't like the cut of his clothes, or his complexion is marred, or he is ungainly on the ballroom floor. But the best reason of all is because you find him attractive," she confided with a wink.

Taken aback by this odd admission, Louise grasped her friend's arm and queried, "If I find a man attractive, why on earth would I decline an introduction?"

Smiling, Ellen leaned close, "To play the flirtation game."

"I don't understand," the sheltered girl replied, confused.

"First, you catch the eye of an attractive stranger. But don't be too bold, or it will put him off," Ellen explained. "Once he notices you, be sure to look away. Then every few minutes, look at him again. The third or fourth time your eyes meet should be encouragement enough. And, just to be sure, after the last glance, lower your eyes and smile to yourself."

"But if the man is a stranger, how do I meet him?"

"He will have to make inquires to find a mutual acquaintance to make the introduction."

"If I find the man attractive, I still don't see why I would refuse to make his acquaintance."

Miss Struthers sighed elaborately and elucidated with the air of authority, "Mother says men enjoy the chase, so refusing to acknowledge a man on his first attempt at meeting you presents him with a challenge.

His pride is delicately bruised. He must find a way to recommend himself. That usually means locating someone with a closer association to you. He may have to go through two or three additional introductions before discovering the person who is a close enough friend that it would be an insult for you to refuse the presentation."

"But wouldn't he be put off by such conceit?" Louise asked.

Ellen shook her head, "Once he succeeds in making your acquaintance, he will be quite proud of himself, thinking he has outwitted you. But all the while, his interest has been piqued, and to satisfy his curiosity he shall be obliged to call on you."

This revelation alarmed Louise. If a man she met this evening called on her, she would have to explain to her parents how they met. She dreaded to think how many hours she would spend on her knees in repentance for attending the ball. They would never allow her to see the man again and she would be forced to renounce her friendship with Ellen. Her father might even beat her. It would be much better not to meet any men at all.

"There is a young man casting glances our way," Ellen observed. "Our eyes have caught a couple of times."

Louise followed the direction of Ellen's gaze and saw Mr. Emmett conversing with another man as both men suddenly looked her way. Recognition flashed in Mr. Emmett's eyes, he spoke again to his companion, and they casually ambled across the room toward the two women.

"Don't look at them," Ellen hissed as she frantically flapped her fan in front of her face. "Do you know either of them?"

"Yes, the shorter man is Mr. Emmett, the tobacconist's son. A jolly man, but Father doesn't approve, so I shan't encourage him."

Ellen considered the approaching gentlemen. "Either the taller man wants to meet you, or he is hoping to meet me through you. You can decide your own mind, but I shall decline an introduction."

"You find him attractive, then?" Louise asked.

"He is attractive enough," the girl remarked, shrugging her shoulder, "but jolly men appeal to me more. You are my dear friend, so please introduce Mr. Emmett. I have no interest in the other man tonight."

Walking up, Mr. Emmett greeted Louise with a slight bow. "Good evening, Miss Jetter.

"Good evening, Mr. Emmett," she answered, dipping a curtsy.

"Miss Louise Jetter, may I introduce my friend, Mr. David Elkin?" he asked.

After a brief hesitation, Louise extended her hand, "I'm pleased to meet you, Mr. Elkin."

"The pleasure is mine, Miss Jetter," he responded with a brief bow over her hand.

Louise turned toward Ellen, "Miss Ellen Struthers, may I introduce Mr. Douglas Emmett?"

Ellen dropped a short curtsy, "Good evening, Mr. Emmett."

"Miss Struthers," he acknowledged, tipping his head.

A gauche pause ensued as it became obvious Louise would not extend the introduction to Mr. Elkin. Bridging the awkwardness, he asked, "May I have the honor of this dance, Miss Jetter?"

Embarrassment flooded her face. "That's very kind of you, Mr. Elkin. I ... I'm afraid I don't know how," she admitted.

Sweetbriar

At his friend's discomfiture of failing to obtain an introduction to Miss Struthers or a dance from Miss Jetter, amusement twinkled in Mr. Emmett's eyes. "May I have the honor, Miss Struthers?" he asked, extending his arm confidently.

"Of course, Mr. Emmett." Smiling sweetly, Ellen placed her hand on his arm, and they meandered toward the center of the ballroom.

"My apologies if I embarrassed you," Mr. Elkin said, fidgeting with his watch fob.

"There is no need to apologize, sir. One would be expected to know how to dance when attending a ball. Unfortunately, such frivolities are not permitted in my father's household. I am staying the week with my friend, Miss Struthers. Otherwise, I would not be here tonight," Louise explained.

His eyes quickly scanned from head to toe, taking in the peacock feather, the elegant dress, and the tapping foot before returning to her face. "Then, if I am to teach you to dance, Miss Jetter, you will have to introduce me to Miss Struthers so I may call tomorrow."

"Teach me to dance?" she murmured in disbelief. "I would love to learn to dance, but Miss Struthers expressly declined to meet you."

He shrugged. "If I cannot call on you at your home or Miss Struthers' home, then meet me elsewhere," he suggested boldly.

Louise gasped, "That would be most improper, Mr. Elkin." Then she quickly snapped her fan open in front of her face to emphasize her point.

"And where is the propriety of attending a public ball without your father's permission? It should not be of great concern for us to meet now that we are acquainted," he persuaded.

Her eyes quickly darted around the room, searching for a way out of the wickedly delightful conversation.

Oh, what she wouldn't give to learn to dance! "I suppose it wouldn't be so very inappropriate if we just happened upon each other unexpectedly. And it would be natural enough to walk about conversing. Do you suppose, though, circumstances would present an opportunity for dancing?" she asked under her breath.

A slow smile spread across his comely features. "A leisurely walk in winter weather can be chilling. If you were overcome with cold, I know of a coffeehouse frequented by aspiring musicians. No doubt that would present opportunity enough."

Louise glanced away. Her heart, thrilling with anticipation, beat fiercely in her breast. The music ended, and Mr. Emmett was returning with Miss Struthers. Breathlessly Louise said, "On the morrow, Miss Struthers will receive visitors until afternoon tea. By late morning she will be too inconvenienced to run an errand with me, but I recall I promised my mother I would purchase her a hank of black yarn. Her mittens are worn, and she needs new."

Mr. Elkin's smile broadened as he said, "On the morrow, in late morning, I shall take a turn around town in my carriage. If I happen to pass you by, it would only be common courtesy to offer you my services."

"If you happened by and if I were cold, I might consider accepting your offer," she replied coyly, tipping her nose in the air.

The next morning Louise walked only a short distance before Mr. Elkin hailed her from his brougham. Seeing the vehicle, she realized he was a man of substance and became self-conscious of her drab attire. But he offered his hand, and after a slight hesitation, she stepped into the elegant carriage.

Mr. Elkin directed the driver to a shop where Louise bought the black wool yarn her mother wanted. Then, instructing the driver to take them to the coffeehouse favored by musicians, her companion explained that instrumentalists gathered there to exchange news and gossip about their trade and would require very little persuasion to play a few tunes.

The jammed public house was a cacophony of unrelated musical scores played on diverse instruments scattered about the room. The low kettledrum rumble of male conversation was punctuated by the higher notes of the serving girls' piping voices. Apprehensive in the unfamiliar, boisterous horde, Louise pressed close to her escort.

Mr. Elkin grabbed a chair, scampered up, and gaining the throng's attention, brashly announced his mission to educate his young companion in the art of dance. He ignored one man's muttered entreaty to allow him, instead, to school her in the art of love. A few musicians came forth, money changed hands, and tables were shifted about to accommodate the couple.

Louise quickly learned the stylized steps of the minuet, and after a quarter-hour, David, as she had come to think of him, suggested she learn the waltz.

"In for a penny, in for a pound," she laughingly agreed but was unprepared for the breathtaking enchantment that raced up her spine when his arm encircled her waist. Timidly, she tried to follow his lead and stumbled.

Smiling, he drew her closer.

Louise wasn't sure if dancing, in itself, was wrong but suspected it was a sin to enjoy the feel of their bodies pressing close together. Tilting her head back to ask him to loosen his hold, she lost the thought at the unfamiliar intensity ablaze in his eyes.

Later, in the carriage, she understood when he unexpectedly dropped a peck of a kiss onto her lips.

Spring 1805, England

"The success of the French Revolution was very short-lived," sniffed the Right Honorable William Pitt, Prime Minister of the United Kingdom.

"Yes, but you must admit, old Boney was crafty when he outmaneuvered his fellow conspirators six years ago," his Parliamentary friend, William Wilberforce, commented. "Most likely Joseph Sieyès never suspected that by drafting their new constitution, the little general would usurp him and secure his own election to First Consul. Then the wily bastard was absolutely brilliant the next year when he revised the bloody document and secured that position for life."

"Bloody hell, Napoleon as First Consul for life was bad enough," complained Pitt. "Now that he has been crowned Emperor of the Empire of the French, there is no doubt he intends to expand that empire for years to come. And if his expansion is to be thwarted, it is up to England to devise the means to defeat him."

"Since Great Britain has been his most resolute adversary, he tries to strangle us by blockading our shores. We need to keep the Royal Navy well manned, and that means impressing sailors, preferably from the ships that trade with France," Wilberforce advised.

"Yes, we must keep our navy strong. We must also support opposition to France by financing whichever continental countries are willing to fight."

Louise came to rue the evening she met the charismatic David Elkin. It had all started so innocently when she consented to the secret rendezvous. He would teach her to dance; what harm could come of that? But one clandestine encounter led to another, and the dancing soon gave way to kissing. Before long, there was no pretense of dancing, and she foolishly believed he intended

Sweetbriar

to marry her. But David had no interest in marriage. Not to her, at least. Not to his lover.

Now, like a caged animal, Louise apprehensively paced the small room and cast fretful glances toward the bed. A wardrobe, vanity and stool, and the big double bed cramped the tiny room. Yesterday she was fetched to the house, and tonight Mrs. Patterson expected her downstairs.

She recoiled when heavy footsteps halted outside her door. Then feminine laughter drifted through the wooden panel like smoke from a fire, and the footsteps receded down the hall.

This morning Louise had met the other young women at breakfast if you could call it that. Breakfast in this establishment was served at 11:00 a.m. Most of the girls were still half asleep, but a couple of them nodded hello.

That was when Mrs. Patterson handed Louise the two evening gowns with décolletage designed to reveal more than conceal. She was wearing a royal blue gown now. The cost of the clothes, along with her room and board, would be deducted from her wages. Tonight, it was time to start earning her wages.

She froze at a light tapping on the door. The soft knock came again, and the voice of a young woman called her name. Reluctantly Louise opened the door a crack.

A petite blond named Emily offered a tentative smile. "Mrs. Patterson thought you'd like someone to talk to for a few minutes. May I come in?"

Stepping back, Louise allowed Emily to slip inside.

"You look fretful, so I guess you could use a friendly chat. 'Ave you ever done this before," she asked cautiously, "you know, offering your favors?"

Louise blushed, dropped her eyes, and shook her head. "Not for pay. My gentleman friend..." her voice broke, and she cleared her throat. "Well, maybe he wasn't much of a gentleman."

Emily took her hand and gave it a squeeze, then plopped on the edge of the bed, the only available place. Louise remained standing but didn't retrieve her hand.

"'Tisn't so bad really," Emily claimed with a toss of her head. "Better 'ere than out on the street. You don't 'ave to take a man tonight, but 'tis best if you do. Listen, you can make it easier on yerself by ignoring the younger men. They be too energetic for all their lack of skill. 'Tis best to save your smiles and kisses for the older men. They be more demanding and imaginative, but they be more 'preciative, too."

Wary eyes grew huge. "What do you mean?"

Again, Emily squeezed her hand, "Don't worry 'bout that now. Older men, once they be done, might fall asleep. Just let them. Treat them right in the morn, and most will give a generous tip that you won't 'ave to split with Madam."

Louise couldn't believe she was having this conversation. Just a few weeks ago, she was cosseted and protected. Then she fell in love.

They heard the front doorbell chime. Emily squeezed her hand again, "Come now, let's see a smile. You stay with me, and I'll 'elp you find someone who won't be too demanding of you tonight." Emily stood, gave Louise a tug toward the door, then released her hand. Slowly, with feet like lead weights, Louise followed.

Gentlemen were already in the elegant salon surveying the salacious young women. Louise stayed close to her new friend, too apprehensive to move from her side.

Emily skirted around the salon, eying men as though she were choosing a bolt of cloth to make a dress. Then she gave a come-hither curl of her fingers, and a dapper man in his mid-thirties approached. He seemed so old that, inwardly, Louise cringed. She felt like a field mouse under the shadow of a hawk, afraid she would be consumed.

"Good evening, ladies. What a pleasure it is to see two such lovely creatures." Then, looking directly at Louise, he said, "I don't believe I've seen you here before. My name is Edward. What might yours be?"

With a throat as dry as sawdust, Louise couldn't force her name out of her mouth. But before it became too awkward, Emily nudged her and said, "'Tis Louise, she 'asn't been with us long."

Edward smiled and took her hand. "I'm delighted to make your acquaintance, Louise. I think we should get to know each other. What do you say?"

Again, Emily nudged her, harder this time, and Louise finally squeaked out, "Oh, yes, Mr.—"

"I'm Edward, and you're Louise," he chuckled. Then he put his arm around her narrow waist, fingers familiarly brushing the side of her breast, and gently urged her toward the stairs. Fear clawed at the pit of her stomach, but she was helpless to prevent the inevitable.

After ascending the stairs, they wandered the full length of the narrow, dimly lit hall. "We can't be roaming around all evening," annoyance evident in his voice. "Which room is yours?"

They were two doors past it. "Oh, well, that room back there. That's my room," she mumbled. Coloring deeply in humiliation, she lowered her head, unable to look at the man beside her.

Puzzled, he thought it odd that she walked past her own door. Once inside, he was further baffled and irritated when she reached to extinguish the oil lamp. "Don't put the light out. It's more enjoyable when we can see what we're doing. And see you, I must. You're so hesitant and blushing, like a true innocent." Edward brushed past her, sat on the bed, kicked off his shoes, and removed his stylish jacket. "Come, girl. Show me your lovely body. Undress for me."

Mortified to be alone in such close proximity with the man and unable to move, she just stared.

"So, you want to play the reluctant, do you? Be as reluctant as you like but unbutton your dress," he demanded in exasperation. "Start with the top one." When she hesitated, he commanded severely, "Do it!"

With trembling fingers, Louise fumbled the buttons. Slowly they came unfastened, first one, and then another. As Edward continued to disrobe, he watched her as greedily as a miser with his gold. When the last button was finally released, Louise's dress slid to the floor.

Suddenly he seized the young woman's hips and drew her one step toward him to stand between his legs, her knees touching the hateful bed. "At this rate, you'll be all night," he said, voice raspy with eager anticipation. Quickly he removed her chemise and pantaloons.

She didn't know if she could endure the stranger's touch but found it oddly erotic that he left her stockings gartered above her knees when he laid her on the bed and explored her secret places. Suddenly, desire surged through her like the swift waters of a flooding river, and thrashing in its tide, she succumbed to the rushing need he aroused.

Early Summer 1805, England

"Derek! Derek!" Brad shouted, sprinting up the rough wooden gangplank of the *Angel Star*. "Where the hell are you?" Tearing off his forest green cutaway coat, Brad spotted the cabin boy coming from below decks. "Move your ass, boy. I have need of you."

Derek O'Malley, Quinn's youngest son, scurried to obey. "Yes, sir?" he inquired.

Sweetbriar

Tossing the boy the coat, Brad strode toward his cabin below deck, removing his buff waistcoat as he went. Cantankerously, he called over his shoulder, "Have Cook heat water for my bath and tell him to be quick about it. Set out clean trousers. Hell, I need a clean shirt and neckcloth, too. Brush out my coat and polish my boots while you're at it."

"Yes, sir. Yes, sir." Derek echoed in his wake. "Is that all, sir?" He scampered to keep up with Brad's longer gait as they entered the cabin.

"No, dammit!" Snatching up and furiously shaking his nearly empty captain's decanter in the boy's face, Brad roared, "How many times have I told you to keep my brandy topped off?"

"W-why never, sir," Derek stuttered in wide-eyed panic.

"Well, I'm telling you now, so move before I throw you overboard, you lazy pup!" Brad thundered.

Flustered, the cabin boy vanished like a puff of smoke in a strong gale, prepared to tell Cook to strain the vegetables off the broth, if necessary, to guarantee the captain had his bath without delay.

Watching the boy race away, Bradley Anderson sat on his bunk and laughed, remembering the harried demands Captain O'Malley had made when Brad was a cabin boy. He had been just as terrified of being thrown overboard.

He hoisted his long legs onto his bunk and laid back. His legs and thighs were smoothly muscled from years of balancing on the swaying deck of a ship and were a fine complement to his broad-shouldered torso and narrow hips. His sinewy arms rippled as he flexed the long, shapely fingers of his brawny hands. He was over 6 feet tall with chestnut brown hair that had a constant windblown look. His hazel eyes were changeable, gray when angry, and slightly green when pleasantly aroused. If there was any flaw in his masculine good looks, it resulted from an aristocratic nose that was somewhat too long.

The mirth of a moment ago faded as quickly as it appeared. Brad had reason to be angry. His first port call was always to arrange for the purchase of tea. The special Rockwell blend was the best British breakfast tea and had a substantial American market. Milton Avery, Earl of Rockwell, negotiated all sales personally, but he had been out of town all week. This afternoon Brad arrived at his lordship's office, as arranged by the clerk, but Lord Rockwell was disinclined to discuss business. He intended to take his daughter riding in the park instead. Disgusted, Brad tried to mask his frustration, but the nobleman noticed and insisted Captain Anderson dine with him that evening, promising to settle the matter over cigars and brandy. Brad accepted as graciously as possible even though it ruined his other plans for the evening.

Soaking in his bath with the hot water and brandy easing the tension from his muscles, Brad shrugged imperceptibly. He could put off his plans for one more evening.

Bradley and the earl relaxed before dinner in a spacious salon overlooking the back garden and enjoyed the last golden rays of the early summer sun. The terrace doors were flung open to entice in the unseasonably warm, rose-scented breeze, and the lace curtains fluttered lazily. Tonight, no fire burned in the grate of the massive marble fireplace, which dominated the room. Lord Rockwell had chosen this room specifically for the calming effect it would have on his guest. The deep plush chairs and silk-covered walls suggested, soothingly, that there would be no talk of commerce before dinner. That would come later in the library, where the somber atmosphere dictated a quick conclusion to business matters.

The tall oak doors from the hallway opened quietly, and the soft rustle of skirts announced a woman's presence in the room. "Ah, there you are, my dear," Lord Rockwell sighed as he rose from his chair. "Captain Anderson," he said, addressing his guest, who had also risen, "this is my daughter, Beth."

Brad was impressed by the young woman whose abundant hair was burnished, more coppery than auburn. It was piled high on her head with soft tendrils escaping to grace the delicate nape of her neck. Slightly taller than average, she had a slender build and firm, high breasts. Intuitively, he imagined the promising figure, the long legs, and slim ankles hiding beneath the skirts of her russet-colored gown. He was captivated by her beauty even before she tilted her brown eyes toward him and smiled coquettishly. "I'm delighted to make your acquaintance, Captain Anderson."

Nodding his head, Brad responded, "And I yours, milady." It occurred to him that, given the time, a man might easily drown in the dark pools of her sparkling eyes. After too long a moment, she lowered her lashes demurely, leaving him bereft.

Abruptly Rockwell intervened, "I presume from your appearance, Beth, that dinner is ready to be served."

Brad took pleasure in the way she swished her skirts when she turned to smile impishly at her father. "Oh, yes, Papa. And I instructed Cook to prepare your favorite dishes. I'm sure you will be pleased."

And pleased he was. Simple and delicious courses satisfied the palate as well as the stomach. Carrot soup with a hint of dill weed came first, and then Yorkshire pudding flavored with meat drippings accompanied the savory joint of roast beef, followed by roasted potatoes and new peas with baby onions, all slathered in fresh country butter.

While dining, both men were content to allow Beth to entertain them with the trivialities that comprised a woman's world. She chatted easily, her discourse intelligent and spiced with a touch of wit, which kept the conversation light and congenial.

With sharp English cheddar, crisp apple tarts, and fragrant tea completing the meal, Brad was beguiled by the surreptitious glances the young lady sent his way over the rim of her teacup as she sipped the soothing brew. But all too soon, Lord Rockwell stood, signaling the end of the evening for his daughter. "Say goodnight now, Beth. Captain Anderson and I have business to discuss."

Moving around the table, Beth dutifully kissed her father on the cheek, "Goodnight, Papa." When she turned toward the American, she caught the faint scent of cedar. "Goodnight, Captain Anderson. It has been a pleasure meeting you," she uttered, extending her hand.

"The pleasure has been mine, Lady Beth," he replied, holding her eyes with his as he brought her hand to his lips for a light kiss. Beth's color heightened, and her bold eyes sparkled as she slowly withdrew her hand before leaving. Brad caught her parting smile as she turned and quietly closed the door behind her. The soft rustle of her skirts echoed in his mind. "Your daughter is enchanting, milord," Brad remarked as his admiring eyes lingered on the closed door. "She must have numerous admirers."

Clearing his throat, Lord Rockwell quietly answered, "Hardly, sir, she is just fourteen." The captain's startled look prompted his lordship to continued, "Many people mistake Beth for being older. She took it upon herself to become the woman of the house after my wife passed away last year. I find no harm in indulging her. But enough of this, you came to talk tea, which can best be done over brandy and cigars."

Milton Avery enjoyed this aspect of his tea business and didn't mind that circumstances necessitated his continued role in commerce. As a young man, he asked his father to help him purchase the tea business, and through long hours of diligent work, the business had grown. In time, Milton married, and his wife produced their daughter, Beth. But it was a difficult birth, and his wife took months to recover. With heavy hearts, they decided against more children.

As the second son of the second son, Milton Avery had never anticipated the Rockwell title descending to him. But his older brother's entire family perished in a cholera epidemic in India six years ago. His father, suffering from a broken heart, withered and died shortly thereafter. The title and lands were entailed to male heirs only, and his unfortunate uncle had sired only females, so at his uncle's death two years ago, Milton Avery became the fourth Earl of Rockwell. That's when he and his wife reconsidered the possibility of another child, a son. To this day, he felt it was the gravest mistake of his life. He lost his wife and the stillborn baby, never asking whether the child was a boy or a girl. He didn't want to know.

The modest Rockwell estate might have provided for his diminished family without the need of retaining the tea business. Still, he needed a way to assuage his grief, and the business was familiar. And the relentless urging of his aunt prevailed upon his sense of family duty to provide dowries for his four female cousins. The amounts were small but depleted the estate. Tenant rents barely covered the expense of maintaining the manor and small staff. If it hadn't been for the tea business, Lord Rockwell couldn't have afforded the London house and staff, which would have presented a distinct disadvantage to finding an acceptable husband for his daughter when the time came.

Seated comfortably before the fire in the library in an oxblood leather chair, Brad glanced around. Apparently, not all British aristocrats were fond of the ceiling-high bookshelves that necessitated a tall rolling ladder. In this library, browsing and selecting a book would be easy work. Two walls had low cabinets topped by shelves that reached only head high. The other two were wainscoted in dark mahogany that complemented a broad, dark desk. When handed a snifter, Brad lazily swirled the cognac and inhaled deeply as he sipped appreciatively. "I commend you on your exceptional taste, milord."

"Thank you, Captain, it's some of the finest France has to offer," acknowledged his host. "Fortunately, my cellar is well stocked, and I hope it will see me through the current hostilities Boney is showing toward the civilized world."

Setting aside his glass, Bradley agreed, "I hope that also, however, France has increased its unfriendly measures against Great Britain, specifically in the area of trade."

"Unfortunately, that is true," conceded Rockwell. "Frankly, it was a related event that called me away from my office recently. Are you aware of the British decision regarding the American merchant vessel, the *Essex*?"

With a shake of his head, Brad encouraged his host to continue.

"As you know," Milton said, "British law forbids merchant vessels from carrying cargo from the French colonies directly to France. To circumvent the law, many vessels, including the *Essex,* made a habit of interrupting their voyage with a stop at an American port. Now, the High Court of Admiralty, citing a precedent

Sweetbriar

set in 1756, has disallowed the legality of this practice and has confiscated the *Essex* and her cargo. I am convinced the situation will worsen before it improves." Lord Rockwell paused to clip the end off a cigar, and between puffs, continued. "Therefore, Captain Anderson...I may be inclined...to negotiate favorably with you...on a large shipment of tea."

"How large?" queried Brad, sipping the brandy.

Having lighted his cigar successfully, Lord Rockwell handed the cigar clipper to Brad and sat back in his chair, "Say enough to fill three ships without room for other cargo."

Bowled over, it was Brad's turn to use the ritual of lighting his cigar to marshal his thoughts. Surrey Trading Company currently had twenty-three ships in active service, each assigned to various ports of call throughout the Atlantic and Mediterranean. Two were used strictly for trade on the American seaboard, these being the oldest ships, still seaworthy but requiring more frequent repairs. Three plied the West Indies primarily for sugar, molasses, and rum. Seven conducted commerce with the Mediterranean countries, one with Ireland, and five each with France and England. Each captain was personally responsible for the cargo of his ship and received a percentage of the profits they made.

If the French blockade of Great Britain worsened, as appeared likely, trade with England would become ever more hazardous, if not impossible. In America, it would push the price of all British goods skyward. Three full shiploads represented twice as much tea as Surrey Trading Company normally imported in an entire year, but at the right price, this offer might be extremely lucrative. On the other hand, if the situation between France and Great Britain improved, it could place himself, the other captains, and Surrey Trading Company in an unprofitable position. So, the question was if tensions eased, might the American market for this tea be expanded to support the increased purchase? With an imperceptible nod of his head, Brad decided it was a chance he was willing to take.

He relaxed back in his chair and sent a plume of cigar smoke swirling toward the high ceiling. "What is the favorable price you had in mind?"

Confident of Captain Anderson's interest, his lordship amiably stated a price scarcely lower than normal.

Brad took his time, sending another plume of smoke upward, and countered with a much lower price.

"I expected a reasonable offer, young man," Lord Rockwell barked out sharply.

"And I have given you a reasonable offer."

"Why that's preposterous. You cut current prices almost by half."

Looking at the older man, Brad responded, "That may be, but you ask me to commit myself and others to a sale double our normal purchase. You may, if you wish, negotiate with each of us separately, but I cannot promise you a total sale of such volume."

The earl glowered into the fire, inherently knowing from past experience that his guest would stand firm on his offer. "Are you prepared to commit to the full amount tonight?"

Without hesitation, Brad nodded, "Yes, milord, I am."

"So be it then," Lord Rockwell said, rising, "I'll expect you in my office tomorrow afternoon."

Startled by the abrupt dismissal, Brad tossed back the last sip of his brandy, stubbed out his cigar, and rose. They shook hands.

Rockwell escorted his guest outside then returned to the library, not completely dissatisfied with the night's transaction. A low price was preferable to three

Sweetbriar

shiploads of tea moldering in a dockside warehouse during a blockade.

Clad in her white flannel nightdress and green woolen dressing gown, Beth quietly crept into the room, tiptoed to her father's chair, and slipped her arms around his neck.

Troubled, he turned, "Beth, are you ill? Why are you still awake so late?"

"I couldn't sleep, Papa. I heard Captain Anderson leave, so I thought I'd come down and talk."

Not since before the death of his wife had Milton Avery taken his daughter onto his lap, but he drew her to him now, "And just what might cause a young girl like you to lose sleep, my child?"

"Papa, do you suppose the captain is married?" Beth inquired, watching her father out of the corner of her eye.

Puzzled, he replied carefully, "I've never given it any thought. Why do you ask?"

"No reason in particular," she shrugged, "but when you see him next, will you invite him to dine with us again?"

"And what schemes have you up your sleeve this time?" her father chuckled, sitting her up straight, and looking her in the eye.

"None at all, Papa," Beth claimed with wide-eyed innocence. "It's just that Captain Anderson is so very handsome and many girls must be vying for his interest—"

Incredulous, Lord Rockwell soundly set his daughter on her feet. "Now listen here, Beth," he said, ruffled, "you're much too young to be thinking about men."

"Don't be foolish, Papa," she laughed. "Aunt Sylvia says a girl is never too young to think about her effect upon men. After all, I've been practicing on you for years."

Glowering at his daughter, he made a mental note to speak to his sister, Sylvia. "Enough of this nonsense, child. My business with Captain Anderson is concluded, and I am not inviting him to dine again. That is final."

Beth pouted and stamped her bare foot, "But I'm not too young. I think he likes me. Did you not notice him kiss my hand?"

"No," he barked.

She flinched at his unexpected outburst, "But, Papa—"

"No!" he shouted, rising from his chair.

Rattled, she stepped back. Her father had never raised his voice to her before. Beth opened her mouth to speak, but the look of contained wrath on his face stopped her. Unexpectedly, she burst into tears. Then, mortified by her tears, she turned and dashed from the room.

Before stepping into the hired cab, Brad saw a curtain flutter in an upstairs window and smiled momentarily as the image of the woman-child he met that evening flashed in his mind. She was young, true, but what a beauty! There was no doubt she would break hearts when formally introduced to London society. If she'd already been out, Brad might have been tempted to ask permission to court her, but it was just as well. The sea was a demanding mistress, and too often, ships were lost with all hands. His conscience wouldn't allow him to consider marriage until he was ready to sail a dockside desk instead of a ship. He might consider a mistress but not a wife.

That thought seeded on the fertile landscape of his consciousness. Many years ago, on one of Brad's earliest voyages, Captain O'Malley had cautioned him away from dockside taverns and their disease-ridden whores, explaining that the first could get a sailor shanghaied, and the second could give him the pox. Over the years, Brad took the warning to heart with hard-won restraint. Then two years ago, a lovely, well-to-do American widow, twelve years his senior, had initiated him into the sensual mysteries of life. When it suited, she took enjoyment from him and gave it in return. But he was only her occasional lover. She had others. So, after eight weeks at sea, Brad felt free to slacken his needs elsewhere. He was acquainted with an establishment that discreetly catered to the high born and wealthy gentry of London, but there was always the risk of disease. The seed of his thought germinated and took root. A mistress would be a better solution. She could satisfy his desires after the lengthy sea voyage as well as bestow all the comforts of home.

Then, recalling his earlier thoughts of the day, Brad consulted his pocket watch in the glow of the carriage lamp and smiled. It wasn't all that late, at least not overly late for a visit to the house that afforded such delightful female companions. Tapping the roof of the carriage, Brad gave instructions to the cabbie and relaxed in pleasant anticipation.

The sensually luxurious house contained lovely, desirable women, skilled in their allurements to men. It was one of the highest-priced brothels in London and well worth the money expended. Brad was graciously welcomed by the proprietress, as were all her patrons. No uncouth scenes in this refined establishment, finances were diplomatically settled prior to admittance to the main salon.

Accepting a glass of wine from a footman, Brad casually surveyed his surroundings. Crystal chandeliers reflected their radiant golden light from opulent velvet draped walls. Music drifted from a small second-floor gallery, feather-light, and soft as down. Few guests and courtesans lingered at this hour, most having retired upstairs long ago. But, as always, there were the late arrivals and women to accommodate them.

A burst of derisive laughter interrupted his thoughts as a man and woman walked toward the stairs. "Don't worry," the woman cooed, "She's new and will come around in time. Just be patient, dearie."

Brad's glance trailed in their wake, and he saw a young woman standing with head high, but scarlet faced, eyes flashing in anger. Approaching from an oblique angle, Brad whispered in her ear, "If looks could kill—"

"Then they would trouble me no more," she snapped.

"Is it as bad as that, fair lady?"

She spun to face him, but her fury died at the mocking amusement in his eyes. Slowly a smile formed on her lips. "And who might you be, kind sir?" she asked.

"Captain Bradley Anderson, at your service," he legged a courtly bow, sweeping low.

"And I am Louise," she rejoined with a deep curtsy.

Both laughed at their impromptu foolishness. His eyes quickly appraised her. An attractive young woman with black hair, cropped short in the French manner. She wore a cobalt dress that mirrored the color of strikingly blue eyes. Eyes that danced in a heart-shaped face. Her sensuous mouth curved in a way that invited a kiss, clearly a woman born to seduce men.

"Captain Bradley Anderson, would you be kind enough to escort me upstairs?" she asked softly, almost shyly.

He felt a quickening in his loins, smiled warmly into her eyes, and tucked her hand under his arm, "It will be my pleasure. No doubt, it will be my very great pleasure," he replied as they moved toward the stairs.

After the door to her room closed behind them, Louise suffered the disturbing mix of angst at the necessity of offering her body to a stranger combined with the now-familiar hankering for his touch. Short hair framed her fragile face, and tetchiness marred her sapphire eyes as he approached.

Gently tracing a finger across her jaw, he bent to kiss her trembling mouth, but she turned her face away. "Don't be afraid," he soothed quietly. "I won't hurt you." She reached for him then, passionately, and the awkward moment passed. Undressing her slowly, Brad paused to kiss the delicate curve of her neck as he caressed her breasts, unconsciously discerning that for a small woman, she had a voluptuous body. When he finished disrobing her, Brad kissed her mouth again, and bending lower ran his tongue around her nipples, finding them already taut with passion.

"I want you, Captain Bradley Anderson," she murmured.

Green eyes glimmered as he drank in the beauty of her sumptuous body, and he undressed hurriedly, revealing his own hard arousal. At first, he took his time to prolong their pleasure, and then when he discovered her ardor matched his own, fervently made love to her. But as was his habit, he withdrew from the woman before spilling his seed.

Temporarily sated, with the young woman curled close to him, her head resting on his shoulder, and her leg thrown across his hips, he asked, "Have you been here long?"

"Mmm, not really,' she replied, her hand sensuously teasing the hair on his chest, "five weeks perhaps, not more."

"And how came you to be here?"

Her hand stopped its lazy movement, and then leisurely started again when she decided to answer. "I come from a good family, but I made the mistake of thinking I was in love. I was intimate with the young man. It was wrong, and I knew it, but it happened anyway." She sighed. "When my parents learned of it, they threw me out of the house. I thought my young man would marry me, but he was already engaged." She rose onto her elbow to look at the American and continued bitterly, "His father brought me here. I was furious when I realized what he intended for me, but he told me I should be grateful he arranged this rather than tossing me into the gutter the way my family had done." She shrugged, "What was I to do?"

Brushing his knuckles across her cheek, Brad asked, "Is that why you were so angry when I first saw you? Was that the man you had been involved with?"

"The viscount? No," she said, anger flaring in her eyes again. "That was Rolf Dunmore, a vile man. Mrs. Patterson does not require any of us to come upstairs with him, even though he pays handsomely high for his pleasures. Alice encourages him because she prefers a woman to a man anyway. But I shall not be the second woman in a man's bed for any price."

"Good God. You mean the man wants two women at the same time?"

Embarrassed, Louise glanced away and sighed. "It's by far the most disgusting thing I've learned since I came here, Captain Bradley Anderson." Then glancing back at him, she smiled slyly and said, "But there are other things I've learned men enjoy that aren't so very disagreeable." She traced her fingers slowly across his chest, following with light, nipping kisses. Tracing lower, she felt his muscles contract beneath her fingers. His breath drew in sharply as she trailed kisses down his taut stomach. Sliding her hand across his thighs, she caressed his manhood.

Louise had learned quickly to use the power sex exerted over men to her advantage. By her willingness to give pleasure, she had acquired some devoted admirers who consistently returned to her rather than seeking another of Madam Patterson's beauties. This limited the number of men she brought to her bed and allowed her a small measure of serenity. But she longed to ensnare one man's passion and enjoy only a solitary lover.

As her kisses moved lower, the man with her now moaned and tangled his fingers in her hair.

Carefully, Brad disentangled himself from the sleeping girl, but as he slipped out of bed, she awakened, sat up, and stretched lazily, unselfconscious of her nudity. She smiled and patted the space he had just vacated. "Come back to bed, Captain Bradley Anderson, and I shall make it worth your while."

Inevitable lust stirred, but he shook his head as he stepped into his trousers. "I have business to attend to, and it is already daylight."

She pouted seductively, "Will you come back again?"

"Do you want me to?" he countered, shrugging into his shirt.

Scooting out of bed, she stood on tiptoe, putting her arms around his neck. "Yes," she whispered and pressed her lips to the pulse beating in his throat.

Placing his hands on her hips, he impulsively asked, "Are you as talented in the kitchen as you are in the bedroom?"

She looked into his eyes and found them more serious than she expected. "Yes, I am an excellent cook," she said with unabashed pride.

He smiled as he disentangled her arms from around his neck and sat on the bed to pull on his socks and Wellingtons. "I'd like to enjoy the pleasures of home while I'm in England. It would be convenient to have a small cottage and a woman to satisfy both of my appetites." He looked at her again, "You could be that woman, Louise."

She sat next to him and sighed dejectedly. "No, I can't be that woman. Madam won't allow it. She's been very clear on that from the beginning. If any of us leave to be with a man, she won't have us back." Louise gazed at him sadly, "And you will sail away. What would become of me then? I'm sorry, but you will have to look elsewhere for your cook and bed partner, Captain Bradley Anderson."

"It is true that I shall sail, but I shall be back next year and for many years to come. At day's end, I won't stop wanting a hearty meal and a woman to warm my bed."

She stood and paced in the small space beside the bed, considering. "And who will care for me when you are gone?" she demanded.

As she passed in front of him, Brad took her hand to stop her pacing. "I shall give you enough money to care for yourself until I return."

Taking his cravat, she slung it around his neck, and while tying an intricate knot, weighed his proposal in her mind. When she finished fussing, she contemplated his eyes, searching for the possible truth of his words. Satisfied, she said, "Then you must speak with Madam Patterson."

Brad smiled, nibbled teasingly at her breast, then lightly smacked her buttock with the palm of his hand as he stood and reached for his vest. "Yes, I'll have a word with her this evening after I've finished with today's business." He let her help him on with his coat, and as he buttoned it, glanced at her in the mirror, "You won't have cause to regret it, Louise. I promise you that." Then he tugged at the front of his coat, brushed his lips quickly across hers, and left.

Returning to the *Angel Star*, he sent messengers to the captains of the other Surrey Trading Company ships, who were all in port. Brad would gamble on a full shipload of tea and let the others dicker for the remainder. Captain O'Malley already had most of his freight confirmed, so he committed to only a small portion. The other three captains found the commodity appealing at the low price Brad had obtained and haggled back and forth for the remainder of the morning before deciding on the final allotments.

With an outline of cargo weights for each ship, Brad arrived at the tea exporter's office. He anticipated leaving the information and returning with the other captains later in the day when the bills of lading were completed, but Lord Rockwell invited him into his office.

"Sit down, Captain, and I'll have the clerk draw up the papers while you wait. It will save you time."

"Thank you, milord." Brad sat in the straight-backed chair across from the exporter. This utilitarian office was in stark contrast to the nobleman's luxurious townhouse. Two straight-backed chairs faced an ancient, scarred desk. A small coal-fired brazier, used in the colder months, squatted idle in the corner. A tall, narrow clock ticked loudly from its perch on a plank shelf. "Thank you for the enjoyable dinner last evening. Your daughter is a lovely and entertaining hostess," Brad commented dutifully.

All morning Milton Avery had re-examined the late-night encounter with his daughter and lamented the loss of his wife. Kathryn would have known how to talk to Beth, how to explain that she was too young to cast her eyes upon the dashing sea captain. When had his child abandoned the fairy tale world of dolls and begun to inhabit the very real world of adults? Her budding interest in men had caught him off guard, and like a thief in the night, had stolen his reason. He regretted his loss of composure last night and realized his daughter was no longer a child but a young girl on the threshold of womanhood. Acknowledging his need to get used to the idea of his little girl growing up, he had decided to start by inviting the man Beth thought she fancied to dinner, reasoning that the American would sail away, and Beth would forget about him. "I shall be sure to mention your compliment to her, Captain. I don't suppose you get many chances to partake of a family meal while in London."

Brad rested one ankle on the opposing knee. "My grandfather was the last Duke of Surrey, so my father obliges me to call on his few remaining relatives and childhood friends, when possible. And I have enough English blue blood in my veins to get more social invitations than I choose to accept," he contradicted.

Surprised by this revelation, Rockwell inquired, "How is it your father didn't inherit the title when your grandfather passed?"

The uncomfortable chair was intended to bring a swift conclusion to business negotiations rather than encourage leisurely conversation. Brad dropped his booted foot to the floor and shifted his weight. "You know how it is here in England for second sons. My grandfather had arranged for an advantageous marriage for my father, but he objected to the woman, so to avoid the match, he emigrated. He founded Surrey Trading Company and eventually met, then married, my mother. When hostilities erupted between our countries, he never questioned his loyalties, America was his home. Fourteen years ago, his older brother died without siring a son, so when the Duke died, the title and estates reverted to the crown."

"Yes, similar circumstances brought the Rockwell title to me, and I may be the last Earl of Rockwell. My wife died trying to give me a son, and I hesitate to remarry until Beth is out and settled." Clarifying, the older man explained, "There should never be more than one female ruling a household, and Beth takes that duty very seriously. She may be my unofficial hostess, but it was my wife's expressed wish for Beth to wait until after her sixteenth birthday to enter the marriage race, and that won't be for two years yet."

A brisk rap on the door preceded the entry of a small, wiry clerk. His fingers were ink-stained, but his manner was as sharp as the nib of his quill. Setting papers on the worktable, he instructed, "Your lordship, sign here and here." Efficiently the clerk sanded and blotted each signature. "And, Captain, you sign here and here." Again, he applied the sand and blotter block, then handed the captain his copy of the bill of lading. "The ladings for the other ships will take longer to complete. When may I expect their captains to arrive?"

Brad glanced at the clock before replying, "I should think another hour or two. Captain O'Malley is already loading and will want his the soonest."

"Thank you, sir." The clerk snatched the exporter's paper from the table and hurried out, his heels clicking crisply on the worn timber floor.

Lord Rockwell cleared his throat, "With a full shipload of tea, your business is done. If you have some time on your hands tonight, Captain, come to the house for dinner."

"Thank you, I appreciate the offer but have other obligations this evening," Brad declined and stood. Curiously, he saw relief spread across his lordship's face as they shook hands. "As always, it is a pleasure doing business with you, milord."

Business was business, and if anything, Madam Patterson was shrewd in business. As a young woman, she had worked in a brothel similar to this when her alluring charms caught the eye of a widowed merchant who was old enough to be her grandfather. She teased him and spurned him. She toyed with him and refused to take him to her bed. In the end, overwrought with desire, he married her. But her amorous appetite was his undoing. Two years into the marriage, his heart gave out. She cheerfully disposed of his mercantile business and refurbished their home to accommodate a different type of business, one familiar to her. And she prospered.

But it was rare for a prostitute to capture more than a fleeting interest from a man. Occasionally, a patron would offer to make one of her girls his mistress, and that was bad for business. A man with a mistress was not a paying customer. She discouraged her girls from accepting these rare offers and emphasized that a man who tired of his mistress would have little regard for her welfare. Mrs. Patterson made sure every girl understood that, if she chose to leave the establishment for any reason other than pregnancy, she would not be allowed to return. It was a harsh rule for the girls, but it was good for business.

When the American was admitted to her house a second time within twenty-four hours, she wasn't surprised. After an extended sea voyage, she supposed his masculine needs took some time to be relieved. But instead of paying for the privilege of visiting her girls, he asked to confer with her personally, and she wondered if he had a complaint to lodge. Reluctantly leading him to her private lounge, she stated, "If you were displeased by your companion last evening, you should have told me what you desired from a woman. We can't satisfy every man's taste, but...."

Sweetbriar

"I have no complaint," Brad assured her as he sat in the proffered chair. "The girl pleased me well enough. It would be convenient to have her to myself while I'm in London, but she tells me once she leaves here, you won't take her back."

"That is true," Madam Patterson confirmed and leaned back in her chair. "It may be convenient for you to have her for a time, but it would be inconvenient for me. If she leaves, she will not be welcomed back."

"Be that as it may, Louise has agreed. It just means I need to make more permanent arrangements than otherwise," he said, "and that may take some time."

The woman reached over and rang a small brass bell, then laced her fingers together under her ample bosom. A servant entered. "Bring Louise to me," she instructed. When the servant left, the madam slowly appraised her guest. He appeared to be a well-bred gentleman and wore fine garments. Perhaps wealthy, perhaps not, she could not determine from just the cut of his clothes.

As Louise entered the room, Madam waved toward a chair as she commented to Brad, "Louise is a sweet girl who came from a proper home." Then, glancing over to the young woman, asked, "Isn't that true, dear?"

"Yes, ma'am."

"If you had not the misfortune to misjudge a man's character, you would have married well, is that not so?"

"I suppose so, ma'am."

"This gentleman says it would be convenient to have you to him while he is in London, but he does not reside here and is not offering marriage. The arrangement would be temporary at best. Don't you think it would be foolhardy to place your trust in him?"

Louise studied Brad, who returned her gaze. "You said I would have a home, and you would provide for me during your absences."

"You have my word on it," Brad confirmed.

Then she stared at Madam Patterson and murmured, "I don't like having a different man every night." Color rose to her face, and she lowered her eyes in embarrassment. "I will trust Mr. Anderson to keep his word."

"Very well," the proprietress said callously. "Go back to the salon."

"No," Brad interjected, "go to your room, Louise. I shall be there shortly."

Fretfully, she glanced from one to the other then quickly slipped out the door.

Anger choked the old whore's throat. "This is not a charitable home for wayward girls. She must earn her keep."

Fury flashed in Brad's gray eyes. "Three days, no more, shall I ask for her to remain here," he said, "and you will be adequately compensated for her stay. But I shall not have her entertain men or even show her face in your salon. Heed me well, madam, for I am not a callow youth or a decrepit old man mooning over the girl. She is now under my protection, and I am unwilling to make allowances. I expect her to be well cared for until I come for her."

The heat of his diatribe quickly burned her anger away. Her shrewd mind changed tactics. "The girl came here with only the clothes on her back. And pitiful enough, they were. Too prim to be of use here. She still owes me for the two gowns and undergarments I gave her," she wheedled.

Disgust flourished on Brad's face. "You'll make good use of the clothes on some other girl," he sneered. "She can come to me with what is hers." Reaching into his pocket, he withdrew silver coins and tossed them on the table. "Payment for her services," and stalked out of the room.

It wasn't easy, but within three days, Brad acquired a small residence in a modest part of town. The walled courtyard promised warm relief from chill winter winds and provided an intimate privacy to the quaint little cottage.

Unsure how long her good fortune would last, Louise accompanied Bradley through the overgrown garden and into the house. A small vestibule opened on one side to a parlor and on the other to a dining room with the kitchen behind. The furnishings were worn but of quality workmanship. He assured her money was available to restore the furniture and to make needed repairs. But Louise remained silent. Then at the back of the house, they entered a femininely decorated bedroom where a lace canopy crowned the mahogany tester bed. A wardrobe and vanity were also mahogany. Creamy white brocade accentuated the dark wood of the chairs and matched the heavy drapes at the window.

"It's lovely," Louise murmured. "I shall be very happy here and do my best to make you happy."

Irritated by her lack of comment up until this time, Brad asked critically, "Will you, Louise? You've been so quiet. I doubt you care for the place at all."

When she turned toward him, unshed tears shimmered in the sapphire blue of her eyes. "You don't know what it means to have a home again. I hated that place," she spat bitterly. Youth and vulnerability marred her somber face. A single tear cascaded down her cheek, but she dashed it away and clasped her arms around Brad's waist, pressing her body close to his. "Please don't ever make me go back to a brothel, I beg you," she pleaded. As his arms enfolded her, she offered herself with a passionate kiss.

Mid-Summer 1805, England

Pacing the floor, Lord Rockwell again questioned Providence for taking his wife from his side and leaving him alone to raise their headstrong daughter. A son he might have guided and counseled but a daughter he would never understand. His lordship knew his frivolous sister, Lady Sylvia, meant well in her desire to assist with Beth's upbringing, but the foolishness she sometimes put in the girl's head infuriated him.

Beth had been sulky since he scolded her for her interest in Captain Anderson, speaking to him with cold politeness only when asked a direct question. He finally explained to her that, contrary to his better judgment, an invitation had been extended to the captain but was declined because of other commitments. Two days later, his daughter boldly suggested he escort her to the docks to see the merchants' ships firsthand, and he adamantly refused. A young girl couldn't possibly understand that riffraff and persons of the lowest nature frequented the area. After days of sullen behavior, Beth suddenly cheered up, giving the impression the incident had ended, so Lord Rockwell gave it no more thought. Until now. Ten minutes ago, his sister burst in, hysterically babbling about a horseback ride, some romantic nonsense of sailors and piracy on the high seas, and that Beth, along with Sylvia's daughter, was missing.

"Sylvia, will you please make your point and tell me what the devil pirates have to do with Beth and Mary?" his lordship demanded curtly.

Abruptly the tears ended, and she indignantly stated, "Milton, you needn't speak to me that way."

Exasperated, Lord Rockwell roared, "Dammit, Sylvia, where is my daughter?"

"I don't know," she wailed. "We were riding and talking of sailors and the privateers that prey upon merchant ships when Beth suddenly called over her shoulder that she was going to see them for herself and off she rode. What she hoped to see, I have no idea." Sylvia flounced into a chair, "Mary knows I always ride the most sedate mares and told me not to worry. She would catch Beth before she did anything rash. That was the last I saw of them. Heavens, Milton, you shouldn't curse at me. How was I to know they would disappear? After all, it was your daughter that ran off. Mine was only trying to stop her."

"Yes, I know, and I apologize for my profanity," he grated out with barely controlled patience. "Please calm yourself and tell me when all this happened. I have a fairly good idea where Beth may be going, and if I'm right, we'd better send men out to search for them immediately. The docks are no place for two young women to be riding around without an escort. If we don't find them soon, there is no telling what harm may befall them."

Lady Sylvia wept again. Icy knives of fear stabbed her quaking heart at the import of his words. She cried shrilly, "Oh, Milton, now you will be upset. I thought this was just a silly prank the girls were playing on me, as they sometimes do. I grazed the mare for a while, waiting for them to return." She dabbed at her eyes with a scrap of fabric she called a handkerchief. "Then I thought, perhaps they expected me to return home, which I did, but they weren't there either. I decided to go back to the area where we'd been riding and ordered the carriage brought around because I was quite tired of horseback. Of course, I couldn't be seen in the carriage wearing my riding habit, so I changed clothes—"

"Yes, yes, Sylvia, I understand all this," Rockwell interrupted with a sinking heart. "Just tell me how long it has been since you saw them last."

"Dear me," she moaned, wringing her hands, "It's been close to two hours now."

"Good God!" Rockwell burst out. "Do you realize what may have happened to them by now?" He turned on his heel and stormed from the room, shouting for his butler and valet, ignoring her exasperated admonition about using the Lord's name in vain.

At least twenty men would be needed, as quickly as possible, to begin the search. But with twenty men or even a hundred, how long would it take? Perhaps he should send word to some of the captains he knew. Anderson, for one, should lend assistance since he had, unwittingly, caused the trouble. In fact, he could send word to all the Surrey Trading Company captains, even that Irishman O'Malley, if he had to.

The clanging clatter of carriage wheels on cobblestones drummed into his brain, '*I must find her! I must find her!*' And Lord Rockwell was hard-pressed not to travel every dockside street in search of his daughter. Common sense advised him to obtain assistance from the merchant captain, but his heart beseeched him to look for her immediately. Scarcely had the carriage stopped moving before his lordship burst out of it and bounded up the wooden gangway of the *Angel Star*, calling at the top of his lungs, "Anderson! Captain Anderson! I have need of you!" Receiving no immediate reply, he grabbed the shirt sleeve of the first man he encountered, demanding, "Where is your captain? If he is here, take me to him at once."

The sailor, a large weather-beaten man, turned flinty eyes on the nobleman and jerked his arm away, "He be in his cabin, find 'im yerself." Aggravation suffused the aristocrat's face at the man's insolence, then quickly abated as he caught sight of Anderson emerging from below decks.

"Lord Rockwell, what's amiss? I heard your call from my quarters."

"I must speak to you at once," his lordship declared. "Privately," he added, coloring slightly because of the request he had to make.

Once inside the captain's cabin, the nobleman outlined the events of the previous weeks, explaining Beth's apparent infatuation with merchant ships in general and touching on her possible infatuation with Bradley Anderson in particular. The pleased surprise on the American's face at this revelation went unnoticed. Lord Rockwell mentioned the sudden disappearance of Beth and her cousin that afternoon and his suspicion of their destination. When he concluded with a request for Captain Anderson and his crew to search for the girls, he flushed deeply.

Brad recalled his attraction to the young noblewoman and momentarily felt a rekindling of his interest in her. To think the chit would be so daring and so stupid to come searching for him just because of one night's light flirtation. She was spirited, that was obvious, and it was a trait he found as appealing as her beauty. He supposed she would someday present a challenge to the unfortunate man foolish enough to fall in love with her. But the disappearance of the girls was disturbing news, and Brad felt the same urgency as Rockwell to find them before it was too late.

Mary and Beth were hopelessly lost. Having left the taverns and unfashionable eating houses behind, along with the rude rejoinders of the inhabitants, they rode side by side, horses' flanks almost touching. Only a tight rein kept the animals from shying in the loud din of the docks. The relentless activity of the burly stevedores and the crude laughter of the sailors increased Mary's apprehension. The young, obviously pampered girls would make easy prey to anyone brash enough, but the possibility of an armed escort within hailing distance created a strong deterrent. Leering stares and coarse jeers satisfied the majority, but the idle bystanders grew increasingly audacious the farther they progressed.

"Beth, please, could we go back now?" Mary inquired uneasily. "We've been truant far too long. I'm sure Mama has already informed your father of our disappearance, and if the gossips learn of this escapade, our reputations will be ruined."

Secretly fearing the truth of her cousin's words but frustrated by her lack of success, Beth retorted, "If it's your reputation you're worried about Mary, perhaps you'd be better off at home. I didn't ask you to join me." Then seeing the pinched hurt on her cousin's face, Beth relented. "We've come this far, Mary, a mile or so more won't hurt. Surely one of these ships belongs to Captain Anderson."

She didn't mention her anxiety that his ship might be anchored out in the river awaiting a loading berth or, worse yet, that he might have already sailed for home. Even though the excursion was foolhardy, Beth was determined to press on, never again expecting to have the opportunity to convey to Captain Anderson the fascination she felt toward him. Besides, they'd made so many turns getting to where they were; Beth didn't have the slightest idea how to get home.

Without warning, a man in ragged clothing grabbed the bridle of Mary's horse and viciously ripped the reins from her hands. Screaming, she frantically clutched the horse's flowing mane to retain her seat as the animal reared. Shocked and frightened, Beth fought for control of her own mount, striking blindly at the intruder with her riding crop. Mary's horse bolted out of control as the attacker suddenly turned his assault upon Beth, seizing hold of her skirts in an effort to dismount her. The terrified horse danced sideways over the cobblestones as Beth savagely whipped at the man with her crop. Trying to protect his face, the man lost his hold and fell to the street.

Heedless of direction, Beth prodded her mount. Panicky tears blurred her vision and were snatched away in the wind as her horse flew over the cobblestones. Her fiery hair, burnished by the late afternoon sun, cascaded down her back as it fell loose from its pins. Looking back over her shoulder, she searched for her cousin in vain. Suddenly the horse reared, its path blocked by stevedores unloading a ship. Caught off balance, Beth lost her grip on the reins and tumbled helplessly to the street. The pain from the fall quickly faded into blackness.

The crew of the *Angel Star*, assisting in the search for the two girls, speculated among themselves as to their identity. Some heard they were the spoiled daughters of respected noblemen but doubted the truth of it. Others considered the possibility they were the wayward daughters of merchants and laughed among themselves. A few thought they might even be high priced whores.

But none could doubt the good breeding of the dark-haired girl brought aboard their ship. Mary wept and pleaded to be taken home but was forced to wait until her uncle and Captain Anderson were located. When the two men arrived, their aggravation boiled over at finding only Mary, who was too hysterical to be of any help in locating Beth. Discouraged, Lord Rockwell escorted her home.

A short time later, the unconscious red-haired girl was carried on board. Taking her in his arms, Brad carried her below to his cabin. She was breathing and didn't appear to be bleeding, but he was unable to determine how badly she was hurt. He tried to feel the back of her head, but the masses of her hair made it difficult to tell if she was injured there. He sent to the galley for fresh warm water and was just wetting a kerchief at the washbasin when the girl stirred.

With a growing sense of unreality, Beth awakened. An oil lamp, swaying from the rafters, cast shifting shadows about the small room. The unfamiliar acrid odors of tar and lamp oil brought bile to her throat. Closing her eyes, she breathed deeply to clear her head and then retched. Clasping a hand to her mouth, she lurched from the narrow bunk onto quivering legs and collapsed on the floor. Uncermoniously, she was hoisted off the deck and hauled, ragtag, to a broad window ledge cluttered with books. A muscular, bronzed arm swept the books aside and quickly unlatched the portlight. Beth clutched frantically at the sill as her head and shoulders were thrust outside.

"If you are going to be sick, please have the courtesy to do so overboard. You've been enough trouble for one day without having to clean up after you," an irate foreign voice declared.

The sight and smell of the oily, fetid water below added the contents of her stomach to the rotting debris strewn across its surface. When her heaving subsided, the man whose arm had been wrapped securely about her waist, drew her safely inside and held her close as he reached to push the portlight closed. Exhausted, Beth leaned against him.

When he spoke again, his voice was gentle, his breath softly tickling her ear, "I can understand your relief at having been rescued, Lady Beth. However, should anyone enter the cabin at this moment, I'm afraid they would misinterpret our embrace.

Still lightheaded, Beth pushed away as she recognized Captain Anderson's voice. Conscious of her torn, soiled clothing and the vile taste in her mouth, which seemed to permeate her entire being, Beth brushed the tangled hair from her face, gathering what dignity she could about her like a cloak, and inquired haughtily, "What are you doing here, Captain Anderson? If my father knew of this—"

"First of all," Brad tersely interrupted, crossing his arms over his chest, "I happen to command this ship, and these are my private quarters. Secondly, your father does know and is on his way here this very minute." Raking his eyes over her, Brad continued sarcastically, "May I suggest, Lady Beth, that you make yourself presentable before he arrives. There is a brush and comb on the wash table along with a bowl of warm water. The mirror is on the inside of the wardrobe door."

Beth's face burned with the hot blood of humiliation.

Bradley crossed the cabin and turned as he opened the door, "I would advise you to remain here, milady. If you come on deck, my crew, which is a rough lot, may well find you indistinguishable from the sort of woman normally found on the docks." A brief bow and he departed.

She was furious. How dare he speak to her in such a manner? She should have known he was not a gentleman. It was only because her father had allowed him to dine with them that she mistook him for someone used to polite society. How could she ever have imagined herself attracted to him? When she told her father how she had been insulted, Captain Anderson would be sorry. No doubt her father would have him arrested.

Crossing the cabin, she snatched up the brush, yanked opened the wardrobe door to use the mirror, and burst into tears at the shocking sight of her reflection. Dirt was smeared across her face, tangled hair tumbled about her shoulders, and bile speckled her grimy, tattered habit and blouse. She would never be able to face her father this way.

Briskly, she dragged the brush through her hair and splashed water on her face to clean it, but there was nothing she could do about her clothes. She discarded the jacket to the riding habit, which helped. In the wardrobe, she found a clothing brush and improved the looks of her skirt by removing some of the dirt. But the bile stains were still on the front of her blouse, and no amount of rubbing would remove them. Again, she searched the wardrobe for anything that might help her out of this predicament. The clean scent of cedar insinuated itself upon her consciousness, and she noticed the entire inside of the wardrobe was lined with thin cedar boards. Burying her face in the clothes and inhaling deeply, she relished the refreshing fragrance. Quickly, before she might change her mind, she took one of the shirts from the wardrobe and replaced her stained blouse. It was too large, the sleeves hung past her fingers, but at least it was clean. Gathering her cast-off jacket and blouse, Beth rushed to the cabin window, unlatched it, and threw the clothes overboard.

Startled by the sound of the cabin door opening, she turned and reached to brush the hair from her face, but her hand was covered by the too-long shirt sleeve. She reached with her other hand to pull up the sleeve, but it was also obscured by a long sleeve. Stretching both hands over her head, Beth let the sleeves slide to her elbows and brushed the hair from her face. That's when she spotted the unrestrained amusement in Bradley Anderson's eyes. Would she forever be humiliated by this man?

She darted to her father's arms and burst into tears. "Oh, Papa, please take me home. I'm so sorry for all the trouble I've been. I've lost Mary, and I don't know how we'll ever find her."

"Hush, child. Mary has been found and is already recovering at home," her father soothed, patting her shoulder. "Now, I think you should thank Captain Anderson for your rescue. We may never have found you and Mary had it not been for the good captain sending his men out to search."

Thank the man who had embarrassed her? Beth couldn't believe her ears. They waited, and she had no alternative but to thank him or faint. She fainted.

Brad caught her, and lifting her into his powerful arms, said, "I'll carry her to your carriage, sir. I'm sure she'll be fine once you get her home."

Lord Rockwell preceded them out of the cabin. Brad adjusted her weight and whispered in her ear, "Don't think you've fooled me, Beth, my love. I know quite well this is a ruse, which I'll gladly play along with so I can hold you in my arms. Just remember to return my shirt when you get home. It's one of my favorites, and I'll enjoy thinking of you whenever I wear it."

She struggled, and Brad quietly reminded her she was supposed to have fainted. He placed her in the carriage, and smoothing the hair away from her face, whispered, "Goodbye, sweet Beth," then ever so lightly; he kissed her temple.

Lord Rockwell climbed in across from Beth, and as soon as the carriage jolted to a start, addressed his daughter, "You may sit up and open your eyes, Beth. You fooled that good man back on his ship, but you aren't fooling me. I know very well you didn't faint."

Beth straightened in her seat and adjusted her skirts, "Papa, he is a disagreeable man—"

Livid with emotion, he interrupted, "That man, and most of his crew, went to considerable trouble to find you and Mary. I dare not think what might have happened to either of you without his assistance."

"Papa, forgive me, please," Beth pleaded, ashamed. "I shall never act so foolishly again." The day's trauma was too much to bear. She threw herself into her father's arms, crying with hard racking sobs, and before arriving home, she fell into an exhausted sleep.

The next morning, the earl insisted Beth write a letter of apology and gratitude to Captain Anderson for his assistance, saying he would deliver the letter himself. Although mortified, Beth did as instructed.

> Dear Captain Anderson,
> After reflecting on the events of yesterday, I write to apologize for my impetuous behavior and for the extreme inconvenience I caused you.
> Kindly forgive me and accept my sincere gratitude.
> Cordially,
> Beth Avery

That evening her father delivered the American's reply:

> Dear Lady Beth,
> Your apology and gratitude are kindly received. It is my earnest wish that your recovery is swift.
> I would encourage you to be more circumspect in the future when riding.
> Your humble servant,
> Bradley Anderson
> PS: Kindly return my shirt.

Arriving home last night, Beth had gone straight to bed. She had no idea what became of the remains of her riding habit or his shirt, thinking the maid had disposed of them. Reluctantly, Beth searched through her wardrobe and found the shirt hanging among her jackets. She caught the faint scent of cedar and recalled this was his scent. She held the shirt to her face and inhaled deeply. His clothes had held the faint aroma of cedar the night he came to dinner, and when he carried her to the carriage yesterday, his coat retained the fresh scent too. She inhaled again, then folded the shirt and placed it in her cedar chest. Smiling, she decided it might have been his shirt once, but it was hers now.

Late Summer 1805, England

Mrs. Patterson contemplated the note in her hand. She hadn't heard from Louise since she left eight weeks ago and hadn't expected to ever hear from her again. But the note said she would arrive shortly. The American sea captain had appeared to have the financial resources to care for a mistress and had exerted some effort to find a home for the girl, so Mrs. Patterson was surprised by the communication. Apparently, things hadn't worked out with her lover, though. It was too bad, but Mrs. Patterson wouldn't take her back. Business was business. She wouldn't let the girls think they could come and go as they pleased.

A soft noise drew her attention. Louise stood in the doorway of the sitting room dressed in a respectable manner. The gown's neckline was decent, and the hemline was almost flush with the floor. Hat, gloves, and reticule were stylish but not expensive in appearance.

"May I come in?" Louise asked.

"By all means, please come in and sit down. Is your man treating you well?" the old madam inquired with sarcasm in her voice.

Settling on the velvet-covered divan, Louise quietly replied, "Yes, the captain treats me well. He sailed back to America, you know."

"I thought as much when I received your note, but I made it clear that once you left here, you could not return," Mrs. Patterson said firmly.

"I don't want to return," the young woman stated. "It's not that at all. It's something else entirely. You see, I need your help. I'm pregnant."

The madam eyed her critically, but due to the high waist and full skirt fashion, divined nothing of the girl's condition. "How am I supposed to be of help? The best course is to send a letter to your man and explain the situation. Sometimes men are agreeable to caring for their bastard children," was her advice.

"That's just it. It's not his child," Louise declared. "I haven't had my menses since before I left here, so it is possibly the offspring of any number of men."

Mrs. Patterson was pensive for a few minutes. "You wouldn't be the first woman to foist another man's bastard onto a gentleman. There is a good chance he would never know."

Louise leaned forward, tense with anxiety, speaking earnestly, "You don't understand. He doesn't release himself inside me. He spills his seed on the bed linens. He will know the child is not his and throw us both into the street." Wringing her hands, she sobbed, "I might as well jump into the Thames today and be done with it."

Mrs. Patterson was silent for a long time, weighing the matter in her mind. "You want to end the pregnancy, is that it, child?" she inquired quietly.

Louise was slumped on the divan, weeping. Without looking up, she nodded her head.

"You know what you are asking is a very dangerous course. Many women die," she counseled.

Struggling to control her emotions, Louise choked out, "I will die anyway if I don't try. Please help me."

The silence was broken only by the sound of weeping, but at length, the madam nodded, "It is a disgusting thing, but I know a woman who will do it. You'll need someone to care for you afterward. You were fond of Emily while you were here, and she is about due for her menses. I'll see if she will accompany you home for a couple of weeks. Leave me now."

Summer/Fall 1805, England

The entrance of William Pitt's secretary was preceded by a discreet tap on the door separating their offices. "Sir, Mr. Wilberforce is here to see you," the man said.

Tossing the latest military and naval reports onto his desk, William Pitt sighed and pressed the bridge of his nose between thumb and forefinger.

"I hope there is more good news than bad in those reports," William Wilberforce asked good-naturedly.

"Austria forced Boney's hand by attacking Bavaria. Seventy thousand troops should have been sufficient, but the French quickly moved one hundred eighty thousand troops from Boulogne. They surrounded the Austrians and forced them to surrender. Austria signed a treaty in Pressburg, in which they relinquished Venetia to the French-dominated Kingdom of Italy and the Tyrol to Bavaria."

"So, we can't expect further assistance from Austria. But we still have the Russians," his friend commented encouragingly.

"That's just the half of it," Pitt sighed, sitting back in his chair and leveling his eyes on Wilberforce's face. "After defeating the Austrians, Boney faced down the superior forces of the Russian army and inflicted twenty-five thousand causalities while sustaining fewer than seven thousand to his own troops. There is just no stopping the French army. The only good news is the little general was forced to abandon his plans to invade our shores."

"Invade England!"

"He won't be able to resurrect that plan for a good long while, if ever," the Prime Minister confided. "Apparently, Vice-Admiral François Rosily was sent to Madrid to replace Admiral Villeneuve, but the prospect of being disgraced must have been too much for the timid French Admiral. Villeneuve made a rapid scramble of the combined French and Spanish fleet out of Cadiz harbor only to be trapped by the Royal Navy.

The Parliamentarian grinned, "Then why the long face? I have no doubt Admiral Lord Nelson and his fleet performed their duty to God and country admirably."

"Yes, admirably," commented Pitt, "thirty-three French and Spanish ships to twenty-seven British vessels. Using unconventional battle tactics, Nelson cut the enemy formation in half, surrounded it, and forced them to fight to the end. Nelson took twenty-two vessels that day, of which ten were sunk, burned, or wrecked while losing none of his own. Of the eleven ships that regained Cadiz, we believe only five are seaworthy. The Battle of Trafalgar was a British victory."

Wilberforce clapped his hands down on his thighs enthusiastically. "Not just a British victory, William, a spectacular British victory. After a naval defeat of this magnitude, I doubt Napoleon will ever again have the opportunity to challenge Britannia at sea."

"Yes, the Royal Navy enjoyed a decisive victory, but at what cost? We lost Nelson in the battle," Pitt revealed. "God rest his soul."

Early Winter 1805, America

"I fear we lost the ship to the French," Charles Anderson remarked. He sat on the far side of the desk at his dockside warehouse office. "You say he sailed a week before you, Brad, and you've been back a week already. Granted, there is any number of things that might have caused a delay, but O'Malley is our most experienced captain, and there's not much that slows him down."

"That's true," Brad agreed, reclining in the chair across from his father. "But since the French started the damnable blockade, the Brits have stepped up impressment. No doubt, it is the only way they can keep their ships manned and retain control of the seas." He leaned farther back, extended his long legs, and crossed his ankles. "And they are excellent sailors. They have it all over the French. Even with the extra canvas, we carry on the *Angel Star*, we are hard-pressed to outrun them. If O'Malley were boarded, it would take longer to cross with a short crew."

"Listen, Brad," Charles shifted in his chair as he changed the conversation to one he knew his son resisted. "I think it's time for you to relinquish your command and learn the shore operations. I want you to settle down and get yourself a wife." He smiled gauchely, "I would like to see you start a family before I die."

The younger man frowned at the familiar request. "I'm not ready to settle down, and I can't think of any woman I'd want to marry. Besides, you were nearly thirty before you married Mother," Brad countered.

"I was thirty because of the repugnant British peer tradition of leaving everything to the firstborn son," he responded in disgust. "As the second son, I had to find my way in the world, and that took time. You don't have that excuse. I'd hand this entire business over to you if you'd just learn the shore operations." Charles mused a moment, "What about that Newton woman out of Salem. She comes from a good family, and she's attractive, as I recall."

"She has the face and no doubt the body of an angel. And she talks incessantly. If I married her, I'd have to cut her tongue out before the wedding night was over." Unexpectedly, the pleasure Louise gave with her mouth and tongue flashed into Brad's mind, and he shifted uncomfortably in the chair. Sitting straighter, Brad argued, "I'm just not ready to marry yet. Give me another year or two."

He was saved from further discourse by a loud knock on the door, followed by Quinn O'Malley's entrance. Relief flooded Charles' face as he rose and clasped the big man's hand. "You are here at last. I had begun to think we'd lost you to the French."

"No, Mr. Anderson, it was the blasted Brits. If they'd had their way, they'd have confiscated my entire ship. Bad enough as it was, they impressed a good portion of my crew and delayed us long enough that we caught the leading edge of a storm. We had the devil to pay fighting it short-handed." O'Malley collapsed into the chair Brad had just vacated. "We'll be getting her unloaded as soon as there's space at the dock," the Irishman concluded wearily.

Chapter II
Spring 1806, England

Confiscated American ships and cargoes, when auctioned, provided lucrative compensation to the crews that preyed upon them. Unfortunately, the small four-pound cannons, which commonly armed merchant vessels, were no match in close confrontations against the larger batteries of privateers or the twelve and sixteen-pound carronades of the Royal and Imperial navies. To avoid seizure, a merchantman's best hope was to slip unnoticed past any sail sighted on the horizon. Numerous American ships trading with England and France had been seized over the past year due to the belligerents' superior firepower. But it was Great Britain's continued impressment of American sailors that rankled the young nation's citizenry.

Rather than retaliate militarily, the Jefferson administration responded economically in April by enacting the Non-Importation Act, which forbade the importation of all British manufactured products that could either be produced in America or obtained from other countries. However, wanting to give the British government the opportunity to rescind their seizure and impressment policies, and thus preserve the American market for British goods, the new law was immediately suspended until November. So New England merchant ships again sailed to Great Britain with American wares, planning to return with their holds full of British goods.

The *Angel Star* made good time crossing the Atlantic. Her extra canvas capacity allowed her to outrun the French ships blockading English shores, and she dropped anchor near the London docks an hour after dawn. Leaving the chief mate to square away the ship, Bradley Anderson and his cabin boy, Derek O'Malley, were rowed ashore. Brad sent Derek off to deliver a message, while Brad jostled his way to the river master's office.

Brawny stevedores loading and offloading ships crowded the docks. Wooden hulled ships, bunched together like a flock of waterfowl, bobbed at rest on the river's surface. Every berth was filled. With luck, the American hoped, some of the ships would sail within a day or so. But at the bustling river master's office, it took until late morning to hear the disappointing news. No berth would be available for almost two weeks. Undeterred, and with ample time to arrange for his return cargo, Brad whistled his way to the Rockwell Trading Company offices to see about a shipment of tea.

"Captain Anderson to see you, milord," the clerk announced at the inner office door.

"Good afternoon, Captain." His lordship came from behind the desk to shake hands, "You must have made good time this year. I wasn't expecting you for another fortnight."

Brad laughed ruefully, "Apparently the river master wasn't expecting me either. He says it will be at least ten days before a berth is available to unload." Brad perched himself on the uncomfortable straight-backed chair. "I'm happy to say that after last year's purchase

Sweetbriar

we were able to expand our market for your product. In fact, my father wants the increased purchase maintained and has outfitted another ship. Except for a few odds and ends, I intend to fill my hold with your tea—provided we can agree on a reasonable price."

"I'm a reasonable man as you well know, Captain, so I'm sure we'll be able to accommodate you." Retreating behind his desk, Lord Rockwell sat. "By the by, there's a small group of us going to my country estate for a few days. Since you won't be rushed to finish your business, why don't you join us?" the older man offered. "The country doesn't offer the enticements of London but will give you the opportunity to enjoy polite society and get you land legs back."

Brad was surprised by the proposal. Through his father's relatives, he often received dinner invitations when in England but had never received an invitation to visit a country estate. "Milord, your offer is very generous, but I shouldn't impose."

"Nonsense young man, I'd welcome your companionship. It seems as if only old men go to the country anymore. Your presence will enliven things a bit. We'll be leaving in two days, say what," his lordship encouraged.

Rockwell's generosity appealed to Brad, but having just arrived in port, he was anxious to see Louise. Deciding to spend a night with her then pass a day or two in the country before cutting the visit short, Brad reluctantly agreed, "You leave me no choice, sir. I'm obliged."

"That's settled then," Rockwell grinned. "Day after tomorrow, come to the house at nine o'clock in the morning. There is room for you in the carriage. Now, let's discuss your tea shipment."

***

Derek O'Malley accepted the slice of sweet bread Louise offered. While he ate it, he delivered the message that his captain was back in England and would come to her within a day or two, then quickly bounded away like a startled stag.

Anticipation of seeing Bradley again set bees to buzzing in Louise's stomach. Eager to prove herself a talented homemaker, she put the house in order and planned the meals for his arrival.

Recovery from the terminated pregnancy had lasted months, and only recently had she regained the weight she had lost. Much of the money Bradley gave her last year was used to pay Emily for nursing Louise back to health. Frugality was required with the money that remained, but she spent extra now to ensure his pleasure with the table she set. His contentment was her only concern.

One night last year, after they made love, Louise teasingly asked Bradley if his wife pleased him in bed as well as she. He lightly replied that he didn't have a wife, but when he did, he expected her to be very lively. At that moment Louise gave herself to him completely, her heart as well as her body. Even though she could never erase from her life the few weeks she had lived and worked in the brothel where Bradley found her, she was determined to win his love.

Their last night together, Louise had been fretful about his leaving but tried to conceal it; he must have known because he was tender in his lovemaking and took extra care to ensure her needs were satisfied. Then he thoughtfully asked for her devotion in his absence instead of callously demanding her faithfulness. These considerations, she believed, indicated his growing affection, and now she sought to bind him to her forever.

Knitting in the front sitting room the day after receiving Bradley's message, clattering carriage wheels alerted Louise to a visitor. Through the window, she witnessed her lover alight from a hired cab and swagger up the tidy path with the late afternoon sun glinting in his tousled hair. Opening the door, she grinned, "If it isn't Captain Bradley Anderson returning home from his travels and just in time to eat the lamb stew I prepared."

"Louise," he swooped her up, twirled her around, and kissed her rapaciously as he kicked the door closed behind them. "Your fine stew will have to wait. I want you first," he breathed hoarsely and carried her to the bedroom. Setting her on the bed, he lay beside her, hitched up on one elbow. "You are beautiful, my pet."

"Bradley, I'm so glad you're home. I've missed you," she whispered.

He lightly kissed her nose, her eyes, and then her mouth. "And I've missed making love to you," he replied, then sat to pull off his boots. Glancing over his shoulder, he saw the shimmer of desire in her eyes and asked softly, "Will you undress for me?"

She smiled as she stood. Undressing for him excited her. Watching his eyes follow her hands, she teased him as she slowly unfastened her bodice. She waited for him to remove his shirt and stand to unfasten his trousers before she untied the ribbon beneath her breasts and let the garment fall to the floor. The astonishment in his eyes gratified her. She had worn nothing beneath her dress and stood before him in exquisite nakedness.

At her shamelessness, lust slammed into his loins forcefully. Brad drew her to the bed and sat her on the edge, then knelt between her legs and placed them over his shoulders. He tantalized her with his tongue and nipped at the seat of her pleasure until she was driven to the edge of reason. Then he stood and began thrusting into her, plunging deep. He clasped her buttocks in his hands, kneading, and she writhed in climax. When her spasms subsided, he withdrew, turned her onto her stomach, and entered her again. He drove into her deeper and faster until fierce cries of ecstasy shattered their rapture as they climaxed in unison.

Their labored breathing slowed as awareness gradually returned. Brad stirred, then turned to face Louise, and drew her into his arms. "You are delightful, my pet, but I can only stay the night. I hate to leave so soon, but I shall be out of town for a few days."

Louise played her fingers through the hair on his chest, "Then take me with you," she pouted. "I've missed you, and all I've thought about lately is the brief time we have together."

Brad brought her hand to his lips and kissed each finger in turn. "I'm sorry, Louise, it will be a week or more before there's dock space for my ship, and Lord Rockwell invited me to his county estate. How would I ever explain your presence? Even the most forward-thinking man would frown on a guest bringing his mistress. I'll be gone for only a few days."

Her greatest fear was losing this man to another woman. Louise sat up and searched his face for deception but found none. "He couldn't accept your mistress, but he would accept your fiancée." Impetuously, she continued, "I will make you a good wife, Bradley. Take me with you."

He grimaced. Untangling himself from her arms, Brad stood and started dressing. Without looking at his mistress, Brad flatly stated, "I shall never marry you." She was speechless. The silence between them lengthened while he finished dressing, then he looked at her and softened his tone, "I shall provide for you until I marry, but I shall not marry you."

Her voice trembled as she asked, "What if we have children? What then?"

A long minute passed while he contemplated her question. "If you have a child by me, I shall provide for it, but I shan't marry you. I don't want to give you a child and shall take greater care in the future to prevent it from happening. I provide you with a home and an income in exchange for your favors. That's all it is, and it should be enough, so don't expect more."

She lay naked on the bed in front of the man who held her heart. But he rejected her love. What a fool she felt. Not knowing if she should rant and rave at him or bury her face in her hands and cry, she did neither. Standing and dressing, she said, "You'll enjoy the lamb stew, Bradley. And I baked bread this morning."

He let his breath out in a sigh, "Thank you, Louise. I've longed for your cooking almost as much as I've longed for your lovemaking."

Then she did cry.

Lord Rockwell, Lady Beth, and Bradley Anderson jostled in the carriage most of the day. Throughout the journey, his lordship drew their attention to points of interest as they bounced along the ancient Roman road, but hardly a word passed between the young lady and the captain.

It piqued Beth that the American acted as if she weren't even in the carriage. He was brooding over something, and Beth wondered if he was as uncomfortable in the situation as she. She had almost forgotten about her idiotic ride to the docks last year, but the thought of seeing *him* again had brought it all back—embarrassed by her torn and dirty riding habit, humiliated by being sick in front of him, and frustrated by being the object of his mirth. She was more mature now and didn't wish to be reminded of her impetuous behavior of last year.

Alone in her room last night, she remembered his shirt and thought she should return it to him. Taking it out of her cedar chest, the fresh cedar scent was heady and brought to mind that it was his scent. Then she recalled his promise to think of her whenever he wore the shirt and was appalled. She didn't want him thinking of her in the disheveled condition she'd been in at the time. She would never return the shirt, she decided. But instead of throwing it away, or even putting it back into her cedar chest, she took off her nightgown and wore the shirt to bed.

But it upset her that Mr. Anderson was joining them for the trip to the country. This was her special time and being thrown into his company for the next week or more was too much to bear. So, she decided to rob him of the opportunity to embarrass her or laugh at her by ignoring him completely.

Brad was in a foul temper. Last night he was completely caught off guard when Louise suggested he marry her. Good God. What could she be thinking? He had met her in a bordello. She was an excellent housekeeper, a wonderful cook, and divine in bed, but that didn't make any difference, she had been a prostitute.

For a few seconds last night, he thought they had passed the crisis, then he made that stupid comment about wanting her cooking almost as much as he wanted her lovemaking. He meant it as a compliment, but she started crying. Damn! What was a man to do with a hysterical woman? She wouldn't let him touch her or comfort her. In fact, she threw him out of the bedroom, slammed the door in his face, and locked it. No amount of reasoning or cajoling opened the door, and Brad left in a sulk. It was a long trek until he found a hack to take him back to the *Angel Star,* and his temper worsened with each step. Perhaps it was for the best to be out of

Sweetbriar

town for a few days, he decided. It would give her time to calm down and come to her senses.

His gray eyes briefly flicked over Beth's face, but there was no recognition in his glance. "You've been very pensive this morning, Mr. Anderson," her sweet voice interrupted his thoughts. "I don't think you heard a word I said. I'm distressed to think my conversation is dull. Perhaps there is a more interesting topic you would care to discuss?"

Embarrassed by his boorish behavior, Brad apologized, "My thoughts were elsewhere. I doubt your conversation is ever dull, milady. I am a dullard for not paying attention and beg your forgiveness. What were you saying that I missed?"

"I only mentioned the other guests who will join us at the manor. My father's sister, Lady Sylvia, and her husband, Viscount Hartford, along with their daughter, Mary. Have you met Lord Hartford or Lady Sylvia before?" Beth inquired.

Brad was thoughtful for a moment then shook his head slightly, "I don't believe I've had the pleasure of meeting the lord or his lady." Then a slight smile touched his lips as a thought occurred to him, "But I may have met their daughter last year. Is she a petite, dark-haired young woman of about your age?"

Blood rushed to Beth's face when she realized he was referring to the ill-fated horseback ride to the docks last year. He must have met Mary before having her escorted home.

"Come to think of it, Lady Beth, I believe you have something of mine that I want back," Brad continued with a sparkle of amusement in his eyes.

"Say what. Beth has something of yours?" Lord Rockwell inquired. "What on earth could my daughter have that belongs to you, sir?"

"I believe Mr. Anderson is mistaken, Papa," Beth interjected hastily, "I have nothing that he could possibly want."

Brad's smile deepened, and he sat straighter as it dawned on him that he might enjoy a week in the country after all.

Unexpectedly, Lord Hartford brought along a second cousin on his mother's side, Viscount Dunmore, a handsome, arrogant aristocrat twenty-eight years of age. He had inherited his title at nineteen, and many opined that he suffered sorely from a lack of guidance, which Lord Hartford was tardily bestowing. As an adolescent, Rolf Dunmore had displayed a propensity toward a carefree, pleasure-seeking lifestyle, and his father had wisely withheld access to the majority of the inheritance until age thirty. But his generous allowance never stretched far enough, especially given his recent association with an older, more decadent group of friends. This visit to the country was punishment for incurring a gambling debt, which required Lord Hartford to extend another loan to the young man, a loan that couldn't be repaid until he received his full birthright.

The guests were gathered in the main salon getting acquainted prior to an early supper. The evening was chilly, and a fire blazed merrily in the large fieldstone fireplace. "Let us not stand on formalities," Lord Rockwell enthused, "we're all here to enjoy ourselves. Hartford, I don't believe you've met Captain Anderson, heir to Surrey Trading Company in America. His grandfather was William Anderson, Duke of Surrey." Brief bows were exchanged. "My sister, Lady Sylvia, and her daughter, Mary."

"Captain, it is a pleasure to see you again," Lady Mary said demurely.

"And this is Viscount Dunmore," Hartford put in.

Sweetbriar

"I'm glad to see another young man come to the country, but I'm surprised you were able to pull yourself away from the entertainments that London offers," Rockwell commented.

With his eyes fixed on Beth, the young nobleman replied cryptically, "Sometimes it is prudent to forsake the contrived pleasures of the city for the natural beauty found in the country." He relished her youthful blush as she lowered her eyes.

Her father, observing the interaction, continued, "You have not met my daughter, Beth. She has acted as my hostess for informal gatherings such as this since the death of my wife, even though she will not come out for another year."

Rolf glanced sharply at Rockwell before politely nodding toward Beth, "My pleasure, Lady Beth." She returned his nod.

Brad had a vague recollection of the name Dunmore but couldn't place the circumstances. Nevertheless, he was uneasy with the scene just played out before him.

The late afternoon was uneventful after the day's long, tiring journey. Casual conversations lagged intermittently among the new acquaintances, and no one was interested in prolonging the evening after supping, so they all retired early.

Beth and Mary shared a room when in the country, as they had since childhood. They enjoyed exchanging confidences, and it was only at bedtime or early in the morning that afforded them the privacy to do so. After dismissing the maids, they assisted each other in preparing for bed.

"Your captain isn't as frightening as I remember," Mary ventured. She sat at the vanity as Beth brushed her hair. "In fact, he isn't frightening at all. Maybe it is just that I was frightened last year. Anyway, I've decided that I approve of him."

"You approve of him? What does that mean?" Beth queried, looking at her cousin in the mirror.

"It means that I like him, and I understand your attraction to him," she replied, blushing prettily. "I'd like him even more if he weren't your beau."

"He is not my beau!" Beth exclaimed. "He may be attractive in a rugged sort of way, but not as attractive as another I've seen."

"You can't possibly mean Lord Dunmore."

"And why not? He's a gentleman, more so than the merchantman. Though his title is less distinguished than my father's, he would still be a more appropriate choice than the American," Beth reasoned.

"If a title is all that matters to you, then you are correct," Mary retorted. "But I've known his lordship for a couple of years now, not very well mind you, but he's been to my parent's home enough times. He puts on a nice face when he wants to, but sometimes I catch him looking at me strangely. I feel exposed, and it makes me ill at ease," Mary confided.

"Sometimes, I think you are ill at ease whenever you receive attention," Beth said kindly. "I think it would do you good to receive more attention. If you 'approve' of Mr. Anderson, why don't we see if we can get Mr. Anderson to 'approve' of you?" Beth suggested.

Mary sniffed in surprise.

"Mary, you'll be coming out in a few months, and if you are as reticent then as you are now, I don't know how you will ever catch a husband," she chided. "You need to smile at him and hold his eyes longer, to a count of three. That gets a man to actually see you as a person, instead of a little china doll. And if he compliments you, be sure to flutter your eyelashes at him."

Mary frowned and twisted her hands in her lap.

"Mary, you may not have been listening to your mother all these years, but I have. We'll have you pour the next time we sit for tea. When handing the cup and saucer over to him, be sure to bend from the waist, so he gets a good look at your bosoms."

Mary stood and began pacing, "Oh Beth, I couldn't do anything like that. I'd die of mortification."

"No, you won't, Mary. Wait and see. I bet you will wrap Mr. Anderson right around your little finger. It's not as if you will be trifling with him too much. He will sail off to America soon enough. Just consider it practice for your coming out. Now, come brush my hair," Beth said, taking her place in front of the mirror, "then we will go to sleep so we can awaken fresh as a daisy in the morning."

During the leisurely breakfast next morning, Lord Dunmore commented on the clear crispness of the air, so unlike smoky London. Rockwell explained that spring mornings often warmed considerably in the afternoon and recommended a picnic as an entertaining diversion for the day. Servants scurried about packing food into baskets and gathering quilts to cover the ground. Grooms saddled horses for the men and hitched the carriage for the women.

Rockwell and Hartford rode ahead to scout a location while Brad and Rolf lingered behind to escort the ladies. When the carriage came around from the stable, Dunmore superciliously mounted his horse, leaving the American to hand the women into the conveyance. In deference to her rank, Lady Sylvia stepped in first, then Mary, and last of all, Beth. As Brad swung into his saddle, Dunmore quickly maneuvered next to Beth, conversing through the window. Riding on the other side of the coach, Brad chatted with Lady Sylvia.

Mary, seated between her mother and cousin, could be seen through neither window, and was left out of both conversations, which satisfied the bashful girl but vexed her younger cousin. Wanting to encourage Mary's sociability, Beth considered switching places with her, but after last night's tête-à-tête, knew Mary was uncomfortable bantering with his lordship. The situation resolved itself when Lady Sylvia suggested to Mr. Anderson that he might prefer the conversation of the younger lady of her household. Ignoring her daughter's protestations, Sylvia shifted to the opposite seat facing the rear of the carriage and shy Mary was obliged to move closer to the window.

Brad rode easily, as much at home on horseback as he was on board ship. Mary enjoyed the smooth grace of horse and man moving as one but was tongue-tied, not knowing how to natter with a man she barely knew.

"Do you come to the country often, Lady Mary?" Brad inquired.

Relaxing and answering the simple question, Mary smiled gratefully, "We come here every spring for Beth's birthday, it's the day after tomorrow, you know."

Startled, he replied, "No, I didn't know. I'm surprised his lordship invited me here. Usually, birthday celebrations are a family affair. Have special festivities been planned that I should be aware of?"

His declaration embarrassed Mary, and she doubted the wisdom of mentioning the forthcoming birthday. "My uncle doesn't believe in making a fuss for birthdays. That may change after Beth comes out, but until then, it's a family dinner followed by music and singing here at the manor house."

"Just dinner and music? Surely his lordship allows gifts. I've never heard of a birthday without gifts."

Mary giggled, "He tries to be nonchalant by leaving a gift on her breakfast plate, refusing to wrap it in fancy paper like the rest of us. She loves to unwrap presents, so I don't know why he is so contrary. Maybe he doesn't want to spoil her."

Sweetbriar

"Heaven forbid an indulgent father spoiling his daughter by wrapping her birthday present in fancy paper," he chuckled then mused a few minutes. "Lady Mary, I find myself at a disadvantage and need your assistance. Lady Beth's birthday comes as a surprise to me, and I am short a gift. You know your cousin's tastes and preferences. Perhaps you can guide me in selecting something appropriate," Brad requested. "I'm sure we can find an excuse to go to the village tomorrow. What do you say?"

This type of conspiracy appealed to her, so she readily acquiesced. "Beth and I always try to find an excuse to go to the village, but my uncle has no patience with our wandering through the shops. I'm sure if you suggested it, he would allow us to go with you and Lord Dunmore."

Not liking to include Dunmore but realizing the impossibility of excluding him, Brad stood in the stirrups and called across the roof of the carriage. "Lord Dunmore, it just came to my attention the young ladies desire an excursion into the village tomorrow, do you care to join us?"

"I can't image what enticements the village of Rockwell may possess, but if it attracts the ladies, it is as good a way to spend the day as any other," he replied, sounding bored. In truth, it irritated him the American thought of it first, but the more Rolf considered the idea, the more he liked it. Lady Beth's smoldering glances and seductive smiles belied the innocence of her youth. In the village, he'd find an opportunity to coax her away from the others and discover the veracity of it for himself.

"Over here, lads, I think we found the perfect spot," Lord Rockwell called. They were close to a small stream with a thick stand of oak trees for shade if it became too warm. The grass was ankle-high, and wild spring meadow flowers bloomed profusely. The sun was warming, but a slight breeze kept it from becoming too balmy. Servants spread blankets on the grass and unpacked food baskets as the young lord handed the ladies from the carriage.

Brad scanned the area admiringly. "This is lovely and reminds me of some of the meadows at home."

Flicking an invisible speck of lint from his pale blue coat, Lord Dunmore commented dryly, "One meadow is much the same as every other."

Beth laughed, "Papa always makes a fuss about finding the perfect picnic spot then brings us here every spring. He knows it's my favorite place and does it to please me." Color rose in Dunmore's face, and Brad turned away to hide his smirk. "Mr. Anderson, why don't you and Mary pick a wildflower bouquet?" Beth suggested.

Brad glanced at Mary, who dropped her eyes and blushed. "It would be my pleasure. Shall we Lady Mary?"

Behind Mr. Anderson's back, Beth fluttered her eyes at Mary to remind her to flirt. They wandered a short distance. Brad picked the flowers that Mary selected, handing each to her amiably. Recognizing her silence as bashfulness, Brad commented, "The fresh air and sunshine are invigorating in spring, wouldn't you agree, Lady Mary?"

Remembering her cousin's admonition, Mary raised her eyes and stared directly at her companion. "Yes, after the long winter, I always look forward to the first spring outing." She felt heat on her face as she colored, but maintained eye contact to the count of three, just as Beth had instructed.

Charmed at her flirtation, Brad deduced she was being encouraged by her cousin to overcome her shyness and decided to play long. "Your eyes are lovelier than

Sweetbriar

the cerulean blue of the sky, milady." She fluttered her eyes. Bemused, Brad remembered being subjected to similar antics when his sisters were young. "Do you have something in your eye?" he inquired, stepping close. He took her chin in his hand and tilted her face back. "Let me look. Perhaps I can find the offending speck."

Embarrassed, Mary quickly confessed, "I have nothing in my eye, Mr. Anderson, and I apologize for toying with you. Please don't attach your affections to me. I am only practicing at flirtation, so I'll be prepared for my coming out."

He smiled, "Lady Mary, under different circumstances, I should be honored to receive your attentions, but at the moment, my amorous interests lie elsewhere."

"They do?" she asked with wide-eyed curiosity.

"Yes. However, if I may assist in your flirtatious education, please do not hesitate to practice on me. I give you my word, my heart is secure."

Mary offered Brad her first genuine adult smile, her eyes sparkled with pleasure, and her face glowed with youthful beauty. "Thank you, Mr. Anderson. I appreciate your kindness." Looking at the bouquet in her hands, she laughed, "And I think we have enough silly wildflowers."

As soon as the offish American and that childish twit Mary wandered across the meadow, Rolf Dunmore sidled next to Beth and suggested they take a crock to the brook to collect water for the bouquet. It was cool in the deep shade of the trees, and Beth shivered as they slowly picked their way toward the stream. "If you are cold, Lady Beth, allow me to drape my coat around your shoulders. I assure you I won't take chill," Dunmore offered.

Rubbing her hands up and down her bare arms, Beth shivered again. "It is cooler than I expected. If you don't mind, I would appreciate it."

Rolf removed his coat, drew it around Beth's shoulders, and snuggled the collar under her chin. Beth caught her breath as his body warmth washed over her. She had never stood this close to a man. He stared intently into her eyes. A slow smile graced his lips as he dipped his head.

Fury surged through Brad's blood as he observed Dunmore nearly kissing the young noblewoman, but he restrained himself from pulling the man away and beating him senseless. "I'm told you have a crock of water for the flowers," he interrupted.

Beth gasped and stepped away, flushing with embarrassment.

Dunmore didn't have the decency to look embarrassed and was clearly aggravated by the interruption. "I was just getting it. It will take only a moment. No need to wait, Mr. Anderson, we will be finished here presently." The nobleman snatched the crock from Beth's hand, lurched down the embankment, and disappeared as he stooped to gather the water.

It flashed in Brad's mind where he had heard the name Dunmore before, recalling the vulgar rake wasn't satisfied with having only one woman in his bed. Realizing Beth's inexperience and reckless nature made her susceptible to corporal dangers to which she was ignorant and seeing the viscount prey upon the innocent girl engorged Brad's ire. He must protect her, he decided, but inconspicuously so the naive girl wouldn't resent his intrusion.

"You're cold, Lady Beth. You will be more comfortable in the sun." Anger still flashed in Brad's gray eyes as he gripped her elbow to escort her back to the picnic site. As they left the shade of the trees, he removed

Sweetbriar

Dunmore's pale blue coat from her shoulders and flung it in the dirt at their feet.

For Beth, all pleasure in the picnic revelry evaporated like a morning mist under a hot summer sun. After the viscount returned with the crock of water, he sullenly mounted his horse and rode off with no explanation. To Beth's aggravation, Mr. Anderson devoted his attention to Mary, who blatantly flirted. The American ignored Beth completely except to cast stormy glances her way. She sulked as she picked at her food, tossing bits and pieces to the chattering squirrels.

In late afternoon they returned to the manor, fatigued from the fresh air and sunshine. Rockwell and Hartford suggested a game of cards. Only Dunmore was interested but, needing a foursome, Lady Sylvia reluctantly consented to play.

Mary asked Mr. Anderson to tell her and Beth about America. Considering his home so similar to England that it would be of little interest to the ladies, Brad gave in to the impulse to thrill them with tales of the western frontier and the savage Indians. He possessed prodigious storytelling abilities. Before long had both young women shivering in abject terror.

The next morning dawned clear and bright. At breakfast, Brad mentioned he, Dunmore, and the young ladies were contemplating a walk into the village and asked if their lordships or ladyship cared to join them. The older men planned a morning of chess, and Lady Sylvia was too drained from the previous day's activities to consider a long walk.

As the four young people prepared for their departure, Brad whispered to Mary, "How well do you know Lord Dunmore?"

She whispered back, "Not well. He comes to see my father occasionally, but he makes me uncomfortable, so I avoid him."

Brad studied her face before continuing in a low voice, "He makes me uncomfortable, also. I'd prefer he not wander off with your cousin. Will you help me keep an eye on them?"

Mary's eyes slid toward the two, "I don't know what she sees in him, but I wish he would go away." Looking back, she continued ruefully, "It was better last year when she had her cap set on you. All we had to do was escape our chaperon and ride to the docks. I fear her flirtation with Lord Dunmore is more dangerous than that." Their conversation quickly terminated as Beth and Dunmore joined them.

"At least the fair weather is holding. We should have a delightful time," Beth enthused as they headed down the lane. "At the mercantile, I want to buy some green embroidery floss and see if they have any appealing lace or ribbon. Maybe we can stop at the milliner and try on a few bonnets. I might even buy one if any are becoming."

"And I'm hoping to find a book of poetry," Mary added. "What about you, gentlemen? What do you fancy?"

"I doubt the little village of Rockwell has much to offer a man of discerning taste," Dunmore sniffed.

"Perhaps the ladies will be kind enough to assist me in finding gifts for my mother and sisters. Gifts improve my chance of a cordial reception when I return home," Brad joked.

"You mean you need to bribe your way into their good graces," his lordship snipped.

Brad and Mary exchanged glances, but Beth didn't seem to notice. "Perhaps you'll find some yarn in a color that pleases," she suggested.

Mary inquired, "Do they like fine things? There's a nice china shop with figurines, and vases, and such."

"Don't be ridiculous, Lady Mary," Dunmore chided, "What would anyone in America do with such frivolous things? I'm sure they would prefer something more practical."

Attempting to check his annoyance, Brad countered, "On the contrary, Dunmore, my parent's estate is quite refined. Fine linens grace the tables, meals are served using crystal, china, and sterling, and the house is situated on a hundred-fifty acres of prime land. Additionally, my mother possesses a beautiful collection of small crystal figurines."

Taken aback at the familiar form of address, his lordship sneered, "That's Lord Dunmore to you, sir."

"And, *Lord* Dunmore," Brad replied condescendingly, "may I remind you that my grandfather was a Duke of the Realm and I am heir to one of the most profitable trading companies in America. I am not a backwater native of some English colony and don't expect to be treated as such."

Blood suffused Rolf's face. His hands clenched into fists. Beth laid her hand on his arm and soothed, "Please, milord, let us not be disagreeable."

He jerked his arm away before realizing the rudeness of the gesture. Then, glancing at Beth, he smiled stiffly. "You may address me as Dunmore if you wish," he stated quietly. She lowered her eyes, pleased by the offer but disturbed by his display of utter pettishness.

Soon they entered the village, and their attention was diverted toward the wares displayed in the shop windows. Beth cheerfully helped Brad choose yarn for his mother and sisters, inquiring about their hair color to ensure she suggested flattering shades. At the milliner, while Beth was preoccupied with bonnets, Mary quietly informed Brad of a flower vase her cousin had admired on numerous occasions.

They wandered here and there in a leisurely fashion, sometimes together and sometimes not, having no plans to investigate the shops with any particular purpose. The shifting mix of the group was so casual it didn't occur to Beth that either Mary or Brad stayed close at hand as they browsed. Conversely, as the sun slipped into the west and they tired of roving the village, Dunmore begrudged the two for frustrating his scheme of persuading the charming red-haired youth to slip away with him.

Beth awoke early on her fifteenth birthday and prodded her cousin, "Mary, wake up. It's my birthday, and I don't want to miss a minute of it." Then shaking harder, "Wake up."

"Beth, please, I trying to sleep. It is still dark out. Just go back to sleep until morning."

"It is morning, sleepyhead." Beth crawled out of bed and threw open the drapes; the early morning light was still a pearly gray. "Mary, I need to talk to you," Beth whispered. "I didn't tell you this before, but when we were on the picnic, in the trees by the stream, I think Dunmore wanted to kiss me."

Mary was instantly awake and sat up, "Beth, what happened? What did he do?"

Beth related the incident, explaining how Mr. Anderson's appearance shattered the moment, "But I believe if he hadn't happened upon us, Dunmore would have kissed me."

Mary threw back the covers and quickly crossed the room, taking Beth's hands, "How fortunate for you that Mr. Anderson went looking for the two of you. I don't think his lordship can be trusted. I told you he makes me uneasy. Please, Beth, stop your reckless flirtation with the man."

Beth sighed, "I know you are right because you have a pure heart. But tell me truly, dear cousin," she asked with barely contained excitement shining in her eyes, "are you not at all curious to find out what it is like to be kissed?"

"Are you more curious about being kissed than desirous of being respected?" Mary angrily retorted. "What type of character does a man possess if he takes such liberties with a girl not yet introduced to society? And what does it say of the girl's virtue?"

Beth paled, stunned by the intensity of her cousin's reply. "You question my virtue?"

Recognizing her advantage, Mary continued earnestly, "Last year, you chased Mr. Anderson to the docks with no escort. This year you openly flirt with the viscount, a man almost twice your age. I don't question your virtue, Beth, but what will Mr. Anderson think?" Beth's eyes widened. "He has a high regard for you, and I don't think he gives his esteem lightly. If I were you, I wouldn't be so fast to toss it aside."

Suddenly Beth felt weak, and for some inexplicable reason, wanted to bury her face in the refreshing fragrance of a cedar scented shirt. "Did Mr. Anderson tell you this?" Beth questioned quietly.

Mary shook her head, thoughtfully, "No, but I have seen him look at you. I believe there is admiration in his eyes." After another few moments, she added, "He led me to believe his affections are engaged."

"And you think his affections are directed toward me?" Beth asked incredulously. Mary nodded. "This requires some serious thought, Mary. I'm not at all sure how I feel about it. The stories he told us about his home are frightening. No genteel woman would ever consider living there." Beth paced as she contemplated this new idea. A few minutes passed, then she stopped in front of her cousin. "You are right about the rashness of flirting with Lord Dunmore. I shall cease immediately. And I shall pay more attention to Mr. Anderson's demeanor. If he has developed a fondness for me, I must discourage him as I have no desire to live in America. Life is precarious enough without constantly fearing Indian raids and massacres. I am an Englishwoman and shall marry an Englishman," she said emphatically.

"Beth, how can you say that? Mama says Mr. Anderson is heir to a fortune and is a splendid catch for any woman. Plus, he is handsome, considerate, and kind. I have no doubt he will make an excellent husband," Mary enthused.

"I admit he is handsome, but I don't know if he is considerate or kind. I'm not sure our temperaments are suited. Besides, he's an American, and my father is a titled Englishman. I want to marry another titled Englishman. I want to feel secure in my home. I want my children to live without fear of being slain by savages."

Then, dismissing the subject, Beth crossed to the bell cord and rang for their maids, "Never mind all this, let's get dressed and see what trifle Father has left on my breakfast plate this year."

Yesterday in the village, Brad covertly purchased a gift for Beth but was unable to find fancy paper to wrap it, so he decided to use one of his monogrammed kerchiefs instead. He used the emerald green ribbon from his purchases to tie the cloth together, thinking it would make an eye-catching foil entwined in her hair. Then he imagined entwining his fingers in the magnificent tresses, surprising himself at the thought.

Entering the dining room, Brad placed his gift with the others piled around Beth's breakfast plate. Lord Hartford and the viscount were having a quietly heated discussion in the farthest corner of the room while most of the other guests milled about waiting for the birthday girl to make her appearance.

Brad accepted a cup of tea from the serving girl as Lord Rockwell ambled over. "I see you found out about Beth's birthday, Captain. I should have told you when I extended the invitation, but I thought if I did, you would decline to join us. Now that Beth is older, I especially feel the loss of my wife's supervision of her and am never quite certain what to do. Please accept my apologies."

"Under other circumstances, I might have been displeased. As it is, I am thankful Providence brought me to your assistance," Brad replied with a glance in the direction of the young lord.

Rockwell followed his gaze, "Is there something you wish to tell me?"

Brad shrugged and sipped his tea before commenting, "Only that I would not place too much trust in the viscount."

The older man clasped his hands behind his back thoughtfully. "He is the relation of my brother-in-law and comes from a good family. Some men are too young when they inherit and need time to grow into their responsibilities. But I only met the man a few days ago. You are levelheaded, so I shall heed your advice until I know the viscount well enough to form my own judgment."

Relieved, Brad responded, "Thank you, milord."

Rockwell clapped him on the shoulder heartily. "We've known each other for a long time, Captain. I suggest you drop the formality and call me Rockwell."

"Thank you, Rockwell," Brad nodded.

Just then, Mary and Beth sashayed into the room, "Good morning, Papa," Beth sang gaily and planted a kiss on his cheek. "Good morning, Mr. Anderson."

"Happy birthday, Lady Beth. Good morning, Lady Mary," he replied with corresponding nods of his head.

They all gathered close to greet the celebrant, and with a little urging, she sat to open her presents. "I don't need to ask who this is from," Beth laughed as she raised the unwrapped gift. It was a golden locket that opened to reveal a miniature of her mother, Lady Kathryn. "Oh, Papa, thank you," she cried as she jumped up, threw her arms around his neck, and hugged him close. "It is so beautiful, and the likeness is exactly as I remember Mama." She passed the open locket around for everyone to admire.

When the locket was returned, her father instructed, "Turn around, Beth, and I will fasten it for you." His voice was gruff with emotion, and moisture glistened in both their eyes as he placed the locket around her swan-like throat.

When Beth sat again, her eyes swept over the gaily wrapped packages scattered around her place setting. "I love opening presents," she exclaimed with childish joy as she wiggled in her chair. Reaching for the largest package, she saw her aunt's calling card pasted to the top. Quickly ripping the paper and opening the box, she found a beautiful emerald green lace shawl. Shawls were the latest fashion. "Auntie, it's lovely. You must have spent countless hours crocheting such a delicate article. Thank you." She stood, draped the garment around her shoulders, and spun slowly with her arms extended, allowing everyone to admire her aunt's handiwork. The shawl stayed draped around her shoulders as she opened the gift from her cousin. "Why, Mary, you told me this book of poetry by Robert Blake was for yourself." Quickly riffling the pages, she stopped to read aloud.

> *"A flower was offered to me;*
> *Such a flower as May never bore.*

*But I said I've a Pretty Rose-tree.
And I passed the sweet flower o'er.*

*Then I went to my Pretty Rose-tree:
To tend her by day and by night.
But my Rose turned away with jealousy:
And her thorns were my only delight."*

Mary leaned over and hugged Beth, "I knew it would please you. I hope it provides you with many enjoyable hours of reading."

Next, she opened a gift from her uncle. It was a box of lace-edged handkerchiefs with her initials embroidered in one corner. "What lovely kerchiefs, Uncle. Thank you. Tell me, did you embroider them yourself?" she playfully inquired.

He colored in embarrassment at her teasing, and everyone joined in the merriment.

"That leaves two, yet I hesitate to accept gifts from gentlemen I hardly know," Beth announced.

Nonplussed, Bradley and Dunmore exchanged glances.

After a pause, she laughed, "The look on your faces is so droll. It would be rude of me to reject such considerations from my guests." Laughter filled the room. Taking the paper-wrapped present, Beth tore it open and discovered an attractive inlaid backgammon board. "Lord Dunmore, thank you for your thoughtfulness, but I don't know how to play backgammon."

"Then it shall be my privilege and pleasure to teach you," he replied with a slight bow. This time it was Beth and Mary who exchanged glances.

Taking a deep breath, Beth said, "Last but not least. Mr. Anderson, I presume the monogram BA indicates your gift."

"It does indeed, milady."

She was surprised to find her hands slightly shaking as she placed the object before her and reached to untie the green bow. "The ribbon is lovely and should look becoming in my hair. That's almost like getting two gifts in one," Beth said with a nervous laugh. When the ribbon was undone, the kerchief fell away and revealed a tall, delicate leaded crystal vase. It was sized to hold one rosebud. "So beautiful," she murmured. Her eyes flew to his face, "How did you know?"

"Know what, milady?" he asked, smiling innocently.

"That I have coveted this vase for the past two years," she whispered, admiring it once more. "When I noticed it missing from the shop window yesterday afternoon, I thought someone had bought it."

Brad laughed lightly, "Someone did buy it. Me. But I must confess that Lady Mary was my advisor," he said, glancing in her direction with an acknowledging nod. "She told me it would please you."

"Oh, it pleases me. I just don't know how I can accept it." She knew its cost from having admired it in the past.

"Of course, you can accept it, my girl," her father interjected. "I don't know about anyone else, but all this fuss has left me famished. Let us eat breakfast, say what."

A maid quickly removed the gifts and wrappings while a serving girl uncovered the platters of breakfast victuals that had been placed on the sideboard.

Once they were served, Lord Dunmore, who was sitting to Beth's right, leaned close and quietly suggested, "After breakfast, we can sit on the terrace, and I'll give you your first backgammon lesson."

From across the table, Mary chimed in, "Lord Dunmore, I also don't know how to play. May I learn too?"

He straightened and caught the American's eye. "I don't suppose you know how to play either?" he asked sarcastically.

Brad lazily replied as he spread jam on his biscuit, "I have some familiarity with the game and am always interested in observing the play of others to see what I might learn." He was secretly pleased to see the disgusted look on the other man's face.

Finishing breakfast, Beth instructed the servants to take the small chess table, inlaid with ivory and ebony, to the terrace along with four chairs. Dunmore sat across from Beth with Mary on his left. Brad chose to stand at Beth's right shoulder between the two women instead of sitting in the fourth chair. As Dunmore arranged the backgammon board, he explained the positioning of the game pieces and the object of the game. Then he demonstrated the movement of the gammons by throwing the dice a few times. After ten minutes of instruction, Beth and Lord Dunmore engaged in a practice game as he expounded on the rules throughout their play.

After a second practice game, Beth wanted to try a game without the benefit of Dunmore's coaching. She was a quick learner and held her own but missed a few crucial moves that would have sent her opponent to the bar. During a follow-up game, Brad couldn't resist leaning down occasionally to whisper strategy in Beth's ear. Her play improved and she almost won the game.

Dunmore was irritated with Anderson for giving guidance to Beth but held his tongue for appearance's sake. As the third game progressed, his annoyance grew each time the American leaned close to her. The communication between the two appeared too intimate to suit the young lord. His play suffered as a result.

When Beth won the game, she clapped her hands, bouncing up and down in her chair gleefully. "Oh,

Dunmore, this game is delightful, shall we play another?" she asked.

"Dear Beth," he said familiarly, "your game is improving but is still quite basic. Let me play against your tutor, and I'll demonstrate more advanced game strategies to you."

Beth glanced at Brad; whose steely gray eyes were fixed on her recent opponent. "Do you want to play Mr. Anderson?" she inquired.

"I doubt his lordship considers me a worthy opponent," Brad began stiffly, then shifted his gaze to Beth and smiled, softening his tone, "but for the sake of your education, I shall gladly submit."

Beth relinquished her chair, moving to sit across from Mary.

Brad sat and casually inquired, "Do you play for stakes?"

"Ten pounds a point, if it is not too rich for your blood," the viscount answered with a smirk.

"I can manage that. You choose to play with doubling, then?" Brad's inquiry challenged.

"I find it makes the game more interesting," was the supercilious reply.

They tossed the dice, and his lordship began the play. He doubled the stakes early in the game before there was a clear advantage and relinquished the doubling die to his opponent. He realized his error when the American declined to double after taking a slight advantage. Aggravated, Lord Dunmore heatedly denounced his opponent for withholding the die. Then, toward the end of the game, with a clear advantage, Brad doubled to four, but the dice turned against him, and the viscount won the game.

"That game wasn't much of a challenge," Brad declared. "Do you care for a rematch?"

Sweetbriar

"As you wish, but the stakes are the same as before, ten pounds per point, and I don't want you withholding the doubling die as you did last game," his lordship demanded.

Again, Dunmore won the toss and after a few plays sent one of Anderson's gammons to the bar. Brad rolled the dice but was unable to place his marker and forfeited his turn. Dunmore doubled and rolled but was able to move to the count of only one die.

Mary interrupted, "I don't understand the purpose of doubling."

Lord Dunmore impatiently explained, "Each game begins with one point, and in this case, a point is worth ten pounds. The stakes of the game increased to two points when I doubled. Mr. Anderson has the right to make the next double, which will be to four points. If a double is refused, the game is forfeit. The last game totaled four points, so my opponent owes me forty pounds. Please take your turn, Mr. Anderson."

After rolling a pair, Brad placed his marker on the board and sent two of Dunmore's gammons to the bar. His lordship placed both of his markers on his next toss, and the play continued with no additional doubling until both players had all their gammons on their home board. Much to his lordship's annoyance, Brad had the advantage and the doubling die. He doubled to four and rolled the dice but was unable to bear off any of his markers. On Dunmore's next turn, he rolled a pair of threes and bore off four markers, giving him the advantage. When Brad bore off only one gammon, Dunmore doubled to eight before rolling the dice. The next few plays were tense as each man came closer to winning; Dunmore with two gammons left and Brad with three. The next roll of the dice would determine the game. Brad hesitated as he contemplated the board.

"Don't be all day about it. You'll either win, or you'll lose. Just toss the dice," his lordship sneered.

Coolly, Brad lifted his eyes from the board and contemplated his opponent. "I double to sixteen," he said and rolled. The dice came to rest with a pair of fives showing. Brad sat back and crossed his arms. "I win," he said. "Minus the forty pounds from the last game, I believe you owe me one hundred-twenty pounds. If you don't have that much cash on hand, I will accept your note."

"One hundred-twenty pounds!" Beth gasped. "That's more than I spend in pin money in ten years."

Dunmore's face heated with anger, "I daresay, we'll play another game and see who wins. Same stakes as before."

In a quietly calm voice, Brad cautioned, "As you choose, milord, I'm quite agreeable. Just be aware, sea voyages have long periods of slack time between shorter periods of frantic activity. During the long periods of boredom, I amuse myself by playing backgammon. Any of my crew would tell you that I win more often than I lose."

Furious and feeling duped, the viscount rose, knocking back his chair. "Rot in hell," he spat and stormed into the house.

Minutes later, a volcanic quarrel erupted from within the manor. A short time after the flow of scorching words abated, a sealed missive was delivered to Bradley. Inside was a bank draft for one hundred-twenty pounds drawn on the account of Lord Hartford.

"What is this?" Brad demanded of the servant.

"His lordship directed me to give it to you, sir," the girl answered.

"But where is Dunmore?" he asked with a frown.

"Oh, Lord Dunmore has left, sir. I don't believe he will return."

Although surprised by the announcement, the three young people, each for their own reasons, were relieved by the abrupt departure.

After dinner that evening, Mary sat to play the pianoforte. Her touch was light and her skill more than adequate for the complicated cords of formal compositions. But after the first piece, Rockwell suggested she play more fashionable melodies.

Then an idea occurred to him, "I say, Anderson, you know that Mary will be coming out in a few months and Beth will come out about this time next year. I have two left feet when it comes to dancing. Would you mind terribly if we moved the furniture back so you could try your hand at teaching these two young ladies a step or two?"

"I quite agree," Lord Hartford chimed in. "Mary has been pestering me for weeks. I do fine with the minuet but am not inclined to embarrass myself with the more robust dances."

Both girls eagerly looked to the American. When he hesitated, Beth leaned close, laid her hand on his arm, and beseeched him with sparkling eyes. "Please say yes, Mr. Anderson," she implored softly. "I would love to learn to dance."

Brad's heart almost stopped. He had been right. A man could drown by gazing into her eyes. Clearing his throat and tearing his eyes away, he acquiesced, "Lady Sylvia, do you wish to play the pianoforte? Lord Hartford and I could demonstrate the minuet to both ladies at the same time."

"Dear no, sir, I have no talent for the instrument," she demurred, batting her fan quickly in front of her face. "I'm afraid you'll have to instruct them one at a time. Mary will play while you teach Beth, and then Beth will play so you can teach Mary."

The servants quickly removed the furniture to the corners of the room to clear a large area in the middle. The older generation hurriedly moved out of the way, as if to hesitate would require them to participate. Mary began a sedate minuet and Brad demonstrated the steps to Beth. She learned quickly and after a second dance traded places with her cousin. Mary overcame her initial nervousness, and soon, she too knew the steps.

Beth's fingers tripped into a popular three-quarter time tune, and she called over to her father, "Papa, may we learn to waltz?"

Milton coughed in surprise and cast his glance toward his male guest. "I don't know that it would be appropriate, Beth. You are still quite young, my child."

"Oh, Milton, really," his sister interjected, "Maybe Beth is too young, but I think Mary would benefit from learning. I hear it has become a more civilized dance in recent years. I would rather Mary learn under my supervision than receive instruction from some dandy out in a moonlit garden one night. You don't mind, do you, Mr. Anderson?"

Brad glanced at Mary's flushed face. "May I have the honor of this dance, Lady Mary?" he inquired.

Smiling, she fluttered her eyelashes. "Yes, you may, Mr. Anderson."

He took her left hand, placed it on his right shoulder, and clasped her other hand in his before encircling her waist with his arm. Slowly he taught her the steps, and as she became more proficient, increased the tempo.

"You must remember to smile, Lady Mary, otherwise your partner will think you aren't enjoying yourself," Brad teased.

"Mr. Anderson, this dance takes my breath away, so I have no thought for my countenance. I must stop before I swoon."

Sweetbriar

They came to a slow standstill and Brad escorted her to her parents. "Your daughter is as light as a feather and will be in great demand," he commented. Lord Hartford beamed with pride and Mary flushed at the compliment.

Beth rushed to join them. "Papa, please, let me learn this dance. I really am not too young, and it is my birthday," she pleaded.

With a sigh, he nodded his head. "I'll never hear the end of it if I don't agree. Very well, if Mr. Anderson hasn't tired of dancing, who am I to object?" Beth turned to Brad expectantly.

"Will you honor me with a dance, Lady Beth?" he inquired dutifully.

"Yes, just as soon as Mary has caught her breath." Turning to her cousin, she urged her to hurry, "You can catch your breath while you play the pianoforte, Mary. I'm sure if you breathe deeply, you'll be fine."

Mary laughed, "Just wait until you've whirled around a few times and see how long it takes you." But she stood and crossed to the instrument.

Beth knew how to place her hands from watching Mary, but she wasn't prepared for the shock of standing so near to her partner. His face was close to hers, and she saw the color of his eyes shift. Instead of the stormy gray of yesterday, they were a darker hazel color. She had never realized a person's eyes were capable of changing color but decided she preferred the greenish cast they now held. As they started to glide faster, she inhaled deeply and caught the slight cedar scent she had come to associate with this man. She closed her eyes to enjoy the fragrance better.

Within his chest, Brad's heartbeat like the wings of a caged bird as he gazed at her face. With her eyes closed and her lips slightly parted, she appeared as if she awaited a lover's kiss. He was tempted to oblige except her father was seated ten feet away. Then he recalled the ire he felt a few days past when he found Rolf Dunmore leaning toward Beth with the same intent in mind. Recoiling at the similarity of their thoughts, he abruptly ended the dance.

Confused, Beth opened her eyes, "Is something wrong? The music hasn't ended. Did I misstep?"

He shuddered a sigh, stepped back, and shook his head, "You dance beautifully, Lady Beth. Please accept my apologies, but it appears it is I who must catch my breath. I am not used to so much activity," he lied and escorted her back to her father.

"Lovely, my dear," Rockwell commented. "You seem to take to dancing quite naturally. I shall have a difficult time making you wait another year for your coming out, but that was your mother's express wish. She believed you needed the maturity of sixteen years before entering the marriage race, and I wholeheartedly agree. Now, why don't you play us a pretty song so we can enjoy your lovely voice?"

Beth reclaimed her place at the pianoforte and began to key the notes of *Three Sisters*. When Brad came to stand beside her, she cast a glance his way and inquired, "Do you sing, Mr. Anderson?"

"I'm told I'm tolerable in duets. Would you oblige?" he countered.

"My dear Mr. Anderson, if you sing as well as you dance, I must question why you would waste your talents sailing the seas. Surely you must have all the American maidens pining for your return." Her gaze was direct but there was amusement in her assertion.

Lowering his voice seductively and leaning close, he replied, "I must confess, sweet Beth, I have yet to meet an American maiden who can hold my interest. I find the simpering manners of many young women irritating. I prefer to hold out for a woman with a bolder personality." His gaze was as direct as hers, but there was no laughter in his tone.

She wasn't quite sure what to make of his statement and directed her eyes back to the pianoforte's keyboard. "I shall play the refrain of *Three Sisters* once, and then we will sing the three verses." With that, she began to play. Her voice was as sweet and clear as the water in a high mountain lake. His voice fluidly blended to give depth.

> *JANE was a Woodman's daughter,*
> *The fairest of the three,*
> *Love in his arms had caught her,*
> *As fast as fast could be;*
> *A Sailor's Son was ANDY,*
> *As brave as brave could be,*
> *And he resolved to marry,*
> *The fairest of the three,*
> *The fairest of the three,*
> *The fairest of the three,*
> *And he resolved to marry,*
> *The fairest of the three.*
>
> *MARIA thought it wiser,*
> *A rich man's wife to be,*
> *And so took a Miser*
> *As old as old could be,*
>
> *LOUISA felt Love's passion,*
> *But wished this world to see*
> *So chose a Lad of Fashion,*
> *The dullest of the three,*
> *The dullest of the three,*
> *The dullest of the three,*
> *So chose a Lad of Fashion,*
> *The dullest of the three.*
>
> *LOUISA's spouse perplexed her,*
> *A Widow soon was she,*

*MARIA's lived and vexed her
As well as well could be.
But JANE possessed true pleasure
With one of low degree,
They were each other's treasure
The happiest of the three,
The happiest of the three,
The happiest of the three,
They were each other's treasure
The happiest of the three.*

"What a foolish song," Beth tittered as they finished. "Why can't a girl find a man to marry who is young, handsome, and wealthy? And why should all men of fashion be dull? Here, let's have a better song. Do you know *I Leave My Heart with Thee*, Mr. Anderson?"

At first, Brad was startled by her question until it dawned on him that she was referring to a song. Then he realized the words to the song reflected his own emerging feelings and bowed politely. "I'm afraid the words have slipped my mind. And I think tomorrow I must return to my ship. By your leave, I shall retire now."

Beth was dumbfounded. One moment they were blending their voices most pleasantly, and the next, he was walking away. If he didn't care to sing again, he could have encouraged her to continue without him. Instead, the vexing man ended the evening while it was still early.

Brad bade goodnight to his host and the other guests then retired to his room. He intended to leave at dawn, but sleep did not come easy as his thoughts kept straying to the sparkling young woman with the deep brown eyes.

***

The first day after Louise threw Bradley Anderson out of her bedroom, she remained incensed. Then she began considering her alternatives and realized she didn't have any that appealed to her. She might be a kept woman, but she was well cared for by a man who imposed few demands. She reasoned that even if he did marry, as the captain of a merchant ship, he would still make frequent trips to England and desire the comforts she provided. So, she awaited his return, hoping to mend the rift between them.

Expecting him to be gone only two or three days, she became concerned after more than a week had passed. What if he didn't come back? Where would she go, and how would she live? Might she find another lover to provide for her? These thoughts plagued her for days, but then the clatter of carriage wheels on the cobblestones outside drew her attention. Bradley and an older, bewhiskered man alighted. With trepidation, Louise greeted the men at her door.

"Good evening, Louise, this is Quinn O'Malley, a friend of mine," Brad said in an offhand manner as he entered the cottage. "I didn't have time to send a message, so I hope you won't be too inconvenienced by serving us supper."

"Not at all...sir." Louise wasn't sure how to address him in the current situation but remembered to drop a quick curtsy to her guests.

"Pleased to make your acquaintance, lass. I appreciate your hospitality. Brad tells me you set a fine table, and I have a hearty appetite," the big man enthused.

"Kindly make yourselves comfortable, gentlemen, it will take a few minutes, but I think you will be satisfied with the food I have to offer. Would you care for a glass of wine while you wait?" she anxiously inquired.

"I'll get it, Louise. You go and prepare the meal. By the way, we'll expect you to join us at the table," Brad informed her.

In the kitchen, she worked quickly to piece together a meal for her unexpected guests. Bradley had never brought anyone to the cottage before and had it not been for their tiff, Louise would consider it a good sign, but her recent worries made her uneasy. Why had he brought the man here? Had she angered Bradley enough to discard her? Did he expect her to accept the older man as a replacement lover? That would be too much for her bruised heart to bear. She sat at the small worktable, placed her head on her arms, and silently wept.

"Are you still angry with me, Louise?" She raised her head and saw Bradley leaning on the door frame with his arms crossed over his chest. "I thought if I gave you some time you would reconcile yourself to the circumstances. Perhaps I'm mistaken, and you would prefer for us to leave."

"Why have you brought that man here?" she questioned quietly, glancing past his shoulder.

He shrugged an embarrassed reply, "I wasn't sure how you would greet me. I thought if I brought a guest, you would be too polite to argue or slam the door in my face." Dropping his arms to his sides, he asked, "Will you forgive me?"

She considered him for a few moments, deciding how to respond. As all women know, the time to ask for favors is when a man is begging forgiveness. "I am so lonely when you are gone that I have an unreasonable need to be with you when you are here. Perhaps if I had a companion, a maid, it would ease my loneliness, and I wouldn't be so demanding."

Brad crossed the room and drew Louise into his arms, holding her head to his chest. "What an oaf I've been to think you would be content here by yourself. A maid is little enough for you to ask. Is there anything else you long for?"

She sighed, "I need a few things but have been hesitant to ask. I will provide you with a small list if it isn't too much trouble?"

Tilting her face up, Brad gazed into her eyes, "Make your list. You shall have what you want. I'm not a miserly man. If I didn't provide for you well enough, you should have told me."

She smiled, thinking that if her lover never intended to marry her, she should use his guilt to safeguard against the future when he no longer wanted her. "Let me finish preparing your dinner. It won't take much longer. You and Mr. O'Malley must be famished, and I don't want to keep you waiting any longer than necessary."

With relief, Brad playfully swatted her bottom. "If you mention that you are out of brandy, Quinn won't stay long after dinner. It's been purgatory staying away from you, my pet."

She laughed, "Then let me finish as quickly as I can, and we will have our meal, then send Mr. O'Malley on his way."

Returning to the parlor, Brad was caught by surprise when Quinn O'Malley demanded, "Do you mean to marry the lass?" When the younger man didn't answer, O'Malley persisted, "It is as plain as the whiskers on my face that you are more than passing acquaintances."

"Louise and I have an understanding," Brad replied curtly. "It is no concern of yours, my friend."

"It may be no concern of mine," his mentor acknowledged, "but you were in my care a good many years, and I think of you as one of my own. You must have known I'd be asking questions when you brought me here."

Sighing, Brad confided, "I met her last year in a brothel. She is a genteel girl who misjudged a man's character and was abandoned by him and disowned by her family. She said her paramour's father took her to the brothel as a kindness. She prefers this arrangement, and we both find it beneficial to our needs."

O'Malley mulled this over and nodded his head. "You know I'm a God-fearing man and don't approve of consorting with women outside the marriage vows. But if you insist on doing it, I guess it is better to keep a mistress than to be visiting bordellos. I've known many a good sailor brought down by the pox. Still, I don't think you'll be wanting your father to know, so we will keep this between the two of us. Just remember where you met her when it comes time to take a wife."

"Don't be worried about that, Quinn. My heart is still my own."

When dinner was served, O'Malley enjoyed the meal in a leisurely manner, much to the consternation of the young couple. He chatted about his family much too long after the repast was finished, and when Louise apologized a second time for not having brandy to serve, he understood the hint to take his leave. "I appreciate your hospitality and may impose upon you again for a nourishing meal. But trust me to have Bradley send a messenger to give you adequate notice, that way you'll be sure to have the brandy on hand," he teased.

After receiving a nod of approval from Bradley, Louise replied, "You are always welcome at my table, sir."

Chapter III
Spring 1807, England

The crossing between America and England was more difficult and dangerous due to the European war. The French attempted and oftentimes succeeded in confiscating the merchant ships and cargoes bound for England. And the British efforts to increase their naval power escalated the impressment of crewmen from ships outbound from England and America.

While evading both Imperial and Royal ships off the southern shores of England, Brad seriously considered following his father's advice about relinquishing command of the *Angel Star* and taking over the shore operations of Surrey Trading Company. Thinking about settling down and taking a wife, a wife who would bear him sons and warm his bed at night, Brad's mind bobbed, like a rudderless ship on a choppy sea, over images of women he knew. He remained discontented in his contemplation until the sextant in his mind directed him to the vision of Beth Avery. He reminisced about teaching her to waltz on her fifteenth birthday, the nearness of her lithe body, and her sensuous countenance as he whirled her around. Her teasing eyes and parted lips had tortured more than one dream in the past year. After close self-examination, Brad determined she was his heart's desire. However, he was in England on business and couldn't very well drop everything to court the girl.

Two years ago, Lady Beth had ridden to the docks in search of him. But he wondered if it had only been a girlish infatuation because last year, she appeared to favor the vile Lord Dunmore over himself. Brad's discontentment returned. It was essential to see Beth again to determine if she returned his esteem, but when he mulled over various ways of finagling an invitation to the Avery home without disclosing his partiality to her father, Brad was stymied.

A knock at his open cabin door broke into his thoughts.

"Sir, the river master's cutter approaches. Do you wish me to go ashore and inform your lady friend that you've arrived?" Derek O'Malley asked, his adolescent voice breaking awkwardly.

Louise. Brad would never marry her, but if he had no wife when he gave up the sea, he might consider taking her to America. However, marriage was his goal, and any way he looked at it, the liaison with Louise was doomed. After marriage, Brad thought it best to have at least one ocean between his wife and ex-mistress. Nevertheless, he wasn't married yet, and Louise remained his for the taking, so Brad sent the young O'Malley off with news of their return.

After leaving the river master's office, Brad proceeded to the tea export office belonging to Lord Rockwell. "Captain Anderson," the clerk announced at his lordship's office door.

"Anderson, it's good to see you again," the nobleman said as he extended his hand. "I wasn't sure you'd get through the blockade, many ships haven't, you know."

"It wasn't easy, Rockwell, and I'm questioning whether or not it will be worth it in the future," Brad replied.

"I think that usurper, Boney, causes more trouble for world-wide commerce than for all the armies of Europe," his lordship commiserated. "Prior to Pitt's untimely death last year, he was working to form a fourth coalition against France. It included Prussia, Russia, and Sweden. The new Prime Minister, William Grenville, was able to hold it together. But Fredrick Wilhelm of Prussia foolishly declared war in August instead of waiting for additional troops from Russia."

"Our President prefers for our country to avoid becoming embroiled in European wars, so I know little of your various intrigues," Brad commented.

"Boney was vicious," Avery declared. "He personally took command of the army and overran Prussia's superior force of two-hundred-fifty thousand troops with only one hundred-sixty thousand French soldiers. And did it in just nineteen days."

"Good lord."

"Word is they inflicted twenty-five thousand casualties, took one-hundred-fifty thousand prisoners, and captured a hundred thousand muskets along with four thousand artillery pieces. Instead of wearing the little general down, Prussia seems to have reinforced France's weaponry, say what," his lordship said wincing. "Then to top it off, he issued a decree from Berlin forbidding all European countries allied with or under the control of France from importing British goods."

"But how strong is his control in other nations? Can he enforce such a decree?" Brad asked.

"He has conquered or allied with every major continental power and no doubt believes he can bring England to her knees by imposing trade restrictions with the nations he controls. Only Portugal has openly refused to join his Continental System, but many other countries secretly flout it," the nobleman replied.

Brad nodded, "England may face additional trading pressure. There's talk in our Congress of ceasing trade with any belligerent country. So far, it's only talk, but if it goes much further, they may make the decision about relinquishing my command for me." Brad shook his head in disgust, "But I'm here now, and the American demand for your premium tea remains robust, so I'm ready to make arrangements for my return voyage."

Glancing at the ponderous clock on its heavy plank shelf, Rockwell shook his head, "Not today, Captain. I'm afraid I don't have the time. My daughter comes out tonight, and I need to return home. I wouldn't have come to the office at all today, except the arrangements for these types of affairs are better left to the servants and the women, my sister in this case," he explained. "Why don't you join us tonight? As I recall, you taught Beth to waltz. It is fitting for you to see her make a successful debut. And it might do you good to get off the ship after so long at sea."

Brad smiled. The suggestion played smoothly into his hope of seeing the coppery haired vixen again. "My sisters have married already, so I haven't attended a coming out for some time, Rockwell. But I enjoy these events, and I am happy to accept."

Beth expected to make a grand entrance, imagining a grand entrance was called for after this past month. It had been a whirlwind of ordering ball gowns and day dresses, and all the other articles of clothing that went with her new social status and tonight represented her formal introduction to society.

Sweetbriar

Lady Sylvia had guided Beth with the preparations for the ball. Her friends and their parents were invited, along with all the eligible young men. Beth decided to dance with every man; after all, it was her ball, so it was only proper for her to dance with them all.

And she would flirt. She had practiced with her fan in front of the mirror and knew just how to accentuate her brown eyes by covering the lower half of her face. She knew precisely how to show surprise or shock or disinterest. She expected to have all the young blades eating out of her hand.

And she would drink champagne. Papa said she could have one glass. Being a grown woman was heavenly.

Dashing Beth's plans for a grand entrance, her father insisted he escort her downstairs before any of the guests arrived. It was her responsibility as the hostess, he explained, to greet her guests. It made no difference to Beth if she greeted the guests, although she would never say as much to her father. Then he said it would give him the greatest pleasure to be her first official escort because, after tonight, he didn't expect ever to have the privilege again. She couldn't refuse such sweet sentiments and descended the staircase on her father's arm, to an audience of none. And moments later, her guests began to arrive.

All Beth's expectations for the evening were met. The champagne tickled her nose and made her light-headed, so she gladly drank only one glass. She danced but never with the same beau twice. And after all the practice with her fan, she barely had time to flirt between sets.

Arriving at Rockwell's townhouse, music and gaiety flowed over Brad. His smiling host exclaimed, "Captain Anderson, I fear you may have arrived too late." The older man's eyes twinkled with pleasure. "Beth has danced every set and still has many admirers waiting. I won't be surprised if she receives multiple marriage proposals from just this one evening."

Brad quickly scanned the crowd and spied the radiant haired nymph in a group of dancers on the far side of the room. Her exquisite loveliness had blossomed as perfectly as a rose in spring. At the sight of her, Brad's breath caught fast in his throat. Finding his voice, he murmured, "In that case, perhaps I should list my advantages and press my suit before her other admirers have a chance."

Rockwell chortled, considering Brad's remark a polite social pleasantry offered to a proud father until he saw Anderson's gaze transfixed upon Beth. Coughing softly, his lordship commented, "Of course, I agreed to let my daughter make the final decision in choosing a husband. It seems reasonable since she will live the rest of her life with the man."

After glancing briefly toward his host, Brad returned his gaze to the young woman. "Then, I shall state my case to your daughter. Please excuse me, Rockwell," he said and strode across the room.

Notes from the harpsichord softly faded as the minuet ended. The young man who partnered with Beth was charming, but not charming enough for a second dance, she thought, annoyed when he didn't escort her off the ballroom floor. Glancing about, she hoped to capture the gaze of another young man when hers was ensnared by a vaguely familiar face. When the man stepped forward, Beth recognized him as the disagreeable Captain Anderson.

"May I have the honor of this dance, Lady Beth?" he asked, bowing slightly from the waist.

Her eyes quickly swept around the room, but she found no one to intervene. Her previous partner politely excused himself, and the strains of the violins flowed in-

Sweetbriar

to a three-quarter time movement. Beth had no choice but to waltz with the American.

"What are you doing here, Captain Anderson? I don't recall seeing your name on the guest list," Beth accused.

"I just arrived in port and your father, remembering that I taught you to dance, invited me," he replied evenly. Drawing her closer, he whispered in her ear, "And you still have my favorite shirt, which I would sorely like back." Hot embarrassment suffused Beth's face. "After all, I did promise to recall how charming you looked in it whenever I wear it."

The audacity of the man! Her eyes flashed, and her color deepened.

"You look flushed, sweet Beth. Perhaps you require some fresh air," Brad suggested as they approached the open terrace door. He tucked her hand under his arm and escorted her out. "Have you thought of me at all these past months?" he queried.

"Of course not, why would I?" she snapped. If he only knew of the times she had buried her face in the soft fabric of his shirt to inhale the fresh cedar scent. Or the night she had dared sleep in it. "Please take me back inside. I shouldn't stay out here with you."

Instead, Brad drew her into his arms and tenderly pressed his lips to hers. Swept away by the sudden thrill, Beth's arms crept around the American's neck. Instinctively she fingered the tousled curls at his nape. His tongue teased at her lips, and when they parted in surprise, he deepened the kiss, drawing her lower lip between his teeth. Euphoria flashed and seared all thought from her mind. Beth almost swooned.

As quickly as the kiss began, it ended. Brad stepped back, his voice husky with desire, "You're right, Beth. You shouldn't remain here with me." He drew a deep, shuddering breath and whispered, "If you stay, I shan't resist making love to you."

Shocked by his words, she slapped his face, then turned and fled inside, where she came face to face with her father.

"Why, Beth, you're flushed. I think you have danced too much. I insist you sit for a while."

"Oh, father! It's not that at all," she cried.

Peering out the terrace doors, his lordship sighted Captain Anderson. Was his interest in Beth serious, the older man wondered? He stared at his daughter again and realized she was flushed not from dancing but from agitation.

"It's not seemly for you to be outside, my child," he scolded. But when she laid her head on his chest, he patted her shoulder. "Run upstairs and cool your face with some water. You'll be fine in a few minutes. When you come back down, you can dance until dawn if you choose." Rockwell released her and gave a nudge to get her going. He watched her pensively a few moments then stepped outside.

"Captain Anderson, I wish to speak to you." The nobleman couched his command as a request, "Please join me in the library."

Brad nodded and followed.

Closing the door behind them, Lord Rockwell waved his guest to a chair but remained standing with his arms crossed over his chest, facing the fireplace broodingly. Anderson was only one generation away from noble English blood—blood more noble than his own, Rockwell conceded. And the American's wealthy father owned a large and profitable import-export business, which the captain would, no doubt, inherit one day. As for bloodline and wealth, the nobleman would not object to a union, if in fact the young man had that in mind. Rockwell turned and stared coldly at Bradley

Anderson, who to his credit, returned the look with a level gaze.

"Explain your behavior," Rockwell snapped with the cold hauteur of his class.

"I meant no disrespect, milord," Bradley replied.

"Then state your intentions toward my daughter!" he demanded.

Brad considered the conversation premature but recognized certain affairs required decisiveness regardless of the timing. He inhaled deeply before responding, "My intentions are honorable, sir. Although I've met your daughter only a few times, I feel a strong attraction. With our common interests in business, I believe this would be an appropriate alliance," Brad replied.

"I don't intend for my daughter to marry a sea captain, young man. I know your future prospects are good, but Beth has an impulsive nature and hasn't always had a sensible example of womanhood since my wife died. My sister tries, but she is a foolish woman without much common sense. Beth needs the steady hand of a husband at her side on a daily basis. A sea captain won't do."

"Sir, you are correct that my prospects are secure. For quite some time, my father has urged me to leave the sea and learn the shore responsibilities of the business. With the French and British disrupting trade so much, I find the idea very appealing. I assure you, I do not intend to continue at sea after I marry," Brad explained.

Rockwell sighed deeply and dropped his arms to his sides. "I have no objections to the marriage provided you quit the sea." Unconsciously, Brad had been holding his breath and now slowly let it out. "However," his lordship stated, "I promised Beth a say in the matter. I shall talk with her tomorrow and see how she feels about it." He paused to contemplate the man before him, then abruptly said, "I have been away from my guests long enough."

"With your lordship's permission," Brad said, rising, "I shall return to my ship. Considering the circumstances, I have several matters to ponder."

"Very well, Captain. Come to my office tomorrow afternoon, and we'll discuss your marriage proposal as well as your tea shipment."

Beth splashed cool water on her face and felt much better. She examined her reflection in the mirror as she dried her face. Did she look different? Does one look different after being kissed? She ran her fingertips lightly over her lips and felt a flutter of excitement in her stomach. She remembered the faint scent of cedar on Mr. Anderson's clothes when he held her close and quickly crossed to her cedar chest. Finding his shirt, she pressed it to her cheeks and inhaled deeply. The giddy feeling returned as if he again held her in his arms.

None of the gentlemen who danced with her tonight looked at her the way he did, and none were daring enough to usher her outside. Captain Anderson was an irksome man. How was she ever going to get him out of her thoughts? She considered kissing someone else but questioned how a woman went about it. It had happened so suddenly. She wondered if she had done something to entice him to kiss her. All she remembered was the annoying conversation about his shirt.

She pressed the shirt to her face and inhaled again. It belonged to her now, and she meant to keep it. She placed it back in her chest and decided to rejoin the festivities. Perhaps another man would kiss her. That would teach the impertinent sea captain a thing or two, she thought, as she descended the stairs.

She would find Mary, Beth decided. Mary had been out for many months now and had probably been kissed. Maybe she knew what a girl did to encourage a man's advances. Slowly Beth wandered through the rooms looking for her cousin. In her search, Beth didn't see Mr. Anderson among the guests. Her father may have thrown him out, she thought, which would serve him right. A gentleman didn't take such liberties with a well-bred woman. Still, she would have preferred to show the captain he wasn't the only man she could kiss.

After dancing until two o'clock, Beth fell into a deep, exhausted sleep. She dreamed each of her dancing partners guided her out of the terrace doors and kissed her. But when each kiss ended, her dancing partner's face was always that of Bradley Anderson.

Slowly she awakened, stretched languidly, and moaned softly. She'd had a wonderful time and anticipated a whole season of dancing, two seasons if she played her cards right. After waiting so long for this time in her life, Beth refused to rush headlong into marriage. After the disastrous escapade along the docks two years ago, Beth had recognized her impetuous nature and decided to show more common sense. It made sense to become acquainted with all the young men before deciding who to marry. After all, once married, there would be little enough time for balls.

A soft knock on her door aroused her from her daydreams, and her maid peeked in to see if Beth was awake. "Milady, your father wants a word with you. Let's get you out of bed and dressed. Oh, shame on you, milady. You wore that shirt to bed again. What would your father say if he knew you slept in a man's shirt?"

"Hush now, don't you dare tell him about this shirt. Dress me just as quickly as you can. Papa hates when I keep him waiting.

As the maid gathered clothing, Beth brushed her hair and washed her face, and after dressing, skipped down the stairs, excited about starting the new day.

"Good morning, Papa," Beth sang as she waltzed into the breakfast room. "How are you today?"

"Just fine, Beth, and you?"

"Papa, you should have told me that dancing all night would give me aches in places I didn't even know I had," she laughed, lightly rolling her shoulders and hips.

Pleased to see her good mood, Rockwell anticipated an easy conversation. "I'm glad you enjoyed yourself. I'm happy to tell you last night was a complete success."

"Papa, it was wonderful. To think I have a whole season of balls and dancing ahead of me," she trilled.

"Yes, well," he cleared his throat and started again. "Beth, when I said the evening was a complete success, I meant that you succeeded in catching the eye of a very eligible suitor."

Her heart leaped. She was elated that someone had already asked permission to court her. The first of many such requests, she hoped.

"I always knew you would be an instant success, but I hadn't expected a proposal on your first night out," his lordship enthused.

The smile faded from Beth's face, and she blinked her eyes, "A proposal? Of marriage? It cannot possibly be true, not yet."

"Yes, my dear, a marriage proposal. And one to which I have no objection." He beamed and patted her hand.

"But father, it's too soon. I can't possibly marry yet," Beth announced.

"Well, you wouldn't marry just yet. After all, your engagement will last a year," her father assured her.

Sweetbriar

"No, father, I cannot. It's too soon. I've only just come out. What about all the balls and operas, and ... and ... fun? I can't possibly get married or even engaged so soon," Beth retorted, vexation creasing her brow.

Looking at his daughter from under his eyebrows, Lord Rockwell quietly asked, "Don't you even want to know the identity of your admirer before rejecting him?"

Beth knew that tone of voice and adjusted her skirts, thinking before she calmly replied, "No, father, I don't. It would mortify me to see the man at another ball, knowing he asked for my hand, and I refused him. I'm afraid I would never forgive him for the embarrassment he caused me. If I don't know his name, then I shall feel perfectly comfortable and shall treat him as if nothing had ever been said." Warming to her subject, she continued, "He'll understand that he asked too soon, Papa, because you'll explain it all to him. Then he'll know the importance of courting me so I can fall in love with him." The idea had taken a firm hold in her mind. "That's it, you know. I shall fall in love with him and not even know it was him," she beamed with conviction.

"You're talking nonsense, girl," her father glowered. "How can you fall in love with the man when you don't even know who he is?"

"It doesn't matter. I'm still young, just give me a while," she requested with a radiant smile, the smile she always used to get her way.

With a sigh, her father nodded his head.

In Rockwell's outer office, awaiting his arrival, Brad slowly paced. He had reservations about offering for Beth so soon. If he had controlled himself, he wouldn't have kissed her. If he hadn't kissed her, she wouldn't have been agitated. And if she hadn't been agitated, her father wouldn't have pressed the issue prematurely.

A wiser course would have been to make the social rounds while in London and court her properly. But seeing Beth flirt with that awkward boy while dancing drove away Brad's common sense, and the way she kissed drove away his good judgment. The kiss promised a passionate nature, and Brad briefly forgot himself, foolishly declaring his eagerness to possess her. And she was justifiably insulted.

Would she reject him for being too forward? Would she accept? Brad raked his fingers through his hair.

Lord Rockwell stood a moment watching Captain Anderson through the shop window. The young man was plainly disturbed. Perhaps he had second thoughts about his marriage proposal. It would be just as well if he did, considering Beth wasn't planning to marry anyone for a while. His lordship didn't blame his young daughter for wanting a year of parties and fun, but he wanted her settled.

"Good afternoon Anderson," Milton Avery said, stepping into the shop. "Come into my office, and we will get this business concluded."

Not sure of which business his lordship spoke, Brad followed and took his customary chair.

"I won't keep you wondering as I can see you are eager to know." Rockwell stood beside Brad, placed a hand on his shoulder, and looked him in the eyes. "Beth isn't ready to commit herself yet. She says she's still young and wants time to enjoy this year's parties and all. It's nothing personal young man." He gave Brad's shoulder two good pats, then walked around his desk and sat.

Brad shifted uncomfortably in the chair and cleared his throat. "Did she give any indication that she would entertain the proposal in the future, or was it a flat rejection?" He could wait a year if need be.

"She didn't even want to know who offered for her. Said it would be too embarrassing socially. If you're truly interested in pursuing your marriage proposal, I suggest you give her some time. Being a grown woman enlivens Beth. She's not ready to settle down yet. I'll keep you in mind before agreeing to another proposal that I promise." Then picking up his spectacles, Rockwell cleared his throat. "Now, let's discuss your tea shipment."

Brad reluctantly turned his thoughts away from marriage and spent the next hour haggling over the price and quantity of tea.

Summer 1807, England

Instead of devoting his time to business, Brad immersed himself in London's social activities. As heir to one of America's most profitable trading companies and a very eligible bachelor, he had no trouble securing invitations to the most prominent homes.

The first time Beth saw him at another party, her eyes widened, and a fierce blush rose up her neck to her cheeks as she unconsciously touched her fingers to her lips.

Brad couldn't suppress a smile, knowing she remembered the feel of his mouth on hers. But he was wiser than to attempt to kiss her again. That night he made it a point to dance with as many young ladies as possible, fulfilling the expectations required of unattached men. Toward the end of the evening, he approached Beth's father, knowing she would return to him at the end of the current dance.

"You have fulfilled your duties to the young ladies in earnest, Captain," Lord Rockwell commented dryly.

"Has your interest in my daughter begun to wane already?"

"On the contrary, your lordship, it has taken great willpower to restrain myself this long. If I am not a dutiful guest, I shall lack the very invitations I need to woo your daughter, as you suggested," Brad countered.

Relieved, his lordship smiled, "You can drop the formality, Anderson. I told you last year you may call me Rockwell. Your interest in Beth hasn't changed that."

Brad nodded his acknowledgment, "Thank you, Rockwell."

"By the by, what do you make of the incident between your American frigate, *Chesapeake* and our fourth-rate warship, *Leopard*?"

The American crossed his arms over his chest as his jaw clamped tight. "My understanding is the *Leopard* made an unprovoked attack against the *Chesapeake*, which could be construed as an act of war."

"Poppycock! It was no such thing. Humphreys hailed your frigate, and your Commodore Barron should have allowed the *Chesapeake* to be searched for Royal Navy deserters," asserted the Englishman.

"Commodore Barron was within his rights to refuse the search without being fired upon," Brad argued. "Three of his men were killed and eighteen more wounded, including Barron. If their decks hadn't been cluttered with stores for their voyage, I dare say an outright battle would have ensued rather than just one gun answering the attack."

His lordship looked sharply at his companion, "You can't deny they found four deserters, Anderson."

Brad uncrossed his arms, "They found only one British deserter—Ratford. The white American and two black freemen may have previously served in the Royal

Navy, but they weren't deserters. Otherwise, they would have hanged from the yardarm alongside Ratford."

"Oh, no," Rockwell contradicted, "we only hang British subjects. If the Americans are found guilty, they'll be lashed, and if they aren't guilty, they'll be returned to your country. Only time will tell."

Their conversation was interrupted as the music ended and Beth's partner escorted her off the ballroom floor. Relaxing, Brad smiled congenially, appreciating her graceful movements. But when Beth frowned at him, Brad tensed. Then his smile completely faded when she snubbed him.

"Papa, you must be fatigued by these late hours, especially after working half the day. I shan't complain if you wish to leave early," she encouraged.

"Attend to your manners, my dear," her father chided. "Mr. Anderson has come to pay his respects."

Beth blushed and lowered her eyes as she turned toward her admirer. "Good evening, Mr. Anderson. I didn't realize you socialized when in England."

"It suits me more this year than in the past. Will you honor me with a dance, Lady Beth?" he asked.

Having no excuse to refuse, it perturbed her to hear the first strains of a waltz. Of all times, why not a minuet? "Of course, Mr. Anderson." She reluctantly placed her hand on his offered arm.

Being careful to hold her at a respectable distance as they glided around the ballroom, Brad politely inquired, "Are you finding London society as invigorating as you anticipated?"

She finally smiled, "Yes, the many events are splendid. The balls and the theater I find most agreeable, but I fear my father doesn't find them as enjoyable as I."

"And the young gentlemen, do you find them agreeable, also?" he asked.

Beth's brow wrinkled quizzically, "I suppose they are agreeable enough. I try not to show any of them too much interest. I've anticipated this year for so long, and I'm not inclined to spoil my pleasure by having my attention monopolized by anyone in particular."

Relieved, she hadn't rejected him for someone else, Brad inquired, "But are you not concerned that you may fail to make a brilliant match if you show no one any particular interest?"

She mused momentarily before replying, "I have been accused at times of being rash in my behavior. And I admit to sometimes acting without great forethought. However, last year I decided that something as important as felicity in marriage deserves the most careful attention. My intention is to know the temperament of the gentlemen who express an interest so I may make as happy a marriage as possible. I mean to know their shortcomings as well as their advantages. I do not want to marry in haste just to repent at leisure. I would much rather take my leisure in choosing an agreeable husband."

This time Brad's smile reached his eyes. "Then do you reject the notion held by many that it is best to know as little as possible about a mate so as not to be aware of their shortcomings? And in being unaware also being able to overlook? Tell me, how is your future spouse supposed to maintain control of his household if you know all his shortcomings? Surely you must allow a man some secrets."

The perceived criticism prickled, "Mr. Anderson, you misunderstand my words. We all have shortcomings, many of which should be overlooked. It is the one that should not be ignored that I wish to discover. That and whether the general congeniality between two people can be sustained throughout a lifetime together."

"And I think, milady, you have given yourself an impossible task. With such an attitude, all the young men will marry and father children before you discover their true nature."

Her eyes flashed, and to prevent her from speaking the retort Brad saw forming, he drew her closer and whirled her around faster. No doubt, the opinion Beth possessed of his temperament wasn't to his advantage. He began to comprehend the difficult business of courtship and resolved on circumspection in the future. He must remember to compliment her on her appearance and choose innocuous topics that wouldn't cause disagreements between them. Brad didn't have the time to risk earning her displeasure and needed for her to think benignly of him before he left for America. Beth hadn't accepted her first marriage proposal, and he hoped she would continue to refuse all others until he returned next spring.

Annoyed with her dancing partner, Beth considered him a pleasant man when he put half a mind to it. Except for the disagreeable conversation, she enjoyed dancing with him. Mr. Anderson boldly held her too close and twirled too fast, stealing her breath away. And the thrill of his unforgettable kiss haunted her. But he had a way about him that constantly exasperated.

The first night she had met him, he was so charming and dashing she had yearned to capture his heart. But afterward, he proved to be a great disappointment. First, it was the disastrous ride to the docks two years ago and his amusement over her humiliation. And last year, he abruptly pleaded exhaustion while waltzing and insisted on retiring early instead of taking pleasure in blending their voices in song. That next morning, barely sparing her two words, he borrowed a horse from her father and took his leave right after breakfast.

Thankfully he was an American, and she a noblewoman determined to marry an Englishman or the challenge of turning his irritating ways more agreeable might be irresistible.

Brad felt stuck between a rock and a hard place. He never realized matters of the heart could get so complicated. His mother and sisters were always so amenable he had assumed all women were. It was bad enough he was making a jumble of things with Beth Avery, why couldn't he find some quietude with his mistress. He provided for her well enough. She had a home, an income, and a day maid. But she wasn't satisfied and was turning into a shrew.

"Bradley Anderson, I asked you a simple question. It shouldn't be difficult to answer. What keeps you out late so many evenings recently?" Louise demanded with growing impatience. She felt it had started last year after he disappeared to some lord's country estate for a week. When Bradley returned, he acted remorseful about their argument by increasing her allowance and finding her a maid, but this year he seemed preoccupied. From the start, he came to her late at night with alarming frequency. Because of his care to not get her with child, Louise had nothing to hold him and feared her future would be bleak indeed if his interest in her withered.

"I didn't know you expected me to account for my time, Louise. Isn't it enough I come to you when I can?" Brad almost winced at the guilt he heard in his voice.

Perceiving the defensive note, Louise changed tactics, "I'm not asking you to account for your time, dear. I just never know any more if I should prepare a meal for you or not. In the past, your habits were more predictable."

He couldn't very well explain to his mistress that his efforts to attract a wife caused his unpredictable schedule. And he'd be damned if he'd forgo the pleasure Louise provided until he was committed to another. "It is best if you do not anticipate me until late. If I go hungry for a night, I won't blame you," he hedged, uncomfortable under her continued scrutiny.

Rarely more than one night passed without Bradley making demands of Louise in the bedroom, so she doubted he kept another mistress. She often wondered how he managed the long weeks at sea and the months away from her but did not want to know if he had an American mistress. "If you would just tell me what keeps you out so often, I would understand, and my mind would be at ease," she implored.

Unable to bear the accusation in her eyes, Brad put his arms around her and held her head to his chest. "It is nothing of consequence," he murmured. "Put your mind at rest. All is well." He prayed the lie wouldn't send him to hell.

The inevitable departure from England couldn't be postponed much longer. Brad had hoped to win Beth's affection and obtain a commitment from her before returning to America. He felt he had made progress. They shared many pleasurable evenings together, and their conversations were satisfying to them both. Recently she had even commented that his companionship pleased her. But Beth dispensed her attentions as freely with other gentlemen, and Brad judged her serious about not settling on any one man this season.

After the Chesapeake-Leopard Affair, President Jefferson had expelled all British ships from American harbors, and the political tensions between the two countries had worsened. Brad worried about the possibility of returning to England to continue his courtship.

Convinced Beth would settle on a man and agree to marry next year; Brad wanted to be that man.

He attended a small soirée at the Rockwell home. The evening hours were evaporating like water boiling from a kettle when Brad made the mistake of asking a waif-like brunette to dance. She attached herself to him, giggling and fluttering her eyelashes as if she had no brain in her head.

"Mr. Anderson, waltzing makes me breathless. I would appreciate a stroll in the garden," she insisted as they drifted smoothly toward the open terrace doors.

The last thing he fancied was a walk in the moonlight with this silly adolescent. Gliding to a stop, Brad took her elbow and escorted her to the door, "Miss Caruthers, if you stand here by the door, you will discover a refreshing breeze. Perhaps a glass of punch will revive you. I'll fetch it and return shortly." His frustration smoldered as he strode across the room. As soon as she had her glass of punch, he intended to return her to her mother and find Beth for that stroll in the moonlight.

"I see you met Priscilla Caruthers, Mr. Anderson," Beth sidled up to him as he poured punch into a small glass. "Do you find her discourse pleasing?" Laughter sparkled in her eyes.

He glanced briefly toward the simpering chit by the door before replying, "Not nearly as satisfying as your conversation. After I return her to her mother, will you take a breath of air with me? I find the room has become rather warm."

Butterflies fluttered in Beth's stomach. These past weeks Mr. Anderson had been an attentive and polite companion, dispelling her concerns that he had a contrary nature. Her father had disclosed to her the American's intention to quit the sea. When he sailed away, she never expected to see him again. Most likely, he wanted

Sweetbriar

to express his farewell. She wondered if he would miss her, knowing she would miss him. "Yes, it has warmed considerably. It would please me to take the air with you."

Excusing himself, Brad delivered the glass of punch to Miss Caruthers, who impatiently tapped her daintily slippered foot. "No breeze exists, Mr. Anderson, but a turn around the gardens will refresh me," she insisted.

"Miss Caruthers, if you feel faint, perhaps you should sit down." Brad took her elbow and escorted her to her mother. "Thank you, Miss Caruthers," he said abruptly and left.

Beth sashayed toward the open doors, and Brad joined her as they stepped outside. A moon bright and full lit the path. They meandered a short distance in silence before she asked, "Will you sail soon, Captain Anderson?"

He nodded in affirmation, "I have delayed too long as it is. Only one thing holds me here."

"What is that?" she whispered.

"You, sweet Beth," he said, slowly drawing her close to see if she would resist. Instead, she tilted her face toward his, and he pressed his lips to hers. Gently, he teased her lips with his tongue. She opened to him, timorously returning his kiss. He held her closer, feeling the rapid beat of her heart against his chest. His passion rose. His lips left hers and drifted to her earlobe, softly nipping. "Marry me, sweet Beth," he murmured.

Trembling from the breathtaking kiss, she came to her senses when he uttered the words. Thinking about the land he called home and the Indian savages, she withdrew from his arms and stared solemnly into his eyes, "No, Mr. Anderson. As an Englishwoman, I feel obliged to marry an Englishman. I am sorry." Turning, she fled swiftly up the path back into the house.

Too stunned to follow, Brad stood transfixed. How could she kiss him the way she did and then refuse his offer of marriage? Having felt her pulse quicken, he didn't believe for a moment she was unaffected. He decided to talk to her father again and see if he might persuade her.

Over the next several days, Milton Avery tried, but she adamantly refused, declaring her preference to wed a fellow countryman.

Disheartened, Captain Bradley Anderson sailed for home.

Chapter IV

England had retaliated against Napoleon's Berlin Decree with Orders in Council, which forbade all trade between the United Kingdom and France or her allies. In no time, French trade suffered under the oppressive blockade imposed by the Royal Navy.

Bonaparte responded by issuing a decree authorizing French warships and privateers to capture, as lawful prizes, any neutral ship sailing from British ports or submitting to search from the Royal Navy on the high seas or paying any tax whatsoever to the British government.

The American government passed the Embargo Act in the misguided hope of stopping France from seizing American ships and inducing England to cease impressment of American sailors. The law prohibited American vessels from landing in foreign ports and required the posting of bonds of guarantee double in value to both the ship and its cargo. Failure to post the bond would result in forfeiture of both ship and cargo, the loss of credit in regard to customs duties, and denial of a ship's owner or captain from giving oath before any customs officer. Unfortunately, the new law was difficult to enforce and did not prohibit the importation of French or British goods to American shores.

With the spring thaw, the combined effects of these international actions were felt severely in the New England states. The economic downturn caused spiraling unemployment and threw the region into depression. Many exporters simply ignored the laws, and parts of Maine openly rebelled by exporting goods overland to Canada.

By March, the frustrated president signed another Embargo Act into law, which prohibited the exportation of any American goods by sea or land and subjected violators to a $10,000 fine plus forfeiture of goods for each offense. The law also allowed port authorities to seize cargoes without a warrant and bring to trial any shipper suspected of contemplating violation of the law.

Still, the embargo was flouted.

Early Spring 1808, America

Charles Anderson called a meeting of his ships' captains to discuss the repercussions of the Embargo Act on their business. All their livelihoods were at stake as each captain earned a percentage of the value of their cargoes, and without cargo, they had no income. After outlining the restrictions and penalties being imposed on shippers, the elder Anderson allowed the men to voice their angst. They were all concerned about the impact the new laws would have on their wages and their families. Men viewed things differently when they had young mouths to feed.

"Does anyone have any suggestions?" Charles asked, bringing the men's attention back to the issue at hand.

"Aye, we could all join the bloody Royal Navy," one man declared. No one at the table found the comment humorous.

Bradley interjected his thoughts, "The new laws say we can't export, but there are no restrictions on importing. We could sail away empty or try to find paying passengers and come back with our holds full. Half a ship's pay is better than none at all." There were a few half-hearted nods around the table.

"We can expand the coastal trade," another captain suggested.

O'Malley snorted, "Us and all the other shippers will be looking to do that. And who do you think will buy our wares? I have no doubt other areas of the country are as hard hit as we. A man has to work to have money to buy our goods." There was a general agreement on that point.

"But what if we intend to work the coastal trade and a storm blows us off course. Who's to say it can't happen. Any port in a storm, I say. If that port happens to be England, France, or Portugal, all's the better," the first captain retorted. This idea elicited an enthusiastic accord.

Brad and his father exchanged glances. The idea had merit for some, but they couldn't all get blown off course. Charles acknowledged quietly, "Smuggling is what some will do. I'm not willing to risk losing my ships. Are you willing to risk your cargo and customs rights?" The scheme immediately lost some of its appeal.

"Well, I for one, don't plan to have my family starve," one captain said. "Canada doesn't have a law against exporting. Maybe I can find cargo there. Or maybe I set sail and work only foreign ports until our esteemed Mr. Jefferson figures out his new laws are bankrupting the nation."

Again, there was a general agreement with these suggestions. They had good export contacts in other countries; it was just a matter of selling foreign goods abroad instead of American goods. The trade laws were bound to change sooner or later because the United States could not maintain an isolationist stance forever.

Charles knew his captains were shrewd men and didn't believe any one course of action was right for all of them, so he would let each man make his own decision regarding his ship and cargo. This practice had worked well in the past, and he felt it would continue to work well in the future. Experience had taught him the importance of getting them all together to examine options and share ideas. Solutions would follow as surely as a river flowed to the sea.

His concern now was for his son. Brad had always been lighthearted and outgoing, but since returning from his last voyage, he had brooded sullenly. Perceiving that Brad endeavored to overcome a disappointment, Charles had provided several occasions to talk, but Brad had chosen to keep his own counsel. More than ever, Charles wanted him to settle down and take a wife, knowing a woman's embrace could do wonders for relieving a man of his worries.

After the other captains dispersed, Brad lingered at the large table, and Charles suspected his son was finally ready to discuss his troubles.

"Father, I'm thinking about some of the ideas we tossed around today. I want your advice concerning my next voyage—"

Interrupting, Charles raised his hand, "I think the current situation presents a perfect opportunity for you to shift your attention to the shore operations. There isn't a need for you to sail again. A good portion of the fleet will probably be out of service for a while anyway. Take yourself a wife and start a family, Brad. It's past time."

"That's just it, Dad," Brad said with a deep sigh, "I finally found the woman I want to marry, and she's in England. I must go back."

If his son had been in higher spirits, Charles would have been elated. "Does she return your affection?"

Brad sighed again, "When I left, she wasn't partial to any man but was insistent she would marry an Englishman. I'm hoping she hasn't found one yet and that I can convince her to change her mind."

Charles considered his son's dilemma. "Young girls often say things to spike a man's interest. Perhaps she told you that so you would find her more desirable," he offered.

Brad shook his head, "I asked her to marry me, and she refused." Pacing, he raked his fingers through his hair, "I know she finds me attractive, and I thought she liked me well enough, but she was firm in her refusal. Even her father couldn't convince her to accept me."

"So, her father was amenable, and her refusal wasn't due to the urging of her family?" Charles questioned.

"Her father is the Earl of Rockwell and considered the match satisfactory provided I retire from the sea." A wistful smile touched his lips, "During our interview, Dad, he sounded much like you."

"Here is my advice to you, son," Charles said, rising, "Write to the earl and determine if she is still unattached. There is no point in sailing to England if she became betrothed over the winter. If her affections aren't engaged elsewhere, then follow your heart. Perhaps she will have changed her mind during your absence. But if she is promised to another or is resolved in her refusal to marry you, then I suggest you give it up and settle on a good American girl."

Shrugging his shoulder, Brad partially agreed, "Writing to Rockwell sounds like a sensible thing to do, so I shall start there. But I am not sure I can surrender the notion of pursuing her if she is still unattached, no matter how many times she turns me down," Brad said grimly.

His father was adamant, "Just the same, son, I won't have you pining over this girl all summer. I expect you to come out of your doldrums and set full sail in society. If you get to know other women, you will discover whether or not you can put this girl out of your mind."

Brad nodded in acquiescence. His father would continue to harp on the issue, and it was easier to accept social invitations than to listen to his father's lectures.

Late Spring 1808, England

Milton Avery studied the letter from Bradley Anderson, pondering whether or not his daughter might have had a change of heart. Last year she had given a poor excuse for declining Anderson's offer of marriage. Rockwell understood her hesitation to marry a foreigner, obliging her to leave England, but the two shared a common language. And Anderson's family, especially his mother and sisters, would provide companionship to Beth until she became established in society.

His daughter hadn't accepted either of the two Englishmen who had offered for her over the winter. One she considered too old and the other too boyish, calling to mind the tale of the three bears. Milton speculated if his daughter would ever find the man who was 'just right.' He perused the letter again.

> *Dear Rockwell,*
> *I have no doubt you are aware of*
> *The recent laws passed by my country*
> *prohibiting the exportation of*
> *American goods. Although we can still*

> *import from your country, the local economy is depressed and the citizenry have little money to spare. I believe most of our ships will remain in foreign waters or American ports until the situation improves on this side of the Atlantic.*
>
> *I have taken advantage of these circumstances to retire from the sea and my father is instructing me in all aspects of our shore operations. I do not anticipate returning to England due to commerce.*
>
> *I wish to inquire after your daughter, whom I hold in high esteem. I pray she is well and declare to you that my affections have not diminished. If she has not accepted another, I ask if I may renew my offer of marriage. If you believe Beth will be more open to the idea of marrying me, I shall immediately sail to England.*
>
> *I await your reply,*
> *Bradley Anderson*

Rockwell had speculated if he would hear from the American again. Most men packed it in and turned their attentions elsewhere after a refusal. Appreciating the man's steadfast heart, Avery knew Anderson was exactly the type of man his daughter needed. A woman would do well to place her trust in such as him.

The nobleman paced the room. He would as soon have Beth married and be another man's worry. The constant social activity was wearing thin after so long. Beth didn't appear to be settling her attentions on anyone and was gathering more admirers each week. After her cousin Mary became engaged, his lordship had hoped Beth would follow suit, but she was content to lead them all on a merry chase. Perhaps he should accept the proposal and let her reconcile herself to it. But he had promised her a say in the matter so he would discuss the letter with her. Ringing for the butler, Milton instructed him to bring Beth to his study.

It was infrequent that Beth's father requested her presence in the library. It was the room he used for solitude and the occasional home business meeting. Except for the morning following her coming out, it was also where he presented her with the marriage proposals she had received. She nervously fingered her skirts, wondering if she had another proposal.

"Good afternoon, Papa, what brings you home so early?"

"Sit down, child. I thought you would like to know I received a letter from Bradley Anderson," he began and paused when he saw a glow of pleasure imbue her face, deducing she wasn't indifferent to the man after all.

"And how is Captain Anderson?" she inquired earnestly. "If he is back in England, you should invite him to dinner. He is affable and makes pleasant conversation."

"No, he's not in England, and he is not Captain Anderson anymore. He decided to devote his time to learning other aspects of his father's business." Noting her obvious disappointment, Rockwell continued, "He asked after you, Beth."

She smiled hesitantly.

"He has a high regard for you, my dear. I must know what your feelings are toward him."

Taking a deep breath to order her scattered thoughts, she replied, "As I said, Mr. Anderson is affable—"

Her father interrupted impatiently, "I'm not asking if you find him an entertaining dinner companion. I'm asking if you consider him a potential husband."

She fidgeted with her skirts, lowering her eyes to hide her feelings. "I believe Mr. Anderson will make a good husband to whomever he decides to marry," she said quietly.

Lord Rockwell relaxed, settling easier in his chair. "Is there any other man you prefer?"

Choosing her words carefully, she replied, "Father, I find no other man more pleasing nor less to my liking as a potential husband."

He mused about this for a few minutes. "Let me put it another way, Beth. Is there anything in particular about Mr. Anderson that you find objectionable?"

Raising her eyes, Beth regarded her father, "Mr. Anderson is not an Englishman, Papa."

Exasperated, Rockwell rose and paced the floor. "What is your insistence on marrying an Englishman? You should be more concerned about a man's character than his nationality."

"Please, Papa," Beth implored, "England is all I know. You are here and Aunt Sylvia and Cousin Mary. You are the only family I have. I shall try very hard to find you an English son-in-law, I promise. Just give me a little more time."

She pleaded so beseechingly he could not refuse. "All right, I shall write to Bradley Anderson and let him know how you feel. But I want your promise to start giving serious consideration to marriage and begin evaluating which of your many admirers you might find agreeable as a husband," he stated. After she meekly agreed, he dismissed her.

Late Summer 1808, England

As the small boat approached the English pier, the altercation with his father replayed in Brad's mind. After waiting months for a reply from Rockwell, the ambiguity had been frustrating.

> *My dear Anderson,*
> *Your recent letter was well received. I am pleased to discover you have assigned your-self to learning other aspects of the import-export trade.*
>
> *It is unfortunate your country has been saddled with onerous laws, and for the sake of all your countrymen, I hope the boot of oppression is soon lifted.*
>
> *My daughter is well, and graciously received your felicitations. I made inquiries of her to determine her mind as it regards you and your proposal. She says there is none she prefers more or less than yourself, but I believe she feels more benevolently toward you than she admitted to me. At the mention of your name, her face shone in a manner I have only seen when a woman's affections are engaged.*
>
> *However, I discovered the source of Her reluctance to consider any but a fellow Englishman as her lifelong partner. She Says England is her home and where her family, such as it is, resides.*
>
> *I fear she is and will continue to be resolute in her decision, so I leave it in your hands to decide whether you wish to pursue what may be a hopeless cause.*
>
> *Dutifully,*
> *Milton Avery,*
> *Earl of Rockwell*

Brad had raked his fingers through his hair that day, tramping the floor, infuriated that Beth might care for him but give herself to another just because he resided in America. The thought of moving to England flitted across his mind, but Brad recognized, if he did, he had no means of supporting a wife without returning to the sea. Rockwell wouldn't allow that, and it wasn't what Brad wanted. He had discovered a propensity toward the operation of his father's business and anticipated someday assuming the leading role.

"Calm yourself, Brad," his father had demanded. "It is obvious her desire to remain in England is stronger than her attraction to you. Forget the girl. There are many fine American women capable of making you a good wife."

It was so like his boyhood days. His father had never understood Brad's abiding need to sail the seas, and just as he had not been able to deny his craving for adventure in his youth, Brad could not deny his burning desire to take Beth as his wife.

"Father, I shall travel to Canada and find passage to England," Brad declared, knowing the only American ships legally permitted to sail for foreign ports did so under the direction of the President. "I must persuade her to marry me. She is the only woman I want."

In Quebec, Brad located a ship bound for London, and refusing to sign on a foreign vessel in any capacity, paid in gold coin for a berth. But throughout the long voyage, Brad paid even more dearly from boredom and his own roiling emotions over the rift with his father and his doubts about succeeding to win Beth's hand.

After the ship set anchor in the Thames River, Brad waited impatiently until late in the afternoon for the captain to order the landing boat. As it finally bumped against the pier, Brad jumped ashore and hurriedly pushed his way through the crowds toward the Rockwell Trading Company headquarters.

"Captain Anderson is here, sir," the secretary announced at the door to his employer's office.

"It's just Mr. Anderson now, Gladwin," Brad corrected the man and nodded toward the nobleman, "Good to see you again, Rockwell."

"So, you decided to come back. I can't help but wonder at the surprise this will give my daughter. Have you settled yourself yet?"

"No, I just stepped ashore a few minutes ago. I didn't want to risk missing you and came directly here," Brad breathed heavily, slowly catching his breath.

"It's just as well you did. I was only this minute preparing to leave. I'll send Gladwin to the ship for your baggage. You can stay at my townhouse tonight if you choose. Tomorrow is soon enough for you to look for lodging. I'd offer you my hospitality, but since discussing your letter with Beth, she has been making an earnest effort to find an admirer she is willing to accept. It would be too awkward to have you constantly about when others are calling. You can visit her as often as she will allow." His lordship smiled broadly, clapping Brad on the shoulder, "I can hardly wait to see Beth's face when you walk in the door."

When they arrived at the Avery residence, the butler informed his lordship that Lady Beth was in the garden gathering roses for a potpourri.

"Please inform my daughter we have a guest this evening. Fetch her to me, but don't mention the name of our guest, Rollins. I want to surprise her," he instructed.

"As you wish, milord," the servant replied.

Leading Brad to the salon, Rockwell poured them both a copita of port wine, "I don't know about you, Anderson, but I could use some fortification for this little reunion."

Silently Brad accepted the tulip-shaped glass, not trusting his ability to voice his agreement. Tossing back the wine, he downed it in one unmannerly gulp.

Eyeballing his guest, Rockwell observed, "I'd say you have it bad, Anderson."

Just then, the door opened. Beth entered, carrying a crystal bowl overflowing with the fragile blooms of sweetbriar roses. Their purifying fragrance instantly permeated the air. "Rollins said we have a dinner guest this evening—" she began, but when Brad turned at the sound of her voice, the bowl of flowers crashed to the floor. She froze in dazed silence.

Rushing to her, Brad gently nudged her aside. "Take care, Lady Beth, the shards are jagged."

"Rollins!" Avery called out. "Have the maid sweep up this mess." Then he asked, "Are you feeling ill, my dear?"

"No, I'm fine. The bowl just slipped out of my fingers," she replied, not taking her eyes from Bradley Anderson's face. *'What is he doing here?'* she thought. *'Surely Father didn't send for him. Why are my hands shaking so?'* "I think I was in the sun for too long. I must sit down," she breathed.

Brad grasped her cold hands in his and led her to the settee, kneeling at her feet. "Perhaps some wine will revive you," he suggested. Her father quickly poured the ruby port into a copita and handed it to Brad. Instead of passing it to Beth, he held it to her lips.

She sipped delicately then took the wineglass from him, "Thank you, Mr. Anderson. I feel much better."

After all the months of trying to forget the American, Beth conceded that none of the men she knew appealed to her so well. She wished he didn't live in a savage country that frightened her. If only America were a tame land, she would gladly give her heart. Bit by bit, Beth gathered her wits, hardening her resolve to remain safe in England.

"What brings you to London? I was under the impression you no longer commanded a merchant ship."

Sitting beside her, Brad cast a glance toward the earl and replied with a partial truth, "You are correct. I did not come for commerce. A few years ago, I acquired a small property here and must dispose of it before it falls into disrepair."

"Then you will return to America soon?" she asked.

Shrugging noncommittally, he replied, "Who can say? I shall remain as long as necessary to achieve my goal."

"Beth," the earl said, drawing her attention, "Mr. Anderson only arrived this afternoon and hasn't yet arranged for lodging so he will sleep the night here. Please have the maid air out a guest room for him."

"Yes, Papa, I'll do that and inform Cook to prepare for three of us at dinner," she rose and gave a glance toward their guest before leaving the room.

During the Atlantic crossing, Brad had brooded over his plans for courting Beth Avery. The diminutive cottage was inadequate for entertaining, which was impossible to do in any event with his mistress underfoot. He determined it best to let a townhouse for the season but intended to stay with Louise until an appropriate residence was located.

He also intended to limit the staff to a cook, needed for hosting dinner parties, and a maid for serving meals and cleaning. He would forgo a butler and valet to conserve funds, not knowing how much time it might take to convince Beth to marry him.

Before leaving England permanently, Bradley had it in mind to end his affair as well. Even if Beth refused him again, he decided against inviting Louise to join him in America because he would never give her what she wanted. She was a decent girl who had exercised poor judgment in the past but who might still have the chance of a better future. Brad considered making a gift of the cottage along with a small amount of money for her to use as a dowry. There were men willing to accept a cast-off woman for the advantages of these possessions. No one need ever know of her time in the brothel.

His thoughts shifted as the hack driver announced their arrival at Brad's destination. He instructed the man to unload his sea chest then hurried up the flower-strewn path.

General mayhem prevailed in the rooms of the modest bungalow. Rugs hung in the back courtyard for beating and airing, furniture jammed the walls for scrubbing and waxing the floors, and draperies soaked in the washtub awaiting attention from the maid. Amid a thorough house cleaning, Louise was on her knees, scrubbing the parlor floor. She sat back on her heels when she heard the front door slam closed.

When Bradley stepped into the room, Louise hurriedly scrambled off the floor. He appeared as shocked by her disheveled home and person as she was to have him standing in the doorway. During the spring, she had waited impatiently for his return, and then worriedly throughout the summer, fearing his ship had been captured by French privateers. The heavy house cleaning helped dissipate the nervous energy her troubled mind created. Louise was relieved Bradley had returned but was flustered to have her lover discover her dressed in a raggedy gown with her hair tied up in a dishtowel like a scullery maid.

Immediately Brad concluded it was an inopportune time to arrive unannounced. If he stayed any time at all, he knew from experience, he'd be asked to move something heavy, then something else, and something else. It had happened often enough with his mother and sisters when they decided in-depth cleanings were needed.

"Where you want this, guv?" the pint-sized hack driver asked, struggling under the considerable weight of Brad's sea chest.

After a few seconds appraising the disordered room, Brad turned on his heel, "Load it back into the cab. I won't be staying."

"Bradley, where are you going?" Louise cried, racing over to clutch his arm. "Please don't leave, you've only just arrived."

Gently, he removed her soapy fingers from the sleeve of his green broadcloth coat, gave her a quick once over, and shook his head. "I'll find lodging elsewhere for a couple of days. Please try to get the house," and yourself, his expression said, "back in order by then. His lips quickly brushed hers, then he strode out the door, down the path, and into the hack. Moments later, he was gone, leaving Louise standing forlornly on the doorstep.

Early Fall 1808, England

Within a fortnight, Brad located an appropriate townhouse, hired his staff, and moved to his new quarters. During this time, he never gave Louise what she considered to be, a satisfactory explanation for needing lodgings of his own. She presumed he had sailed on a delayed merchant voyage, and Brad did not disabuse her of this notion, being neither genuinely deceitful nor legitimately truthful.

Wanting her lover to reside with her, Louise refuted Bradley's claim that he needed to entertain, saying their lovemaking should be all the entertainment he needed. And as a lover, she enthusiastically made her point, which pricked Brad's conscience like the sharp tines of a pitchfork.

But marriage to Beth was his goal. He needed to engage her heart before proposing again, and that necessi-

Sweetbriar

tated time and familiarity. He called on her often, but so did other men. He danced with her frequently at balls, but so did other men. He delighted her in many ways, but so did other men. And she encouraged them all, which disconcerted Brad.

Determined to separate Beth from her many admirers, Brad invited her and the earl to dine. The delicious roasted goose elicited compliments from both his guests.

Relaxing by the parlor fire following the repast, Rockwell appeared as if he might fall asleep in his chair but was in no hurry to depart. Drowsily, he stated, "I've been in this house before. It used to be owned by the proprietor of a textile factory, but he died last year. Do you know what happened to his family? He had a wife and two young sons."

"I didn't inquire about the circumstances of the house or family," Brad responded, "and the solicitor didn't offer any explanation, so I can't say what became of them."

"As I recall, the wife had a somewhat despondent nature, and he built her a reflecting pond in the garden. All black tile in the pool and planted with a variety of white flowers and silver-leafed vegetation. Looked charming at night, especially after the moon rose," Rockwell commented sleepily.

"Mr. Anderson, you didn't mention such a treasure existed," Beth enthused.

"I am surprised at the revelation," he replied. "I was more interested in finding a house to suit than in looking at the landscape. I suppose we could take a peek at the pond if your father cares to show it to us."

But the older man declined. "The grounds here are small. You'll have no trouble finding it. Look just past the terrace, behind some shrubbery. It's a secluded spot. There's a bench, making it convenient to sit and gaze at the reflections in the pond. I always thought it a strange thing to build for a woman with melancholy, but he said it relieved his wife's mind. Pour me a glass of port, and I'll sit here by the fire until you return."

Beth and Brad's eyes briefly caught before she cast hers down, so she didn't notice the smile that skittered across his face. "If it's as lovely as your father recalls, it would be a shame to miss it. Shall we look?"

"I suppose we could for just a minute. If you don't mind, Papa," she asked hesitantly.

"No, no," he said, waving his hand. "Mr. Anderson is right. If it is still there, it would be a shame to miss it. I've seen it several times, and I'm comfortable right where I sit. Go on now."

Brad handed the man a crystal goblet of wine then escorted the young woman to the terrace doors. The drapes had been pulled, but rather than open them, Brad pushed the fabric aside to unlatch the doors, letting the curtain fall back into place after they passed through.

A waxing quarter moon cast its faint light on the short path. Past tall shrubs to the left, they found the spot. Rounding the pond, Brad guided Beth to the bench where they sat. It was a peaceful place, quiet except for the sound of crickets and one boisterous tree frog. The scent of aromatic blooms wafted in the air. It was so exquisite a place neither was inclined to talk at first. They gazed at the white reflections in the dark pool, watching the ripples created from the breeze of their movements. As the air stilled, so did the water, the mirrored reflections were perfect in their delicate beauty.

After a few minutes, Beth softly sighed, "I can understand how a disturbed mind would find peace sitting here. The man was thoughtful, having this built for his wife."

Brad took her hand and brought it to his lips, kissing her fingers lightly, "The elegance of this garden is but a shadow to your radiant beauty, sweet Beth." He drew her close, placing his lips on hers. When she leaned into him, he put his arms around her and nibbled her lower lip. She responded, opening to him. Deepening the kiss, he explored her mouth tantalizingly slow. Returning his kiss, Beth unconsciously fingered the hair behind Brad's ear. Forcibly restraining himself, Brad pulled away.

Breathless, Beth found the courage to look at her companion and saw his eyes sparkling green in the moonlight. "Your eyes are so changeable, Mr. Anderson," she whispered. "I've never seen anything like it before. Usually, they are hazel in color and sometimes gray. But here under the moon, they appear green." With soft amazement, she inquired, "How can that be?"

His only answer was to draw her into another deep, needy kiss. Beth accepted his lips and the fluttering thrill when their tongues leisurely dueled. The few other times she had been kissed was nothing like this. No other man was daring enough to do more than press his lips to hers. Succumbing to the sensual sensations, she was powerless to stop him.

Ending the kiss, Brad huskily whispered as he pressed her head to his chest, "I had better return you to your father before I forget myself entirely."

His declaration and the hammering of his heart enthralled Beth. She sighed and moved away. "Yes, Mr. Anderson, I believe it is time for us to return." Standing, she stumbled on quivering legs, then steadied as Brad's arm encircled her waist.

Indoors, Rockwell stood by the fire wishing to be home in bed. But, even more, he wished for his daughter to be settled before his time on earth came to an end. Feeling confident of her attachment to the American, Avery thought a kiss or two in the moonlight might loosen her resolve and speed her toward marriage. "Was the reflecting pool still there?" he asked as the young couple entered the room.

"Papa, the reflecting pool is beautiful and so peaceful. When I marry, I shall ask my husband to build me a pond and garden just like it. It will be the perfect place to find solace if I should ever be vexed by him," she declared.

The two gentlemen shared a look and a quiet chuckle at her statement. "Let's hope you won't have too much need for solace," her father stated. "Are you ready to go home now, dear?"

"Yes, Papa. Thank you for dinner, Mr. Anderson. By the by, Mary and Peter will return from their honeymoon soon. No doubt Peter's parents will throw them a magnificent ball, but I am planning a cozy welcome home dinner. I have no doubt Mary will enjoy seeing you again. You must come dine with us."

"Seeing your cousin again will be delightful, and I look forward to meeting her husband," Brad replied. "Just tell me when and I shall be there."

"Thursday next. In the evening about six o'clock. It will be a small party with only Lord and Lady Hartford, and the newlyweds. You won't mind a quiet evening, will you, Mr. Anderson?" she asked.

"I find quiet evenings in your company very agreeable, sweet Beth," he replied courteously.

His lordship was tired and wanted to go home, but Beth was playing backgammon with Viscount Dunmore. They were at his sister's home relaxing after dinner near the fire in their large, elegant game room. Since Mary and Peter had left on their honeymoon, Beth insisted on frequent visits, saying it eased her aunt's loneliness, but

Sweetbriar

Beth devoted more attention to the young lord than her aunt.

The Averys didn't move in the same circles as the viscount, and until a short time ago, had only seen him twice since Beth's fifteenth birthday. Both times Rolf Dunmore had interrupted the Hartford's evening entertainment to confer briefly with his cousin. Subsequent to those visits, Hartford confided his doubts of ever seeing the younger man after he came into his full legacy. But apparently, Rockwell's brother-in-law had been mistaken. Dunmore had inherited recently and visited the Hartford household almost as frequently as Beth.

"I say, Rockwell," Lord Hartford commented with a glance toward the young pair, "I haven't seen Dunmore so much in all the years since his father died as I've seen him since Mary's wedding. I believe he is enamored of your daughter, and it would please me to see him married. Has Beth expressed an interest in anyone in particular?"

Milton shook his head, "It's hard to say, girls don't confide in their fathers the way they do their mothers. At one point, I thought she was interested in a gentleman, but she has since refused his offer. If you think there is something brewing between these two, I suppose it's time for you to tell me about the man."

Hartford cleared his throat, shifting uneasily in his chair, "He was wild in the past, but I think it was the influence of a fast crowd on an impressionable youth. I've tried to provide guidance over the last few years and think he's improved. Since coming into his own, he is taking more responsibility for his actions. Why now he often spends a peaceful evening with us," Hartford chuckled.

"I'm more concerned about him spending peaceful evenings with my daughter," Rockwell retorted. "What are the wild ways that he has supposedly relinquished?"

He sipped his brandy nonchalantly, but the firelight on his face reflected the significance of his inquiry.

His host nodded toward the game players, "Gambling for one. He came to me a few times to borrow against his inheritance."

Rockwell didn't like the sound of that. "What else?"

Sighing deeply, Hartford continued, "Once I had to extricate him from a delicate situation involving a gentleman's daughter. They were commoners. She was an ambitious creature and thought she could trap him into an ill-advised marriage. There's been no more trouble of that nature, and he was much younger at the time. I daresay he learned his lesson."

This was disturbing to Lord Rockwell, who believed a man's character was formed early and not easily changed. He would keep an eye on the situation. As much as he wanted his daughter married, he wanted more for her to be happy. A husband of weak character would bring her nothing but grief.

They looked over as Dunmore crowed delightedly, "I win again, Lady Beth, and you must pay up." Laying his palm on his chest, he said, "I insist you allow *me* to escort you to the opera tomorrow evening."

Beth flicked her fan open and fluttered it quickly in front of her face, "I think you cheated, sir." But there was laughter in her voice, and her eyes glittered wickedly. She turned toward her father, "Papa, I made a foolish wager and promised the viscount I would attend the theater with him tomorrow evening."

Milton glowered at his daughter. "That won't be possible, Beth. You've had me out every evening this week, and I am too fatigued to consider another late night. And you know I won't permit you to go without a chaperon," he informed them.

"But, Papa, you let me go with Mary and Peter when they were engaged. And we won't be alone," she said.

Dunmore confirmed her statement, "A good friend of mine recently became engaged and asked me to join them tomorrow night. There will be the four of us and perhaps as many as six. I believe he asked his brother and sister-in-law to come, but I'm not sure they will. All of us can stop by your home, and you will have the opportunity to meet them. They are quite respectable, although commoners," the young nobleman said snobbishly.

It was true Rockwell had allowed Beth to join Mary and Peter a few times, but that was more or less with Beth being their chaperon. Still, he supposed there was safety in numbers.

"Please, Papa?"

"Oh, very well, Beth," he sighed. "But you must return home immediately after the play. I don't want you stopping at a coffeehouse afterward. I'll have Rollins wait up for you and report to me what time you arrive home. And I expect all of you to stay together, Dunmore. Do I make myself clear?"

"Yes, sir, and thank you," he replied, smiling.

The young couple accompanying the viscount the next evening impressed Milton Avery. They were well-spoken, and the woman was garbed in a becoming gown under a Spencer jacket of a stylish but modest cut. Her fiancé was dashing and solicitous. Assuring the earl they would all sit together and deliver Beth home at a reasonable hour, and the four set off in the viscount's carriage.

Traveling a short distance, the carriage turned away from the direction of the opera house, but Beth chatting with the nice couple, didn't notice. After a while, she realized they hadn't arrived at their destination and peered out the window. Not recognizing the neighborhood, she turned to her escort, "Lord Dunmore, your coachman must be lost, this isn't the way to the theater."

The young couple nudged each other and laughed softly.

Patting her hand, Rolf smiled, "I'm sure you have seen that hideous opera at least twice so you can't possibly mind that we changed our plans for this evening. Please don't be upset, or I shall be disappointed to find that you don't have an adventurous spirit."

Beth smiled hesitantly, noticing the young couple sitting across from her seemed unconcerned. Impulsively, she snapped her fan open to cover the lower half of her face, and the sparkle in her eyes intensified, "Dunmore, far be it from me to disappoint you and your friends. I suppose one night's entertainment is as good as another."

"That's the spirit, my girl." He reached into his coat pocket and extracted a black half-face mask. "And we shall take care that your father doesn't discover our little deception."

The woman across the seat tied a similar mask onto her face, then unbuttoned her Spencer jacket and took it off, revealing a shockingly low-cut gown. She smiled at Beth, "You'll find this evening so much more entertaining than the theater. Let his lordship tie your mask for you."

Feeling uneasy, Beth shifted in her seat and turned her back toward the viscount. He positioned the mask and tied it securely then dropped his hands to her arms. When he placed his lips on the nape of her neck, Beth gasped at the unexpected contact. The other woman giggled and turned away.

The gaming house fascinated Beth, never knowing such places existed. Elegantly dressed men and women, both young and old, crowded the light-filled rooms. Fine jewels sparked from ears, throats, wrists, and fingers, dazzling the eye. The cacophony of eager gamblers, lusty serving wenches, and shrill game hawkers was deafening, the games of chance numerous and varied.

Some card games, such as whist, Beth recognized, but most were unfamiliar, and the dice games made no sense to her at all. But she liked the roulette tables. The clicking of the spinning disks sounded like carriage wheels rolling over cobblestones. The clattering of the small spheres bouncing before they came to rest was like the rapid clacking of Spanish castanets. Beth flushed with excitement when Rolf leaned close, explaining the game and giving her coins to wager. In a short time, her coins disappeared, and she pouted about her losses. But he laughed and continued to play, raking in more than either of them lost.

Later, he called her Lady Luck, took her hand and led her to a dice table. He beseeched her to blow on the cubes before he tossed them. And each time he won; the spectators cheered louder. Caught up in the exhilaration of the moment, Beth didn't mind him hugging her and kissing her cheek. When he tired of the game, she accepted the goblet of celebratory wine he offered. The thrill of seeing him win made her giddier than the wine, and she enthusiastically encouraged him to play another game of chance.

However, the hours of darkness grew short, and not wanting to anger the earl by a late homecoming, Rolf declined. The night's escapade to test Beth's willingness to play along with his schemes had succeeded. She participated eagerly, even accepting his mild advances. When the time came to take a wife, he wanted a complacent woman. And he suspected Beth's dowry would be hefty. That was important, too.

Holding her hand, they wandered through the rooms, searching for their companions, and found the two sitting grimly at a card table. Their luck had not been equal to the viscount's. Obstinate about recouping their heavy losses, they belligerently insisted on staying. Unable to change their minds, Rolf and Beth left without them.

Alone in the carriage, Rolf reached around Beth's head to untie the face mask. Then he tried to draw her close, but she skittered away, ill at ease in the shadowed intimacy of the conveyance. So, he contented himself with holding her hand on the short journey to her home. He handed her out in a gentlemanly manner and escorted her to the door, where the disgruntled butler received her.

Returning to the carriage, Dunmore directed his driver to deliver him to Madam Patterson's salon.

"Captain Anderson, it's a pleasure to see you again." Mary smiled as she turned toward her husband, "Peter, may I introduce Captain Anderson?"

"It is Mr. Anderson now," Brad explained, "I turned my ship over to others. It's not commerce that brings me to England this year." His eyes drifted momentarily toward Beth before shifting back to the newlyweds.

"Peter Lipton," the man said, extending his hand.

"Bradley Anderson," the American replied. "Please accept my congratulations on your marriage, Mr. Lipton." Peter beamed delightedly at the compliment. "And best wishes to you, Lady Mary." She blushed prettily.

"If you don't mind, gentlemen," Beth interjected, draping her arm around her cousin's shoulders, "Mary and I haven't had a chat since before the wedding. Would you mind terribly?"

"Not at all," they consented then crossed the room to join their host.

Beth led Mary to the opposite corner, where they sat with their heads together. "You look so happy, Mary. I'd say you find married life agreeable."

Coloring deeply, Mary advised, "All I shall say on this subject, dear cousin, is to find a man who loves you with all his heart and do your best to return his affection. Then you will know abiding happiness."

Beth smiled, "That is easy for you to say, Mary. Your Mr. Lipton was smitten by your beauty the instant he first saw you. I doubt I will ever be so fortunate."

Mary peered at her cousin keenly, "Perhaps you are unaware, but I think you just refuse to see. In this very room, you may find your key to happiness." Her look traveled to the grouping of men.

"What? Mr. Anderson?" Beth whispered. "I dare say he has let me know of his attraction. But you, of all people, know my concerns from that quarter." Beth sighed deeply, "I do prefer him above all others but find it a hopeless case. As soon as he concludes the sale of some property, he will be gone. I'm determined to forget about him and settle on a nice English gentleman."

"You are foolish!" her companion exclaimed. "True love from a man's heart is an invaluable gift."

Becoming heated in defense of her obstinacy, Beth hissed, "But it does nothing to stop the shriek of marauding Indians. Nor does it protect against—"

"Mary, my dear," Lord and Lady Hartford cried in unison, entering the room. The interrupted conversation evaporated from Beth's mind. Welcoming embraces were quickly exchanged as the butler announced dinner.

During the evening, Peter and Mary joyously expounded about the towns and countryside they had traveled through on their honeymoon. The world, as viewed through the mists of their newfound love, was a clear, bright, and shining place. The fields were greener, the sky bluer, and the air fresher.

Often throughout the meal, as Beth glanced around the table, her eyes collided with those of Bradley Anderson. He was unusually quiet and pensive. She mistakenly thought him bored listening to the raptures of the newlyweds. His intense scrutiny grew increasingly uncomfortable. By the end of the meal, Beth welcomed the reprieve afforded by the custom of women leaving the men at the table.

Later, when the men joined the ladies in the parlor, Brad requested Beth sing duets with him. She played the pianoforte as they blended their voices in a variety of songs, which satisfactorily ended the evening for all.

The following week Brad called upon Beth unannounced and showed her a letter.

> Dear Brad,
>
> I wish it were with glad tidings that I pick up my quill, but it is with a heavy heart that I write.
>
> Your father has felt the burden of our nation's ruined economy weighing upon him. Many of his poor captains have chosen to violate the embargo and two ships, along with their cargoes, have been seized.
>
> Although we can withstand The financial loss ourselves, the families of these men are hard-pressed.
>
> Charles has worried himself sick Over these circumstances and recently collapsed from the strain. He has been bled twice but remains weak and bedridden. I fear for his life.
>
> Please return home as soon as

> *possible. The business needs your*
> *guiding hand, and I need your support.*
> *I remain your loving mother,*
> *Suzanne Anderson*

Beth handed the letter back to Brad, "Mr. Anderson, what will you do?"

He paced the room, "I must return home immediately and see what can be done for my father—if he still lives. Someone needs to take the reins of his business and sort out the troubles there. He has competent men, but every business needs strong leadership." Sitting by her side, Brad took her hands, stating, "I haven't finished what I came to England to do."

"The property that you came to sell," she misunderstood, "is that not something you can leave in the hands of a solicitor?"

Brad shook his head, dismissively. "The property is nothing. I can dispose of it in a matter of days if I choose." Searching her face, he continued, "You must know how I feel about you. Before I leave, please tell me you return my affection."

Lowering her eyes, Beth refused to tell him what she wanted to say and what he longed to hear. "Mr. Anderson, I admire you greatly and value your friendship—"

"I don't want only your friendship, sweet Beth. I want you as my wife," he declared. "I won't ask you for a decision now because your answer is in your face. But your eyes and your kisses tell me another story."

She was embarrassed by his candor.

"Please tell me you won't accept another man's proposal before I have a chance to return," Brad begged.

Too agitated to sit, she rose and wandered slowly around the room, touching various objects as she mulled over his request. He wasn't asking her to accept him. Only that she not commit to another. Her intention had always been to wait at least two years before choosing a husband, and only nineteen months had passed since her introduction to society. Complying with his request wouldn't be too difficult, she concluded.

"Mr. Anderson, I won't mislead you. If you intended to live in England, I would be more amenable toward you. But you do not, so I see no hope for us."

Disappointment flickered in his eyes.

"However, I am disinclined to accept any man this year, so from that respect, I shall honor your request."

He crossed to her, took her gently by the shoulders, and kissed her tenderly. Her lips parted. Brad encircled her with his arms and drank of her sweetness. Then, holding her close, whispered in her ear, "Think of me every day as I shall think of you." He released her. "Goodbye, sweet Beth."

"You leave so soon?" she asked, surprised.

"There is a ship sailing on the morrow. I have barely enough time to close the house and write recommendations for the servants. I shan't call on you again before leaving," he replied.

Shaken by the imminence of his abrupt departure, her voice quavered, "Farewell, Mr. Anderson. I shall pray for your father's swift recovery." Fearing she would never again see his face or hear his voice, or worse, ever again feel his kiss, her heart shattered as he walked out the door. Gasping in distress, Beth stumbled to her bedroom, where she fell on her bed and cried bitterly into her pillow.

Late Fall 1808, England

The Christmas holiday swiftly approached, and Beth sorted through the social invitations she had received. It was the height of the season, and as much as she would like to attend all the functions, her father

Sweetbriar

tired of the frenzied festivities too easily. She would accept only the activities most likely to be attended by her more devoted admirers. She had promised her father to decide on a husband by spring but found it difficult to determine who would be most suitable.

There were a few titled men available, but some were so class conscious. Beth had overheard a duke's son whisper to his friend that he found her appealing, but *his* father wouldn't consider the Earl of Rockwell's daughter because *her* father worked in trade. She was mortified. As if her father's business was dishonorable. No matter, the son, like the duke, was priggish.

When Beth speculated about accepting a military man, her aunt explained that military wives were uprooted frequently and had long periods of separation from their husbands. The life described severely tarnished the dashing good looks of the young officers.

She even considered some untitled wealthy gentlemen. If she married a commoner, she would retain the privilege of being referred to as Lady Beth, but disappointingly, her daughters would lose that advantage.

If only Bradley Anderson hadn't shown up for those few short weeks, disturbing her mind and entangling her heart. But he was gone, and she had to choose soon.

Aunt Sylvia had suggested Beth narrow her focus in the direction of a particular nobleman. Viscount Dunmore was older than she desired, thirty years to her seventeen, but he was companionable. He called on her often but no more frequently than other admirers. Since they hadn't risked further escapades to the gaming house, or anywhere else for that matter, Beth questioned if her reluctance to allow him to kiss her that night had squelched any serious interest on his part. She wondered if his kiss would thrill her as much as the American's. She hoped so. That would break the enchantment she felt for Bradley Anderson. At the ball this evening, Beth would allow the viscount to walk her in the shrubbery and satisfy her curiosity.

Quickly she finished sorting the invitations into two piles, one to accept and one to decline. She would send her responses tomorrow. Presently she needed to dress for this evening's ball.

Her pale green gown had a knee-length cutaway over-jacket of emerald green. She supposed it would be flattering to entwine a matching green ribbon in her hair. As she removed the ribbon from the drawer in her wardrobe, she spied the handkerchief with the BA monogram. Bradley Anderson had wrapped her fifteenth birthday gift in the soft cloth and tied it with the green ribbon. That evening he had held her in his arms as he taught her to waltz, she remembered. A knot rose in her throat, but she swallowed it down. Smoothing the square of fabric and replacing the ribbon on top, she closed the drawer. The ribbon would not adorn her hair this night. Instead, a few extra curls would do.

Surveying the crowded ballroom, fruitlessly searching for her cousin's familiar face, Beth was disappointed. Mary and Peter didn't attend the dances as often now that they were married. Recently few opportunities allowed for the long, girlish talks the two women had enjoyed so much, and Beth missed the insightful perspective her cousin provided about the men they met.

"Lady Beth," a young officer of her acquaintance inquired, "May I have the honor of a dance this evening?" She recalled he wasn't graceful on his feet but had no excuse to decline his request. "A minuet would be delightful, sir," she replied, scanning the room.

He cleared his throat. "I rather had a waltz in mind," he said as the familiar strains began.

Resigned to the inevitable, Beth placed her hand on his offered arm.

As they clumsily glided around the room, he complimented her appearance and made mundane small talk, which did not require more than a smile or a nod in response. Before the music ended, he maneuvered her close to the double doors leading to the terrace. "Perhaps you'll take the air with me, Lady Beth," he suggested.

She preferred to avoid his advances. "The dancing has left me parched, would you mind bringing me a glass of punch instead?" she asked sweetly, working her fan in front of her face.

His eyes narrowed, but he bowed politely, "As you wish," and left to fetch the refreshment.

Hearing a derisive laugh, Beth turned and smiled in pleasure. "Lord Dunmore, I hoped you would be here this evening."

He leaned close, softly cooing, "Isn't that curious, Lady Beth. I also hoped our paths would cross." Glancing up, he grimaced, "And if I'm not mistaken, your lieutenant will return shortly. Are you thirsty, or do you prefer to avoid him?"

"You are wicked, sir," Beth smiled, "and I prefer to avoid him."

He took her elbow, ushering her through the doors onto the terrace. Beth shivered in the cold. She had tied a shawl loosely around her shoulders while she danced and now drew it closer. They followed the path through the shrubbery in silence, picking their way carefully in the shadows. She shivered again as they moved into a more secluded area.

"You're cold, my dear. Perhaps I can warm you," the viscount murmured, drawing her into his arms. She felt his breath on her hair and tilted her face up to his. His reptilian eyes glittered in the darkness as he lowered his head, and cautiously brought his mouth to hers. When her lips parted, he explored deeply, deciding it would be all the more interesting if she had a passionate nature.

She experienced none of the fluttering thrill in her heart as his tongue stroked hers. As he crushed her in his arms, a suffocating panic rose. She thrashed about, but he didn't release her. Instead, he trailed small, nipping kisses along the soft skin of her throat to her shoulder. Then he bit her.

She struggled harder. "Please release me, sir," she hissed.

His arms loosened, and he held her lightly by the shoulders. "Forgive my fervor, but my passion grows each time we meet." His voice softly coaxed as he rubbed his hands up and down her arms. "Your radiant beauty draws me as the flame draws the moth." Rolf had given great consideration to the words, knowing inexperienced girls needed to hear romantic phrases before giving themselves to a man. He wanted her and her dowry. Until he had both, he would play the attentive lover. Feeling her relax, Dunmore released his hold.

She smiled hesitantly, "I forgive you, milord."

He placed a finger on her lips to still her words, "My name is Rolf, and I want to hear it from your lips."

"I forgive you, Rolf," she complied then leaned forward for another kiss.

He was cunning enough to touch her lips tenderly and give her just the barest tip of his tongue before ending the kiss. "I had better return you to the ballroom before your father notices your absence." Satisfied with his progress for the evening, Dunmore guided her toward the music.

The lieutenant felt foolish standing by the door holding two glasses of punch. Lady Beth wasn't where he left her, and she wasn't dancing either. He should have returned her to her father, as expected, but the hope of walking her in the moonlight and stealing a few

Sweetbriar

kisses was too tempting to resist. He discarded the punch in the bushes with a quick flick of his wrist, irritated with the girl for putting him in this situation. He intended to get an explanation and decided to engage her father in conversation until she returned.

"Lord Rockwell, excuse me, sir," the lieutenant said, sidling up to the older gentleman. "After dancing with your daughter, she asked me to fetch her some punch. I left her standing by the terrace doors and am embarrassed to say that now I can't find her. I let her for only a minute."

They both quickly scanned the room. "You have nothing to worry about, young man. There she is across the hall," Rockwell said as Beth entered through the garden door. "I think she just stepped outside for a moment."

They saw Lord Dunmore enter behind Beth, lean close to whisper in her ear, take her elbow and lead her onto the dance floor.

"Well, I never!" sputtered the soldier. "Lord Rockwell, I dare say, you'll want to put a stop to that," he exclaimed as a flush reddened his cheeks.

Startled by the man's vehemence, Avery asked, "Put a stop to what?"

"If you value your daughter's reputation, you'll think twice about allowing her to stroll in the shrubbery with Viscount Dunmore."

Warily, his lordship inquired as to why.

"The man is a known cad," was the emphatic reply. "Not more than three months ago, he befriended Major Wilkins of my regiment. The major has a young wife who is pretty but painfully shy. The viscount was blatant in his seduction of her and braggadocios to boot. He turned the major into a laughingstock. The worst of it is he didn't even care for the girl. Only a wager he'd made with some of the men, who had it in for Major Wilkins, prompted his actions. It was disgraceful."

"This is alarming news if what you say is true," Lord Rockwell countered seriously. "The viscount is a kinsman of my brother-in-law, and I've heard nothing rumored about an affair. Are you sure of your facts?"

The soldier's flush deepened, "You don't need to take my word for it, milord," he replied resentfully. "You can verify my story with the regimental commander. The men lost all respect for the poor Major, which forced him to apply for a transfer to a northern regiment. I don't doubt the whole sordid mess has ruined his career."

Milton Avery put his hand on the lieutenant's arm, "I shall talk to your commander, young man, so you had better hope he verifies what you told me, or you'll suffer for your slander." The soldier's eyes widened, and Lord Rockwell softened his tone, "And if he corroborates your story, I'll put in a good word for you, as you will have done me a great service. Now excuse me, I must take my daughter home."

The next day in a short interview with the regimental commander, the information relayed by the young lieutenant was confirmed.

Chapter V
Early Spring 1809, America

Throughout the winter Charles Anderson slowly recuperated, thankful for the time early the previous year when his son had learned the shore-based operations of the business. When Brad arrived home from England, he took on the responsibilities of the day to day functions, consulting Charles only on important matters. The older man knew that if business had been brisk, his son would have been overwhelmed, but with the embargo, Brad had managed well.

Now, if he would only manage his personal life as competently. He needed to settle down and forget this nonsense with the British girl. Charles wanted and needed his son here. If the chit didn't love him enough to leave England, then America possessed a plethora of fashionably sophisticated women from which to choose. But Bradley was obstinately blind to them all.

The embargoes that had devastated the United States economy had been replaced in the final days of the Jefferson presidency with the Non-Intercourse Act, which opened foreign markets for American goods, except to France and Great Britain. But when the British envoy, the Honorable David Erskine, affirmed the impending rescission of the British Orders in Council, President Madison withdrew the restriction from American ships sailing to England.

With commerce between the two countries again open, Brad determined his best course was to return to the sea. After weeks of arguing over the issue, Charles seethed and lost all patience when Brad renewed his campaign for commanding a ship. "I will not give you the *Angel Star*, or any other ship for that matter, to sail back to England. You belong here, and here is where you'll stay, by God!" Emphasizing his words, Charles pounded his fist on the desk, rattling a small lantern sitting in the corner.

"Father, I won't have you dictate to me. My courtship of Beth Avery was progressing well. But being a dutiful son, I threw it over and came home when you needed me." Brad was as furious as his father. "You should know by now I intend to live my life on my terms. I'm sorry if that displeases you. But if you won't give me a ship to command, then I'll hire on elsewhere."

Charles blanched, falling back into his chair. "I don't have a ship to give you, even if I did approve of your leaving. We have too many captains as it is. Don't forget, Bradley, two ships were confiscated. These men need work. They've been loyal to me, and I intend to return that loyalty."

Stubbornly, the young man glared at his father. Willful as a boy, Brad was mulishly stubborn as a man.

Charles sighed in capitulation, "If you insist on going, then talk to O'Malley. He's leaving within the week. He can always use an extra hand."

"You want me to sign on as a seaman?" Brad exclaimed in astonishment.

Blood rushed back into Charles' face as he ground out angrily, "Sign on as a seaman or pay as a passenger. The choice is yours, dammit."

A sharp rap at the door preceded O'Malley's entrance, his impatience to sail evident in his weathered face. "Good afternoon, gentlemen. We're just about ready. The merchandise is all on board, and the stores are being loaded as we speak. I calculate we should put out to sea in three days' time."

"As I said, Brad, the choice is yours. Which shall it be?" Resigned to his son's departure, Charles wasn't going to make it easy.

"And what choice is that, laddie?" the old salt asked.

"I'm returning to London. Father says I can sign on with your crew or pay as a passenger," Brad spat out bitterly, wiping the smile off Quinn's face.

After a moment, he voiced his thoughts, "You know I can always use an extra hand. I have a chief mate and all my officers, but I'm willing to take you on as an additional third mate. At least you'd eat and sleep with the other officers instead of with the crew."

Brad's briny expletive irritated his father, and O'Malley eyed the younger man with equal annoyance. "You know me well, young Anderson. I expect a cooperative attitude among my officers. If you don't think you can make the shift, then I don't want you on board."

Struggling to swallow his ire, Brad yielded, "Aye, Captain. Third mate, it is. When do I report for duty?"

The big man sniffed in a lungful of air, "I want you onboard by dawn. You can report to the chief mate."

"Aye, aye, sir," Brad exploded as he turned and stormed out, slamming the door behind him.

Clearing his throat, the big man asked, "What's that all about, Mr. Anderson?"

Charles stood, pacing the room with his hands clasped behind his back, "Bradley won't listen to reason.

Twice now, that English girl has turned him down, but he refuses to admit defeat. I need your help, O'Malley. He listens to you. Knock some sense into him if you must. Just give me your word that you will bring him back when you return. I don't want to lose him. He is my only son.

Quinn snatched off his cap and scratched his head, then jammed the cap back on and gave it a tug to settle it firmly. "Damned if I know how to change his mind once he sets its course. But I give you my word. When we dock here again, he'll be on board. What it'll take to keep him here, though, is another matter."

Clapping his trusted employee on the shoulder, Charles entreated, "Just bring him home, Quinn, that's all I ask."

Late Spring/Early Summer 1809, England

Within a few days of sailing, Brad set aside his bruised pride. The other officers demanded less of him than he expected, and there was insufficient work to keep his mind occupied. In his spare time, he fashioned decorative gifts out of cordage for his mother and sisters. They liked to use the intricately knotted pads in place of trivets in the kitchen. As a young sailor, he had learned the imaginative skill to fill time during the idle dog days of long voyages. His hands were occupied, but his mind was not. It churned. Deliberately neglecting to visit his father before sailing, Brad felt the weight of the estrangement.

After being left to his own devices for most of the journey, he was invited into O'Malley's cabin to play backgammon during the few days it took for the ship to round the southern shores of England. Quinn was a formidable opponent, having been Brad's original instructor. But Brad recognized the games were just an excuse for his mentor to provide him with sorely needed counsel. Talking with Quinn helped Brad understand the futility of his single-minded devotion to Beth Avery, and he realized if she rejected him again, he would have no choice but to accept it.

After the ship set anchor, Brad apprehensively made his way to the Rockwell Trading Company offices, preferring to inquire after Beth before approaching her directly. At the end of the block, he witnessed Rockwell exit a carriage and enter his place of business, relieving Brad of the necessity of taking a hack to the Avery residence.

When the American entered the reception area, Milton Avery glanced away from the papers he was reviewing with his secretary. Like a lighted firecracker, astonishment exploded upon his face. "Anderson, I didn't expect you so soon. Only three weeks have passed since I posted my letter."

"What letter?"

The welcoming smile faded from Avery's face. "If my letter didn't bring you, what did?"

Nodding toward the door to the nobleman's inner office, Brad requested, "May I speak with you privately, Rockwell?"

"Yes, of course." His lordship removed a key from his vest pocket and unlocked the door. They settled into their respective chairs on either side of the desk. "Did your father survive?" Avery inquired.

Stiffening slightly, Brad nodded, "Yes, he recovered and is back to work. And you, sir, are you and your daughter well?"

"Yes, we are in good health, which most likely brings us to the point of your arrival in England." Rockwell smiled, "And the subject of my letter to you."

"Please don't tell me she is betrothed," Brad groaned, slumping forward and dropping his head into his hands.

"That depends. You see, I wrote to inform you that if you renewed your marriage proposal, it would be accepted."

Like the morning sun rising over a mountain top, elation rose in Brad's face. Too ecstatic to remain seated, he catapulted out of his chair, leaned over the desk, and grabbed the older man's hand, shaking it enthusiastically. "Thank you, sir. Thank you. Your daughter has made me the happiest of men."

"Sit down, Anderson, there's something you need to know," Rockwell said as embarrassment crept into his face.

Cautiously, Brad sat, not liking the tone of voice he heard.

"I was mistaken in believing Beth should be consulted on a subject as serious as matrimony and have taken matters into my own hands," Avery stated. "I have no doubt she would have accepted you last year if you had intended to remain in England. To me, it seems a frivolous thing to reject a bonafide offer on the trivial pretense of wanting to stay close to her dwindling family. A woman needs to make the best match she can and cleave to her husband. I've become concerned that, in her desire to remain in England, she will make an inappropriate match. She doesn't know I wrote to you. So, knowing she hasn't agreed to the marriage, are you still willing to become engaged?"

Soberly, Brad mulled this over in his head for a few minutes. "I am confident of Beth's fondness for me. Last year she intimated that she would be amenable toward me, except for my intention of living in America. My intentions have not changed. I want to wed Beth, but I am troubled that she has not accepted it freely." After a moment's silence, he mused aloud, "My home is not so very different from what she knows of England, and my family will welcome her warmly." More silence ensued as Brad contemplated the situation. "You know I love your daughter, so I shall accept the risk that she will come to love America as much as I."

Rockwell nodded, smiling, "The ultimate gift a woman should hope for is a steadfast husband who loves her. I'll arrange for us to meet the solicitor tomorrow, and we'll settle the terms of the engagement. I suggest we complete the legalities before informing Beth. She can be intractable at times, and I'd rather not allow her the opportunity to defy me on this."

Brad stood and paced the small area in front of the desk with his arms crossed over his chest. "My mother and sisters have always been content with letting their husbands make major decisions, so I do not have the experience to determine if this is the best course of action."

"Beth didn't have the advantage of a mother to guide her, and I have always been too lenient, so she learned to be headstrong. But in this, I think it best to present her with a fait accompli."

"Then, I shall defer to your superior judgment, Rockwell."

In the rose garden selecting fresh blooms for the dining room, Beth spotted her father approaching from the house. He had been out all morning on business, and she hadn't expected him to return so early. Kissing his cheek, she greeted, "Hello, Papa. Isn't the weather perfect for this time of year? Why don't we have Maude serve us tea in the gazebo today?"

"That would be enjoyable. However, we have a guest joining us, so I already instructed her to serve us in the drawing-room," he replied.

"Papa, I wanted time alone with you today to share some wonderful news, but I suppose I can just tell you outright and spare you the guessing game I had planned." After a suspenseful breath, she continued with a satisfied smile on her face, "I've decided to marry Rolf Dunmore."

If she expected to please her father, she couldn't have been more mistaken. His face turned an apoplectic crimson, and he breathed deeply several times to gain control. "You are half right, Beth, you will marry. But you will not marry Dunmore," he said forcefully. Observing the confusion on her face, Rockwell guided his daughter to the carved stone bench at the side of the path. There he took her hands in his. "It's time we talked about your future, child."

"Oh, father! I'm not a child anymore. I'm to be eighteen soon. I'm a grown woman if I do say so myself."

"My point exactly, Beth."

When he cleared his throat, she received the distinct impression he didn't know where to start, so she quickly interjected, "Rolf came by the house this morning and proposed to me. He would have talked to you first, but you weren't home. I've accepted him, Papa. I thought you would be pleased that I finally settled on someone."

"I have no intention of allowing you to marry that demon." Searching her face, he asked frankly, "Do you love him?"

She lowered her eyes. "He is an agreeable man, and I have no doubt that in time I will give him my heart as well as my hand," she acknowledged.

Relieved, her father declared, "You will give that man neither your hand nor your heart. Not now! Not ever!"

Startled speechless by his vehemence, she gaped.

"For reasons which are far too indelicate to discuss with an unwed girl, I will never approve of Viscount

Dunmore as a husband for you. Never," he emphasized. "And it is too late for you to choose another man."

"I don't understand," she exclaimed. "I already told Rolf I would marry him. He's coming back in the morning to discuss the terms of my dowry with you."

Sighing profoundly, Lord Rockwell revealed his decision, "I already settled the terms of your dowry and accepted an offer of marriage for you. We were at the solicitor's office this morning."

"But you always said I would be the one to decide who to marry," Beth cried, snatching her hands away and springing from the bench.

Her father's stern voice broke through her agitated thoughts. "If you had ever been inclined toward one man, I would have gladly accepted your choice, but you encouraged them all. When I suspected you might settle on Dunmore, I decided enough was enough. He has too many reprehensible habits to be acceptable. Take a few minutes to reconcile yourself to your engagement, for my decision is final. Your future husband will arrive shortly, and I expect you to receive him graciously, as required of any newly betrothed woman."

"And just who is my 'future husband'?" she asked, dripping sarcasm.

"Bradley Anderson."

Beth's knees gave out, and she plopped onto the bench, stunned. Under different circumstances, she would have joyfully accepted Bradley Anderson's proposal. He was a gentleman, wealthy, and handsome. She couldn't deny any of that. If the elder Mr. Anderson had remained loyal to the crown, he would be a duke, and the title would eventually descend to his son. They would live in England, and she would someday become a duchess. But that wasn't to be.

Time and again, Beth had endeavored in vain to forget the American's spine-tingling kisses. She felt none of that thrill when Rolf kissed her but thought it didn't matter. She wasn't prepared to abandon her decision to marry the viscount, but her pleading went unheeded. Beth's father firmly insisted she go to her room and prepare to receive their guest.

Restlessly, Beth pondered why her father chose to force a marriage she didn't want. Although forty-six years of age, he was a vigorous man with a relatively good build. His pale blue eyes were clear, and the only outward indication of aging was the thinning of his salt and pepper hair. She didn't think it health or age that decided him to marry her off to the American.

Nor did she think financial difficulties caused her father's decision. He always encouraged her to dress in the height of fashion and escorted her to all the gala activities due a woman of her station. How could she possibly forsake the theater, the balls, the luncheons, and all her friends to live in America?

And that was the crux of the matter. Marriage to Bradley Anderson was unacceptable because she would have to live in his country, fearful every day of the Indians who possessed a blood lust for all civilized folk. The notion revolted her.

Beth decided good behavior was called for this afternoon to calm her father. But as soon as possible, she meant to inform Bradley Anderson, in blunt and specific terms, that she was not agreeable to their impending marriage. She was determined to find a way out and believed a long engagement would present the means.

A hesitant knock on the door interrupted her thoughts, and Millie, her maid, entered. "S'cuse milady, will you be wantin' to change 'fore tea? Mr. Anderson has already arrived."

"Yes, I must change. The blue muslin will be fine. And hurry, Millie, Papa will be displeased at my tardiness."

Standing by the fireplace, Brad crossed the room when Beth entered and raised her hand to his lips for a light kiss on her fingertips. He allowed his eyes to travel over her possessively. No one had ever stared at her so insolently before, and she blushed from the heat of his gaze.

Her father coughed politely, "Perhaps you will pour the tea, Beth. Anderson has brought us some news that I think we should discuss."

"And what news has Mr. Anderson brought that you would need to discuss with me?"

"Please, Beth, let us not stand on such formalities," Brad said, tucking her hand into the crook of his arm and guiding her to the settee. "My name is Bradley, and those close to me refer to me as Brad."

She flushed again, realizing her hope of maintaining formalities was wasted. As she sat to pour, Beth noticed a small package next to her teacup and glanced at the American.

"Please accept this token of my affection," he said, sitting beside her.

With trembling hands, she removed the wrapping. Inside the jewelers' box lay a beautiful ring. It was heart-shaped with a large solitaire ruby surrounded by small diamonds.

"It was the wedding ring of my great-grandmother, the last dowager Duchess of Surrey," he informed her. "I chose it as your engagement ring."

Setting it on the table, she poured the tea. "Then it's a pity a Duchess won't wear it," she stated rudely. "What is your news, Mr. Anderson?"

She knew she hit her mark from the offended expression on his face. But her victory withered on the vine when he calmly stated, "Word just arrived that after your parliament rescinded the Erskine Agreement, the United States re-instated the boycott against England. Political tensions are high, and there is talk of war. I know most women prefer long engagements with all the accompanying festivities, but I feel it imperative we marry as soon as decently possible and return to America."

Blood drained from Beth's face, dulling her vision, and leaving her lightheaded. Her father's voice sounded far away when he suggested Bradley take her outside for a breath of air. Scarcely aware of being led down the path to the rose garden or sitting on the garden bench, she revived as Brad chafed her hands. Shuddering a sigh, she looked at him as she moistened her lips.

Finding the gesture provocative, Brad stood, drew her into his arms, and kissed her possessively.

Swaying against him, she felt the hard length of his body against hers and jolted when he slid his hands below her waist and pressed their hips close. Wrenching loose, she pushed him away, "Take your hands off me."

Releasing her, she stumbled backward, but he reached out and caught her before she fell. Then he smiled, caressing her body with his eyes. Enraged, she slapped his face. "I will not marry you," she hissed.

Cold anger flashed abruptly in his eyes. They glinted like chips of gray ice, sending a tremor of fear quivering along Beth's spine. In a deadly quiet voice, Brad responded, "I hoped you would be pleased by our engagement or, at the very least, reconciled to the idea. As it is, circumstances dictate that we wed as soon as possible. The matter is settled."

Stamping her foot in frustration, Beth cried, "But I don't want to leave England." Unexpectedly, tears spurted from her eyes, and she sobbed loudly, covering her face with her hands.

His anger dissipated as Brad gathered her into his arms.

She cried against his shoulder for a time, then regaining control, astonished them both by whispering, "Kiss me, Bradley."

When his mouth closed over hers, she hungrily consumed the taste of him and felt the surge of an unknown yearning. As his nipping kisses drifted to her neck and shoulders, she trembled with pleasure and pressed her body closer to his. When he loosened his embrace, her reason slowly returned.

Tousled hair fell over his forehead, passion flushed his face, and his green eyes gleamed with compelling intensity. "I love you, sweet Beth, and desperately want you to return my love. Please say that you do."

Unsure of her emotions, she stepped back to put a small distance between them. "I don't know what I feel for you, but I know how I feel about leaving the safety of my home. Please don't make me marry against my will."

It was as if she threw cold water in his face. "I'm sorry you feel that way, but what is done is done. We will marry," he said firmly, then turned on his heel and strode back toward the house.

Abandoned, Beth collapsed onto the garden bench and wept.

Watching his future son-in-law stride up the garden path alone, Rockwell perceived his disappointment. When Brad entered the room, the nobleman suggested they go to the library for a brandy.

Brad silently followed his host, and when seated with cognac in hand, took a long swallow. "Frankly, Rockwell, when you suggested we settle the nuptial agreement before informing your daughter, I had my doubts about the wisdom of it. But now I'm relieved to have a legally binding contract in place. Otherwise, I'd be tempted to board the first ship out of England, regardless of its destination," Brad said dejectedly.

"Mm, as bad as that, was it?" his lordship asked. "Give her a few days to get used to the idea. I suppose it did come as a bit of a shock to her." After a thoughtful pause, he added, "Just so you know, when I arrived home this afternoon, she told me that just this morning, she decided to marry someone else."

Brad's head snapped around, and he stared at Milton Avery with narrowed eyes. "Are you regretting your decision to have me marry her? If so, perhaps it would be better all around to dissolve our contract," Brad suggested, choking on words that constricted his heart. He tossed back the remaining brandy and slammed the snifter on the table in disgust.

"On the contrary, her choice would have been her ruin. I am more thankful than ever that you arrived when you did. And I think we should move along with the wedding as quickly as possible. It will be best to announce your engagement at Beth's birthday party week after next. The invitations have been delivered already."

"What about the banns?"

"We'll post banns for three weeks in the *Gazette* and read them in the parish for three consecutive Sundays. These things can be set in motion immediately. I will ask Father Stilton to schedule the wedding directly following the service on the third Sunday. With such short notice that will provide the best probability of having the majority of guests Beth will want in attendance. I'll call on my sister tomorrow and recruit her to organize everything. She was a dynamo when it came to putting together Mary's wedding."

"Thank you, Rockwell, I appreciate your understanding." Breathing deeply to calm himself, Brad shifted the conversation. "If you don't mind, I want to take Beth to your country estate for a few days following the ceremony. We won't have time for a proper honeymoon, and it will provide her with the chance to make her farewells to the neighborhood."

"That's a splendid idea. I know she will appreciate it. Now, why don't we find out if she has composed herself and is ready to be civil?"

Needing to end his liaison, Brad called on a solicitor about transferring title to the cottage and settling some cash on Louise. When asked, he shamefully admitted he didn't know her surname. She had always just been Louise.

Since his arrival in England, Brad hadn't visited her and would have preferred to avoid the necessity of seeing her at all. But that wasn't possible, nor would it have been honorable. Putting off the inevitable encounter, day after day, until he could delay no longer, he intended only a brief meeting to explain the terms of the settlement, followed by a speedy departure. Then he could attend the engagement celebration at the Avery home that evening free of encumbrances.

Arriving at her cottage unannounced, Louise caught him off guard when she flew into his arms and captured his mouth in a deeply searing kiss. Before he could disentangle himself from her arms, she deftly undid the buttons of his short-fall trousers, slipped her hand in, and grasped his manhood. Unable to prevent his body's sudden response to her amorous ambush, out of habit, Brad picked her up and carried her to the bedroom. When he set her on her feet, she dropped to her knees and took his rigid appendage into her mouth, sucking gently, and flicking her tongue, assailing his senses. Incapable of resisting the erotic sensations, he closed his eyes and gave himself over to the tantalizing pleasure. Afterward, he sank to the bed and threw his arm over his eyes, breathing heavily. Louise quickly shed her clothing, straddled him, and guided his still firm organ inside her.

Abruptly, logic returned. He hadn't come for sex, but to end the long-standing affair. Growling, he hastily lifted her off his torso and stood to adjust his clothing.

But highly aroused, she wanted her needs satisfied. "What are you doing, Bradley? We are not done yet," she asserted as she tried to pull him back onto the bed.

"Louise, stop! I didn't come here to make love to you," Brad exclaimed.

"What do you mean you didn't come here to make love? That is always why you come here. That is what we are doing right now. We are making love, and I want you. Come back to bed," she demanded in frustration, pulling on his hands.

He shook her aside and tried to button his pants, "No, Louise. We need to talk."

Furious, she lunged at him, striking his chest with her small fists, crying wildly, "I do not want to talk! Talk between lovers is never good. Men only want to speak of things women don't want to hear."

This attack astonished Brad almost as much as the unexpected sexual encounter. Familiar with her occasional fiery temper displays, Brad understood it would take time to soothe her. Wanting her in a reasonable state of mind to tell her about the settlement, he had no doubt she would accept the end of their affair once she understood he was providing for her future. He grabbed her wrists to stop the pounding, but she incoherently continued to struggle.

Kicking out with her foot, she landed a solid blow to his shin. Cursing, he stumbled back, tangled in his loosened britches, then fell to the bed with Louise on top of him. He rolled to pin her, only to have her frenzied grappling renew the desire in his loins.

Louise stilled when she felt his hard arousal and triumphantly touched her lips to his. Losing restraint, he sullenly nudged her thighs apart and buried himself in her moist flesh, willfully taking what she offered.

Climbing toward her peak, Louise locked her legs firmly around her lover's hips to prevent him from withdrawing before his release. Too late, Brad realized he couldn't break her hold and couldn't stop his seed from spilling inside her.

While their breath still rasped harshly in their throats, Louise lowered her legs. Angrily, Brad stood, snatched her dress off the floor, and threw it on the bed. "Get dressed. We need to talk," he callously said as he adjusted his garments and buttoned his pants. With a glance in the mirror to ensure he was presentable, he stalked out of the room.

Her deliberate seduction sickened him. Self-disgust, a most unfamiliar and disturbing emotion, engulfed him. He grimaced. Having always considered integrity a cornerstone of his character, he paced the small parlor while he waited for Louise, castigating himself for his deplorable behavior.

Twenty minutes later, she came out of the bedroom, dressed and composed. Her pale face suffered from the most woebegone expression imaginable. Her eyes shimmering with unshed tears, she sat across from her lover and asked, "What do you wish to speak to me about, Bradley?"

"I'm getting married soon," he stated.

Tears welled and spilled over, but she sat motionlessly.

More gently, he continued, "I want you to have this house, Louise. It is your home. I'll also provide you with money for a small dowry so you can marry."

With her heart breaking, she nodded her understanding.

Removing a card from his coat pocket, he handed it to her, "This is the solicitor's card. His name is Gregory Thompson, and he is located on Fleet Street. If you show this card, someone can direct you there."

"I know how to read, Bradley. I came from a good home," she stated with dignity.

Only women from better homes were fortunate enough to receive an education. He was ashamed he hadn't known even this much about her. "I'm sorry, Louise. I know this hurts, but I was truthful with you from the beginning."

She nodded and stood, "Goodbye, Mr. Anderson," she said, then staggered back to her bedroom.

Belatedly Brad recognized the mistake of visiting Louise today of all days. His intention to talk to her briefly before returning to his hotel and changing into evening clothes would have allowed him to arrive at the Avery home early. Instead, he was compelled to bathe the scent of Louise from his body before facing his fiancée, making him overly late arriving at their engagement festivities.

He wandered through the salon and ballroom, searching for Beth. Lady Mary approached, displeasure evident in her usually placid face, "How good of you to join us, Mr. Anderson. Attending this little soirée hasn't caused you too much inconvenience, I trust."

He winced at the scorn in her voice. "I was unavoidably delayed. I hope Beth isn't too upset by my tardiness."

"Upset?" Mary echoed, raising her eyebrows in astonishment. "To say the least! May I remind you the *Gazette* already posted the banns. Everyone noticed your absence at dinner. Beth was mortified. And poor Uncle Milton. Do you have any idea how awkward it was for him to announce his daughter's betrothal to a man who didn't even have the courtesy to make an appearance?"

Flinching from the legitimacy of her diatribe, Brad reined in his irritation. "Where is she?" he asked. "I can't find her."

"Such a strange evening this turns out to be." Brad and Mary turned at the interruption. "First, the groom-to-be is absent for the engagement announcement, and now the bride-to-be has disappeared. All the young men have been eager to dance with Lady Beth tonight, perhaps it was all too much, and she needed some fresh air."

Obviously, too much wine had loosened this guest's tongue. "Perhaps it is you who needs the fresh air, sir," Brad snapped, turned on his heel and headed toward the garden doors.

Edward chortled gleefully. "Perhaps I do," he muttered under his breath and followed.

Mary hastened to find her uncle. She wasn't sure what Mr. Anderson would find if her impetuous cousin was in the garden but worried it wouldn't be good.

Beth was resigned but not reconciled to her fate. Brad had been an attentive fiancé the past ten days, but if he truly loved her, she reasoned, he would have been at her side for the formal announcement of their engagement.

Since their betrothal, Beth's father had allowed Brad to escort her to social functions without the benefit of a chaperon. That first evening, alone in the carriage with him, her nerves had been atwitter with anticipation of stolen kisses. He sat close, casually draped his arm over her shoulders, and chatted of inconsequential things. As the carriage stopped in front of the opera house, Brad brushed his lips lightly over hers, stepped down, and handed her out. It was almost as if his passion had wilted as soon as the heart-shaped ring adorned her finger.

But during subsequent evening rides, he was more forward in his advances, at first softly kissing her hair and later her lips. As his ardor increased, he kissed her neck and shoulders, sending her senses reeling. And last night, while nibbling her lower lip, he lightly brushed his thumb over the tip of her breast. It hardened and aroused her with a spine-tingling thrill that terrified.

The viscount stopped in the shadows, drew her close, and interrupted her disturbing thoughts. It was scandalous to stroll in the garden with Rolf tonight, but Beth didn't care. Brad wasn't here and would never know.

Dunmore took her hands in his. "My love, we've enjoyed so little time together since your father ruined our plans to marry, and soon you'll leave for America."

"Rolf, I don't want to live in America. I don't know what to do. Neither Father nor Auntie seems to care about my happiness anymore."

"I care about your happiness." Lowering his mouth to her ear, he whispered seductively, "Come away with me tonight, we'll elope."

"How can we elope? There are banns to be read, and I have nowhere to stay until that is done. Think of the scandal."

"It is you I want. If you stay with me, your father will have no choice but to allow our marriage, my love," he said, leaning close and kissing her deeply.

"How charming," Brad's abrasive voice nearly caused Beth to leap out of her skin.

Rolf released her abruptly, standing as far away as politely possible.

"Tell me, Dunmore, did my eyes deceive me, or were you seducing my fiancée?" There was no mistaking

Sweetbriar

the fatal tone in Brad's voice or the loathing in his turbulent gray eyes.

Rolf inclined his head, "Lady Beth and I were merely exchanging farewells."

Startled, Beth glared at him sharply. "What do you mean, Rolf?" she asked in confusion, knowing he had just asked her to elope. But she received no reply.

For a long minute, Brad stared at the nobleman, who refused to return his gaze. "You're lying, Dunmore," Bradley asserted in a barely audible voice. "You attempted to take advantage of a naive woman, but I understand that's a well-known trait of yours."

"How dare you," his adversary hissed.

Baring his left hand and stepping forward, Brad countered, "How dare you," and slapped Dunmore's face with his glove.

Beth gasped, wide-eyed.

"Anderson!" Rockwell exclaimed from behind.

Brad turned slightly to acknowledge his presence. Raising an eyebrow, he also acknowledged Edward's attendance. "Rockwell, will you act as my second?" Brad inquired his face like chiseled granite in the moonlight.

Milton Avery shifted his gaze from Anderson to his daughter and finally to Dunmore. Sneering disgustedly at the viscount, he replied, "Yes, of course. I'm honor-bound to do so."

Rushing to her father, Beth pleaded, "No, father, you can't. Rolf wants to marry me."

"Silence, Beth!" he ground out harshly. "If not for your foolishness, this would not be necessary." Then he sighed and softened his tone, explaining, "You see, dear, the viscount is not the sort of man to marry an inexperienced girl, except maybe for her dowry."

"No, father, I don't believe it," she insisted.

Brad addressed Dunmore, "Name your second."

"Edward, you witnessed the insult, will you act as my second?"

"Of course, what else are friends for?"

Rolf clapped his crony on the shoulder. "Come then, we have arrangements to make," and without a backward glance, the two men stamped up the garden path.

After their departure, Brad addressed his future father-in-law, "If you don't mind, Rockwell, I would like a word with my fiancée."

Glancing at her pale face, his lordship released his arm from her grasp. "I have no objection," he replied, then turned and left.

As Brad glowered at Beth in silence, she unconsciously retreated. The juniper hedgerow brought her up short. Taking one quick step forward, Brad roughly grabbed her by the shoulders and demanded, "Is this the type of behavior I can expect from you as my wife?" When she didn't answer, he shook her once. "Is it, my love?" he mocked in imitation of the viscount.

"No," she whispered, barely finding her voice.

"Then what can I expect?"

"Brad, please."

He pulled her against him, his lips hard and cruel as he took possession of her beguiling mouth.

Deep in her belly, warm excitement fluttered. Her knees weakened, and a thrill raced up her spine as her betrothed devoured her neck and shoulders hungrily. The hard length of his body pressed close to hers. Her heart hammered wildly.

Releasing her, Brad's voice was frigid despite his passion. "Come, my love, we're keeping our guests waiting. I'm sure they are anxious to witness the happiness we share in our betrothal." He grasped her wrist, keelhauling her behind him as he stalked up the path.

She struggled. "No, Brad. By now everyone will have heard about the duel. I can't possibly face them knowing what they're thinking."

He stopped, yanked her close, and scowled, "You should have thought of the consequences earlier. I don't like this any more than you, but unless you want to add to the gossip, stop struggling and put a smile on your face." Breathing deeply to gain control over his rage, Brad looped her arm through his and continued up the path.

As they entered the ballroom, the overly animated chatter died. Brad gazed at his fiancée with a smile that did not reach his eyes and suggested, "Shall we dance, my love?" Having no choice, she followed his lead as he whirled her around the room to the strains of a waltz.

Slowly the guests resumed their meaningless prattle.

Looking at the woman in his arms, Brad asked unsympathetically, "Must you appear so forlorn? From your countenance, anyone would think the gallows awaited you."

"Brad, please let me sit." Mercifully the music ended with her request, and he guided her to a chair. Gesturing to a roving footman, he nipped two flutes of champagne and toasted, "To your every wish, my love." But his eyes remained chips of ice.

Wanting to fling the champagne in his face, Beth hesitated, fearing his possible reaction. Instead, she lowered her eyes and sipped the wine.

By the time the last of the guests departed, Beth's nerves vibrated as tautly as an overwound violin string. Hearing her father invite Bradley to the library for a glass of brandy, she retired to her room, exhausted from the events of the evening. Thoughts of sleep did nothing to ease the bitterness in her heart. Brad's untimely arrival caused more gossip than his earlier absence. Then, as if nothing was amiss, he hovered about her solicitously while his stormy gray eyes betrayed the fury he firmly restrained.

Millie just finished brushing out Beth's hair when her father rapped on the bedroom door and entered. He dismissed the maid with a toss of his head. "Bradley just left, and since you had retired, asked me to give you this birthday present. He meant to give it to you when he arrived, but under the circumstances, he forgot."

Resentment surged through her veins. "Just leave it. I'll get to it later."

He placed the diminutive package on her vanity and dropped a kiss on her brow before leaving.

Beth was tempted to throw the package away unopened, but curiosity won out. Inside was an exquisite ruby and diamond brooch fashioned in the shape of a heart to match the ring she wore on her finger. Beneath the pin, a card read, "A gift from my heart. Affectionately, Brad." She threw herself on the bed and burst into tears.

The next day developed into a waking nightmare. When Beth arrived for breakfast at the usual hour, her father had already departed to make dueling arrangements with Rolf's second. She barely started eating when the first visitors arrived, compelling her to submit to their embarrassing questions. More visitors entered before the first went away, and so it continued all morning. Beth learned how swiftly word spread around town and how quickly reputations were ruined. The horrifying truth was if Brad decided to break their engagement, she doubted any man of her acquaintance would agree to marry her.

At noon her aunt and cousin made an appearance, and future visitors were turned away at the door with the explanation that Lady Beth was about town making final wedding arrangements.

Sweetbriar

Returning home that evening, disappointment pricked when Beth discovered her father had retired early, leaving instructions not to be disturbed.

Brad and Lord Rockwell arrived separately at Hyde Park at dawn. Dew lay heavy on the ground, and foggy mists swirled in the chill air. The Honorable Judge Turner, who had reluctantly agreed to officiate, waited stoically. Rolf and Edward arrived ten minutes later.

The judge glared sternly at the viscount and the American. "I understand there is a point of honor to settle here. Before we commence, I ask you to reconsider the need for this duel and reconcile your differences."

Rolf inclined his head sharply, "Mr. Anderson insulted me before witnesses. I am obliged to defend my honor."

When Brad remained silent, Judge Turner shook his head resignedly. "Lord Rockford, are you acting as second for Mr. Anderson?" the judge asked.

"I am," he acknowledged.

"And you, Mr. Sanders. Are you acting as second for Lord Dunmore?"

"Yes, sir," Edward replied.

The official gestured toward his servant, "I brought dueling pistols as requested. Examine them carefully and load them to your own satisfaction. The recommended powder charge is thirty grains."

The seconds each examined the matching guns. The .50 caliber flintlocks were constructed of browned barrels with full black walnut stocks. Silver inlay decorated the relief carving in the fine-grained wood.

Lord Rockwell measured the powder and selected a round ball and soft cotton patch. Ramming the load home, he then used the smaller flask to prime the pan. Ensuring enough of the finer powder lay adjacent to the flash hole, he closed the frizzen. After Edward followed the same procedure, they turned toward Judge Turner and acknowledged their satisfaction with the weapons.

"Lord Dunmore and Mr. Anderson, accept your weapons and stand back to back. Take your paces to my count of ten and on command turn and fire. One... two...three...four... five...six...seven...eight...nine...te—"

Before the command to turn, his lordship spun around but slipped on the soggy grass, causing his shot to veer off course. Instead of the killing wound to the chest he intended, the bullet deflected as it passed through the heavy material of the loose cape on Brad's coat as he turned to face his opponent. It lost velocity and lodged just under the skin on his left side. Straightening from the staggering blow, Brad looked Dunmore square in the eyes and took deadly aim. Disbelieving shock spread across Rolf's face as he comprehended that his haste would cost him his life. But Brad lowered the pistol slightly as he pulled the trigger, and the bullet gouged a groove into the grass between Dunmore's feet. Wetness stained the crotch of his lordship's trousers, and his face reddened from the humiliation of losing his bladder.

"The question of honor is settled to my satisfaction," the American stated icily. Handing the still-smoking pistol to Judge Turner, Brad strode to his waiting carriage, gave instructions to the cabbie, and quit the park.

Beth was nervously entertaining Captain O'Malley when Lord Rockwell returned home. Surprised by the unexpected visit, he asked crossly, "Early for a morning call, is it not, Captain?"

"My apologies, your lordship," O'Malley said. "I heard rumors of a duel between Brad and another man. I must talk him out of this madness. He wasn't at his lodgings, and I hoped to find him here."

"Oh, father, please. What news have you of Rolf? Is he alive?" Beth pleaded for assurance. "Captain O'Malley says Brad is skilled with the pistol and I doubt Rolf has any experience with them. I couldn't bear it if he is dead on my account."

"You should not you concern yourself with the viscount!" he roared, and she cringed. "He is not your betrothed. He is nothing more than a scoundrel. If not for Anderson's sense of fair play, that villain, Dunmore, would be dead this very minute, which would serve him right."

Urgently the captain interjected, "Please your lordship, where may I find Brad?"

Dropping his shoulders in a deep sigh, the nobleman replied, "I'm sorry, I don't know. Perhaps he went to find you or maybe a doctor. He might be wounded, but I can't say for sure. He left too quickly after Dunmore's deplorable conduct this morning."

"Thank you, sir. Again, my apologies for disturbing your household so early," O'Malley bowed and left.

Milton Avery glared at his daughter. "Dunmore is a scoundrel, and your infatuation with that man has disturbed me for some time. After the events of this morning, I forbid you to associate with him. I need not remind you that shortly you will wed Bradley Anderson. Henceforth, I expect you to act accordingly." He turned on his heel, called for his breakfast to be served in his bedroom, and trudged up the stairs.

Brad slid his gaze over Louise's body, enjoying the translucent glow of her skin, so inviting to touch. Her beauty always heightened after lovemaking. He hadn't intended to make love to her when he arrived, hadn't even realized he gave her address to the cabbie.

Dazed when he left the park, he was swaying on his feet by the time he knocked on her door. Shocked at the bloodstains on his clothes, Louise quickly guided him to the kitchen, sat him in a chair, helped him out of his coat and shirt, and examined the wound. It had bled freely, then clotted, and gave the impression of being worse than it was. As she felt the bullet just under his skin, Brad groaned. After fortifying him with brandy, she removed the bullet without too much effort. He hissed through his teeth when she doused the wound with brandy before bandaging his side. Then, silently taking his hand, Louise led him to the bedroom and embraced him, offering the only comfort she knew how to give.

Noticing his gaze and feeling his gentle touch, tenderness swelled in her breast for this man she loved. "Bradley, I've felt you draw away from me for some time and suspected you intended to marry. If your betrothed returned your love, I might accept your decision, but the fact that you came to me today tells me she does not. Do you love her so much that I mean nothing to you?" Brimming tears accented her sapphire eyes and sparkled like crystals against the glow of her skin.

"In time, I hope Beth will love me. For now, it is enough that she will be my wife."

To hear the woman's name cross his lips tore at Louise's heart, but still, she wanted to be a part of his life. "Let me go to America so I can be near you if you have need of my solace," she offered.

Pounding on the front door of the house interrupted their conversation. "Bradley Anderson, open this door!" O'Malley bellowed.

Sitting up, Brad reached for his pants, flinching at the pain in his side. "I'm sorry, Louise, I shouldn't have come here today. You deserve better than what I can give you. Find yourself a husband and have children. I know that is what you want."

"I want you, Bradley," she pleaded, clutching his arm.

The pounding sounded again, "Open this door before I break it down!"

Brad shook her off, "Goodbye, Louise." He buttoned his pants and pulled on his boots, then headed for the front door before O'Malley followed through on his threat.

When Brad flung the door open, his old friend's face reddened in righteous anger at the sight of the younger man's disheveled state and bare chest. "By God, man, I should throttle you. First, you fight a duel over the woman you profess to love, and then you fornicate with your mistress!" The bloodied bandage binding Brad's waist registered in Quinn's mind. "My God, you're shot, man! How bad is it?" he asked, gripping Brad's shoulders.

"I'll live, if that's what you want to know unless you kill me for my reprehensible behavior," Brad responded. He turned back into the house to retrieve his ruined shirt and coat from the kitchen.

O'Malley followed close on his heels. His indignation returned, "I should tie you in the bilge of the ship until your wedding, is what I should do. I don't know what type of man you're turning into, but I don't like it. You dishonor your bride to say nothing of that poor lass in there," he scolded, jabbing a thumb toward the deeper regions of the cottage. "What is she supposed to do now?" Then, as a new thought tripped into his mind, he demanded hotly, "You don't intend to keep her after you're married, do you?"

There was only so much Brad would take from his friend and felt O'Malley crossed the line. With fists raised, Brad spun around. Only the stabbing pain in his side kept him from landing a punch in his mentor's face. Paling from the burning pain as much as from his aggravation, Brad lowered his fists. "I've provided for her. Gave her this house and money for a dowry," he spat through gritted teeth. "Not that it's any concern of yours." Wincing, he shrugged into his bloodied shirt and groaned out loud when O'Malley silently helped him with the coat.

"Let me take you back to the ship and have a look at that wound," Quinn offered as they walked outside. Brad nodded, and they clambered into the waiting cab.

The morning dawned clear and bright with the heady fragrance of mid-summer flowers wafting on the gentle breeze and the humming of energetic bees harmonizing with the singsong chirping of robins. Beth greeted the day with despondency. Brad with cheerful expectancy.

For all of Lady Sylvia's iron efficiency in making the hasty wedding arrangements, she wept as she drew the veil over Beth's face. Unmindful of the tears, Lady Sylvia fussed over the bride, ensuring her train spread perfectly, and her veil draped gracefully. Glancing swiftly at Mary, the matron of honor and only attendant, Sylvia made last-minute adjustments to her gown. Then she told Milton all was ready and allowed herself to be escorted to her pew.

With the first strains of the wedding march and the rustle of the guests rising, Brad turned toward the front of the church. Lady Mary glided slowly up the aisle. Long moments later, Beth appeared on her father's arm. A crown of baby's breath and rosebuds entwined the radiant hair curled atop her head. She appeared ethereal under the soft transparency of her veil. The empire gown of flowing white satin boasted long sleeves and a modest neckline, but the weight of the lengthy train pulled the gown's skirt fittingly close to her body. Brad's breath caught as if a chicken bone was stuck fast in his throat, and his heart labored in his chest as Beth, virginal and seductive, glided toward him.

The ceremony was agony, the closeness of the veil suffocating. Feeling faint, Beth's mind retreated. Dimly she heard the priest clear his throat.

"Lady Beth," he whispered, "if you intend to wed Mr. Anderson, please say 'I do.'"

Swallowing the hysterical laughter bubbling in her chest, Beth spoke the appropriate words, oblivious that her near-hysteria gave her the appearance of smiling joyfully.

An answering smile spread over Brad's face and glowed in his eyes as he took Beth for his wife.

Aware the wedding festivities would continue well into the night; Brad had reserved the finest rooms in London's most exclusive hotel. After the reception, they would be driven over in his lordship's closed carriage.

The congratulatory toasting continued for over an hour following the seven-course dinner. Brad wanted to slip away shortly after the first waltz but discovered every man present requesting a dance of the bride. By seven o'clock, the groom doubted he and Beth would ever visit their bridal suite unless he intervened. Recognizing the closing stanza of a cotillion, Brad impatiently strode onto the ballroom floor, swept his bride up into his arms, and marched from the room. Quickly recovering from their initial astonishment, the amused guests rushed after the couple, sending them on their way in a shower of rice.

With a struggling bride cradled in his arms, Brad stepped into the carriage and heard Quinn O'Malley exclaim, "By Jove, man, you should have done that hours ago."

Settling with Beth on his lap, Brad was surprised when she immediately disentangled herself from his arms and stood before him. "How dare you humiliate me? Everyone will talk about your vulgar behavior!" she cried furiously. The carriage lurched forward, throwing her into his arms again.

Brad laughed, "Oh Beth, you enchant me," and leaned in to kiss her.

Further infuriated, she slapped his face, and from his expression, feared violent retribution.

But he eyed her reproachfully. Then unexpectedly drew her close and kissed her, lovingly possessing her mouth. Beth held no control over the rapid beating of her heart or the wild fluttering in her stomach. An unfamiliar yearning tingled through her body as his hands glided over her, stroking, caressing. Enthralled by their rising passion, neither noticed the motionless carriage until the coachman tapped politely on the door and announced, "Sir and madam, you've arrived."

Blushing deeply, Beth allowed her husband to hand her out and escort her into the hotel. At the doorway to their suite, he swept her into his arms again and carried her through the sitting room directly into the bedroom, where he deposited her on the bed. "I'll entertain myself with a glass of brandy while you prepare for bed, sweet Beth. If you are terribly inconvenienced for lack of your maid, my services are at your disposal." When she didn't respond, he bowed and turned to leave.

"Bradley!" she shrieked, nervously clenching and unclenching the skirt of her gown. Then she cleared her throat to gain control of her voice, "May I have a servant to attend to my toilette? The buttons of my dress are in the back, and I should never be able to—"

"I'm your husband now," he quietly interrupted, "and am perfectly capable of helping you unbutton your dress." When he took her hand and raised her to her feet, her eyes widened. "Why are you frightened? I'm not going to hurt you. Not intentionally, at least."

Her eyes flared. "What do you mean, 'not intentionally'?" she whispered.

Eying her curiously, he gently asked, "You do know what happens when a woman loses her virginity, don't you?"

Flushing, she cast her eyes down and shook her head, too embarrassed to speak or look at her husband. The way he fondled her in the carriage gave her the impression that something more physical would ensue, but she had no clear idea to what extent.

"Didn't your aunt or your cousin talk to you about this?" Again, she shook her head. Brad shifted uncomfortably and heaved a sigh. He placed his fingers under Beth's chin and tilted her face, gazing intently into the depths of her eyes. Her guileless innocence gave his conscience a twinge of unease as he asked himself what it was like to bed a virgin. Again, he sighed then quietly promised, "Beth, I give you my word, I shall be a considerate lover. Will you trust that I will be as gentle as possible and believe it is my desire to give you pleasure in our marriage bed?"

Nervously she ran her tongue over her lips to moisten them, unaware of the provocative nature of the gesture. "I'll try," she whispered.

Watching her, burning desire flared in Brad's loins. He lowered his mouth, covering her parted lips. As he drew her into his arms, he lightly sucked Beth's lower lip into his mouth and then slowly released it, scraping it through his teeth. Her body quivered, and he deepened the kiss.

Without breaking their embrace, Brad unbuttoned the back of her wedding dress. He loosened the bodice, and his lips burned a trail to her ear, then along her neck and across her shoulder as the gown slid from her arms. The bodice fell away from her torso as the last button loosened. The sheerest lawn chemise barely obscured her body and did nothing to conceal her arousal. When Brad bent lower and sucked a taut nipple through the delicate fabric, she whimpered as she tangled her fingers in his hair, weak from the delicious sensations he awakened.

Pushing the dress over her hips and discarding it, Brad lifted her in his arms and placed her on the bed. His green eyes burned brightly as he gazed at her disheveled beauty.

Embarrassed, she covered her breasts with her arms.

"Don't cover yourself, sweet Beth," he softly commanded.

But she sobbed and turned her back to him, drawing her knees up. Hearing him disrobe, she squeezed her eyes tightly shut.

Brad sat on the bed for a minute, then lay beside his wife, placed a hand on her shoulder, and gently turned her onto her back. He lightly kissed her closed eyes, then her lips. As he explored her mouth, he took her hand, uncurled her fingers, and placed her palm on his chest.

Her eyes flew open and she gasped, snatching her hand away.

Quietly he chided, "Don't pull away, love. I want you to touch me."

With her eyes locked on his, Beth hesitantly placed her hand on his chest. The hair felt crisp and sensual as her palm lightly brushed across his firm muscles, surprising her. They kissed again. The growing heat suffusing Beth's body flared when Brad gently slid his hand under her chemise and rolled her taut nipple between his thumb and fingers.

He shifted and drew his wife across his chest, then easily wrested the chemise over her head and off her arms. She thrilled to the feel of her bare breasts against

Sweetbriar

his chest. As his tongue plundered her mouth, his hands continued their fiery exploration. Then he shifted his weight again and suckled at her breast.

Beth breathed his name as desire engulfed her.

The ribbon fastening her lower undergarment loosened, and Brad slid his hand on the flesh of her hip. Gathering her close, he turned her onto her side and pressed the hardness of his manhood against her. His hands caressed her bare buttocks. His fingers traced the seam of her bottom, then slid down her thigh and drew her leg over his hip. Now he touched and teased the lips of her womanhood, moist but not yet adequately aroused for his entry. He tugged the undergarment off her legs, shifting her onto her back again. He stopped his ministrations, then ran his hands through her hair and gazed at her flushed face.

Her breathing slowed, and she became aware of his scrutiny. Opening her eyes, she whispered, "Why are you looking at me?"

"My sweet Beth, you are so beautiful, why shouldn't I look at you?" he murmured huskily. Then taking the hand she still rested on his chest, guided it lower. She felt the firm muscles of his abdomen, and then he curled her fingers around his engorged organ. She tried to pull away, but his hand held hers firmly in place. "It would give me great pleasure to have you stroke me," he said as he gently thrust. "Just lightly grasp me with your hand," he instructed, then released her hand and gently thrust again. She squeezed him lightly, unsure of what to do. "Oh, yes. That's good," he groaned against her mouth and thrust again.

Stroking his hand over her breasts and down her stomach, Brad twined his fingertips in the nest of curls above her thighs. His fingers found the nub of her womanhood. He massaged her slowly at first, then more vigorously as her hips undulated. His mouth left hers to taste her neck and shoulders. She moaned in pleasure. He could feel her wetness now and knew she neared an ecstasy she didn't yet know existed. Moving lower, his lips found her breasts, and his tongue tantalized her nipples. Her hips thrust with every ragged breath. He nipped at her, and she cried out. Her body tensing as an exquisite release exploded within her.

Beth's body melted into the featherbed, and Brad moved over her, kneeing her thighs apart. "I've wanted this since the first moment I saw you, Beth," he breathed in her ear. Slowly, he intruded upon her entrance but was hindered by her maidenhead. He clasped her hands over her head, entwining their fingers, and covered her mouth in a deep, passionate kiss. Then he buried his face in her hair and thrust deep.

Shrieking in pain, she struggled against him, sobbing in anguish.

"Hush, Beth, hush. Lie still, you're only making it worse," Brad crooned in her ear. "Hush, lie still, it won't hurt for long."

His words penetrated her pain, and she quieted, but tears streamed from her eyes. He released her hands, and supporting himself on his elbows, brushed the tears from her face. He kissed her lips gently, then her tear-spiked eyelashes.

She opened her eyes and stared into her husband's face, comprehending his concern.

"Are you all right, Beth? Is the pain lessening?"

Hitching a sob, she nodded and in a small, broken voice replied, "Yes, it's better, I shall be fine. Will it always be like this, Brad?"

His eyes blazed with desire. "No, sweet Beth, just this once. From now on, I can only give you pleasure." He shifted slightly to gauge her reaction, and she winced. "I haven't slackened my desires yet, but if you are still in pain, I'll withdraw and leave you be tonight.

Sweetbriar

But if you think you can bear it, I'd like to move inside you." His strained voice confirmed his need for her.

The emotion on his face and in his voice knotted her throat. Unable to speak, she instead caressed his cheek and offered him her lips.

A groan escaped his mouth as his lips met hers. He moved slowly, fearful of hurting her further. She responded and moved in sync with his thrusts. She broke their kiss and nibbled at his earlobe, driving him into a frenzy.

He thrust faster and deeper, arousing his young bride's passions. Time passed as they climbed toward the pinnacle, and in shattering cries of ecstasy, tumbled together into the abyss.

The next day Beth wondered if many nights would be like her wedding night. After their initial coupling, Brad awakened her twice during the night to slacken his need, then again, this morning. And she learned that each time could be different.

She had fallen asleep in his arms with her head nestled in the hollow of his shoulder, floating on a blissful cloud. When she awoke, he whispered that he was her stallion and wanted her to ride him. He lifted her astride his hard shaft. She was grateful the candles had guttered, and the velvety cloak of darkness concealed her wanton response. That wild and rapturous ride shattered her world, leaving her adrift in a void without time or substance.

The next time she awoke, Brad lay snuggled at her back with his arms encircling her, fondling her breasts. He kissed her shoulder and neck, and as he made love to her, kneaded the nub of her womanhood with his fingers. The floating ecstasy became an exhilarating crash of brutal seas upon the rocky headland of their joining. Then, lying breathlessly on its shore, consciousness dissipated into the oblivion of a deep and dreamless slumber.

In the morning when he reached for her, she grumbled about the soreness she felt, and Brad showed her how to please him with her hands while he returned the favor. Afterward, he confided to her that there were many other ways of experiencing pleasure as husband and wife, and that over time, he would teach her. She assumed he expected an enthusiastic pupil.

Chagrined at breakfast by her ravishing hunger and the laughing glint in Brad's eyes as he watched her eat, Beth noted his healthy appetite as well. With the long journey to Rockwell manor ahead, she set her embarrassment aside and ate heartily.

That night, after being jostled in the carriage for hours, all Beth wanted was a soft bed and a good night's sleep. The bed was soft, and her sleep was deep.

But it was intermittently interrupted by her husband's caresses.

Although Brad had anticipated staying only a week, they remained a month in the country, taking leisurely strolls through the countryside, visiting with the neighbors, and taking pleasure in each other. Beth set aside her apprehensions about the future and lived each day with carefree abandon.

Toward the end of their stay, Brad surprised her with an alfresco luncheon for two in Beth's favorite meadow. He lounged beside her and playfully fed her tender morsels and tidbits, liberally interspersed with lingering kisses and affectionate caresses. As the sun lowered in the western sky, he took her hand and led her into the concealing shelter of the trees where they made love. The burbling stream, the twittering birds, and the sweet fragrance of the crushed grass mingled with the ecstasy they shared and brought Beth the most exquisite joy. Afterward, she wept against her husband's chest, and for the first time, professed her love for him.

Exulting deep in his heart, Brad held her close and gently stroked her hair, murmuring soothing assurances of his eternal love and devotion.

And for a time, Beth was content.

Late Summer 1809, England

The newlyweds returned to London, to the Rockwell home, with scant fanfare. It was the off social season of family holidays to the country or ocean beaches, and there was scarce to occupy Beth's time or thoughts but preparations for the terrifying voyage to a savage land across the sea. Not reconciled to leaving England, she repeatedly pleaded with Brad to remain until spring. He steadfastly refused, patiently explaining time and again his apprehension over the tumultuous political situation between their two countries and the need for his return. Her anxiety increased each day until she detested her husband for being American. As her resentment grew, she dreaded the nights he reached for her and despised her body for responding to his touch. She became morose, and Brad avoided her by spending time at the docks or aboard ship.

Two weeks passed, then Captain O'Malley joined them for breakfast one morning. He had delayed sailing for as long as possible, he explained, and announced his intention of getting underway that afternoon. The day of their departure had arrived.

From the first moment Beth set foot on board ship, she felt queasy. After the quietude of the country, the clamorous and disorderly bustle of the London docks grated on her nerves. The tangy air of the river provided small relief from the odors of rotting garbage, unwashed bodies, and tar. Especially the tar. Decidedly sick by the time they reached open seas, she couldn't decide which was worse, the small stuffy cabin with its smell of lamp oil and tar or the rolling of the horizon when on deck. Daily she prayed for the blessed relief of sleep but, in her illness, even that eluded her. Unable to eat, or retain anything she attempted to eat, Beth lost weight at an alarming rate.

At first, Brad chided her for her poor seamanship, but after a week, he grew apprehensive. He asked the cook to prepare a tray of hardtack and cheese and took it to her in the cabin, urging her to eat. But she weakly declined. Unable to remain silent, Brad broached the topic of his concern. "Beth, you need to eat. I'm concerned for you, and I'm also concerned about the baby."

Perplexed, Beth asked, "What baby? I don't understand."

Picking his wife up and settling her in his lap Brad shared his private thought, "Sweet Beth, we've been married seven weeks now, and you've not bled. I can only assume you are with child."

Distressed that he should mention such a private subject, Beth buried her head in her husband's shoulder, sluggishly calculating the passage of time and cursing her lightheadedness. At length, she determined her husband was correct because nine weeks had passed since her last menses.

Muffled against his neck, Beth exclaimed, "Oh, Brad! What am I to do?" and burst into tears.

Piteously she wailed while Brad held her, tenderly stroking her hair and crooning softly to her as if she were a lost child. After a time, she calmed, and from sheer exhaustion, fell wearily asleep in his arms.

At twilight, she awoke. Brad slept, still cradling her. Beth lightly kissed the corner of his mouth and tried to ease herself off his lap, but he tightened his arms.

Opening one eye, he smiled, "Did you sleep well?"

She smiled back, "Yes, and it appears you did, too."

Sweetbriar

"Hush, woman," he said mockingly, "Don't you recognize a man deep in thought when you see one?"

"You can't fool me, Brad, you were sound asleep."

"I was only daydreaming about having a baby in the house," he stated lightheartedly. Then on a serious note, he inquired, "And talking about babies, how do you feel?"

Beth thought for a moment before replying, "I feel better, and the uneasiness in my stomach is not quite so persistent. The sleep did me good. Perhaps some fresh air and a hot cup of tea will help."

"Fresh air will help, no doubt of that," Brad partially agreed, "but you need to be able to keep solid food down before ingesting any liquids. After you eat the hardtack and cheese, I'll see if Cook has warm broth. If a cup agrees with you, I'll have him add barley and vegetables for a more nourishing soup."

Brad carried Beth out onto the deck. The night was dim, illuminated only by the full moon, misted by high, thin clouds. Without the horizon dipping and swaying in the distance, Beth enjoyed her meal of hardtack and cheese followed by chicken barley soup. She surprised Brad by the quantity she consumed over the course of the night.

For a while, Captain O'Malley conversed with them and suggested Beth take her main nourishment on deck at night while the horizon was veiled from sight and sleep during the day since food didn't agree with her then.

That started a new regime for Beth. Long enchanted nights on deck conversing with Brad and various officers while the fresh salt air whet her appetite. She ate numerous small meals in the hours of darkness and then slept during the day with the gentle roll of the ship soothing her slumber.

Over the next three weeks, Beth's health improved. As the combination of seasickness and morning sickness subsided, she gained weight, though the discomfort of swollen ankles and feet replaced her previous illness. She relieved this by traipsing around deck barefoot. Conscious such blatant behavior could not be condoned; she gradually enjoyed the secret of her unconventional freedom more each night. With her skirts trailing about her feet, she was convinced no one noticed but didn't realize her husband, along with the captain and officers, were bemused by her unexpected performance, chalking it up to the eccentricities of a woman in the family way.

As the wind stiffened, the sea acquired a rough chop, and storm clouds showed their billowy heads on the horizon. All hands turned to secure the ship in anticipation of the inevitable blow, except for one seasoned seaman who stood watch in the crow's nest. Captain O'Malley ordered maximum canvas in the hope of outracing the approaching tempest.

Concerned, Quinn stopped Brad as he came on deck after looking in on Beth. "How's the young missus holding up in this weather? With full canvas, it's rough but not near as rough as it will be if we find ourselves in the middle of that squall. It's a widowmaker if I ever saw one."

Slapping him on the back, Brad smiled, "Don't worry about Beth, she's sleeping soundly. You just keep us ahead of that storm, and we won't have to worry about Beth or the widow maker."

Quinn heartily replied, "That I intend to do, laddie. Neptune himself can't stop us now, or my name's not Quinn O'Malley."

No sooner did the words escape his mouth than the ship heavily shuddered as it yawed. A commotion broke out forward as one of the two cannons careened across the deck, pinning a crewman against the gunwale as he screamed in agony. Brad and O'Malley fought against the heaving deck heedless of men scrambling in all directions. The ship pitched again, causing the big gun to again slam against the sagging sailor, cruelly crushing the life from him.

"Anderson! See to that cannon before someone else gets hurt!" The captain yelled above the tumult.

"Grab those lines, men!" Brad called, as the ship righted herself. "Heave to. She's coming back. Work with the roll. Work dammit, heave to!" Minutes dragged by as they struggled against the lurching of the lumbering cannon as it careened back and forth with the lunging roll of the ship in the tossing waves. Minutes passed as they strained against the ropes holding the cannon. "We almost have it now, men. Pull! Pull!" At last, the behemoth slid back into position. "That's good, men. Tie her down."

With the cannon secured, Bradley, panting and sweating, lurched toward O'Malley and the injured seaman. "How is he?" Brad asked, "Does he have a chance to pull through?"

Standing, Quinn shook his head and flatly stated, "No, he's dead. And it's my fault. I shouldn't have tempted the fates with my rash words."

Anger suffused Brad's face as he stood facing his friend. "This was an accident, nothing more," he ground out harshly. "What you said had no part in it. Understand, Quinn. It was just an accident."

Momentarily they stood transfixed, eyes locked. Then Quinn shifted his gaze to the approaching storm clouds. "Aye, laddie, it was just an accident," he whispered, unbelieving.

"I'll get him below. The sailmaker won't be able to make a shroud until after the storm." The captain nodded, and Brad snagged a sailor to help take the dead man below.

After stowing the body in a corner of the crews' hold, Brad looked in on Beth. She had been flung about the small cabin and wailed uncontrollably. He didn't have time to calm her fears. Every hand was needed on deck. Picking her up from the floor, he helped her to the bunk. "I'm needed above. I'm sorry I can't stay with you, Beth, but I can tie you onto the bunk, so you won't toss about."

She clutched at him and screamed hysterically, "Don't leave me! I don't want to die alone!" Then she started slapping and hitting him in panic. "I knew if I left England, I would die! You did this to me!"

Her frenzy unnerved Brad. He tried to grab her hands, but she was too quick as she rained blows about his head. He shook her shoulders as she continued her attack. Finally, in desperation, he slapped her face.

The shock brought her to her senses. She stopped beating at him, but the terror was stark on her face. "I hate you!" she spat.

"Beth, please, let me tie you onto the bunk. You'll be safe from injury." He rummaged under the bunk and pulled out a length of hemp rope. Forcing her to lie down, he tied her torso securely, leaving her arms and legs free. "I'm sorry, Beth. They need me on deck. Please understand this is the best I can do for now." He tried to kiss her, but she turned her face away. "I'll return when I can. Try to stay calm," he said, then left.

Beth never forgot the horror of those long hours as the ship yawed and pitched on the furious seas. Brad returned a few times, but she wouldn't face him. He never stayed long, just long enough to reassure himself she was still safely tied in place. For a while, she vaguely heard men shouting as they battled the wind, then the leading edge of the tempest broke over them. The hysteria didn't return, but her terror grew as evening approached. Between the dense clouds and the deepening night, all light faded from the tiny room.

The wailing wind whistled through the rigging as the ship lurched and rolled in the roiling waves and the cloudburst pelted the portlight and luminescent flashes flickered for dazzling moments casting faint shadows in the tiny room followed by despondent darkness and the rumbling growl of thunder and gusts howled and rain slashed in the inky gloom splintered by blinding bolts and barking blasts and pitch blackness as the squall screamed and shrieked in fury, and the ship trembled and shuddered in the cresting waters and the deluge slapped a steady staccato and fire bolts crashed and cracked a continuous cacophony that shattered the ominous hours with rumblings that ruptured and reverberated in the restless exhaustion of night.

The only illumination came from the increasingly frequent flashes of lightning as rain pelted the portlight. At one point, Brad came into the cabin and sat by Beth, dripping cold water.

"Will you please light the lantern so I can see? It's more frightening in the dark," she said in a small disembodied voice as thunder rumbled.

"I'm sorry it's too dangerous in these rough seas. If the lantern smashed, a fire might start. But I can sit with you for a while. The sails are furled, and now it's just a matter of riding out the storm." He held her hand.

"Will we come through this?" she asked.

"No reason why not," he replied. "Captain O'Malley is experienced and has a capable crew. I'm more concerned about you than the storm."

"Is it often like this?"

"It's not uncommon, but we had hoped to avoid the beginning of the storm season," Brad explained. "It arrived early this year. We probably should have set sail a fortnight before we did. O'Malley was ready, but I wanted you to have as much time with your family as possible, so I urged him to delay. I'm sorry, Beth, I never meant to put you in danger."

Frustration and anger rose in her voice, "How can you say that, Bradley Anderson! Just taking me to America puts me in danger!"

Her irrational declaration started him, "What do you mean? How does taking you to America put you in danger?"

"Why, the Indian savages, of course! I never forgot the stories you told us at Rockwell Manor when we visited for my fifteenth birthday." Her voice raised a notch. "I promised myself I would never leave the safety of my homeland. Now here I am in the middle of the Atlantic Ocean, tied to a bed in the hopes we'll survive this storm, knowing worse is to come as soon as we sight land," she wailed.

Her disclosure stunned Brad. "Is that why you kept refusing to marry me? Because of some Indian stories I told? Beth, they were just tall tales. Over on the frontier, the Indians are warlike, but at home, we rarely see any. We'll live in a city, much like London, only smaller. The few Indians that come to town want to trade, not pillage and kill." If his wife hadn't been tied to the bunk, Brad would have lifted her into his arms. Instead, he slid to his knees beside her and brushed the hair away from her face. "Sweet Beth, you'll be perfectly safe." He showered small, comforting kisses on her tear-stained cheeks.

She brought her hands up to cradle his face. "Is this the truth, Brad?" she asked, wishing she could observe his face to determine his sincerity.

"I vow to you it's the truth," he said gravely.

"Oh, Brad," she cried in relief. "If it's the truth, I shan't dread living in America. I shall be happy as your wife." And she kissed him with all the love she held in her heart.

Fall 1809, America

The staccato rap on the door diverted Governor William Harrison from his perusal of President Madison's most recent missive. "Come," he ordered curtly.

Colonel Michaels briskly marched to the front of the desk and saluted smartly. "You sent for me, sir."

"Yes, Michaels," Harrison said as he tossed the President's letter on the desk. "It appears our new President is concerned about the tactic I used to negotiate the treaty for the three million acres in the Illinois and Indiana regions."

"I don't know why he should be concerned, sir. The Kickapoo and Wea are the primary inhabitants of the area, but the treaty included the Delaware, Eel River, Miami, and Pottawatomie tribes as well."

"He doesn't like that I negotiated the treaties with the tribes willing to sell the land, then used them to influence the other tribes to acquiesce. But I was sent here to get land to satisfy the insatiable thirst of the multitudes wanting to settle out here, and that is what I intend to accomplish," the governor asserted. "How much progress has been made on the land around the Wabash River?"

"The Pottawatomie, Eel River and Miami tribes accepted the initial payments and the large subsidies you promised at Fort Wayne. But the Miami were opposed to the treaty and weren't happy that the Wea were excluded from the powwow," the colonel stated. "Apparently, the Pottawatomie chiefs pressured the Miami to accept the treaty in reciprocity for the Potawatomie's previous acceptance of treaties that hadn't been as advantageous."

"Then, over the winter months, we had better obtain acceptance from the Wea. Promise them even greater subsidies, if necessary, to convince the Kickapoo to accept the treaty." Harrison ordered. "Acquiescence by the Kickapoo is imperative because they are closely allied with the Shawnee."

"Why not just include the Shawnee in the negotiations?"

Glancing sharply at the colonel, Harrison scathingly replied, "Because the Miami war chief, Little Turtle, convinced the Shawnee to vacate the area if you understand what I mean. If we include the Shawnee now, it could aggravate the Miami, who as you mentioned, were opposed to the treaty."

"If you don't mind my saying so, sir, I think it is a mistake to exclude the Shawnee," Colonel Michaels advised.

"I do mind you saying so," snapped the governor. "Forget the Shawnee."

But excluding the Shawnee was a mistake.

Chapter VI
Early Winter 1810, America

Dr. Rutherford arrived at Anna Louise Jetter's cottage; grateful the New Year's cold snap had moderated. Uneasy about taking a woman pregnant in her eighth month on a two-hour journey, he was relieved it wasn't snowing anymore. As he clambered from the sleigh, Anna Louise appeared in the doorway.

"Good day, Dr. Rutherford. I packed a small valise to get me by for three or four days, as you instructed. I boxed all the rest up, and it's ready for shipment. After all this work, I hope the lady of the house finds me suitable."

"I'm sure she will, Mrs. Jetter. As I told you, she is homesick and needs someone from her own country to perk her up. And she insists on having a wet nurse, says it is a common practice in England."

"Only among the upper crust," Anna Louise commented as the doctor helped her into the sleigh. "We commoners nurse our babies."

"Be that as it may, I'm sure you will get along fine. Now settle yourself comfortably. It will be a long ride.

Here's a lap robe, I want you to stay warm. We can always stop at a roadside inn if you start to feel a chill," he instructed.

"Thank you, doctor. I'm sure I will be just fine. In fact, I'm excited today has finally arrived and to be on my way."

As he flicked the reins, he cautioned, "Don't get so excited you cause that baby to give us trouble. I want you to sit back and relax. Try to sleep. I'll awaken you in plenty of time to refresh yourself."

"I will try, but I doubt it will do much good," she sighed. "The baby's movements are so robust it doesn't allow me to get much sleep at all." Dutifully, Anna Louise sat back, closing her eyes.

Almost two hours later, Dr. Rutherford gently nudged her, "Mrs. Jetter, are you awake? We'll be arriving soon."

Sleepily, she opened her eyes. "My apologies, Dr. Rutherford, I must have dozed off for a few minutes," she said, stretching politely. "Have we traveled far?" Looking around, she saw the changed landscape. They were traversing an expansive open meadow. On the rise, in the near distance, stood a large colonial house with smoke emitting from its numerous chimneys.

The doctor chuckled, "You needed the rest, but we shall arrive soon. I thought you'd like to rub the sleep from your eyes. That's the Anderson house just up ahead."

"And who are the Andersons?" Anna Louise asked in alarm.

"Charles and Suzanne Anderson. You will stay with them," he replied.

Sighing in relief, she sat back. "Suzanne. I like that. If she's as cheerful as her name, I am sure we will get along quite well."

"I do not doubt that. The senior Mrs. Anderson is a truly charming woman. But you will only remain here a few days until we ascertain your position is secure with the young Mrs. Anderson. With you due so soon, I'll feel better knowing a woman experienced in childbirth is close at hand," he explained.

"The young Mrs. Anderson?" Anna Louise queried.

"Yes, Beth is married to Bradley Anderson, the son of Charles and Suzanne."

"I see," she choked out as panic seized her throat. "And the younger Mrs. Anderson wants the wet nurse and companion?"

"Yes, she is due to give birth about two or three weeks after you. Young Anderson disappointed quite a few matrons in the vicinity when he brought her back from England this past fall. More than one mother had her eye on him as a prospective son-in-law. Needless to say, Beth Anderson wasn't received with open arms by a lot of people, regardless of her heritage. Her father is a nobleman of some sort. But mostly, her delicate condition has isolated her from society, so she will welcome your companionship."

Anna Louise scarcely heard a word Dr. Rutherford said. The horrible fact that she might find herself living in Bradley's home abhorred her. How could she be a companion to his wife, especially when she was big with child? His child! Worse than that, how could she ever face Bradley? As the memory of their last two times together flashed clearly in her mind, her heart sank.

She had known of his impending marriage, having read the banns in the *Gazette*. The despair of losing him caused her to trick him into impregnating her. At least at the time, she had hoped for a pregnancy, obliging him to provide for her and the child. Then, when he so generously gave her the house and money for a dowry, she regretted her actions. But what was done was done.

With a baby growing inside her, it was too late to find a husband. When the solicitor explained that her benefactor would not return to England, she instructed him to sell the cottage. Immigrating to America, Anna Louise had hoped to start life anew by passing herself off as the widow Jetter.

It had been the local midwife who mentioned Dr. Rutherford's search for a nursemaid and companion for one of his patients, and to Anna Louise, it had seemed an ideal situation. Shortly after she met Dr. Rutherford, he arranged for her to meet the expectant mother. Anna Louise couldn't very well ask the good doctor to turn the sleigh around now. Not without a reasonable explanation. An explanation impossible to provide as the sleigh halted in front of the house. Inconceivably, Anna Louise realized she must go through an interview with the Anderson women.

At their knock, a young servant girl admitted them and led them to a parlor where a group of women busily sewed and knitted. Handing her cloak to the young maid, Anna Louise took the proffered chair, sitting close to the fire. The elder Mrs. Anderson, a lovely fiftyish matron, introduced her two married daughters, Katie Tully and Sarah Barker, the latter obviously pregnant, then the younger Mrs. Anderson, who appeared genuinely pleased to meet her fellow countrywoman.

Dr. Rutherford declined refreshment, excused himself, and departed.

While Katie poured tea and passed around the cups and saucers, Beth asked, "In what area of England did you reside, Mrs. Jetter?"

"London, ma'am," she replied.

"That's delightful. I come from London, also. Perhaps it is ridiculous for me to expect us to know any of the same people, but we should try to find out if we do," Beth suggested.

Not wanting to engage in a game of 'do you know' with the wife of her ex-lover and fearful of making a connection sooner or later, Anna Louise demurred, "I'm sure I don't know any of the same people you know, milady. I am just a shop keeper's daughter."

Surprised to hear the respectful form of address, Beth smiled, "What makes you address me as 'milady'? Here in America, I am Mrs. Anderson."

Glancing around the room at the other women, Anna Louise blushed, "Dr. Rutherford mentioned you were the daughter of a nobleman."

Coming to stand next to their guest, Beth took her hands. "Yes, the Earl of Rockwell is my father, and the last time I saw him, he still worked at his import-export business. So, you see, we aren't so very different, you and I," she said with a smile. "I think we will get along fine, Anna Louise."

"If you say so, milady," she murmured.

"I do say so, and I insist you call me Beth. We shall become great friends. As much as I love my mother-in-law and sisters-in-law," she indicated the other women in the room, "the truth is, my husband and I live in the city, so we don't see his family very often."

Anna Louise shifted uncomfortably in her chair, "Milady, it would be unseemly for me to address you by your given name."

"All right, then you may address me as Mrs. Anderson. Do you wish for me to refer to you as Mrs. Jetter?" Beth inquired formally.

"Oh, no, milady . . . I mean Mrs. Anderson, if it pleases you, you may use my given name," she allowed.

"Thank you, Anna Louise. You have such a lovely name. Now, instead of staying here, why don't you come home with me tomorrow? I've made up my mind. You shall do wonderfully," Beth enthused.

But Anna Louise declined to commit. "I think you should discuss this with your husband before I consider moving my things into your home. He may not consider me an appropriate choice at all. You know nothing about me, Mrs. Anderson."

"Is there something about you I should know that would make me believe Mr. Anderson would not approve of you?" she teased.

Anna Louise fidgeted with her skirts as she glanced around the room at the other women, all alert to the conversation.

Attuned to the discomfort of their guest, Suzanne offered, "Why don't you show Mrs. Jetter to her room where you can talk more privately."

Agreeing, Beth placed her teacup on the table and escorted Anna Louise up the stairs.

In the small guest room, Beth crossed to the window, gazing out as she asked, "Why are you concerned my husband might find you unsuitable as nursemaid and companion?" When she received no answer, Beth turned, and sizing the woman up, persisted gently, "You can tell me your secret, Anna Louise. It will be safe with me."

Shaking her head, Anna Louise stood silently with tears threatening. How could she possibly tell Mrs. Anderson that she was pregnant with her husband's child?

Misunderstanding the woman's reluctance, Beth offered, "Is it because you never married your baby's father?"

Vainly she tried to swallow a sob and choked as tears trickled from her eyes.

Beth guided her to the bed, sitting beside her, patting her hand. "There, there. Don't let it concern you. As far as I'm concerned, you are Mrs. Jetter now and forever. Don't worry about my husband. He rarely refuses

Sweetbriar

me anything, and when I tell him how much I like you, I know he will welcome you into our household."

Anna Louise threw herself onto the pillows and sobbed while Beth soothingly patted her shoulder. When she calmed, Anna Louise sat up, "I will remain here until after your husband has met me. Only if he approves will I join your household."

Beth frowned, confused by the woman's continued hesitation, "Very well. I expect my husband to return tomorrow. He has been away to the capital to meet with the governor. You and my in-laws will dine with us tomorrow evening."

"Very well, Mrs. Anderson," she agreed meekly.

"Then dry your face, and let's rejoin the others. I'm sure they want to get to know you."

Anna Louise nodded and brushed the tears from her face. Taking a calming breath, she followed Beth from the room.

The next day Beth returned home to prepare for her husband's arrival. Eager to tell him her exciting news, and hearing his voice in the yard below, she hurried to meet him as he entered the house. "Oh, Brad, I've so much news to tell you. Dr. Rutherford has been so sweet and kind. He found a wet nurse. Best of all, she is an Englishwoman and will make me a wonderful companion."

Taking his wife into his arms, Brad kissed her to silence. "Is this any way to greet your husband after two long weeks, sweet Beth? I've missed you, so can you spare the time to say, 'I love you and thought you would never return' before talking about nursemaids?" Brad asked teasingly.

"Brad, you know I love you, and I have missed you beyond belief," Beth said, holding him as close as her rounded midriff would allow. "But this is so important to me. Anna Louise is such a well-mannered woman. Both your mother and I are quite taken with her, and I know you will like her, too."

"I'm sure I will," he said, "But right now, all I can think about is a hot bath. Please have the servants heat some water."

"I've already taken care of it. You go upstairs, and I'll have the water brought up."

Half an hour later, Brad rose out of the bathwater, and Beth took a moment to slyly admire his body before handing him a towel. "Darling, I hope you don't mind, but I've invited your parents and Anna Louise to dinner tonight." Brad groaned. "She was adamant about meeting you before allowing me to retain her services, even though I assured her you would acquiesce to my wishes. She is due to give birth within a month, so I feel it is essential she settle with us as soon as possible.

"You know my mother and sisters never used a wet nurse, but if you want one, that is fine with me. If you are satisfied with this woman, I have no objections. I had hoped for a quiet, relaxing evening after traveling all day," he grumbled, "but since that is not to be, I had better dress."

"Let me help," Beth offered, walking to the wardrobe to select a suit and shirt.

While Brad dressed, Beth fidgeted on the bed. "Our guests will arrive soon, and I want to discuss something with you beforehand." He mumbled an acknowledgment as he draped his cravat around his neck. "As wonderful as your mother and sisters have been, I am still lonely."

"Yes, I know. After your confinement, you will have more opportunities to socialize," he assured her.

Hesitantly studying him, she continued, "You don't know how much I enjoyed chatting with Anna Louise.

Sweetbriar

She has a delightful way of speaking, and for a while, I felt as if I were home again."

Brad's hands stilled. Quietly he commented, "If by 'home' you mean England, I can understand and if this woman brings you so much pleasure, then by all means, engage her services. But please remember this is your home now, not London."

"You misunderstand me," she objected with exasperation bleeding into her voice.

"Then what do you mean?" he asked, testily wrestling with the neckcloth. "I said whatever makes you happy is agreeable to me."

Turning away from him because of her embarrassment, Beth shyly expounded, "But you don't understand, and I don't know how to say this politely. She calls herself Mrs. Jetter...."

"Are you trying to tell me this woman will soon give birth to a child without the sanction of marriage?" he asked humorously. Apprehensively, Beth nodded, and Brad chuckled, "Sweet Beth, do you take me for a simpleton? Why else would a young, companionable woman be willing to accept a position as a nursemaid? I presume her lover deserted her, but I trust your judgment. After all, women know best in these matters."

"Thank you, Brad. I like her so much," Beth said with relief. "Now you best hurry, I hear sleigh bells, our guests are arriving." She rose and rushed happily from the room.

As Brad entered the parlor, his smile died, and anger flamed as hot as the fires of hell in his eyes as he recognized Louise chatting with his wife and parents. Beth hastened to his side, looping her arm through his, "Dear, I'd like you to meet Anna Louise Jetter. Anna Louise, this is my husband, Bradley Anderson."

Avoiding his stony countenance, Anna Louise murmured, "I'm pleased to meet you, Mr. Anderson."

Extricating his arm from his wife's grasp, Brad clasped his arms over his chest to keep from bodily removing the woman from his home. "Anna Louise Jetter?" he repeated harshly.

Peering at him nervously, Anna Louise nodded, quietly confirming, "Yes, Mr. Anderson, that is my full given name."

"I see. And you are prepared to come into this household and act as nursemaid to *my* child and companion to *my* wife. Is that correct?" he snapped.

Taken aback by his rudeness, Suzanne interrupted, "Brad, Dr. Rutherford recommended Mrs. Jetter and vouched for her character. Beth and I are both satisfied as to her suitability, so I think you should welcome her graciously."

"Apparently, I displease Mr. Anderson in some way," Anna Louise said, standing. "Perhaps it would be best if I left now."

"Tell me, *Mrs.* Jetter, where is *Mr.* Jetter?" he demanded.

A shocked silence filled the room. Anna Louise's eyes widened and flashed toward Beth, then she tossed her head, "If you must know, there is no Mr. Jetter." Lying, she continued, "I found myself in this condition before I knew of his betrothal to another."

A sick suspicion slowly formed in Brad's gut.

"Brad, I don't understand. You said if I found Anna Louise agreeable, you had no objections. Now with no explanation at all, you exhibit dissatisfaction with my decision." Beth's eyes shimmered in frustration.

Taking a deep breath and forcing his eyes away from his former mistress, Brad looked at his wife. Her distress softened his heart, "My apologies, Beth. Of course, the decision is yours to make." Then turning stiffly toward Louise, he continued frostily, "Mrs. Jetter, will you accept my apologies and allow me to welcome you as a member of my household? My *wife* tells me your conversation gives her pleasure, and *my wife's happiness* is of the utmost concern to me," he emphasized.

Returning his direct stare, Anna Louise replied, "No need to apologize, Mr. Anderson. I understand well your concern and assure you the happiness of your household concerns me also. It is the reason I insisted upon meeting you prior to accepting the position."

"Then it's settled," Suzanne concluded the conversation, "as I knew it should have been yesterday. With Beth's permission, I will arrange to have Mrs. Jetter's possessions sent for tomorrow. With two expectant mothers, an extra helping hand will be appreciated, so I'll stay on for a few days until Anna Louise is settled."

The serving girl, hovering in the doorway, saw her opportunity, "Mrs. Anderson, ma'am, dinner is served." Her interruption eased the tension-filled room.

"Thank you. We'll be in presently."

But dinner was an uneasy affair. Uncomfortably aware of the scathing glances thrown her way from Bradley's icy gray eyes, Anna Louise just picked at her food.

By way of conversation, Beth enticed only monosyllabic grunts from her husband, leaving her bewildered.

Suzanne tried to mask the evening's awkwardness by recounting her family's recent activities to Brad, but he paid no attention.

And Charles, conscious of the simmering undercurrents between his son and their female guest, provided only occasional remarks to fill ungainly silences.

Brad doggedly consumed his meal, preoccupied with his own disturbing thoughts. Excusing himself abruptly, he retired to his study. In the appalling stillness following his departure, Charles politely excused himself to follow his offspring.

When Charles entered the study, his son was leaning on the mantle, staring into the fire, holding a snifter of brandy in his left hand. He appeared unaware of his father's presence.

"Do you care to discuss it with me, or do you prefer to brood about it on your own?" Charles asked, pouring himself a brandy.

Absently, Brad queried, "Discuss what?"

"Mrs. Jetter," he replied.

Brad visibly stiffened, then slowly turned toward his father. His eyes were burning points of anger, and his voice was glacial, "And what is there to discuss about Mrs. Jetter?"

Instantly, matching anger flared in Charles' eyes, "You are not the first man to find yourself in an impossible situation. I take it you have previously had the pleasure of meeting the girl."

The innuendo was not lost on Brad, and he relented slightly, "Yes, I have met her before."

"And have you any idea who the father of her child is?" Charles asked bluntly.

Walking swiftly to the brandy decanter, Brad refilled his snifter. "How should I know? I've only seen her twice in the past year. I can assure you, the woman has no reason to be in her current predicament. I left her well enough situated to find a decent husband," bitterness evident in his voice.

Surprised, Charles responded, "I see. In that case, I doubt she was just a passing fancy. How well do you know her?"

"Just a passing fancy? No, she was my English mistress for four years."

Disgusted, Charles tossed back his brandy, refilled the snifter, and asked, "Since she hasn't already disclosed your past relationship to your wife, do you think she intends to?"

Sweetbriar

Dropping heavily into a chair, elbows on his knees, Brad glowered into the fire as if he hadn't heard. After several minutes he sat back and sighed, "Knowing Louise, it's hard to tell. I don't think she would deliberately reveal our past, but she can have a volatile temper at times." Then Brad angrily pounded his fist on the arm of the chair, "Damn it all! How should I know what she will do? I never expected her to do this, to show up in my own home."

Sternly his father advised, "Brad, the decision is yours. Your mother and Beth, especially Beth, like the girl. You will have hell to pay trying to convince them to dismiss her. On the other hand, depending on her discretion, or lack thereof, you might have more trouble on your hands if she stays. Why don't you find an opportunity to speak with her and determine exactly what she has in mind?"

Brad snorted, "I don't see where I have any choice in the matter. I love my wife, as you well know. I'm afraid of anything coming between us, and if anything could, it would be Louise." His heart squeezed in anguish at the thought.

The next few days bustled with activity as the women settled Mrs. Jetter and made final preparations in the nursery. Beth wouldn't hear of Anna Louise eating in the kitchen with the rest of the staff, insisting she was more of a companion than a servant. But, wanting to avoid contact with the man of the house as much as possible, Anna Louise asked to take her meals in her room. She used the excuse that it would be necessary to do so after the babies were born, so it was best to start that routine immediately. This prevented Brad from having any conversation with her that might ease his misgivings.

Upon his return from England, Brad had progressively assumed more of the business responsibilities from his father. Each morning he went to the Surrey Trading Company offices but, since Louise's arrival, he found it difficult to concentrate on the work at hand. The uncertainty of having her in his home, the nagging question regarding the paternity of her child, and his concern for Beth's impending delivery all contributed to his building frustration. Worse, through it all, he recognized his wife's improved contentment since her countrywoman had joined the household.

Arriving home the first evening after his mother's departure, Brad found Louise alone in the parlor, putting the finishing stitches in another of the dozens of baby garments being prepared.

As she bit the thread off the last knot, she raised her eyes to find him leaning in the doorway with a pensive expression on his face.

As their eyes met, he straightened. "Have you seen *my wife*?" he inquired.

Knowing he goaded her by asking after 'his wife' instead of using Mrs. Anderson's given name, she refused to rise to the bait. "She fatigued herself over the past few days, so I insisted she rests. You'll find her in your bedchamber," she replied evenly until her voice caught on the last word.

Brad needed to discuss the untenable situation but couldn't chance an interruption. He glanced back out the parlor doors into the foyer and up the stairs to assure their privacy.

"Do you wish to speak with me, Mr. Anderson?" she asked, setting aside the baby garment as she stood.

"You know damn good and well I do, Louise," he spat harshly in a quiet tone so none of the servants would hear.

"Mr. Anderson, please address me as Mrs. Jetter," she urged with a glance past his shoulder.

He swiftly advanced into the room and grasped her arm roughly, his anger turning his eyes to hot gray coals. "Do you mock me, woman!" he demanded.

Cringing, she hissed back in a whisper, "No. My concern is someone will overhear your familiarity and realize we are not strangers to each other."

That sensible reply cooled his anger slightly, and he released her arm. "What are you doing here? Why aren't you in England where I left you?"

Gesturing to her swollen belly, she calmly stated, "I couldn't stay without a husband."

"I left you the means to get yourself a husband," he reminded her contemptuously.

Bitterly, she replied, "What man wants to marry a woman pregnant with another man's child?"

His eyes swept over her. "Were your other lovers not as conscientious as I to prevent this?"

She sucked in her breath, resisting the urge to slap his face. "There were no others. You know when this happened as well as I," she replied hotly.

His worst fears confirmed. He turned away, raking his hands through his hair, muttering, "Christ! What a disaster."

She barked out a bleak laugh, "To say the least."

Spinning back to face her, he again demanded, "What are you doing here, in this house? How dare you flaunt your condition to me?"

Unable to control the shaking in her legs, Anna Louise sat abruptly. "I had no idea this was my destination. Dr. Rutherford told me an Englishwoman desired a wet nurse and companion. If I had known it was your wife, I would have remained in Salem. If I could have refused to stay, I would have, but Mrs. Anderson made up her mind the moment she set eyes on me," Anna Louise explained grimly.

Brad sighed, accepting the truth of her words, "Yes, Beth is impulsive and determined when it suits her."

After a minute of uncomfortable silence, while Brad paced, the girl offered, "Your wife is a kind and beautiful woman, Bradley. You chose well."

His pacing stopped at the acknowledgment, which appeared sincere.

Anna Louise continued, "With your permission, I will stay until your child is weaned then return to Salem. Your wife doesn't ever need to know about us or the paternity of my baby."

He resumed pacing the floor, apprehensive about allowing her to stay. Her intent might not be to destroy his marriage, but a situation such as this could so easily get out of control. '*Hell,*" he thought resentfully, "*it is already out of control!*' Too close to Beth's delivery time to find another nursemaid, they had no chance of finding another Englishwoman. Grudgingly he admitted, "I don't have a choice, do I?" Looking at her distended belly, he grimaced, "Let's hope that child takes after you in appearance." Then he turned on his heel and stalked out of the room.

He raced up the stairs two at a time. Quietly opening the door to their bedroom, Brad saw his wife open her eyes and smile sleepily at the sound of his entry. Crossing to the bed, he sat and kissed her, "How is my sweet Beth? Mrs. Jetter tells me you are fatigued."

"It was just the excitement of getting the nursery ready. Anna Louise gave me no choice about taking a nap. She is a gem, Brad. I don't know how I would get through this without her."

Uncomfortable having his wife praise his former mistress, Brad admonished, "She is paid to look after

Sweetbriar

you. It's fine that you enjoy your time with her, just remember she is still your servant."

Beth sighed, "She may be a servant, but I think she will also become my friend."

"In time, you will meet other women and have many friends," he assured her. "Now, do you feel like going downstairs, or would you prefer we have dinner sent up?"

She blushed knowing what dinner served in their bedchamber inevitably led to. "I suppose we could have dinner here. If we are very careful," she replied.

He nuzzled her neck, knowing it sent chills racing along her spine, "Perhaps it's time you learn another way for us to find marital gratification?" he suggested and nipped her earlobe.

"How many more ways are there?" she asked breathlessly.

"Tonight, we'll have dessert first, and then we'll have dinner," he said. Drawing her petticoats above her waist, he removed her pantaloons and then astonished his wife when he knelt between her thighs and hungrily partook of her soft inner flesh.

Then she astonished herself when she shyly asked if she could pleasure him in a like manner. And, learning from his whispered encouragements, pleasure him she did.

The household settled into a comfortable routine. After Brad left for work in the morning, Beth and Anna Louise spent time sewing or knitting in the parlor and occasionally entertained Brad's mother or one of his sisters. Dr. Rutherford stopped by more frequently to assure himself both women were well. Before Brad returned in the evening, Anna Louise retired to her room adjacent to the nursery to eat her evening meal. Still in love with Bradley despite all her heartache, she preferred to avoid seeing him act the attentive husband to his wife. He had no reason to come to the nursery, so for the next fortnight, she didn't see him at all.

Then came the night in mid-February when her waters broke, and she knew her time was at hand. At just past midnight, she wrapped a blanket around her shoulders, walked down the hall, and gently tapped on Anderson's bedroom door. Bedclothes rustled, and a few seconds later, Brad cracked opened the door.

"It's my time, Bradley," she whispered.

He grabbed his robe, donning it as he stepped into the hallway, softly closing the door behind him. "She hasn't slept well lately. I'd prefer not to disturb her," he quietly explained. "Go back to bed. I'll send for the doctor." He paused, then asked, "Do you want me to send for my mother, also?"

Visibly relieved at the suggestion, she agreed, "Yes, please."

He nodded and set out to wake the servants.

The following hours tormented everyone. The manservant went off to rouse Dr. Rutherford and Suzanne Anderson, in that order. The cook heated water and prepared food, although no one could bear to eat with the muffled shrieks coming from the second-floor room. The girl's screaming contractions completely unnerved Beth, and Suzanne insisted Brad keep her out of the birthing room. Cradled in his lap, Beth tearfully related the vague memories she had of her mother's death and her fears of childbirth. He soothed her as best he could but didn't tell her he shared her worries.

At midday, the lusty wail of a newborn babe replaced the agonized cries of the mother. Beth wanted to fly up the stairs to the nursery, but Brad restrained her, suggesting she wait until his mother or Dr. Rutherford called for her.

When the doctor finally appeared, he gave Brad a bad shock when he announced, "You have a healthy son."

"What!" Brad's head snapped up.

The doctor held up his hands apologetically, and his shoulders sagged. "I'm sorry. I'm bone tired and just said what I usually say after a birthing. Let me clarify. Mrs. Jetter has a healthy son." Looking at Brad and Beth standing side by side, he said, "In two or three weeks, I will be telling you that you have a healthy son or daughter, too. You can see the infant now, but don't stay long because Mrs. Jetter needs her rest."

Beth tugged Brad's hand, "Come with me, darling," she insisted when he hesitated. Hand in hand, they ascended the stairs and stood together at the foot of Anna Louise's bed. Nursing the baby, she crooned to him and stroked his tiny cheek. Although exhausted, her face glowed with joy. Brad was thunderstruck when she raised her eyes to his. No words were needed to convey her thought, *'Here is your son.'*

Awed by the sight before her, Beth didn't notice the sparks flying between her husband and the new mother. Fortunately, Suzanne was in the nursery, or she might have seen the silent exchange. However, the moment passed when Brad's mother bustled back into the room.

"Now that you've seen the baby, out with the two of you. Mrs. Jetter needs to rest. I'll just sit with the baby awhile," she said, taking the tiny bundle from Anna Louise. "It's been long enough since I held one in my arms," glancing at Brad as if chiding him for not providing her with a grandchild long ago.

Still holding Beth's hand, Brad squeezed it, and they quietly withdrew, closing the door behind them. In the hall, he pulled his wife into his arms as he drew a deep breath to calm the pounding of his heart. He could share with no one what he felt when he saw Louise suckling his son. He loved Beth unequivocally and regretted this emotion had not been reserved for the birth of their child. He knew he would feel it again as strongly in a few weeks' time but instinctively knew it wouldn't be the same as this first time.

Again, the household settled into a new routine when three weeks later, another midnight awakening signaled the commencement of Beth's travail. The manservant left to summon the doctor and Brad's mother, but Dr. Rutherford was across the county tending to a farmer suffering from a kick in the head by his mule. It was Anna Louise who initially held Beth's hands as the contractions squeezed her ruthlessly. Charles and Suzanne arrived at dawn, anticipating another afternoon birth, but Beth was not as fortunate as Anna Louise. She labored throughout the day and into the night, her strength waning as each never-ending hour crawled sluggishly past.

Charles tried his best to distract his son, but they all fretted as time wore on. Anna Louise and Suzanne sent word to the men periodically but refused to take respite from their caregiving. If Dr. Rutherford had attended the birthing, perhaps it would have been easier, but they did the best they could with Suzanne's limited knowledge. Twenty agonizing, screaming, sweating hours after her labor began, Beth was delivered of a daughter. The small girl mewed so listlessly; they feared for her life until Anna Louise assured them the baby's suckling was strong. Now Suzanne's concern was all for Beth, who bled profusely. She weakened further, and fearing her daughter-in-law would die, Suzanne sent downstairs for Brad.

Meeting him in the hallway, she advised him his daughter appeared well, but his wife's condition was grave. Pale as death, he entered the room. His eyes quickly swept over Louise sitting in a chair on the far side of the bed nursing his daughter, then lowered to gaze upon his wife's white face.

Sitting on the bed, he took her hand and lightly kissed her lips. Her eyes fluttered open, then closed again. "Sweet Beth," he said at a loss for words.

Her eyes opened again. In a voice so faint Brad needed to lean close to hear, she murmured, "I'm sorry. I wanted to give you a son."

He quietly reassured her, "You gave me a beautiful daughter, who we will both cherish, my love. Now rest and regain your strength."

Weakly she shook her head, "I'm going to die, Brad, just like my mother." Then she closed her eyes and sighed softly.

Shocked by her words, Brad gathered her into his arms, sobbing, "Don't leave me, Beth, please! I love you with all my heart and soul and can't bear to live without you. If you die, I will die with you. Please, my sweet Beth, stay with me!"

Hot tears soaked her hair. Beth knew they weren't hers. Lifting her hand, she touched Brad's face, fingering the dampness. She remembered her father's devastation when her mother died. Brad's body shuddered over hers as he wept, and Beth resolved to live.

Turning her face toward his, she kissed his cheek, then asked, "Have you seen our baby?"

Her faint voice brought him back to his senses. He eased her onto the pillows. The ghost of a smile graced her lips as she weakly brushed the tears from his face. Unable to speak, Brad shook his head, and as one, they turned toward Anna Louise.

She sat in anguished silence, her heart breaking at the scene she had witnessed. The personal intensity of it was more intimate than anything she had ever experienced. Observing the man she cherished professing his eternal love to his dying wife was unbearable. She stood, and coming around the bed, handed the now sleeping baby to Bradley.

Brad laid the child in Beth's arms and kissed them both lightly on the forehead. "You have made me the happiest of men."

Choking back a sob, Anna Louise stumbled blindly from the room.

Neither Brad nor Beth noticed her departure as they gazed at the tiny miracle their love had produced. After a few minutes, Beth slept. Easing himself up, Brad shifted to sit in the chair next to the bed. An hour later, when the doctor arrived, Brad was still huddled there, holding Beth's hand, watching her breathe, and willing her to live.

Spring 1810, America

Word reached the States that the Emperor of France had issued a decree reiterating that all vessels navigating under the flag of the United States and owned, in whole or in part, by any citizen of that Power which entered any port of the Empire, its colonies, or countries occupied by its armies were subject to seizure. The only exceptions were vessels not carrying cargo or merchandise and charged only with dispatches or commissions of the United States government.

In further efforts to motivate France and Britain to stop seizing American ships, new legislation was passed that allowed lifting all embargoes against either country if America's neutral shipping rights were recognized. The law also continued to impose all embargoes against whichever country continued its attacks.

Seizing this opportunity to further his Continental System and destroy Britain's economy, Napoleon sent a message to President Madison acknowledging American merchant ships as neutral carriers. Although not a supporter of the law, Madison grudgingly agreed. It soon became apparent Bonaparte had no intention of keeping his promise, and the law's parameters were not enforced.

But the British were highly offended by these exchanges, damaging international relations. Tensions continued to mount between the United States and Great Britain.

Beth's recovery was precariously slow and not at all assured. Extra servants were hired to attend her every moment throughout the days and nights. Brad remained in the sick room continuously, which made the nursing of his wife more difficult. Suzanne and Charles urged him to return to work, but he refused.

A week passed before Beth regained enough strength to express her desire to name their daughter Kathryn Suzanne after her and Brad's mothers. Relieved from his worried suffering, Brad broke down and cried, then relented, and returned to work.

Another week passed before Beth was sufficiently strong to hold her baby in her arms. She rallied enough to be propped up on pillows so her husband could see her and the child together. The perfect love on his face at the sight of them, she knew, would live in her heart forever. But the exertion was too much; she relapsed for many days afterward.

When Brad arrived home in the evenings, he immediately dismissed the attending servants and sat with his wife in quietude for the hour before dinner. After he ate, Brad visited the nursery for a few minutes to hold his daughter, and then returned to Beth until retiring to the guest room down the hall, which he occupied while his wife recuperated.

Because Bradley persisted in ignoring Anna Louise and her baby boy, she felt compelled to confront him. If he would only hold Andy in his arms, she felt sure the baby's enchanting smile would capture the man's heart. Even though Bradley didn't love her, Anna Louise wanted him to love their son. But when Bradley visited the nursery, all his attention was focused on his daughter, as if little Andy didn't exist.

Sometimes, when Brad quit the sick room, Anna Louise stood in the hallway holding her son and attempted to engage him in conversation. Uncomfortable in her presence, Brad preferred to avoid her whenever possible. But this night, it was not possible.

"Mr. Anderson, look how big my little Andy has grown," she beamed, bouncing the baby in her arms. Her blue eyes sparkled with mischief. "He's two months old today. Do you not think he is becoming quite the little man?"

A servant exiting Beth's room overheard this comment. Knowing it would appear unnatural for him to ignore Louise and her gurgling baby, he took a step closer as if to admire the boy.

"I can't decide if he takes after me or his father," she mocked.

Alarmed at her statement, he looked closer. The baby had a thatch of black hair and crystal blue eyes. Beyond that, who could say what he would look like in years to come? With a furtive glance at the servant girl, who hovered outside the sick-room door, Brad observed, "I can't comment on any resemblance to his father, but he appears to favor your hair and eyes, Mrs. Jetter."

Her lively eyes danced with amusement. "If I possessed a likeness of my late husband, I would show it to you. I'm sure you would notice a similarity in his nose and mouth," she teased.

Blood rushed to Brad's face as he peered closer, but he could not determine if any similarity to his own

Sweetbriar

countenance existed. "If you say so," he growled then turned on his heel.

As he opened the door to his temporary bedroom, Anna Louise clutched his arm and hissed, "Bradley Anderson, don't walk away from me!"

"What do you want?" he hissed back, gray eyes flashing fire, relieved the young servant had descended the stairs.

"I want you to hold our son," she said, keeping her voice low. "I want you to see our son smile and hear our son's sweet cooing," she insisted.

"No, Louise. You have a son. My wife and I have a daughter," he stated harshly before retreating into his room and closing the door behind him.

Furious, Brad wanted Louise and her baby out of his house, but Beth was too weak to nurse Kathryn, and too much time had passed for her to have milk still. As soon as his daughter was weaned, he intended to send Louise back to England or as far away from his household as possible. He would fulfill his obligations to the boy, provide for his schooling, and help him in trade when the time came, but he did not want to form an attachment.

After arriving in America, the Andersons had socialized very little before Beth's confinement. She hadn't developed any close friendships. His mother and sisters visited each week, but Beth depended on Louise for most of her companionship. It concerned Brad that his wife felt such a kinship with the woman. He wanted to find a way to separate Beth from her 'dear Anna Louise' as she referred to her just this evening but feared the bond might be hard to break. Louise had promised to keep silent about the paternity of her son, but Brad suspected she would expose him as the father if she felt driven to do so. He paced late into the night, examining his options.

The next evening when Brad visited the nursery, he made a point of looking at baby Andy. The result extended far beyond Anna Louise's intention. Bradley let the small tyke hold his finger. Burbling, the baby gripped firmly and shook his arms, smiling at Brad with shining eyes. After a few moments, Brad picked the boy up then felt the knife twist in his heart. *His* son. Not Louise's son but *his* son. As quickly as the acknowledgment blasted into his mind, all the conflicting emotions washed over him. Love for the life he held in his arms, anger at himself and Louise for giving the baby life, and fear that Beth would learn he had fathered the boy and hate him for it. He trembled. Laying the baby in his crib Brad left without a word, never even looking at his daughter.

Alone in his room, he anguished over the situation. The boy was his, but he wasn't at the same time. He wanted his son. He wanted to acknowledge the boy as his son. But any effort to do so would drive his wife from him. Winning her love had been everything to Brad. He could never live without her. Yet he must find some way to have both his wife and his son.

The Shawnee chief known as the Prophet was a religious leader advocating a return to the ancestral Indian lifestyle. A large confederacy of diverse tribes had grown around his teachings. His brother, Tecumseh, emerged as a prominent leader of this confederacy and was vehemently opposed to the 1809 land sale, which had been negotiated at Fort Wayne.

Tecumseh revived an idea advocated years earlier by other Indian leaders espousing the notion that the land was owned collectively by all Indians and could not be sold by individual tribes. Throughout the year, he traveled extensively, urging other tribes to resist the terms of the Fort Wayne treaty. Then in August, accompanied by four hundred like-minded warriors, Tecumseh rode to the home of Governor Harrison.

Hearing the commotion, Harrison stepped onto his second-floor balcony. Seeing the warriors gathered in the clearing in front of his house, he called out, "Colonel Michaels, come quickly!" When the colonel stood at his side, the governor ordered, "Send your aide to Vincennes to alert the garrison. I want them dispatched here to Grouseland immediately!"

"Yes, sir!" After instructing his man to return posthaste with every able-bodied man in the garrison, the colonel returned to the balcony. "What do we do until the garrison arrives, Governor?"

Looking severely at Colonel Michaels, Harrison rolled his shoulders. "We parley," he said and turned on his heels. Descending the stairs, the two men confidently strode out the front door onto the landing.

Tecumseh and the Pottawatomie chief, Winnimac, sat atop their war ponies and exchanged brief greetings with the white men, then dismounted. The two Americans anticipated lengthy verbal greetings before serious discussions began, but surprisingly, Tecumseh quickly dispensed with these formalities.

"All tribes are as brothers to the Great Spirit, and as brothers, are one nation," he intoned solemnly. "The lands of our nation cannot be sold to the Great White Father by one tribe or another, as all Indians own the land."

"On the contrary," Governor Harrison argued, "if the Great Spirit wanted all Indians to be one nation, he would have given all the tribes one language. But different tribes have different languages because they are separate nations. Each nation has the right to negotiate treaties with the Great White Father."

This reply, coupled with the arrival of the garrison soldiers, dissatisfied and disturbed the gathered braves.

"Your Great White Father cannot parley for land with individual tribes and expect all tribes of the Indian nation to abide by your treaty," disagreed Tecumseh.

"He does expect all tribes to honor the treaties of the other tribes. You are all separate nations."

"We are one nation!" insisted the Shawnee chief. "You must set aside your treaty and forbid the white man to settle on our lands."

Harrison was adamant, "Individual Indian nations can sell the lands, and the land now belongs to the Great White Father. It is his wish for the white man to settle the land."

Tecumseh turned toward his followers. Addressing them in his native tongue, he translated the gist of his exchange with the white chief. Then the situation became explosive when, in an impassioned speech, Tecumseh called for the death of Harrison and the massacre of the town's inhabitants. At the answering war cries, the governor drew his sword, and the soldiers moved to surround him.

But Chief Winnimac, who respected Harrison, calmly argued against Tecumseh and urged the warriors to return to their homes in peace. After many tense minutes, his reasoning prevailed.

Tecumseh was angry, though. "We leave now, Harrison, but set aside your treaty and return the land to the Indian nation, or my followers will ally with the British to drive the white man from our land."

"On behalf of the Great White Father, I refuse to nullify the treaty or to relinquish the land," Harrison replied.

War whoops echoed loudly as the horde of Indians leaped upon their ponies and departed.

Sweetbriar
Summer 1810, America

Slowly Beth reclaimed her health. By early summer, she left her bed for an hour or two each day. By late summer, she spent several hours a day in the nursery attending to the babies with Anna Louise. She walked downstairs to dine with Brad in the evenings, but the exertion of climbing the stairs afterward fatigued her, so she didn't join him in the nursery at night.

The babies were almost six months old. Beth was amazed by how quickly they grew and the personalities they displayed, never thinking babies possessed likes or dislikes, or dispositions similar to adults. Little Andy was a happy boy, full of laughing playfulness, demanding attention, while Kathryn was quietly well-behaved, content to play in her crib. Beth suspected she would be a shy girl like her cousin Mary, and remembering her own impulsive youth, was relieved. Because of the differing personalities, it was only natural for more attention to be devoted to the boisterous Andy. Beth formed a strong attachment, and from their evening conversations, she realized her husband shared a fondness for the boy. He was as proud of him as he was of his daughter.

Wanting to give Brad a son of his own but deathly afraid to chance another pregnancy, Beth fretted. The doctor had assured them that with time, as Beth regained her strength, another baby might be considered. He explained that first babies often caused long, hard labor and that subsequent births were usually easier. His only caution was for Beth to recover all her health and strength before expanding the family.

But for Beth, another idea began to form in her mind.

Summer 1810, England

Spencer Perceval, who had been Prime Minister of Great Britain for the past year, looked with disgust at his Foreign Secretary, Lord Bathurst. News of Napoleon's expansion of the French empire continued to infuriate and depress both politicians.

"When, and more importantly, how are we to check this man's voracious appetite for conquering the world?" the Prime Minister demanded.

"We need to form another continental coalition," Bathurst stated.

"And how do you propose forming another coalition?" Spencer fumed. "France controls the Swiss Confederation, the Confederation of the Rhine, the Duchy of Warsaw, and the Kingdom of Italy." Scarcely drawing a breath, he continued, "His older brother, Joseph, is King of Spain, his younger brother, Jerome, is King of Westphalia. One brother-in-law is King of Naples, and the other rules the Principality of Lucca and Piombino. Plus, they are allied with Russia and Austria, although the latter's allegiance is weak."

Reluctantly, Lord Bathurst informed the Prime Minister, "The alliance with Austria is about to become stronger."

Spencer Perceval paused in the act of opening his snuff box. "What do you mean?" he inquired apprehensively.

"You know rumors say that Empress Josephine submitted to an abortion in her youth, which left her barren," Bathurst commented. "Boney was willing to overlook her condition years ago when he wanted closer connections to her influential family."

"What has that to do with Austria?"

Bathurst cleared his throat and shifted in his chair, "With most of Europe under France's dominion, Boney now has the aspiration to found a dynasty. Word just arrived that he divorced Josephine and intends to marry the Austrian Archduchess, Marie-Louise.

Appalled, the Prime Minister tossed his unopened snuff box onto his desk and stared broodingly out the window.

Late Fall 1810, America

As the winter Christmas season approached, Bradley Anderson savored his many reasons for rejoicing. He had assumed command of Surrey Trading Company, allowing his father more leisure time in his old age. Beth had recovered her health, and after many assurances that he could prevent a pregnancy, welcomed him back to her bed. They started socializing with other affluent families in the area, and the numerous acquaintances reduced Beth's dependency on the companionship of Louise. For this, especially, Brad gave thanks.

Andy took his first unassisted steps, laughing happily at the encouragement he received. Kathryn crawled about, and both babies mumbled their first words. Wanting to surprise Brad, Beth taught Kathryn to say 'papa' and thought it cute when little Andy mimicked her. It mortified Brad and embarrassed Anna Louise, but the moment passed when Beth tickled the boy and said, "Do you want a papa too, little Andy?"

This exchange solidified the vague idea that flitted around in her mind. The next day Beth asked Anna Louise what prospects she held for her son.

"I don't rightly know, Mrs. Anderson. I can expect no notice from my family, and I have no notion of what I can expect from his father's family. I suppose after Kathryn is weaned, I will search for a position as governess and hope for some patronage from my employers," was her considered reply.

"Anna Louise," Beth said, surprised, "I didn't know you'd been educated."

The nursemaid colored. "No reason for you to know. I have no one to write to and no reason to sit with ciphers. The few minutes before bed is the only time I have for idle enjoyments. Then I only read my bible. I like to think the good Lord will take that into account and forgive my past indiscretions."

Beth considered this conversation for many days. Even though they referred to Anna Louise as Mrs. Jetter, without a husband, her son's legitimacy would always be questioned. With a basic education, which his mother could provide, Andy would find suitable employment. But the stigma of bastard was hard to overcome. It would limit the boy's ability to succeed in life. He would not be acceptable to respectable families when it was time to marry. Loving Andy as if he were her own, Beth hoped he might fill the void she felt existed between herself and Brad.

He professed a son was unimportant. He loved Kathryn; of that, she possessed no doubt. But she saw the way his eyes followed Andy at times and the pleasure on her husband's face when a new milestone or accomplishment was achieved. Brad could offer respectability and advantages to Andy that eluded the nursemaid's capabilities. Deciding to talk to her husband, Beth wanted to persuade him to adopt little Andy. She didn't think Anna Louise would mind so much if they allowed her to remain as governess to both Andy and Kathryn.

Beth thought out all her arguments then waited until Brad was mellowed one night by their lovemaking before broaching the subject. Her head nestled in the hollow of his shoulder with his arm loosely enfolding her. "Brad, don't go to sleep yet. I want to talk to you about something that has preyed upon my mind for some time now," she nudged him slightly to rouse him.

He gave her a light squeeze replying sleepily, "Talk to me in the morning, Beth. I'm sure it can wait." He started to turn over, but Beth held him in place.

"I want to talk to you about a son," she said, which immediately caught his attention.

"If you want another baby, Beth, you should have told me that a half-hour ago. I would much rather have the pleasure of spilling my seed in you than on the bed linens."

She rose on her elbow to look him in the face. "Brad," she whispered, "what if we could have a son without risking another pregnancy?"

Confused in his half-sleep state, he asked, "And how, pray tell, are we to have a son without you having a baby, Beth?"

"You could adopt little Andy."

That shocked him fully awake. "And what does Lou— Mrs. Jetter have to say about this?" he demanded, sitting up.

"I haven't spoken to her yet. I thought it better if we discussed it first." Arranging her thoughts, she explained, "Don't you see, darling, it makes perfect sense. I love the boy, and you are fond of him, too. You can offer him advantages and respectability far superior to anything Anna Louise will ever be able to provide. If you adopt him as a baby, we will be the only family he ever knows."

Gravely, Brad considered his wife. He would love nothing better than to adopt his son, but he doubted Louise would ever consent. He was also concerned that making the request would anger her enough to disclose the truth. "I doubt the woman will feel kindly about leaving her son behind after her services are no longer required," he responded.

Sitting up beside her husband, Beth earnestly argued her points, "Her services might be extended for years to come. She is educated and can act as governess to Andy and Kathryn. It's not as if she would give him up forever. She would live right here with us and watch him grow to adulthood. But he could grow up as our son instead of as hers. Please, Brad," she beseeched.

He stood, slipped into his robe, and paced the room, scrubbing his hands over his face and through his tousled hair. He acknowledged the logic of her arguments but questioned if they were persuasive enough to convince the boy's mother. Perhaps if Beth gradually introduced the concept of relinquishing Andy, Louise might be more receptive than if asked outright.

He also vaguely wondered if he would be open to his wife's suggestion if the boy in question were from another man's loins. In some ways, he supposed, all men wanted a son to carry on his name, but Brad was as concerned as Beth about risking another pregnancy.

The only part of the plan he resisted was having Louise remain as governess to his children but thought there wasn't any way around it. Silently he nodded, deciding less risk existed in attempting to adopt Andy and having Louise remain in his household than taking the chance of losing his wife in childbirth.

Returning to the bed, he took Beth's hands in his, absently rubbing her fingers with his thumbs. "I think it is necessary for Mrs. Jetter to understand the advantages that will accrue to a son of ours, before asking for her consent in giving us Andy. It will take time and subtlety on your part. You are a perceptive woman, Beth. You need to gauge her thoughts and feelings. Determine when she is most conducive to accepting our proposal. Take care not to rush the process. If handled well, Andy can be ours by his first birthday."

Beth hugged him. "Oh, Brad, thank you. I hope in time, you will love him as if he were your own son. I already do," she said.

Guilt clawed at his heart. Brad held his wife close so she wouldn't see it in his eyes.

Chapter VII
Late Winter 1811, America

Details of the arrangements made by President Madison with British spy John Henry filled the broadsheets for weeks, much to Madison's embarrassment. And United States taxpayers, especially in Massachusetts, balked at the disclosures.

Henry, born in Ireland, immigrated to Philadelphia in 1793, where for a time, he edited *Brown's Philadelphia Gazette*. Then he served over three years in the United States military but resigned his commission in 1801 to settle on a farm in northern Vermont. He remained there for five years of farming, studying law, and writing the occasional editorial article against the Republican form of government.

Sir James Craig, Governor-General of Canada, having read many of these articles, employed John Henry in 1809 to investigate the extent of dissatisfaction New Englanders felt toward their national government. For three months, Henry prowled Boston gleaning information and reporting his findings to Craig in a series of letters. He asserted that, in the event of war between the United States and Great Britain, Massachusetts would most likely take the lead in establishing a northern confederacy that might be persuaded to ally itself with Britain.

The Governor-General, it was reported, had promised John Henry a position with the Canadian government in return for this information but died before fulfilling his promise. Failing to obtain his reward after petitioning London, Henry returned to the United States.

Newspaper accounts stated that, in exchange for the exorbitant sum of fifty thousand dollars, Henry divulged the entire affair to President Madison and provided him with copies of the correspondence to support his story.

However, President Madison was outraged by the duplicity this incident implied and immediately closed all trade with the United Kingdom, exacerbating the ill-will already existing between the two countries.

Ironically, when the content of the letters was disclosed, the information they contained had been readily available in various New England newspapers, if Congress and the President had been inclined to read them.

After Brad consented to Beth's plan for adopting Andy, she undertook the delicate task of convincing Anna Louise to accept the idea. First, Beth related stories to her companion about the many years Brad had spent at sea, of his prolonged courtship, and their eventual marriage. She felt a few pangs of pity when Anna Louise became introspective during these conversations but decided it was because the other woman's love affair had not ended as well.

After a few days, Beth gave an account of her father-in-law handing over Surrey Trading Company to his son, expounding upon the satisfaction her husband obtained in running one of the largest shipping companies in the state. Beth explained that before Kathryn's birth,

Brad often talked about the day he would take his son into the business. Only they didn't have a son.

The first week of the new year, after attending the engagement party for the mayor's daughter, Beth detailed for Anna Louise all the event's festivities. The foremost guests in attendance included the entire town council, local bankers, the newspaper owner, numerous business owners, a state senator, and even the governor, plus all their wives. The circle of influence the Andersons enjoyed impressed Anna Louise.

Later that week, Beth started speculating about the male children of their friends, saying it was never too early to consider her daughter's prospects. Although these conversations disturbed the nursemaid, Beth persisted, firmly believing her scheme was in Andy's best interests.

Toward the end of January, after the babies went down for their nap, Beth hovered over Andy's crib contemplating the sleeping boy. "What will become of poor little Andy, Anna Louise?" she asked.

"What do you mean, Mrs. Anderson?"

Turning from the crib, Beth indicated with a tilt of her head that they should relocate to the drawing-room, and once situated with their handwork, she continued the conversation. "I sometimes wonder about the prospects for your son. He will grow up benefiting from the advantages an influential family bestows. But what then? The son of a nursemaid or even a governess will never be accepted into the best homes. I'm afraid his expectations are limited, even with the recommendations of someone such as my husband. It must be hard for a young man so close to the upper echelons of society to be forever excluded."

Anna Louise smoothed her knitting on her lap, avoiding eye contact with her employer. She gnawed her lower lip for a time. "I haven't given it any thought before now. I acknowledge what you say is true." Falling silent, she industriously concentrated on her knitting, lost in thought. After a while, she remarked, "There is nothing dishonorable in being the son of a servant, Mrs. Anderson. It will be important for me to make clear to Andy, early in life, that he is of a lesser class and to align his anticipations accordingly."

Beth left the statement unfurled between them, allowing it to billow fully with significance.

"Andy's father is of your class. If he had married me instead of—" Agitated, she threw down her knitting and paced the floor. "Andy should be able to enjoy the privileges his father could bestow, but it is impossible for him to acknowledge his son in the current circumstances."

Surprised by the girl's vehemence, Beth reached out to grasp for the brass ring of her goal. "It is my fervent desire for my husband to have a son, but I almost died giving birth to Kathryn."

Still pacing in agitation, Anna Louise absently inquired, "Are you willing to risk your life again, Mrs. Anderson, just to provide an heir?"

"I would prefer to provide an heir without risking my life," she replied quietly. "But it all depends on you, Anna Louise."

Startled, the servant spun on her heel. Standing before Beth with her hands on her hips, suspicion dawned in her eyes. Her voice rose as she choked out the words, "He wants to take Andy away from me, doesn't he?"

"No one wants to take Andy away from you," Beth stated as she stood and clasped her companion's shoulders. "But I am asking you, as my friend, to allow my husband to adopt him. I am determined Brad should have a son, so please spare me the dangers of another birth. I swear to you, Anna Louise, you will remain here as governess to Andy and Kathryn. You will see Andy grow into a man capable of benefiting from all the advantages and respectability my husband can bestow on a son. Please do this for me," she pleaded.

A keening sounded as racking sobs broke free, and Anna Louise buried her face in her hands. Beth guided the girl to the chaise, sat beside her, and let her cry as they rocked to and fro. After Anna Louise quieted, she lifted her tear-stained face. "Will you allow me to speak privately with Mr. Anderson when he returns home this evening?"

"As soon as he arrives, I shall send for you."

Blue eyes flashed fire. "I think under the circumstances, Mrs. Anderson, you should send him to me," Anna Louise hissed furiously.

Surprised by the fierceness of the demand, Beth nodded her acquiescence.

Too distraught to remain in Beth's presence, Anna Louise snatched up her knitting and stormed off to the nursery. Andy was all she had. All she ever expected to have. How could she give him up? But how could she not allow him to have the life Bradley offered? If she permitted his adoption at this young age, her son would never remember that she was his mother. He would grow up saying 'mama' to Beth Anderson.

She trod the floorboards of her bedroom all afternoon, crossing the threshold into the nursery several times to gaze at her sleeping boy. But it was the man he would become that she saw. Which man would it be, the confident son of the rich and influential Bradley Anderson or the bastard son of a governess, dependent on the largess of a benefactor? When the babies awoke, she dressed them and sent them downstairs with the maid after pleading a headache instead of the heartache she felt.

As the afternoon sky deepened to a lavender evening, Bradley knocked gently on the nursery door, en-

Sweetbriar

tered, then hesitated with his back to the closed portal. In shivering silence, Anna Louise surveyed him, wondering how it was possible to love and hate him simultaneously.

"How dare you have your wife ask for my son? You didn't even have the decency to ask for yourself," she spat bitterly at him, turning her back. "How long did it take you to convince her of your scheme?" she tossed over her shoulder.

"It was Beth's idea to adopt Andy, not mine. But you are right about the other. I knew she would be better at the asking than I," he calmly admitted.

She whirled around, flew at him, slapping his shoulders and chest in frustration, demanding, "You kept me for four years then discarded me. Will you take my son and discard me again?" He stood there and took her abuse until her fury withered. Weeping, she leaned her forehead on his chest, "I love you, Bradley, and Andy is all I have to show for it."

Encircling her with his arms, Brad kissed the top of her head. "I'm sorry for never loving you, Louise, but I love Andy. I want the best for him. As my son, I can give him a life far different from what he will have as your son." Loosening his arms, he lifted her chin, looking into her shimmering blue eyes. "On my word of honor, I will not send you away. You will stay here and be a part of his life. That is the most I can promise you, Louise, but please give me my son," he implored.

Again, tears welled in her eyes. Silently she nodded.

Brad leaned down and chastely kissed her quivering mouth. "Thank you," he breathed against her lips.

Desperately, she clung to him, then taking full passionate possession of his mouth, she demanded an answering response and accepted the obliging solace of his kiss.

***

Leaving Kathryn with Anna Louise, Brad and Beth took Andy to visit the elder Andersons. When they disclosed their intention of adopting the boy, Charles and Suzanne were dumbfounded. But childbirth, being one of the more common causes of death for married women, made it impossible to dispute the reasoning behind their decision. Suzanne understood better than Charles why Beth would accept the other woman's son instead of risking another birth, although she questioned in her mind why Brad might willingly forgo siring a son of his own.

Not as reticent as his wife, Charles wanted a few questions answered. After the women retired from the dining table, as the men shared cigars and brandy, he probed. "You are a grown man and can make your own decisions in life, Brad, but have you no doubts about adopting the nursemaid's son?"

"You needn't concern yourself, Dad," Brad smiled. "It was Beth's suggestion. I'm in complete agreement and am happy to do this."

Shaking his head, Charles commented, "From your own admission to me last year, the girl has loose morals. You know nothing of the father. If there is bad blood involved, there is no telling how the boy might turn out. He could be more trouble than he's worth."

Anger suffused Brad's face at his father's words. He pushed back from the table, "You don't know anything about her or Andy's paternity. She's a decent enough girl. And I do know something about his father."

Charles raised his hand to still the angry words, "I understand Beth's reluctance to have more children, but why adopt the boy? You could name Sarah's son as your heir. At least your nephew is a blood relation."

As quickly as the blood had rushed into Brad's face, it drained away, leaving him pale. So quietly that

Charles strained to hear his son's words, Brad revealed the truth, "Andy *is* a blood relation. He is *my* son."

Shocked, Charles slumped back in his chair as if punched. "Does your wife know of this?" he asked in disbelief.

"No, and I don't intend that she ever will," Brad replied.

Sitting forward and leaning close, Charles advised, "Then after the adoption, dismiss the girl. Ship her back to England, if you can."

Standing, Brad paced, "Nothing would please me better, Father. I have been uncomfortable having her around Beth from the beginning, but I have no choice. I promised her she could stay."

Charles gripped his son's arm as he passed close, "That was unwise. You must send her away as soon as possible. Beth has other friends now. She won't miss the girl's companionship for long. It's too risky for her to remain."

Solemnly Brad reiterated, "I gave her my word. It was the only way she would agree."

The older man pushed the arm he held away in disgust. "You fool! How could you be so reckless? Trouble will come of this. You mark my words."

The piercing wail of a cranky boy punctuated this statement, lending it a more ominous nuance. A maid quickly appeared, "'S'cuse, Mr. Anderson, your wife says the young master is tired and should be put to bed. She wants to know if you will stay the night."

Brad nodded, "Yes, it's too late to return to the city with a bawling baby. Put Andy down to sleep. He can share the bed with my wife and me."

"Yes, sir," she curtsied and left to follow his instructions.

"Bradley," his father cautioned, "You must find a way to get rid of the girl. The sooner, the better."

The lines around Brad's mouth hardened, "I may be a fool in your eyes, Father, but I am not dishonorable. I gave my word she would see her child grow into a man. I mean to keep it. Now, if you don't mind, I would like to kiss my son goodnight. I'll join you and the ladies shortly."

After tucking Andy into bed, Brad returned to the parlor and overheard his mother's query, "If it's true the boy's father is a gentleman, why is she willing to give him up for adoption without informing the man of Andy's existence? Has he completely refused to acknowledge the boy?"

Beth shrugged, shaking her head, "She has only said that Andy's father is of our social class. I'm sure if she anticipated assistance from that quarter, she would take advantage of it. It is clear to me she has no hope of a better life for Andy than the one we can provide."

Taking his wife's hand, Brad sat, "I believe Beth is correct in her assessment that Mrs. Jetter perceives the adoption offers the best opportunity for Andy's future. I spoke with our attorney, Father. The papers will be complete next week. Andrew Jetter becomes Andrew Anderson on his first birthday. That same week we will host an adoption celebration for our friends and relatives and post notices in the newspaper."

Charles remained silent but scowled.

Brad smiled at his wife, "Although smaller than I had hoped, our family will be complete. I am satisfied."

"Thank you, Brad," she replied, love and relief evident in her eyes.

Later that evening, after retiring to their bedroom, Suzanne sought more enlightenment from her husband. "I can understand their hesitation to have another baby, but I am astounded that Brad is so agreeable to adopting a stranger's child. Surely you must have discussed this after dinner. Did he explain his thinking at all?"

Kicking off his shoes and removing his shirt, Charles grumbled, "His mind is set, so it makes no difference what his reasons are."

"Charles, please tell me what you make of all this? Andy is a sweet enough boy, but for Bradley to adopt the nursemaid's son just doesn't seem appropriate. I would appreciate having you help me to understand."

He slid his nightshirt over his head and heaved a sigh before answering. "Suzanne, there are aspects of Brad's character that, as a father, I find dreadfully disappointing. It is not right for me to expose these flaws to you and cause disillusionment in your only son. It is better for you to accept his decision and believe it was made as a selfless act of love toward his wife. Now let it be."

It perturbed Suzanne when Charles protected her from what he considered unpleasant aspects of life but knew it was useless to pursue a topic he closed. Still, she wished her husband would confide in her. Suzanne loved her offspring and recognized they, like everyone else in the world, had faults. She wasn't a child incapable of comprehending the frailties of human nature and didn't think admitting to them would cause her any undue misery. But for the sake of marital accord, she kept her thoughts to herself.

Spring 1811

The frigate *HMS Guerriere* stopped the *USS Spitfire* off Sandy Hook, New Jersey on May first and impressed their master-apprentice, John Diggio, a citizen of Maine. In response, Secretary of the Navy, Paul Hamilton, ordered the *USS President* and the *USS Argus* to patrol the coastal areas from the Carolinas to New York in search of the *Guerriere*. About noon on May sixteenth the *USS President* caught sight of a ship off the North Carolina coast. As he lowered his spyglass,

Commodore John Rodgers gave instructions to his second in command, "Come about and give chase. I believe it may be the *Guerriere*."

Aboard *HMS Little Belt* Captain Arthur Bingham, also peering through his telescope, called down to the quartermaster on the lower deck, "Signal that ship and request she identify herself."

A few minutes passed before the quartermaster shouted back, "Sir, she doesn't reply. Should we continue signaling?"

But after carefully studying the ship though his glass, Bingham declined, "That won't be necessary, she flies the blue pennant. She's American, and I prefer to avoid a confrontation. Let us be on our way."

The *President*, having a greater canvas capacity, drew closer, and by mid-afternoon Commodore Rodgers determined the ship was not the *Guerrier*. But wanting to know who she was, continued the pursuit. By evening the Americans closed, but the ships were at such an angle to each other that, in the fading light, *Little Belt* appeared larger than her four hundred sixty tons. At fifteen hundred seventy-six tons, Commodore Rodgers did not realize *President's* fifty-eight guns far exceeded the firepower of *Little Belt's* twenty.

As nightfall approached, fearing an attack, Bingham decided to identify his ship by hoisting his colors, but the darkening sky prevented Rodgers from making the identification. As the *Little Belt* came about, both commanders gave the standard hail, 'What ship is that?' Each believing he hailed first neither replied, so both hailed again.

Later, the Americans claimed *Little Belt* fired one cannon, hitting the *President's* mast, and injuring a man. So, Rodgers ordered a shot over the bow of *Little Belt,* but it fell short, hitting the ship. An answering broadside from the British began a battle that, according to Rodgers, lasted a mere fifteen minutes.

The British disputed this account of the incident. Bingham alleged the *President* shot a full broadside after the second hail, and only then did he respond in kind. *Little Belt* suffered ten dead and twenty-two wounded in the confrontation that Bingham claimed lasted three-quarters of an hour.

The following morning Lieutenant John Creighton from the *President* went aboard the *Little Belt* and apologized for the 'unfortunate affair' and offered safe passage to any port in the United States. But Bingham adamantly refused, accusing the Americans of acting out of revenge for the Chesapeake-Leopard Affair of four years ago.

They parted ways, but the incident added to the explosive powder keg of international relations.

S*ummer 1811, America*

"Anna Louise," Beth excitedly entered the nursery one August morning, "the children have received their first social invitation." Handing over a notecard, she said, "Look here, Mrs. Delaney's youngest son is two now, and she wants to start socializing him. She suggests we take Andy and Kathryn to visit today, saying they can play building blocks while we have tea."

Mrs. Delaney was the banker's wife. Pleased by the invitation, Anna Louise felt it was the validation she had needed to be comfortable with her decision of having allowed Bradley to adopt her son. Within a year or two, she calculated, none of the city's prominent families would even remember Andy's adoption. Everyone would think of him only as the young Anderson boy.

The banker's wife received Beth warmly and briefly admired her children as they gathered in the parlor.

Then Mrs. Delaney turned to Anna Louise, "The servants have their tea in the kitchen. The maid will show you the way. Mrs. Anderson and I will watch the children for the next half hour."

Although the dismissal was meant kindly, Anna Louise flushed in humiliation. Treated almost as a guest in the Anderson household, she was allowed to direct the maids for minor conveniences and took her meals in her room, not the kitchen. But hearing no contradiction from Mrs. Anderson, she gave a brief curtsy and followed the maid out of the room.

"Please don't mind Mrs. Delaney," the maid offered, seeing the high color in the nursemaid's face, "she is a thoughtful woman for the most part."

"You do your employer honor. She is lucky to have you," Anna Louise responded, mollified.

As they entered the below-stairs kitchen, the maid said, "Let me introduce you around. We are an informal lot if you don't mind. Chet is the butler. And Cook is...well, Cook." They chuckled. "Liz is the nursemaid, and I'm Emily," she concluded.

"I am Anna Louise, nursemaid to Mrs. Bradley Anderson."

They all nodded hello. Liz, a mature woman, most likely had not been employed as a wet nurse, Anna Louise surmised. Cook was advanced in years, and Emily quite young. Chet, the most interesting of them all, appeared only a few years older than herself. Understanding how servant romances developed, she supposed Chet would eventually pay court to the young Emily, but he courteously held the chair for Anna Louise before sitting next to her. Chatting in a relaxed and friendly manner, Chet Lambert was well informed about the families who mingled with the Delaneys, as was expected and kept them amused with his antidotes.

Sweetbriar

In turn, Anna Louise found her lack of information for gossip embarrassing.

The half-hour flitted by and ended when Chet directed Emily on some minor housekeeping detail, then offered to escort their guest back to the parlor himself. At the top of the stairs, he halted, stilling her with a quick touch on her arm, "Sunday is my half-day. May I call on you?"

Taken by surprise, Anna Louise hesitated. After loving Bradley for so long, the thought of encouraging another man had never entered her head.

Chet cleared his throat uncomfortably. "Forgive me. I am too forward. A woman as lovely as you must already have an admirer."

Anna Louise smiled uncertainly and placed her hand on his arm, "Not at all. It would please me to see you again."

Her beauty and hesitant smile pierced his heart, and he beamed in return. "Then I shall call for you at the service door at noon. We can stroll the neighborhood if that's agreeable to you."

She usually accompanied Mrs. Anderson when she left the house and never used the back door but knew servants never considered calling at the front entrance. "At noon, it is," she agreed then followed him back to her young charges.

Mrs. Delaney ignored the children while Mrs. Anderson struggled to hold the squirming Kathryn on her lap, nervously watching the boys throw blocks at each other. Anna Louise hurried over to the youngsters and crouched just as a block struck her back, preventing it from hitting Andy in the face. Angrily she turned, took another block out of Master Delaney's hand, and lightly slapped it. "You don't throw blocks at people," she admonished.

"See here, girl," Mrs. Delaney admonished abruptly, "Don't be slapping my boy. He's just playing."

Kathryn fussed, trying to wiggle off her mother's lap. Beth strove to hold her. The baby began sniveling and stiffly straightened her small body, trying to slide to the floor. "Perhaps we should go now, Anna Louise. This has been quite a stimulating day for the children."

Breaking free, Kathryn ran to her nursemaid. "Aw-naw," she cried, holding out her arms. Anna Louise picked her up and took Andy by the hand. Digging in his feet, he wailed, throwing a block and smashing a vase. Water and flowers splattered across the floor.

"I am so sorry," Beth exclaimed as she hurried over to pick up Andy. "Behave, young man," she said and swatted his bottom. He squalled louder and pounded his tiny fists on her chest. "I'm sorry, Mrs. Delaney," she said again and turned Andy around in her arms. "We had best leave. Thank you so much for the invitation. We will reciprocate within a few days." With both babies howling Beth and Anna Louise made their escape.

Once in the carriage, Anna Louise unbuttoned her bodice and allowed Kathryn to suckle. Within minutes she fell asleep. Passing the girl to her mother, Anna Louise took the cranky boy and repeated the process. Soon he too slept. As she buttoned her dress, she casually requested, "Mrs. Anderson, I haven't been in the habit of taking a half-day, but with your permission, I'd like to do so this Sunday."

"You are more than welcome to the time off. All the other servants take a half-day. It isn't an inconvenience." It was not an unusual request for a servant to make, but Beth's inquisitiveness prompted her to ask, "Is there something you wish to do that requires the carriage? If so, I'll speak to the coachman."

Shaking her head, Anna Louise declined the offer, "The Delaney's butler invited me for a stroll in the neighborhood."

Beth thought a moment, trying to remember what she might have heard about the man. "As I recall, a couple of months ago, Mrs. Delaney told me their elderly butler suddenly collapsed and died. It disrupted the family for weeks on end because he was married to their cook, and she was beside herself with grief. I suppose the current butler has only been with them for a few weeks. Would you like me to make inquiries about him?"

"Oh no, Mrs. Anderson, the Delaneys might wonder why you asked. I wouldn't want to cause anyone concern. We've only just met. I'm not at all sure that either of us will want to cultivate a friendship. I just wanted you to know that I'll take my half-day on Sunday, that's all."

"Perhaps you should start taking your half-day every week," Beth suggested. "It would do you good to get out of the house for a while. You are still young and should have friends of your own, maybe even think about getting married someday."

A rueful grimace crossed Anna Louise's face, "Twice before I hoped to marry. Both times the men disappointed me. I won't be that foolish again. Men think only of themselves. I would rather devote myself to Andy and Kathryn, whom I can depend upon to return my affections."

"You can't be serious. Undoubtedly, some unscrupulous men would take advantage of a woman. My Brad saved me from such a man before we married. He even fought a duel of honor because of it. But I believe most men are like my husband, considerate of women in general and steadfast in their love when they give it. Unfortunately, you did not meet such men," Beth pronounced.

With a disdainful sniff, Anna Louise countered, "And perhaps even men such as your husband sometimes find it impossible not to take advantage of a women's unfortunate situation."

Offended Beth retorted, "I don't know about other men, but I know my husband. He would never take advantage of a woman, especially if she found herself in circumstances beyond her control. If anything, he would go out of his way to assist a woman in need."

Anna Louise gave a mocking laugh. "You don't know men as I know them, Mrs. Anderson. Your husband may be better than most, but he is still a man. And all men have their failings when it comes to women. Some just more than others."

Beth sighed in sympathy for the acrimony she heard in the other woman's voice, "I'm sorry your experiences with two men have left you disenchanted with them all. For your sake, I hope someday you meet the man who will prove his love to you."

Turning to look out the carriage window, Anna Louise set her lips firmly together silently aware that, for the second time, she had come too close to revealing more than she should to Bradley Anderson's wife.

The Sunday morning mists slowly dissipated as Anna Louise berated herself for agreeing to walk out with the Delaney's butler. While pregnant with Andy, she had given up thoughts of men. Then, all she hoped for was to find work that would permit her to raise her baby as best she could. But now her son belonged to the Andersons, and she would spend the afternoon with Chet.

His friendly conversation and droll antidotes over tea in the Delaney's cozy kitchen had put her at ease. And his unexpected request to call flattered her into accepting without forethought. The exchange with Mrs. Anderson during the carriage ride home reminded her of all the reasons she should have declined. But for two days she vacillated, and now it was too late to send a note of regret. She would have to see him. It thrilled and intimidated at the same time.

What if he asked questions or wanted to know about her past? She hadn't given any thought to that before this very moment. She would just have to keep him talking about himself, she decided.

Usually, habit sent Anna Louise to the early church service, so she was available to care for the children while the Andersons attended the later service. Today she remained at home, devoting the extra time to curling the short hair around her face and neck. Foolishly she changed dresses three times. Not having sewn a new dress in almost two years, all her gowns were faded—all the more reason she should have refused the invitation.

Looking in the mirror one last time before going downstairs, Anna Louise feathered her black hair softly around her face, while curls at the nape of her neck escaped from her poke bonnet. Although the children were nursing less, the high waist of her gown emphasized her breasts. Fortunately, the bodice, which exposed most of her upper chest, wasn't cut too low for current fashion. The recent trend of wearing skirts at ankle length caused the toes of her black shoes to peek out from beneath the hem. It would have to do.

Knowing her bonnet would elicit a comment from Bradley, which she preferred to avoid, Anna Louise hurried downstairs to elude the Andersons before they returned from church. Passing through the kitchen, she snatched a biscuit before going around to the servants' entrance, where she sat on the bench just inside the door. Agitated, she tried nibbling at the bread in her hands, but her fingers nervously crumbled most of it onto her lap. When the bell sounded, Anna Louise bolted to the door, then hesitated. It wouldn't do for the man to know she waited for him. Brushing the last of the crumbs from her skirt, she squared her shoulders and opened the door.

Chet patiently stood on the far side of the threshold with his back to the door as he surveyed the graveled drive. Just large enough for the delivery wagons to unload supplies, it had a carriage house on the far side. His observations told him the residence was comparable to the Delaney's. Hearing the door open, he turned. She was as lovely as he remembered. "Good afternoon, Anna Louise," he said with a tip of his hat.

"Good afternoon, Chet," she replied.

Not as bold in her appraisal of him as he was of her, she noticed he was almost as tall as Bradley but with a broader build. As they strolled the neighborhood, she took quick peeks from under lowered lashes. His straight blond hair clipped unfashionably short, emphasized his clear blue eyes. His sensuous mouth, with full lips curving upward in natural good humor, accented his lantern jaw. His dark suit was common but relatively new, making her more conscious of her faded dress.

They spoke of the weather, a safe topic for both, but of too short duration. A shuffling silence followed as they sauntered, then Chet broke it. "I hail from the Boston area, but I can tell from your accent you are British. Did you come to America with Mrs. Anderson?" he inquired.

Precisely the type of question she wanted to forestall. She countered, "How did you come to work for Mr. and Mrs. Delaney if you lived in Boston?"

Not recognizing the evasion, Chet happily explained, "I was recommended by Mr. Delaney's sister. I worked in her household for a time. Their butler is just a few years older than I, so the arrangement didn't offer much opportunity for advancement. When Mr. Delaney wrote to his sister about the death of their butler, she suggested I take the position. It was exceedingly considerate of her to think of me. I had no family to hold me in Boston, so I accepted. One town seemed as good as another at the time."

"That's true," she agreed, "when one has only oneself to consider, it is best to take a chance on improving one's prospects in life. Have you been satisfied with your choice?"

Chet smiled, motioning her to the shade of a tree where they sat. "I have been satisfied enough until now. What about you, are you happy as nursemaid to the Anderson twins?"

An embarrassing flush rose in her face. Obviously, he didn't know Andy and Kathryn weren't twins. Or that she was Andy's birth mother. Flustered by his question and tongue-tied, Anna Louise sprang to her feet. "I must return home," she muttered as she swiftly strode away.

Confused by her reaction to his question, Chet leaped up and sped after her. "Please forgive me, Anna. I don't know what I said to upset you."

She shook her head and kept walking. Not knowing how else to stop her flight, he planted himself in her path. Not anticipating his maneuver, Anna Louise marched right into him, the speed of her gait knocking him back. She blinked in surprise.

His hands lightly grasped her shoulders to steady them both. Intoxicated by her nearness, Chet quickly brushed his lips against hers. The kiss was so sudden Anna Louise doubted it really happened. She was still gathering her wits when he pleaded, "Please don't walk away from me. I couldn't bear it if you did. I don't know what to make of it, but I've fallen in love with you."

"How can you say you are in love with me?" she exclaimed, shaken by his words. "You don't even know me."

He dropped his hands to his side and hitched his shoulder, "I don't know, but it's true. I think it happened that first day when you smiled at me. You have filled my mind every waking moment since."

The intense sincerity of his words touched her heart. She searched his eyes, then lowered hers. "Chet, you don't know anything about me, and if you did, I doubt you would speak of love. There are things in my past that would disgust you, so please let me pass," she said quietly.

He contemplated her for a moment then stepped aside, "I will walk you home, and with your permission, call on you again next Sunday."

She glanced at him and shook her head, "It's a mistake to see me again, Chet."

"I've made mistakes in the past and have no doubt I will make them in the future. When you know me, you'll find I'm an understanding and compassionate man. We are, none of us, so fortunate as to be without sin."

Facing him, she declared forcefully, "Some sins are more forgivable than others."

"I'll stop by at noon," he persisted.

Sighing, she shook her head again, "Do as you wish, but I won't see you."

They continued walking in silence, and as she opened the back door to Anderson's residence, he reiterated, "Next Sunday at twelve o'clock, Anna."

Three weeks passed as Anna Louise stubbornly refused to acknowledge her admirer, not even bothering to send him word of her rejection through the maid who came to fetch her. Each Sunday, Cook told her, he sat on the vestibule bench, patiently waiting for her, until evening's long shadows obliged him to abandon his post. Enduring the older woman's tsks and sniffs without comment, Anna Louise was relieved when the rains came so Chet would stop his persistent vigilance.

The nursery door opened, and Bradley entered, as was his habit after returning from church. He crouched low to hug and kiss his children before turning his attention to the nursemaid. "You are a hard-hearted woman, Louise," he said quietly. "But I suppose that is to be expected after two failed love affairs."

Startled, she quickly crossed to the open door and glanced up and down the hall to assure herself no one overheard his comment. Closing the door, she turned to face him, "What are you talking about?"

"I'm talking about the young man," he said, standing, "who comes to the back door every Sunday just to sit unattended on the bench."

Color rose to her cheeks. "How do you know about that, and what concern is it of yours?" she demanded.

"I know because Cook isn't as heartless as you. She wanted my permission to invite him into the kitchen for a warming cup of tea." Brad crossed his arms over his chest, "I think having tea with the man is the least you can do after he walked a mile in this downpour to see you."

Anna Louise gasped, her hand creeping to her throat, "Chet came today? But the weather is terrible. He couldn't possibly have come today."

"Oh, he's here, down in the kitchen right now. But if you don't want to see him, I'll forbid him to come again. I doubt he'll persist if I threaten to complain to his employer. Good positions are hard to come by, especially without a letter of reference."

"You wouldn't," she entreated. "He doesn't deserve to lose his job just because—"

"Because he is infatuated with a cold-hearted woman," he finished for her.

She looked at her clasped hands, twisting her fingers in distress. "I'll see him," she whispered.

"That's considerate of you," he responded derisively. "I'll tell Cook to feed him while he's here, I don't want his death of cold on my conscience." Herding his children to the door, Brad threw over his shoulder, "Wear your new blue dress. It flatters your eyes."

Pleased by the unexpected compliment, Anna Louise quickly reminded herself he was another woman's husband. Since coming into his household, other than the one passionate kiss, she had forced from him after agreeing to Andy's adoption, Bradley had never so much as touched her hand and always carefully kept a few feet of distance between them. But she had chosen the sapphire fabric for the gown precisely because it matched her eyes, intensifying their attractiveness, so she crossed to her bedroom and changed clothes.

When Anna Louise entered the kitchen, she found Bradley conversing with her guest. It was bad enough her former lover knew about her admirer. She didn't want him lingering in the kitchen to scrutinize her interaction with the man. The self-satisfied expression on Bradley's face when he noticed Chet's pleasure at seeing her enter the room dumbfounded her. Sitting at the scarred table, she threw an insolent look to her employer, who took the hint.

"As I was saying, if this downpour continues, as I expect it will, you'll be smart to take a cab home. You will be of no use to the Delaneys if you take sick, and the price of a hack is little enough compared to wages lost due to illness."

"Thank you, Mr. Anderson. I'll take your advice," promised Chet.

With a nod to Chet and a glance toward Anna Louise, Brad quit the room.

"Mr. Anderson is very considerate in giving his advice," Chet ventured as he took a seat at the table.

Anna Louise huffed a curt reply, "More considerate than you. Did you think your repeated calls would go unnoticed?"

Aware the cook overheard the rebuff; Chet questioned the wisdom of coming into the kitchen. "I only wanted your notice," he whispered earnestly.

"And a girl with half a head on her shoulders would appreciate the compliment," Cook blurted, which pleased Chet.

Wanting to throw her hands up in surrender, Anna Louise observed sarcastically, "I've noticed of late the meals served to me have been of poor quality and often cold. If you will cease your tacit incivility toward me and allow me decent food again, I will be more agreeable toward Chet in the future."

Cook placed a bowl of steaming soup before the man, replying with an insincere smile, "I don't know why you should complain about my cooking when the rest of the household is satisfied. Tell me, sir," she asked, "is the soup cold or lacking in flavor?"

Enjoying the interchange between the old woman and the young, Chet tasted the barley and vegetable broth, knowing which servant to appease, "The soup is delicious and hot, exactly the thing to ward off a chill. Perhaps a bowl will warm Anna's cold demeanor toward us, Cook."

With Chet solidifying the cook's good graces for future use, Anna Louise conceded the fight. "Very well, I'll have a bowl of soup. It will be the first hot, nourishing food served to me in weeks." She couldn't resist sheepishly returning the smiles she saw on the faces of her companions.

She savored the pungent fragrance of the steaming broth the cook placed before her, and when her appetite slackened, set her spoon aside, glancing over at her guest. The intense solemnity of his gaze was disconcerting, but he quickly masked it as he shifted his eyes to study his fingernails.

No secrets were long kept from household staff who improved their status among other servants by sharing secrets. From the look on Chet's face, Anna Louise guessed his interest in the gossip he had undoubtedly heard. With no intention of satisfying his curiosity, she resumed their conversation of three weeks ago.

"The last time we met, you mentioned that you had no family to hold you in Boston. Have you no family at all?"

Chet looked up, smiling with sparkling eyes, all the solemn thoughts of a moment ago wholly forgotten. "I had no brothers or sisters, and my mother died when I was ten."

To keep the conversation directed away from her, Anna Louise plied Chet with question after question about his background while divulging little of her own over the course of the afternoon. She learned his father had been a teacher at one of Boston's best schools, which explained Chet's education and manners. After completing his studies, his father's influence secured Chet a position at the school. But when his father died, the young man felt confined by the bureaucracy of the establishment and decided to strike out on his own. He worked for Mr. Delaney's sister about eighteen months before being recommended to replace the deceased butler.

Chet didn't confide to Anna Louise his desire to start a school of his own using the small inheritance he had saved. Now, this was a dream he hoped to realize sooner rather than later. Utterly in love, he wanted to marry this girl, which meant he needed the means and respectability of the position as headmaster to provide her with the type of home he believed she deserved.

Late Fall 1811, America

The solitary rider huddled deeper into his greatcoat and tugged the collar up higher, hoping to keep the drizzling rain from dripping down his neck. It was days like this that built the house of his discontent brick by brick. No matter what the weather, the town's mail must be delivered, and it was his job to do it. He dismounted, climbed the stairs of the front stoop, and rapped the knocker against the door twice. Without a word, the postal carrier shoved a letter into the servant's hand when the door opened, then retraced his steps, mounted his horse, and resignedly clomped down the road.

Silently, the manservant closed the door and placed the letter on the entry table, knowing Mr. Anderson would attend to it when he returned home.

That evening, as Brad shed his hat and gloves, he saw the letter. Picking it up, he noted it was addressed to Beth. "Where shall I find my wife?" he inquired of the butler.

Helping his employer off with his coat, the man replied, "She came down from the nursery about half an hour ago. I believe she is in the parlor."

Brad tapped the letter on his fingertips and went in search of Beth. She was neither in the parlor nor the dining room. "Have you seen my wife?" he asked the maid who was setting the table for the evening meal.

"She is in the kitchen, sir," she said as she bobbed a quick curtsy, "instructing Cook about the holiday menus."

"Please let her know I am home and will be in the parlor."

"Yes, sir," she bobbed again and headed for the kitchen.

He was kneeling before the fire, poker in hand when Beth hurried into the room. "Good evening, darling," she said. As Brad stood, she tilted her face so he could peck her cheek, but setting the poker aside, he grabbed her close and nuzzled her neck, sending chills down her spine. Giggling, she tried to squirm away. Brad clutched her and captured her lips with his. When he released his wife, she was breathless and flushed. He whistled in good-humored satisfaction and anticipated the evening to come. She smoothed her skirts and glanced sheepishly toward the door, hoping no one had observed their embrace.

"You have a letter, Beth," he said, gesturing with his hand toward the mantle where he'd place the letter before stoking the fire.

Curious, Beth took it then smiled gleefully. "It's from Mary," she exclaimed, recognizing the handwriting. Breaking the seal, she quickly perused the letter. Beth's countenance suddenly stilled. "Oh, Brad, Rolf Dunmore has disgraced himself," she said sadly.

"I'm not in the least bit surprised," Brad sniffed. "How did he manage that?"

"Mary doesn't give the details but says it stems from about the time of our wedding. For some reason, people started calling him Diaper Dunmore behind his back, and he became a laughingstock around town."

Brad smiled maliciously, recalling Dunmore had lost his bladder during the dueling incident in Hyde Park. "It is no worse than he deserves. What else?"

"He has become a drunkard and has lost vast sums of money by gambling it away. He has depleted his inheritance. Mary says if he doesn't soon find a woman with a substantial dowry to wed, then Uncle will need to buy him a commission in the army." She fanned her face with the letter as she gazed at her husband, "With his reputation, I don't see much hope of him finding an heiress."

"As I said," Brad reiterated, "It's no worse than he deserves."

"How can you say that?" Beth exclaimed.

"The man was always a rake and a scoundrel. Now he proves to be a wastrel and a drunkard to boot. He is not fit to be in polite society." Seeing her exasperation, Brad changed the subject, "Is there any other news?"

Glancing back at the letter, Beth read quickly. "Mary says that since we sailed from England, my father has been socializing more." Then her eyebrows shot up, "He has been keeping company with a widow in her mid-thirties, and it's rumored he intends to marry her!"

Concerned by the shock on her face, Brad took her elbow and escorted her to the couch. "He mentioned to me a few years ago that he wouldn't consider another marriage until you were settled. He gave me the impression he wanted an heir."

"An heir? Surely he is too old."

Brad couldn't help laughing as he sat next to his wife, "I should think not, sweet Beth. Your father was still a vigorous man when we last saw him. I dare say any number of eligible women would be pleased to produce an heir for him."

Beth blushed in consternation, "But Kathryn is almost two years old. Brad, if Papa succeeds, his granddaughter will be older than his son."

Patting her hand, Brad consoled her, "Such is life. Try to look at it from his point of view. If your father has no heir when he dies, his title and estate will revert to the crown. Additionally, there will be no one to carry on his tea business."

Beth sighed, "I suppose you are correct. It is just that he was so devastated by Mama's death. It never occurred to me he would consider another marriage."

"I assume Mary mentions this to prepare you for an announcement from your father," her husband suggested.

"Then, I shall write to Papa and assure him of my desire for his happiness."

"Your assurance, no doubt, will ease your father's mind and speed him toward conjugal bliss," Brad said, kissing his wife's temple. "And speaking of conjugal bliss, shall I instruct Cook to serve dinner in our bedchamber this evening?"

Tecumseh, whose name meant 'Shooting Star,' traveled extensively in his efforts to recruit additional allies. When a comet appeared in the sky, he told his followers it was a sign from the Great Spirit, and they accepted it as a good omen.

Following the murder of some white settlers, the Indian chief again met with Governor Harrison at Grouseland, assuring the American that he and his band desired peace with the United States. But Harrison believed Tecumseh was only trying to delay a confrontation until he built a stronger confederacy among the Five Civilized Tribes in the south. And though many of the tribes ignored Tecumseh's entreaties, a faction of the Creeks, known as the Red Sticks, joined his call to arms.

Shortly after meeting with Tecumseh, Harrison appointed his secretary, John Gibson, as acting-governor and left the territory to attend to business in Kentucky. Gibson, who had lived among the Miami for many years, soon learned of Tecumseh's plans for war. He called out the territory's militia and sent letters to Harrison requesting his immediate return.

When Harrison came back, he brought a small contingent of army regulars and took command of the militia. He apprised his superiors in Washington, D.C. of the situation, and attempting to maintain peace. They authorized him to face the Indian confederacy in a show of force. The American command of approximately one thousand men consisted of two-hundred-fifty army regulars from the Fourth US Infantry Regiment, one hundred Kentucky volunteers, and nearly six hundred Indiana militia, including two companies of Indiana Rangers.

On October third, while awaiting supplies from the town of Vincennes, the Americans camped and began building Fort Harrison. But within a week, the Indians ambushed a scouting party and inflicted several casualties. This prevented the soldiers from further foraging. Their supplies quickly dwindled, requiring them to cut rations until new provisions arrived. On October twenty-ninth, with provender in hand, Harrison's army resumed their advance on the Indian stronghold of Prophetstown.

Late on November sixth, Tecumseh's brother, Chief Prophet, sent some of his trusted braves to meet the Americans as they approached his town. They carried a white flag and requested the Americans parley with them the next day. Harrison agreed and moved his men to a hill near the confluence of the Wabash and Tippecanoe Rivers. They camped in battle array and posted sentinels throughout the night. However, Harrison did not order the building of defensive works, believing the shallow creek on the east and the steep embankment on the west sides of the hill provided enough protection.

The Indians had fortified their town, but their defenses were weak. Fearing an imminent attack, panic set in. The Winnebago encouraged a sneak attack against the Americans, but before leaving to travel south, Tecumseh had instructed his brother to maintain peace until his return. After consulting the spirits, Chief Prophet decided the best course of action was to kill Harrison in his tent.

A Negro wagon driver, who had defected from the Americans to the Shawnee during the expedition, agreed to lead the warriors. The Prophet cast spells to protect his brethren from harm and confuse the Americans. But in the pre-dawn hours, sentinels detected the advancing warriors. Gunshots rang out. The awakening soldiers were nearly surrounded. The first skirmishes flared up on the northern perimeter, but soon fierce fighting blazed at the southern point of the hill. Several commanding officers died in the surprise attack, and without leadership, the defenders on the south perimeter fell back. Indians followed the retreating forces into camp. Ensign John Tipton regrouped the soldiers, and with the help of two reserve companies under the command of Captain Rodd, repulsed the attackers, and sealed the breach.

The Indians charged several more times, targeting both the north and south ends of the encampment, but the Americans had overcome their surprise. The regulars reinforced the militia units, and the soldiers held their line. As the sun rose, the Indians ran low on ammunition and slowly withdrew.

The angry braves challenged the Prophet and accused him of deceit because his spells had not confused the Americans for more than a short time and did not prevent the death of many warriors. The chief insisted they launch a second assault and offered to cast new spells. His followers refused.

When Harrison sent a small scouting party to Prophetstown the next day, they found it deserted except for one old woman too ill to run away. Sparing the woman, Harrison ordered the town burned, and all the cooking implements destroyed. They confiscated everything of value, including five thousand bushels of corn and beans. Without food or the means to cook it, the old woman and the Indians of the confederacy would be hard-pressed to survive the winter.

As word of the Battle of Tippecanoe slowly reached the American public, outrage flared against the British for supplying the tribes with firearms and inciting them to violence. International tensions, already close to flashpoint, heated further as the war hawks in Congress passed resolutions against the British for their interference in American domestic affairs.

Chapter VIII
Spring 1812, America

Standing before Mr. Delaney's library door, Chet Lambert nervously smoothed his coat as yesterday's conversation with Anna Louise came to mind. She'd caught him staring at her as he sometimes did when he speculated about the secrets she held. He had learned early on not to ask even the most casual question about the life she left behind in England, and though Anna discussed many topics with him, she discouraged the subject of her life in the Anderson household.

Chet longed for a more intimate relationship with Anna but was stymied in its accomplishment. The few Sunday afternoons he was not able to call on her, he sent notes of apology with assurances of his affection. The acknowledging replies always expressed her regrets at not seeing him but never gave an indication she felt more than friendship toward him.

Was her past as shameful as she intimated so many months ago? Or only too painful for her to revisit? He didn't want to believe the servants' gossip that it was her son the Andersons had adopted. Why would they adopt the son of their nursemaid? And why, even if the boy was illegitimate as some speculated, would a loving mother give her only child away?

That was when Anna Louise broke into his thoughts. "Chet, I find it disturbing the way you look at me sometimes."

"My apologies," he said, staring down at his fingernails. "I don't mean to be impolite, but you are such a mystery to me, Anna."

Glancing away from the man sitting beside her, Anna Louise murmured, "I can assure you, if you knew my secrets, you would lose your fondness for me."

"Not 'fondness,' my dearest," he insisted, taking her hand, "it is love divine."

"Please don't say such things to me," she pleaded but allowed him to continue holding her hand.

Leaning close, Chet whispered in her ear, "There will come a time, and I hope it is soon when I shall not only declare my love for you but ask—"

Standing abruptly, she interrupted, "Are you serious about opening a school?"

He nodded, sitting straighter, "In the morning I shall request an hour of Mr. Delaney's time to review my plan. I've spent seven months working out the details and think I've done as much as possible short of laying money down for a building." Warming to his subject, he elaborated, "If I can find a location that provides living quarters for me in addition to the classroom, I believe I have enough money saved to get me through the first year. I hope Mr. Delaney agrees with my idea to start with day classes and expand into a boarding school in the future. That will allow me to add staff as the need arises."

"But how will you find students?" she asked, sitting again.

This, of course, was the key, but Chet shrugged confidently, "My position with Mr. Delaney gives me knowledge of the most affluent and influential families around. If I can initially persuade a few of these families to place their sons in my school, I know I can be successful in time. And once I'm prepared to take in boarders, my school will be able to attract students from as far away as Boston and Salem."

She laid her hand on Chet's arm and looked into his eyes with concern, "But are you sure it is wise to discuss this with Mr. Delaney? He is your employer, after all."

Smiling, Chet placed his hand over hers, "I'm hoping Mr. Delaney will recommend me to his friends. Besides, I need a banker. He is as good as they come."

But Chet understood and shared her concern as he stood before the door. It was time to see if his dreams would pass the reality of a close examination by the banker. His employer had granted Chet a short meeting before the dinner hour. He warily knocked on Mr. Delaney's library door.

"Come in, Lambert. No need to be hesitant since you requested this interview." Chet entered, and Mr. Delaney inquired, "Are there troubles with the staff? It seems as if every other year, we end up with a maid in the family way and have all the hassle of getting her to 'fess up to the culprit responsible. I'd just as soon you'd take care of those unpleasantries for me," the banker said.

"Sir, your household is blessed with serenity among the staff. I came to request you review a business plan for opening a new school." Chet's response startled the portly man.

Disgusted, he stood, "I'm surprised you agreed to approach me this way. If whoever put the plan together doesn't have enough faith in it to bring it to me personally, I can't see why I should waste my time with it."

"Mr. Delaney, please hear me out. This is my business plan. I want to open the school," Chet hurriedly explained.

Slowly the big man resumed his seat, "Are you dissatisfied with your position here, Lambert? If it's higher pay you want, I'm open to discussion. You haven't been here a year, and yet I am satisfied with your performance. The household seems to be running smoother since you arrived."

"Thank you for the compliment, Mr. Delaney. If I wanted more pay, I would ask for it without quibbling. However, my desire is to establish a new school. I was educated to be a teacher and feel it is time I resume my trade. Will you please go through my business plan and tell me if you think it is feasible?" he requested levelly.

Eyeballing his butler critically, the banker silently held out his hand. When handed the portfolio, he perused it page by page, reading swiftly. Chet held his breath as the minutes ticked away. The few minutes felt like an eternity before Mr. Delaney snapped the book closed and handed it back. "Your plan is well thought out. Only one or two items need more consideration. The biggest question that comes to mind is how you plan to attract students."

"Sir, would you consider becoming my first patron? I would waive the fee for your oldest son if you pay the fee for your middle son," Chet offered.

A pause of at least five seconds passed before a low chuckle rumbled from the seated man, "By my word, Lambert, if I do that, I'll not only lose an excellent butler, but I'll have to recommend your school to everyone I know." The chuckle became an outright laugh as the man heaved his bulk out of his chair. He clapped Chet on the shoulder, "Tomorrow morning, I want you to ride to my office with me. We'll discuss this in more detail as one businessman to another. I'm not giving you any guarantees I'll buy into this venture, but at least I'll give it serious consideration."

A huge sigh of relief exploded from Chet as a grin spread across his face, "Thank you, Mr. Delaney Thank you. I appreciate—"

"Don't thank me yet, young man," the banker interrupted, holding up his hand. "Tomorrow, you will find out just how hard a businessman I am. I expect every 'i' and every 't' to be dotted and crossed before I agree to anything," he emphasized.

"Yes, Mr. Delaney," Chet acknowledged, but his grin remained.

In Mr. Delaney's office the next day, the two men discussed the business plan in detail. Concerned Chet Lambert would expend most of his capital on the purchase of a building, the banker suggested the man lease property instead, then provided letters of introduction to a few property owners who might have appropriate buildings available.

For over an hour, they discussed the children of various families. Mr. Delaney cautioned against approaching larger families who would find it less expensive to hire a tutor than pay a flat fee for each child. Then the banker promised to provide a reference letter for Lambert to use when approaching the fathers of his potential students.

The list of supplies was short but costly. Slates, chalk, benches, and tables would do for the younger children, but the older boys needed paper, ink, and quills to become proficient in the written word. Again, the banker recommended reliable and trustworthy businessmen to provide these needed supplies.

But to accomplish the first order of business, locating a building, Chet needed time to contact the men who owned them. He agreed to exchange his Sunday half days for time during the week, promising if he located a building quickly, to fulfill his butler duties until a replacement was hired and trained. Mr. Delaney thought three months adequate time, so by Chet's reckoning, he would have most of the summer to prepare the building and obtain the furnishings and supplies before opening the school in late summer or early fall.

Within a year, he anticipated being positioned well enough to ask for Anna's hand in marriage.

Expecting the Andersons home from church at any minute, Anna Louise hurriedly dressed Andy and Kathryn for the monthly visit to their grandparent's home. On visiting day, Mr. and Mrs. Anderson liked the children to be ready to leave without delay. But the nursemaid was behind schedule.

She'd received a discouraging letter from Chet. It was May, and with all the erratic and uncertain rumors of war, property owners hesitated to commit to a long lease. No doubt, they anticipated charging the government exorbitant rates for housing troops or supplies if the rumors bore fruit. Chet conveyed his anxiety over the possibility of losing his position in the Delaney household before securing a property, saying Mr. Delaney had interviewed several men and would likely settle on a replacement within a week. Knowing the housekeeper's Sunday visits took her past the Delaney home, Anna Louise had taken the time to dash off an encouraging reply.

The rapid sound of boots bounding up the stairs alerted her that her tardiness was discovered. Bradley's tall frame filled the nursery doorway, "Did you forget to wind your clock, Louise?" Impatience and irritation were evident in his voice. "We've waited in the carriage a good ten minutes. I know Beth asked the maid to remind you of our visit to my parents today."

Finishing the last button on Kathryn's coat, she turned the child around and patted her bottom, "Give your daddy a kiss." Walking into her bedroom, she tossed over her shoulder, "Let me get my cloak and bonnet. Then I'll be ready."

Brad followed but stopped in the doorway separating the two rooms, "I thought you spent your Sunday afternoons with the Delaney's butler. What's his name? Chad or something, isn't it?"

With fingers pausing momentarily on her bonnet ribbons, Anna Louise shifted her gaze in the mirror to look at Bradley's reflection. "His name is Chet Lambert, Mr. Anderson," she said icily. "I won't see him for a while as he is occupied elsewhere."

"I'm surprised you let him get away, Louise," Brad commented, crossing his arms and leaning on the door frame. "He gave me the impression he was steadfast in his attraction to you."

Angrily she finished tying the bow beneath her chin, turning with her hands on her hips, "You are insufferable, Bradley Anderson. I'll have you know Chet loves me."

A supercilious smile slowly spread across his face, "He's a lucky man indeed, Louise, if he's captured your heart. Before he showed up last year, I thought you'd sworn off men forever. But they say, 'three's a charm.' Let me be the first to offer you best wishes for happiness."

Brushing past him, she replied sourly, "You can keep your felicitations. They won't be needed." She lifted Andy and kissed his cheek. "How's my little boy? Are you ready to go see your grandparents?"

Brad reached over and stole Andy out of her arms, "Come, son, I'll let you ride on my shoulders." He lifted the boy over his head, and casting Louise a disdainful

Sweetbriar

frown, ducked out the door leaving her to bring Kathryn.

Before stepping into the carriage, Brad handed Andy to Beth, and once seated next to his wife, took Kathryn onto his lap and left Anna Louise to scramble into the carriage unassisted. Holding his wife's hand, Brad pressed her fingers to his lips while staring at the nursemaid seated across from them. His gesture made it plain that he had his family, and she didn't belong.

"Anna Louise," Beth said, "I'm surprised you're joining us today. I thought you spent time with that nice Mr. Lambert on Sunday afternoons."

Looking out the window, Anna Louise set her lips firmly together.

Brad replied for her, "Mrs. Jetter tells me the man is occupied elsewhere these days."

"Yes, that's right, I remember now," Beth said. "Mrs. Delaney told me how inconvenient it is to lose him. Apparently, he intends to open a school, and she is put out because her husband is lending his assistance instead of 'keeping him in his place' to use her words. Why a congenial man like Mr. Delaney married a woman like that is beyond me."

"I didn't know your beau was a scholar, Mrs. Jetter," Brad broke in. Recognizing a serendipitous opportunity, he continued, "Mr. Delaney must be impressed with the man to risk helping him open a school in these uncertain times. Perhaps I should call on the gentlemen to lend my support."

Before the nursemaid's objection to his interference escaped her lips, Beth inquired, "How could you help, darling? The man is opening a school, not a merchant shop."

Smiling indulgently, Brad replied, "Perhaps I'll sponsor an orphan or two. A good education goes a long way toward overcoming poverty. And if the boys are diligent, I can put them to work when they complete their studies."

"That's very liberal of you, Mr. Anderson," Anna Louise said, caught unaware by his munificence.

"And for you, dear Mrs. Jetter, I shall bring my influence to bear on others to sponsor children," Brad declared. "Don't you agree, Beth, that we should exert ourselves to help Mrs. Jetter's gentleman friend succeed?"

"Your generosity is one of the things I love about you, Brad," his wife enthused. "Promise you will call on Mr. Delaney and Mr. Lambert first thing tomorrow."

Chuckling, Brad agreed, "Anything to keep the women in my life happy."

Late Spring/Early Summer 1812

The murder of Prime Minister Spencer Perceval ended Great Britain's staunch refusal to honor America's neutrality. On June sixteenth Lord Castlereagh announced to Parliament the repeal of the 1807 Orders in Council. But their concessions came too late.

President Madison had delivered his war message to Congress on June first. Many in Congress believed England's attention on the war in Europe would force an early end to the conflict in America, stressing a short war would have the additional benefit of permitting the United States to wrest valuable farmland away from Canada. On the eighteenth of June, after more than two weeks of debate, Mr. Madison had his war. The United States of America would fight its second war of independence against the United Kingdom of Great Britain and Ireland.

Summer 1812, America

Lying on her bed, Beth wondered why she was so fatigued. All the recent talk of war had brought on stomach upset, and indigestion caused her to lose her appetite. She was tired and wanted to indulge in a short nap before her husband returned home from work. Congress had approved the use of privateers, and Brad was leaving for Boston in the morning to obtain Letters of Marque for the Surrey Trading Company captains who chose to support the war effort. Anticipating the demands in bed his imminent journey would produce that evening; she wanted to be rested.

No sooner did Beth drift off to sleep than an unfamiliar male voice awakened her. Puzzled, she arose, opened her bedroom door, and stepped into the hall. The voice came from the nursery.

"You are being unreasonable," Chet said in exasperation. "I deserve a better explanation than that. I understand your hesitation to leave a good position, but I'm asking you to marry me."

Originally Chet had thought marriage was out of the question for at least a year, but circumstances had changed. Mr. Delaney and Mr. Anderson put their heads together and hatched the idea of using a large house for the school, which would accommodate a few boarding students in addition to the day students. They found a house with six big bedrooms on the second floor and a few smaller bedrooms on the third. Chet would situate the classroom on the main floor where two good sized rooms would be combined by removing a wall.

But he needed help. A wife and one servant would suffice for now. Almost any good servant would do, but for a wife he wanted Anna. He loved her and sought to marry her as soon as possible.

"Did you hear me? I asked you to marry me," Chet persisted.

"I can't. I promised to stay until the children are grown."

Drawing a deep breath, he patiently argued, "No one would hold you to that promise. You have an offer of marriage. I am sure Mr. and Mrs. Anderson will understand."

"*You* do not understand," she countered. "If you knew anything at all about me, you would know why I must stay."

Curious, Beth crept closer, too embarrassed to reveal herself but unable to stop eavesdropping. If concern over Andy prevented her nursemaid from accepting the man's offer, Beth would reassure Anna Louise she could visit Andy whenever she chose.

"That's just it. I don't know anything about you, so I can't understand," Chet calmly replied. "I've waited for you to trust me and think it's time. What is the secret you are so afraid to tell me? Is it that Andy is your son? That's what all the gossips say."

Quietly, Anna Louise nodded. "Yes, Andy is my son," she whispered.

His breath exploded as if punched out of his lungs. "I haven't wanted to believe the rumors." After a moment's pause, he heedlessly continued, "I don't care if you have a dozen children. I love you and want to marry you. But why on earth did you let Mr. Anderson adopt your son?"

"You want to know my secrets?" she hissed passionately. "I'll tell you, and then we'll see how enduring your love is. I was Bradley Anderson's mistress for four years, and it is he who fathered Andy."

Scandalized by the shocking revelation, Beth silently clutched at her throat, attempting to breathe. '*Brad and Anna Louise! Could it possibly be true?*' she thought as vertigo tunneled her vision to pinpoints of dizzying sparks. Blindly, Beth groped down the hall to her bedroom and locked the door behind her. Frantically her mind raced as events of the past two years flashed through her mind.

Anna Louise insisting she meet Brad before accepting the position as nursemaid; her husband rudely inquiring if Anna Louise intended to be companion to his wife and wet nurse to his child; Brad's obvious fondness for the son of their servant and his easy acquiescence to Beth's idea of adopting the boy. It began to make sense.

Then her mind stretched further back to the night of their engagement party when Brad had arrived hours late, saying he'd been unavoidably detained. Hot, seething rage erupted like a volcano. It spewed comprehension, molten as lava, into her brain. The engagement party was only a week before their wedding, and Andy was only three weeks older than Kathryn. The man Beth loved and thought she knew so well had played her false and then had dared to allow that woman into their home. All the years he paid court to her, he had been lying in the arms of another woman. The saber-sharp knife of betrayal sliced through her heart, wounding to the depths of her being. Beth fell across the bed as wretched tears of anguish racked her soul.

Slowly reason returned and with it questions of doubt. Had the two lovers contrived for Anna Louise to be the wet nurse as a ruse while they continued their affair? Even now, did the woman refuse to marry Mr. Lambert in hopes of winning Brad for herself?

Hopelessly alone, Beth realized everyone she trusted to console and guide her lived in England while she was in America, a land that, at one time, she had hoped never to see. Rising, she breathed deeply to calm her aching heart, and going to the basin, splashed cool water on her face. "I must think clearly to find a way out of this mess," she whispered to herself. After a moment, she knew. "I shall return home to Father."

With this resolution, Beth sat on the bed to plan her escape. As fond as she was of Andy, she would leave the bastard to her husband and his whore. But Kathryn was hers. It would be more difficult to travel with a child, but Beth wouldn't leave her daughter to be raised by the harlot. As a plan took shape in her head, she breathed easier. She would pretend all was well until she was ready to flee. "No," Beth murmured, "I flee not in shame but righteously leave of my own volition."

So absorbed was she in her thoughts, Beth didn't hear the doorknob rattle. Brad knocked and called her name, wrenching her back to the present. Startled, she cried, "Just a moment," as she rose from the bed to cross the room and unlock the door.

His initial irritation at finding the door locked changed to concern when Brad saw his wife's face. "Sweet Beth, are you all right? You don't look well."

Offended by the endearment, she turned away, "I don't feel well."

"Shall I send for Dr. Rutherford?"

"No, I want to be alone," she replied tersely, crossing to the bed and reclining with her back to her husband.

The silence lasted long enough that Beth thought he had withdrawn until she felt his hand on her shoulder. "Perhaps I should delay my journey. I don't like the thought of leaving if you are ill."

She reached over and placed her hand over his, "I shall be fine. I'm just upset with all the talk of war."

Sitting on the edge of the bed, Brad turned his wife toward him and realized her face was tear-stained. He drew her into his arms, pressing her head to his chest, "My poor sweet Beth, you are caught in the middle, aren't you? British born and American wed. Let me comfort you. I'll have dinner served to us up here."

After learning the horrible truth, Beth couldn't bear to endure her husband's embrace, and knowing dinner in their bedroom always lead to intimacies, she objected. "I am too upset and have lost my appetite. I'd rather not eat at all. Perhaps I'll feel better tomorrow, but tonight I want to be alone. Would you mind sleeping in the guest bedroom?"

Except for the time following Kathryn's birth, they had always slept together. Brad stared into her eyes, not seeing the love he anticipated, but hostility, as if he were an enemy. Shaken, he asked incredulously, "Are you serious?"

She pulled away. "You'll leave in the morning for a fortnight. I'm sure by the time you return, all will be well with me, but tonight I'd rather be alone. Please."

Puzzled, he studied her in silence for a long minute before concealing his disgruntlement, "If it makes you feel better, Beth, I shall do as you ask."

Turning away, she mumbled her gratitude. At a loss for words, Brad gently kissed her temple and quit the room.

Next morning, long after the household bustled to life, Beth remained in bed, impeding the manservant from packing his master's traveling case. An hour past Brad's intended departure, he strode into the room and hurriedly rifled through his wardrobe, yanking out clothes, which he handed through the door to the servant.

Beth continued to feign sleep, but Brad shook her shoulder, letting her know he wasn't fooled. "I don't know what has come over you, but I would appreciate a farewell kiss."

With a great sigh and rustle of bedclothes, she turned and tilted her cheek toward her husband. Easing onto the bed, Brad clasped her hands and studied her face. For the briefest of moments, he saw deep emotional pain before she cloaked it with a cool, speculative gaze. Perceiving the distance that had grown between them in the span of one night, apprehension squirmed in his belly like writhing snakes.

"The night Kathryn was born, I thought the worst torture on earth would be to have death snatch you away from me. But the thought of losing your love is worse torture. You are the only woman I have ever loved or ever shall love."

Something primal shifted in the depths of her eyes. She sat up, kissed him with familiar zeal, then lay back on the pillows, "Goodbye, Brad, safe journey."

But the river of unease washing through him remained as he took his leave.

Beth stayed in bed while her mind scrambled about examining one alternative after another. Her husband's heartfelt declaration put to rest her fears that his affair with the nursemaid had continued throughout their marriage. But it did not negate his deceit. Perhaps if he had confessed the affair in the beginning, she could have forgiven him, but he had allowed her to befriend his former mistress and accepted the woman, along with his bastard son, into their home. Even if he agreed to turn the woman out, Andy would be there as a constant reminder of his perfidy. It was beyond her forbearance to endure.

As evening approached, Beth again determined Kathryn's and her future would be in England. She preferred to avoid seeing Anna Louise but needed clothing for her child, and not wanting to risk alerting the servants to her plan, decided to take as little as possible. Ringing for the maid, she requested two valises be brought from the attic, then she steeled herself and walked to the nursery.

The children, dressed for bed, ran to their mother, happy to see her again. Beth stooped to hug and kiss them both. "How are my little darlings tonight?" she asked the children, surprised her voice sounded normal.

"They both missed you today, Mrs. Anderson," Anna Louise commented. "I hope you are feeling better."

"Yes, I am well."

"Your husband was distressed about leaving this morning. I am sure a letter from you will relieve his mind."

"Yes, I shall write before I leave. I've decided to take Kathryn to visit her grandparents for a few days. Please pack clothing for her tonight as we'll leave at first light," Beth instructed.

"Are you sure you are well enough, Mrs. Anderson? Perhaps you should wait a few days."

For the first time since entering the nursery, Beth looked directly at the nursemaid, "I am well enough to care for one child but not for two. I want Andy to stay here with you."

The maid clattered in with the smaller of the two satchels and placed it in the middle of the room.

"Will you be gone long?" Anna Louise asked.

"I don't know yet. Just pack whatever will fit in this bag. I'll send a note in a few days letting you know my intentions," she replied, then left with the maid to pack the other case with her own clothing.

Early next morning, Beth and Kathryn climbed into the carriage and jaunted off toward the Anderson's home. They journeyed barely two miles before Beth tapped the roof and instructed the driver to take them to the post coach station instead. From there, she mailed two letters, one to her husband and one to Anna Louise, then took the post coach to Plymouth, hoping to find passage to Canada and eventually to England.

***

Panic set in as Anna Louise read her letter from Beth. She never intended for Bradley's wife to know of their affair, but it was obvious Mrs. Anderson had learned the truth. She dreaded to think what the second missive contained. It was addressed to Mr. Anderson. Expecting him to be gone a fortnight, just three days had passed since his departure. It was obvious Mrs. Anderson intended a long head start before her husband became aware of her flight. Anna Louise needed to send immediate word to her employer and decided to forward Beth's letter along with one of her own.

'Dear Mr. Anderson,' she began then stopped. She wondered when Bradley had become Mr. Anderson. It flowed so naturally onto the page. Anna Louise realized she thought of him not as Bradley anymore but as Mr. Anderson. That gave her pause for even deeper reflection. Setting the quill aside, she stood and paced the room. If Mr. Anderson was no longer Bradley in her mind, how did she think of Chet? And, of course, he was Chet, not Mr. Lambert. She questioned whether she no longer loved Mr. Anderson and loved Chet instead. And the truth revealed itself.

Mr. Anderson had rescued her from the life of prostitution she abhorred but had substituted another type of prostitution. It was more agreeable but no less a life of sexual favors in exchange for monetary value. It wasn't until he disclosed his unmarried state that she conceived herself in love with him. And even then, her original thought was only to entice him into marriage. When she felt him drifting away to another woman, she fooled herself into thinking she loved the man when, in fact, she only feared a future without his protection.

With thoughts of Chet, serene happiness permeated her breast. For months, as Sunday approached each week, she felt expectancy in anticipation of seeing him, followed by lonely disappointment if he was kept away. When the pursuit of his dream for opening a school required Chet to forgo his Sunday afternoon visits, it was his weekly letters that sustained her. And, the other day, after callously divulging some of her dark past, instead of turning on his heel and stalking out, Chet sat and shed angry tears before kneeling at her feet, professing his love, and asking anew for her hand in marriage. What a fool she had been to reject him. The anguish she endured after his departure was because she had denied her own heart's desire.

With swift and graceful movements, Anna Louise returned to the desk, set aside her first letter, and wrote a new one.

> *Dearest Chet,*
>   *Of all the shameful experiences of my life my greatest regret is my despicable treatment of your kind and loving heart.*
>   *Please forgive me.*
>   *Yours always,*
>   *Anna*

If he truly loved her enough to offer marriage again, she would marry him immediately. If that meant never seeing her son again, so be it. She loved Chet and wanted to share his life.

Then, with a clarity of mind Anna Louise had never felt before, she wrote to her former lover.

After the long, humid day finalizing numerous Letters of Marque for the captains of various ships, Brad wanted only to disrobe and soak in a refreshing bath, it being too hot to consider eating until after the sunset. The innkeeper passed him a thick letter. Seeing it was from his household, but not his wife, Brad tossed it on the table in his room. It could wait until later.

To cool off, he lingered longer than usual in the bathing tub before dressing and going downstairs for dinner. The recent outbreak of war had filled the Capitol with out-of-towners who came to seek their fortunes from the government's coffers. With his work completed, Brad took the time to enjoy an extra mug of ale while he conversed with the other men at his table. By the time he climbed the stairs to his room, the letter was forgotten.

Next morning, as Bradley dressed, he spied the small packet on the table, decided to read it with breakfast, and put it in his coat pocket. But the inn was as crowded as the previous night, necessitating Brad to share a table and conversation with strangers. The letter was forgotten.

Strolling along the avenue after breakfast, peering into shop windows, Brad was rewarded when he spied an intricately carved ivory bracelet, which he purchased for Beth. Satisfied with the gift, he put it in his pocket and discovered the letter. Unfolding the outer letter, he read:

> Dear Mr. Anderson,
> The day after you left for Boston Mrs. Anderson took Kathryn, supposedly, for a visit to your parents. But today I received a letter from your wife indicating she knew the truth about Andy's paternity.
> This disclosure, coming on the heels of her strange illness and abrupt departure, leads me to believe she overheard a conversation between Mr. Lambert and me, in which I foolishly told him the truth. I won't explain my reasons for the conversation, as you may perceive them of your own accord.
> At the same time my letter arrived,

> so did another addressed to you, and it is enclosed. From the handwriting on the exterior there can be no doubt it is from Mrs. Anderson.
>
> No one knows of these circumstances and without your permission I hesitate to take anyone into my confidence. Please return home immediately or, if the enclosed letter from your wife indicates a different course of action, at least send me instructions.
>
> I would give anything for this harm to be undone. Please forgive me.
>
> A. L. Jetter

The world ceased to exist as Brad's trembling hands frantically broke the seal on the smaller correspondence.

> Dear Brad,
>
> I find myself in an unbearable situation that can only be remedied by leaving. It is humiliating to know I've lived for over two years in close proximity to your mistress. Perhaps the affair didn't continue after our marriage, only the two of you are privy to that knowledge, but it is obvious it lasted past the date of our engagement because Andy is only three weeks older than Kathryn. How could you lie with another woman so close to the date we were to marry?
>
> More importantly, how am I to awaken every morning and look upon the byproduct of your infidelity? Without Andy's presence, perhaps in time, I would forget your duplicity. I find it sadly ironic it was I who suggested you adopt the boy

Conversely, I am unable to forsake the greatest expression of the love we shared and have Kathryn with me. She is my sole consolation.

I intend to return to my father's home and shall write again after I secure passage.

Please do not follow me.
     Goodbye,
     Beth

With heart quaking in disbelief, moisture blurred Brad's vision. For long minutes he stood, unaware of the jostling from the milling crowd, but when his mind grasped her intention, his chest constricted in terror. They were at war with Britain! There was no safe passage to England. Every American and British ship sailing the world was fair game to the opposing belligerent. Beth had no concept of the danger.

Sharp awareness of his surroundings flooded back. Running, Brad wildly pushed through the throng. At the inn, he sent to the stable for his gelding then quickly stuffed his possessions into his saddlebags. After hastily settling his account with the innkeeper, Brad was away as fast as his horse could maneuver through traffic. Soon the city was left behind. Loosening the reins, his horse surged ahead. Miles flew by. After a time, the winded animal stumbled, alerting the rider to his mount's fatigue. Slowing to an easier canter, Brad's mind cleared. He began to consider a rational course of action.

First, he needed to determine a starting point in his search. If Beth had gone to his parent's house and stole away from there, it might be impossible to track her. But if their driver took her elsewhere, it might provide some clue. Brad examined the exterior of her letter, disappointed to find the postmark was from the post station closest to their home. If the letter had been mailed en route, it would have indicated a direction, but she had been too clever for that. Knowing Beth kept only a small amount of pin money handy, preferring to have merchants bill her husband for her purchases, Brad reasoned she was incapable of traveling far.

As possibilities sifted through his mind, Brad's confidence in finding Beth grew. With his fears diminished, he thought more clearly, and logical steps for locating his wife and daughter emerged.

The almost single-minded pursuit of seafaring was the basis of New England's economy, so the region had suffered dramatically from five years of on-again, off-again embargoes. New England editors derisively reversed the spelling of the word and published satirical cartoons referring to the 'O-Grab-Me' policies of Mr. Jefferson, and his successor, Mr. Madison.

Opposition to the war was especially strong among the French, Irish, and German immigrants inhabiting Baltimore where several riots broke out, and the offices of the *Federal Republican* newspaper were destroyed. People thought to be sympathetic to the British were assaulted, and the war hawk city officials did naught to stop the violence.

But not all New Englanders opposed the war. Vice President Elbridge Gerry and Secretary of War William Eustis were from Massachusetts. General Henry Dearborn was from New Hampshire. Naval officers Isaac Hull, Charles Morris, and Oliver Hazard Perry all hailed from New England. More of the all-important privateers were sanctioned in the New England states than from any other area of the country.

Soon after the beginning of the war, two American schooners, the *Sophia* and the *Island Packet,* were seized by the British in the St. Lawrence River. By July twelfth, United States General William Hull's army invaded Upper Canada at Sandwich. Then, on July seventeenth the British captured Fort Michilimackinac in the Michigan Territory.

The small village of Sackets Harbor in Jefferson County, New York was the home of a major naval shipyard, headquarters of the United States Navy, and a significant base of operations for the United States Army. On July seventeenth the brig *USS Oneida* and the shore batteries of Sackets Harbor successfully repulsed five attacking British ships.

Noisy Plymouth harbor was a frightful place to bring a child, but Beth had no alternative, having only herself to care for Kathryn. And Beth hoped the little girl's presence would be a shield from ruffians who might accost a lone woman. But late in the afternoon on the second day of searching, Beth began to despair of finding a ship. So far, only one captain, bound for Maine, was willing to take them on board, but his leering, gap-tooth snicker dissuaded her from accepting his offer.

If circumstances forced them overland from Plymouth to Canada, penury would require Beth to sell her heart-shaped brooch to finance the trip. That would leave only her ruby engagement ring with which to purchase passage home. Dispirited, she decided to ask the innkeeper to recommend a reputable jeweler.

They lodged at the inn Brad used when business brought him to Plymouth, and the innkeeper had agreed to mail a bill for their room and board to Mr. Anderson. She knew travel arrangements must be secured before he received the demand for payment.

"Mama," Kathryn tugged at Beth's hand, "Mama, I want up."

For many hours Beth had alternated between carrying her daughter and having her walk. "Walk just a while longer, sweetheart. We don't have much farther to go," she encouraged.

Planting her feet, Kathryn pulled her hand out of Beth's grasp and crossed her arms over her chest in the same manner as her father, "No, Mama."

"Kathryn, please, my arms ache from holding you. It isn't much farther. You can skip if you like," Beth cajoled.

Thrusting her lower lip out, Kathryn shook her head and stamped her foot, "No, Mama."

Taken by surprise, the weary mother wondered what had become of her complacent daughter. Crouching in front of Kathryn, Beth took hold of her shoulders. "You've been so good. Don't spoil it now by misbehaving." She pointed up the dock. "See that ship right there? You can walk that far. Now let's go," she said, standing and holding out her hand. But the child began crying.

Losing all patience, Beth snapped, "Please stop crying, Kathryn," and in frustration, took the girl's hand and tugged her along.

But the little girl struggled and wailed at the top of her lungs, "I want my daddy! I want my daddy!"

The child's cry destroyed Beth's self-control. Picking her daughter up, Beth hugged her close. "I know, sweetheart, I know. I want your daddy, too," she admitted. With one hand, Beth quickly dashed at her tears and choked back her sobs, knowing she couldn't fall to pieces.

But Kathryn continued her tantrum, and passersby turned to stare. Realizing there was no point in trying to inquire about passage on the next schooner with Kathryn carrying on, Beth stepped into the street to return to her lodging. Suddenly, she was grabbed and forcibly dragged aside. A horse hauling a heavily laden wagon crashed by, almost running them over. Unable to suppress her fright, Beth sank to her knees, sobbing as she clutched her child to her breast.

Quieting at her mama's discomposure, Kathryn stroked her mother's hair.

"Come, let me help you," a man's voice said as he took Kathryn out of Beth's arms. Holding the baby, he reached down and helped her to her feet. "Are you all right? I hope you weren't hurt when I pulled you out of the way."

"I'm fine." Beth shakily wiped at her face to dry it.

The man handed her a large linen handkerchief, "Here, use this."

"Thank you," she whispered, taking the cloth.

Eying her curiously, the man commented, "You must be the Englishwoman I've heard about."

The statement caught her attention. "What do you mean?"

He shrugged nonchalantly, "It's being talked about in all the dockside taverns, the lovely, young British matron searching for a way home." At her shocked expression, he explained, "Sailors rarely see women of refinement on the docks. They are bound to comment on it."

Color rose in Beth's cheeks at the thought of being the topic of coarse remarks in common rooms.

Noticing her embarrassment, the man kindheartedly informed her, "During wartime, you won't find passage, and it would be dangerous even if you could. Have you not noticed the additional guns these ships carry? They aren't just the defensive guns used by merchants wanting to escape seizure. Most of these ships will be privateers by month's end. They'll sail with the intent of plundering British cargoes."

The hot color of a moment ago drained from Beth's face. "How foolish and naive I've been," she murmured.

Shifting Kathryn to his other hip, the man took Beth's elbow, "Let me escort you to your lodgings. The docks aren't safe for a lone woman and young child." They turned toward town, and the man introduced himself, "I'm Paul Atherton, by the way."

The introduction offended Beth, something a common woman might expect, but not someone of culture. Ill at ease, she did not reply with her own name.

"My apologies for being forward. Under the circumstances, I just thought you might want to know."

A glance at the man confirmed his discomfort. Of medium build, he appeared younger than Beth. Or perhaps his bright red hair and freckled face just lent him the air of youth.

"Thank you for your assistance, Mr. Atherton," Beth muttered. After a short pause, she conceded softly, "I am Mrs. Bradley Anderson, and you are carrying my daughter, Kathryn."

"I'm sorry for your misfortune, Mrs. Anderson. It must be horrible to suddenly find yourself residing in the wrong country at the outbreak of war," he said compassionately.

"Yes, it is Mr. Atherton. Do you suppose if I made my way to Canada, my prospects for getting to England would improve?"

He shrugged his reply, "England's eyes have been turned to Europe for so long there is no telling how aggressively they'll fight this war or how short of time the conflict might last. Crossing the ocean presents the greatest danger at this point. My advice is to stay in America and wait it out.

The silence between them grew again as Beth digested his words. Her limited financial resources made staying on this side of the Atlantic impossible.

As if reading her mind, he asked, "Do you have friends or relatives who would take you in?"

Another glance toward him, and she shook her head, "None that would sympathize with my position."

He nodded his understanding. "It is never easy for a woman on her own, especially with a child to care for."

"You are right, Mr. Atherton, and I must think of Kathryn now." Beth resolved, "I shall travel north as quickly as possible and find a way to cross into Canada. At least there we shall be among my countrymen, and with their sympathies, have a better chance of getting home." A few paces farther on, Beth turned toward the redheaded man and took her daughter into her arms. "This is where we are staying. Thank you for your assistance. You are most kind."

He tipped his hat in farewell then reconsidered. "Mrs. Anderson, perhaps I can be of further help. If you take the post coach north, you'll travel for weeks and run the risk of thievery along the way."

"Yes, but it is a risk I must take."

"I've been here on personal business but reside in New York," he explained. "My carriage is large enough for you and your daughter. If you care to join me, your trip will be shortened considerably."

"But I don't even know you, sir," Beth blurted, shocked at the suggestion.

He flushed deeply and stammered, "My sister is traveling with me. That's why I brought the carriage instead of riding horseback."

Appraising the man beside her, Beth ruminated, "If I may meet your sister, I shall consider your offer."

"With your permission, I shall bring Jane to make your acquaintance tomorrow morning."

"Yes, Mr. Atherton, tomorrow morning at ten o'clock will be fine," Beth replied.

The journey was a long, arduous ride, harder for the horse than the man. When Bradley finally arrived

Sweetbriar

home, weary and dusty, his first concern was for information about his wife. But Louise could tell him no more than what had been said in her missive. He ordered a fresh horse saddled then interviewed the carriage driver, learning what trifling the man knew. He rode out again without pausing for a bath or change of clothes.

At the post coach station, he learned a young matron had purchased tickets to Plymouth for herself and a small girl. Then Brad continued to his parent's house.

Entering his father's study, the surprise on the older man's face told Brad how astounded Charles was at his son's disheveled appearance. But the astonishment quickly became scowling anger when Brad related the circumstances of his wife's abrupt departure.

Sounding like a shot, Charles' hands slammed on his desk as he leaned forward, bellowing, "How could you allow such a thing to happen? You knew how risky it was to keep that girl around Beth. You should have sent her packing ages ago."

"Don't you think I wanted to, Father!" Brad yelled back. The two men stared at each other in hostile silence. It was Brad who shifted his eyes first. "It's too late for recriminations. God only knows what calamities might befall them if I don't find them soon. I came here tonight to tell you I'll leave for Plymouth at dawn. Here are the Letters of Marque," Brad said, handing over the thick packet. "Will you please distribute them?"

Controlling his anger, Charles sat, "What makes you think they'll still be in Plymouth? And how do you plan to find them?"

Raking his fingers through his hair, Brad trod the floor as he reflected out loud, "In her letter, Beth said she intends to return to her father. You and I both know she won't find a ship bound for England in Plymouth. The most logical course is for her to travel to Canada and buy passage from there. The Plymouth harbormaster should be able to tell me if a woman and girl-child were passengers on any ship headed north. With luck, I'll overtake them before they get to Canada and certainly before they sail for England."

"Take Derrick O'Malley with you," Charles advised. "The lad may be useful."

"I'd prefer the father to the son. At least Quinn would recognize Beth. But he's been chomping at the bit to strike one against the British. No doubt he'll sail the moment you hand him that Marque," Brad replied.

"I'll tell him to put in at Plymouth, and you can have him take you north if need be. I'm sure he'll find enough fair game on the return trip," Charles offered.

"Thank you, Dad," Brad said humbly.

Taking a deep, calming breath, Charles said, "Find Beth and Kathryn. Bring them safely home. And while you're gone, I'll take care of Mrs. Jetter." Brad opened his mouth to protest, but Charles held up his hand, "Don't argue with me on this. You will never repair your marriage while that woman is in your home. She has to go."

"What about Andy?" Brad asked. "In her letter, Beth said she couldn't bear to look at him again, but he is my son, and I love him."

Charles stood, hands clasped behind his back, pacing. "It will take some thought on what to do in the short term. Beth loved the boy before all this happened, perhaps in time, she will change her mind. If not, you'll need to send him to boarding school as soon as he is old enough."

Brad brightened with this thought, "When the time comes, I know which school to use."

Charles quit pacing and frowned at his son scathingly, "Then it is only the next three years we need concern ourselves with."

As Suzanne Anderson entered the room, the delight of seeing her son faded as she took in his disreputable state. "Bradley, you're filthy!" she admonished. "You need a bath and fresh clothes. You can't sit at dinner looking the way you do."

"I won't be staying, Mother. In fact, I was just leaving," he interrupted before she could ring for the maid.

"But I was told you arrived just half an hour ago, and you look exhausted."

"Suzanne," her husband's sharp voice stopped her, "Brad needs to leave."

With an easy smile, Brad crossed to his mother and kissed her cheek, "I don't mean to disappoint you, Mother, but I have urgent business that needs attending. I'll see you again as soon as I can."

"If you insist," she acquiesced, "but when you get home, take a bath and get some rest. And ask Beth to bring the children for a visit, it's been over a month since I've seen them."

In the heavy silence, Charles interjected, "Brad, have Mrs. Jetter bring Andy out tomorrow."

"What about Beth and Kathryn?" Suzanne questioned, peering at her son sharply.

"Sorry, Mother, but they are in Plymouth for a while. I'll bring them to see you when they return."

"What are you not telling me, dear?" Suzanne inquired, placing her hand on Brad's arm.

"Don't worry. I'll see you again soon," he evaded the question with another peck on her cheek and left.

His mother was right about his exhaustion. Brad thought, riding through the twilight. But instead of turning toward home, he pressed on to the O'Malley residence.

Derrick, not having married, lived with his parents, but it was the elder man Brad came to see. The family was at dinner, and the maid led him to the study, saying she would inform her master of his presence.

As much as O'Malley loved his food, he was more excited by the prospect of privateering and appeared almost immediately. "By the saints, man," Quinn blurted at the sight of Brad's dirty clothes, "you didn't need to come tonight. The blasted papers could have waited until tomorrow. It's not as if twelve hours will win or lose the war."

Brad wearily waved the big man toward his oversized chair. "My apologies, Quinn, I didn't bring your Marque. Father will get it to you tomorrow. I have more urgent business to discuss with you tonight."

Curious what could be more important than war and the profits to be made by capturing British merchant ships, Quinn sat, patiently awaiting Brad's news.

"Before I tell you what I came to say, I want you to know I've just come from a confrontation with my father and am in no mood for a tongue lashing from you."

O'Malley's eyebrows shot up in surprise.

Unable to hide his feelings, Brad choked out in a strangled voice, "Beth left me. She found out about Louise and Andy, so she took Kathryn and left."

Appalled but confused by the unexpected disclosures, Quinn sat forward. "What do you mean she found out? Found out what? And what is this about Andy?"

Leaning his head against the back of the chair and closing his eyes, Brad shuddered as he fought for control of his emotions. "Didn't you know, Quinn? I thought you would have figured it out. Andy is not only my adopted son. You remember my British mistress, don't you? Andy is my son by Louise.

The older man's face reddened as he stood. "You mean to tell me you brought that woman home and have had her and your bastard son living right under your wife's nose!" he roared.

Sweetbriar

The thought raced across Brad's mind that perhaps, for the first time in eighteen years, Quinn O'Malley might strike him. He quickly jumped to his feet and faced his longtime friend. "I didn't ask her to come. She came to America on her own. Beth needed a wet nurse, and the doctor found Louise. After Beth met her, there wasn't any stopping it."

This time it was O'Malley who ended the silent, hostile stare. Puffing out his breath, he asked quietly, "How long have they been gone?"

"Ten days. It took less time than anticipated to get the Letters of Marque. Thank God. I believe Beth went to Plymouth hoping to find a ship headed for Canada."

Sitting again, O'Malley rolled the information around his brain. "If she found a ship, the best we can do is follow, but if she is traveling overland, it will be more difficult to find her."

"My thoughts precisely," Brad responded. "Derrick and I shall ride to Plymouth tomorrow and ask the harbormaster about ships with passengers sailing north. If it appears she left by sea, I'll wait for you there. Otherwise, I'll leave word for you with the harbormaster. If overland is the more likely route, as I believe it is, I want you to stop at every American port northward on the off chance of finding them."

"And what will you and Derrick be doing?" Quinn asked.

"First, we'll try to trace them in Plymouth. If we can find where they stayed, there is the possibility we'll have some idea of where and how they are traveling."

The older man nodded his head then crossed to the door, where he shouted for his youngest son.

When Bradley arrived home late that night, Anna Louise handed him a letter with a Plymouth postmark. The hand addressing the letter was unfamiliar. Breaking the seal, Brad discovered a bill for room and board from the innkeeper. A grim smile crossed his lips. He had a starting place for his search.

The harbormaster, a chatty character, was more than happy to discuss the Englishwoman who had wandered the docks for two days inquiring about passage north. He smugly assured Brad that had she come into his office, he, the harbormaster, would have informed her no reputable captain would take her and the child on board during wartime. As the man passed on gossip he'd gleaned from dockside taverns; Brad was hard-pressed to remain civil. Writing a short note to Quinn O'Malley, Brad asked the harbormaster to deliver it to the captain when he arrived. Then Brad and Derrick headed to the inn.

"Mr. Anderson, I'm glad to see you," the innkeeper smiled. "I hadn't expected you to come personally about the bill for your wife and daughter. Will you be staying long?"

"My companion and I shall stay the night only. But right now, I need to speak with you about Mrs. Anderson. May I come into your office?" Brad asked.

"Yes, of course," the innkeeper said uneasily. "I trust Mrs. Anderson and your daughter are well."

Brad ignored the inquiry, telling Derrick to settle their belongings in the room, then followed the innkeeper into his office. "Mr. Adams," Brad began uncomfortably as he sat in the proffered chair, "my wife and daughter are traveling north with the intention of reaching Canada. What can you tell me of Mrs. Anderson's plans?"

"Don't you know?" he asked bluntly, thinking a man should know his wife's travel agenda.

"If I knew I wouldn't ask," Brad retorted, mortified by the question. Breathing deeply to calm the gathering storm in his gut, Brad continued, "Please tell me everything you know about their stay here. Perhaps some inconsequential thing will provide me with a clue on how to locate them."

"Well, sir," the dismayed man stammered, "Mrs. Anderson said she would stay only a few days and to mail the bill to you."

"Yes, Mr. Adams, I have the bill and will settle it on the morrow when I leave. What else can you tell me?" Brad asked impatiently.

"Well, not much. The day they left, she asked me to get a hack. I can give you the driver's name and location if that will help."

"Yes, it will be most helpful."

Mr. Adams wrote the name on a piece of paper as another thought occurred to him, "I don't know if it is of any consequence, but Mrs. Anderson asked me to recommend a jeweler."

This information sank like a stone to the pit of Brad's stomach. He hadn't thought to examine Beth's jewelry to determine if anything was missing. That would explain how she planned to pay for passage to England. "Please give me the jeweler's name and address, too."

Sending Derrick to make inquires of the hack driver, Brad went in search of the jeweler, and as he feared, Beth had procured money for her journey. The jeweler in possession of the heirloom brooch demanded a small fortune, but after an exchange of money, the heart-shaped ruby pin resided safely in Brad's pocket. However, the jeweler was ignorant of any information concerning Beth's travel intentions.

Derrick's news was more encouraging. The hack driver had delivered a woman and child to the home of a well-to-do widow six days ago. But when Derrick knocked on the woman's door requesting information, he was turned away.

By late evening, through acquaintances, Brad secured an invitation to see the widow, but not until the following day.

At first, the good woman hesitated to give information to the two gentlemen, presuming the young mother had been abused by her husband. Brad assured her that was not the case. Then twisting the truth, he said his wife fled because she was British born, and he supported the American war effort by licensing his ships as privateers. The widow relented, disclosing Beth and Kathryn had traveled north in the company of the widow's nephew and niece. Their destination was the small river town of Plattsburg in upper New York.

Leapfrogging northward, Brad and Derrick rode swiftly, first one then the other, pausing at farms and towns and way stations and hostelries and scattered taverns along the way, hastily seeking intelligence of the brougham carrying the man and his sister and the English matron and her daughter, and the two men came together late in the night and exchanged information as they gobbled a quick bite and grabbed less than a handful of hours of sleep and forsaking early morning meals renewed the search before dawn greeted the day, they rode hard again and again and again, over roads and fields and tree-covered hills, across bridges and through streams slow mile after tortuously slow mile, they sped only as swiftly as the tired steeds could stride, and they gained ground by day and by night and by day and by agonizing night they drew closer and closer.

And the carriage eluded them.

They were two days behind when they reached the village. The lustrous glove of night gripped the land, and anxious to find the home of Mr. and Miss Atherton, Brad wanted to press forward, but Derrick O'Malley urged him to put up for the night. A bath, fresh clothes, and a new day, he suggested, would improve the Atherton's reception of them.

Jane Atherton had endeared herself to Beth during the journey north because of her patience with the increasingly cantankerous Kathryn. Every day the child repeatedly asked when she would see her daddy again, and when told to stop asking, asked over and over when she would see Andy again. Until told to hush. Then the unhappy girl cried.

It became necessary to confide to the Athertons that Beth had left her husband, but she could not bring herself to elucidate on her reasons. The blistering pain of his deceit was a wound too raw to share with her new friends. Receiving no explanation for the flight from Massachusetts, the Athertons concluded it was because of the war.

"Mrs. Anderson," Paul said, "Jane and I talked again last night. We think you should remain here a few weeks before venturing over to Canada. For all we know, our respective governments are already settling their differences, and you won't feel so compelled to return to England."

Due to the Atherton's belief in Mr. Franklin's adage 'Early to bed, early to rise,' they were eating breakfast shortly after the cock crowed.

"Mr. Atherton and dear Miss Atherton, I appreciate your offer and would accept under different circumstances, but I must find someone to take me across the river as soon as possible. While the war persists, I doubt my husband will follow me there."

The brother and sister shared a bewildered expression, and Jane asked, "Wouldn't you return home to your husband if the war ended?"

The silence grew uncomfortable, then Kathryn pointed out the window and cried excitedly, "Daddy! Daddy!"

Looking out, Beth viewed two men on horseback cantering up the drive. The younger man she didn't recognize but the older man was her husband. Quickly she grabbed Kathryn, and speaking over her shoulder, urgently implored, "Don't let him know we are here. Say we have already gone to Canada." Then hushing her child by covering her mouth, Beth sped up the stairs. A loud thumping on the front door thundered in her ears as she closed and locked her bedroom door. A quick peek from behind the curtain revealed the younger man still astride his horse.

The cottage door was opened by a man about Beth's age and a plain woman about a dozen years older. "Hello, my name is Bradley Anderson. I apologize for disturbing your household so early. Your aunt in Plymouth told me my wife and daughter traveled with you from Massachusetts. May I inquire if they are still here?"

Jane stepped forward, "I'm sorry, Mr. Anderson, they have gone into Canada."

The snakes in Brad's stomach writhed, twisting into a tight knot. "Can you tell me who took them or their destination?"

"No, Mr. Anderson," Paul Atherton asserted. "She swore us to secrecy. She doesn't want you to follow her. Now, please leave."

The words hit Brad with the force of a blow, staggering him. "They are my wife and daughter," he choked out.

"And they've gone," the young man said, closing the door.

Overcome with failure and fatigue, Brad staggered off the porch and slumped against the hitching rail.

Derrick dismounted and rushed over to support him before he fell.

Hidden by the drape, Beth watched, stunned to see the unfamiliar young man assisting her husband. Brad placed his hand on the saddle horn and rested his head against the saddle momentarily. It took two attempts for him to get his foot in the stirrup, and only the help of the unknown man allowed Brad to mount his horse. He had always sat a horse so proudly. Beth's heart ached to see his shoulders hunched forward in defeat as he rode away.

Summer/Fall 1812

Secretary of War, William Eustis, gave the Governor of Michigan Territory, Brigadier-General William Hull, supreme command of the Fourth US Infantry under Lieutenant-Colonel James Miller, three regiments of Ohio militia, and some small detachments of Michigan volunteers. His orders—secure the Northwest Territories against Indians incited to violence by the British and invade Canada from Ft. Detroit. Although short of supplies, the army crossed over into Canada intending to attack Ft. Amherstberg.

Hull sent Major Thomas Van Horn and two hundred recruits to meet a company of Ohio volunteers who waited at Miami Rapids with three hundred head of cattle and seventy packhorses of essential provisions. En route, while fording the creek at Brownstown, Van Horn's party was viciously attacked by the Shawnee war chief, Tecumseh, and two dozen warriors. The Major ordered a retreat to regroup, but his untrained men scattered in panic. By the end of the day, half his men were lost—eighteen dead, twelve wounded, and seventy deserted. Only one of the attackers was fatally wounded.

Meanwhile, General Hull learned Ft. Michilimackinac had fallen to the enemy and feared the Indians would flock to the British, so he abandoned his Canadian campaign and retreated to Ft. Detroit.

Still needing provisions, Hull ordered Lieutenant-Colonel James Miller, along with six hundred troops, to escort the supply train north. Before arriving at their destination, the detachment confronted the enemy's Forty-first Regiment, a combined British-Canadian-Indian force of two hundred. The American advantage in strength of arms was aided early on by confusion among their foe, forcing their retreat. But the British rallied and stood fast, awaiting another American onslaught. However, having sustained heavy casualties, Miller allowed his opponents to withdraw. Although a tactical victory for the Americans, Colonel Miller's failure to follow through turned the Battle of Oakwoods into a strategic loss a few days later. Ignoring orders, the Americans returned to Fort Detroit without the supply train.

Major-General Isaac Brock, the British commander in Upper Canada, arrived at Ft. Amherstberg on the same day as Tecumseh and two hundred of his warriors. The two leaders quickly established a rapport, ensuring cooperation between their forces. They devised several ruses to deceive the Americans at Ft. Detroit into believing the British force was far superior in strength. Then Brock sent a surrender demand to General Hull, stating he did not want to wage a war of extermination but would not be able to control the savagery of his Indian allies once fighting commenced.

On August fifteenth, the British commenced bombarding Ft. Detroit from across the Detroit River. As American casualties mounted, Hull despaired. His daughter and grandchild resided within the fort. The next day, fearing a slaughter by the Indians, Hull ordered the white flag of surrender hoisted. He asked for three days to agree upon the terms of surrender, but

Brock gave him only three hours. The American capitulation included Hull's entire army, thirty cannon, three hundred rifles, twenty-five hundred muskets, and the supply convoy still waiting at Miami Rapids.

The fall of Fort Detroit encouraged more Indian attacks on American settlements and isolated military outposts.

A few days after the fall of Fort Detroit, during the afternoon of August nineteenth, about four hundred miles southeast of Halifax, Nova Scotia, the *USS Constitution* engaged the *HMS Guerriere*. They exchanged broadsides for half an hour before the American ship closed on her enemy's beam. Another shot sent *Guerriere's* mizzen mast overboard, and coming around to the other side, the *Constitution* rained down grapeshot and musket fire. As the two ships cleared each other, the *Guerriere* lost her fore and main masts over the side, leaving her an unmanageable wreck. Too badly damaged to save, *Guerriere's* captors removed the crew and set fire to the ship.

Late Summer 1812, America

During the long, miserable ride from Plattsburg, Brad reflected on his life and saw a man who had exhibited casual disregard for others. As a youth, he defied his father to pursue a life at sea, settling down only when it was convenient to his own desires. He sought pleasure from one young woman while courting another. He took to wife a noblewoman who wanted only to remain in England, then brought her to America. Worst of all, he allowed his desire to acknowledge his son to jeopardize the happiness of everyone involved.

And what did he have to show for the single-minded pursuit of his desires? Beth fled the country with Kathryn. Louise married, taking Andy to live in her new home. And his father was forced to resume the responsibilities at the helm of Surrey Trading Company.

Before arriving back home, Brad's determination to live life on his own terms without consideration for others had withered and died. But once again, he was inconveniencing others to satisfy his desires, and swore to himself it would be the last time.

"We're ready to get underway," Quinn O'Malley informed Brad as he came topside. Aboard the *Angel Star,* they headed out to patrol the mouth of the St. Lawrence River. Brad theorized his wife would find passage in Montreal and intended to stop every outbound merchant ship until he found her. In reality, he knew it was a slim chance. O'Malley had agreed to a thirty-day search, provided that if she weren't found by then, he would seek a prize of war for his crew.

The sunrise painted the waters of the harbor golden as they slipped out to sea.

Late Summer 1812, Canada

Beth could deny the truth no longer. All the restraint her husband had exercised during their lovemaking had been for naught. She was with child. And she dreaded another ocean voyage while pregnant as much as she feared another labor to deliver the baby.

Her impetuous, reckless nature had the better of her again. Her resolve to sail for England wavered. She loved her husband despite his faults. He had followed her to Plattsburg, and only chance had prevented him from finding her. Only the burning humiliation she felt at his betrayal had kept her from chasing after him as he rode off.

She wanted to write to Brad, asking him to send Anna Louise and Andy away, never wanting to see the nursemaid again and not wanting Andy as an eternal reminder of her husband's deceit. But Beth questioned if Brad would renounce his bastard son.

Besides, she didn't have the time to write. The ship's captain said he would sail the day after tomorrow. She needed to be on board by tomorrow evening if England was her destination. The turmoil she felt about the decision she had to make was evident in her pacing and the constant worrying of the heart-shaped ruby ring on her finger. The ring the captain had agreed to accept as payment for their passage. All she had to do was decide.

They had been at sea for almost five weeks with nothing to show for it. None of the ships they had hailed knew of a woman seeking passage to England. The crewmen of the privateer were justifiably disgruntled. They were at sea for the money to be made from the ships they captured, and too many rich prizes had been allowed to pass.

At two o'clock, the lookout called out a sighting of another merchantman on the horizon headed their way. It was the fifth sighting in as many days.

"It's time to give the men their reward. We'll take this one home with us," O'Malley informed Brad.

The implacable expression on Quinn's face brooked no argument, and Brad knew better than to oppose the skipper in front of his crew. He coursed his fingers through his hair in frustration, then crossed his arms over his chest and gave a silent nod.

The *Angel Star* sailing without cargo was swifter than the British ship and closed the distance by half-past four. They hoisted their colors and opened fire. The shot was high, taking the main-royal mast down.

Their opponent returned fire with negligible effect as most of their cannonballs fell short, either from an inexperienced crew or inferior cannon powder or most likely a combination of both.

Adjusting to the swell of the sea, the next volley from the *Angel Star* lowered and blew away the fore topmast. Built for speed and maneuverability, the American ship danced in and out of range, hailing down destruction while avoiding severe damage herself. Within fifteen minutes more, the British lost their main-topmast and mizzen-topgallant mast then struck her colors. The lives of men had more value than the commodities in the holds.

"You might as well take a crew over and start earning your keep, Brad," Quinn instructed. "See if they need help with the wounded. As soon as you have the deck cleared, we'll head for home."

"Aye, Captain."

Beth had been disheartened at the dismal, tiny cabin the captain provided. Off the galley, it was used to store extra provisions, and the shelves lining three sides of the room were full. Two string hammocks hung from stout hooks overhead and a chipped chamber pot hunkered in one corner. With barely enough room for their two valises, it was a great deal less than expected. She prayed for a swift voyage.

Financial reality had tipped the scales on her decision to continue to England. She had no money. The last of it went to the innkeeper, who complained that Beth shorted him sixpence for their last meal. Had she not accepted passage on this ship, she would have been stranded.

The trip downriver had been smooth but roughened as they came into the Gulf of St. Lawrence. Morning sickness returned. Beth didn't know how she would care for Kathryn in the weeks ahead. But from sheer exhaustion, she slept.

In the dream, she holds Mama's teacup. It is soothing. Mama. Beth sips. The tea is warm and fragrant. Soothing. Mama. Beth smiles. But Mama's eyes are sad. 'I didn't choose to leave,' she says and disintegrates into dust. Beth shivers. She stands alone in the mist-shrouded graveyard. She sets the teacup on Mama's gravestone. The words on the stone shimmer in the shadow of the bare oak tree. Beloved Wife. Her Mama's voice accuses, 'I didn't choose to leave.' The oak tree is her father. She picks up Mama's teacup and sips. The tea is warm and fragrant. Soothing. She smiles. But Papa slowly shakes his head. 'She didn't choose to leave,' he says and walks away. Beth sets the teacup on Mama's gravestone. She feels uneasy. She sees the morning light seeping through the golden clouds over the calm blue water. Brad's ship approaches. He steps ashore. 'Beloved wife,' he says. Beth picks up Mama's teacup and sips. The tea is warm and fragrant. Soothing. 'She didn't choose to leave,' he says. Beth sets the teacup on Mama's gravestone. Sinister clouds rumble in the distance. She is unsettled. The thundering black clouds drown out his words, but she sees his mouth form the words. 'Beloved wife.'

Suddenly, a crack and boom sounded across the water. Beth awakened, dreading a storm. But alarm quickly replaced her anxiety as the ship shuddered with the discharge of cannon. The deafening noise immobilized Beth with panic, and Kathryn shrieked in terror. They crouched on the rough planks, screaming in fear. The ship reverberated time and again as the damage continued. Insensible to the passage of time, with Kathryn clasped tightly in her arms, Beth rocked to and fro, wailing. Her wrong bullheadedness, she realized, would be the death of them.

When Brad and his men boarded the British ship, his first order was to transport the wounded to the *Angel Star*. The dead could wait. Next, he quickly demanded the usual assurances from the defeated skipper for his cooperation in bringing the ship to an American port. Then he requested the bills of lading and other essential papers in the ship's strongbox. They would give an impression of the value of this prize of war.

The captain led Brad to his cabin, placed the strongbox on the table, and handed over the key. It turned smoothly in the lock, and Brad sat to examine the contents. When he opened the lid, he spied the ruby ring resting on top of the papers. Snatching it up, Brad scrambled to his feet, sending his chair flying.

"Where did you get this?" he demanded.

Confused by the heated question, the unlucky skipper didn't answer fast enough.

Grabbing the man by the coat and shaking him, Brad roared, "Tell me how you came by this ring or by God, I'll kill you where you stand!"

Struggling against the madman holding him, the captain howled, "The woman gave it to me. It was all she had."

Frighteningly soft, Brad queried from between gritted teeth, "Where are they?"

"In the galley's spare storage room."

"Take me to them," he ordered, pushing the man away.

Scrambling, the captain led Brad to the galley and pointed to a closed door, "In there."

Brad crossed the small galley and opened the door. Huddled in the corner were his hysterical wife and child. He knelt and placed a hand gently on her shoulder, "You're safe now, sweet Beth."

"Daddy!" Kathryn cried and threw herself into her father's arms, clinging to his neck.

Terror slowly receded from Beth's eyes as recognition dawned. "Brad?" she whispered. "Oh, Brad." She dropped her head onto her knees and sobbed again from sheer relief.

Sitting back on his heels, unsure of himself for the first time in his life, Brad asked, "Will you let me take you home?"

She raised her head and frowned at him bleakly. "Are *they* still there?"

"No."

"Is either of them coming back?"

"No," he said without hesitation.

"Then, I shall come home."

Epilogue
Fall 1813, America

The war continued. It had been waging for over a year with land and sea battles fought and lost on both sides, but little accomplished toward ending the hostilities. With France opposing Great Britain, the island nation was unable to bring her full force to bear against America. So, the war continued.

But Beth was at peace. She had her family and her home. In April, after an easy labor, she was overjoyed to deliver a son. Milton Charles Anderson was healthy, happy, and doted upon by everyone. Even Andy when he came to visit.

Beth had learned that Chet Lambert married Anna Louise and took Andy to live with them. It wasn't until after Milton's birth that Beth inquired after them. Reluctant at first to discuss the subject, Brad finally disclosed that he was providing for the boy financially but hadn't seen him since before bringing Beth and Kathryn home. Then her husband surprised her by revealing he had allowed Chet Lambert to adopt Andy. The boy was no longer Brad's son.

It took a fortnight of contemplation for Beth to comprehend the sacrifice her husband had made to prove his love. And it was an offering she was unable to accept. Writing to Mr. Lambert, she asked him to bring Andy for a visit.

Now one Sunday a month, Andy's new father brought him, and after the visits, Brad was particularly considerate in his lovemaking. Beth understood it was his way of expressing his appreciation.

For Brad, these family changes were only the outward manifestation of the more profound alteration that had taken place in him. He was always considerate now. Even in business, he allowed the needs and desires of others to have some bearing on his decisions and actions. Never again did Brad risk losing his family or the love of his wife to satisfy his own desires.

The End

Excerpt from *Brewer's Betrothal: A Love Triangle Romance*
Due out in October 2020

One day after another, Duncan and Audra rode southeast toward Duxbury, Massachusetts. Together, they traveled slower than Duncan could have traveled alone, but he did not begrudge the delay. They journeyed companionably, mostly in silence, occasionally in easy conversation. Escaping the oppressive dominance of her father seemed to have released the shackles impeding Audra's speech.

Audra—he no longer thought her given name in his mind only. He now freely spoke the dulcet sound aloud when he addressed her. They had agreed to the informality of using each other's Christian names during their journey. It seemed a very small familiarity when compared to the tortured intimacy they shared each night.

They kept to country roads rather than main thoroughfares. To avoid awkward explanations to innkeepers, who might remember and comment on an unmarried man and woman traveling together, they posed as husband and wife. This meant each night they occupied one room—and one bed.

That first night, Duncan's intent of sleeping in the common room had been thwarted when he'd learned the inn was not a coach stop and had no need of accommodating travelers by allowing them to bed down in the taproom.

When the mantle clock struck twelve, the barkeep complained loudly about the hour. His wife, still in good humor, merrily shooed the last of the patrons on their way. She then offered to share the light of her candle to guide Duncan to his room.

Leaving the bitter dregs in the bottom of his mug, he followed her upstairs. Standing outside the door, the thought occurred to him to remain in the hallway for the night, huddled in his woolen cloak, but he recalled his cloak was in the room with Audra.

Sounds of footsteps on the stair tread spurred him to action. He knocked on the door. "Miss Bishop," he whispered, and then looked warily over his shoulder. It wouldn't do to call his 'wife' Miss Bishop. A little louder, he said, "Audra, it is I, Duncan. Please open the door."

He heard the lock release, and then the panel swung open. It was dark inside the room. Only the lighter color of the garment that draped Audra's form told him where she stood. He closed the door behind him, blocking out all semblance of light. The enclosed space felt too intimate. He heard the rustle of fabric, and with it, the urge to know what she wore—nightdress or petticoat.

His loins tingled with desire. "I must sleep in here tonight to avoid—"

"I understand," she murmured.

"I will use my cloak and sleep on the floor."

"That is not necessary, Duncan. The bed is large."

He no longer felt a mere prickle of desire. It was now a full-fledged leap of his cock. "You don't mean that," he said, his voice sounding strained.

She stepped closer. The unique scent of her—spice, musk, and warm woman—drifted to him. "Will you loosen my stays?"

He was unable to move or make a sound. Hell, he couldn't breathe.

"I can't reach around to undo them myself and wearing the wretched thing makes sleep impossible," she said, turning around and stepping backward. She bumped into him.

Duncan emitted a strangling sound, but reached up, and with much fumbling in the dark room, untied the ribbons.

As he helped her remove the contraption, he heard a slight humming that sounded like she felt blessed relief—or pleasurable anticipation.

His erection hardened painfully as he realized she now wore only her shift. Without deliberate intention, his hands reached for her, encircled her waist.

A door down the hallway slammed shut, jolting them both.

He released her and Audra moved away. Duncan breathed again, his lungs bellowing in and out to replenish depleted oxygen.

The bedclothes whispered as Audra settled in. Out of the darkness, her voice came softly, seductively. "You may undress down to your small clothes, if you wish."

His heart raced. Searing blood coursed through his body. "I think not," he croaked, and then cleared his throat. "I'll remove my boots and lie atop the blankets." *And hope the night's chill will cool my ardor.*

But when he awoke after too little sleep, his cock was hard—and in his arms slept the woman of his dreams.

***

Helping Audra in and out of her corset each morning and night was a courtesy he found more trying with each passing day. His nature was sensual man, not saintly monk. The reservoir of his restraint evaporated a little more each time the dark-haired siren innocently presented the back of her unclothed person to the ministrations of his nimble fingers. He feared that soon his self-control would be no more than a dry lakebed of forbearance. Even now, he struggled against the unprincipled temptation to remove not only the constraint of her stays but of his honor as well.

Denying the desire stirring in his loins, Duncan's fingers trembled. The dim candlelight frustrated his attempt to hurry the task of loosening her ties before he disgraced himself by dishonoring the woman standing before him.

She raised her arms so he could slide the garment up and off her body, leaving her standing in her chemise. Freed from the restrictive bonds, he heard Audra sigh. But unlike the seven previous nights, instead of moving away, she remained standing in front of him.

Slowly, seemingly with deliberate intent, she drew the decorative combs from her hair and let the midnight tresses cascade to her waist. She then scooped the entire mass forward, baring her neck and one shoulder to his gaze. Tipping her head, she glanced back at him with a wicked gleam in her eyes.

Succumbing to the white-hot need within, Duncan groaned low and deep, as his arms slid around Audra's waist. She startled when he pulled her delectable backside against the rigidity of his arousal. Ravenously, he tasted the sweet, milky-white flesh at the juncture of her neck and shoulder. She settled her head back against him.

Warm, erotically so, Audra's skin held the sensuous scent of willing woman, a scent that belonged solely to her. Duncan's hands slid up to cup her breasts. She moaned, arched her back, and pressed herself more firmly into his grasp. Through the thin fabric of her lawn chemise, he found and fingered her nipples; felt them crinkle into welcoming buds. She shivered and murmured his name.

Contact the author:
PaulaJudithJohnson@gmail.com

Visit my website:
www.PaulaJudithJohnson.com